"Katie, what's wrong?"

Katie shook her head, unwilling to confess the truth.

"Tell me," Micah urged with a look of concern.

Katie briefly held his gaze before she looked down, anywhere but at him. He was so handsome that he stole her breath every time she saw him. The ease of their conversation had only brought home to her how much she wished things were different, that he wasn't a widower who only wanted a mother for his children.

"I'm fine, Micah." Katie unwrapped the quilt and offered it to him.

His blue gaze seemed to regard her thoughtfully. "I don't need it, but *danki*."

She nodded and stood. She felt anxious suddenly, and she wished that the storm would pass so that she could be on her way home—and away from Micah.

Katie wished that *Gott* had chosen a different path for her.

One that didn't include a dead fiancé. or his older brother, who clearly had loved his wife too much to fall in love again.

Rebecca Kertz was first introduced to the Amish when her husband took a job with an Amish construction crew. She enjoyed watching the Amish foreman's children at play and swapping recipes with his wife. Rebecca resides in Delaware with her husband and dog. She has a strong faith in God and feels blessed to have family nearby. Besides writing, she enjoys reading, doing crafts and visiting Lancaster County.

Jackie Stef began immersing herself in Amish culture at a young age and wrote her first Amish story at eleven years old. When she's not busy writing, she enjoys photography, playing with her pets and exploring the back roads of Lancaster County. She lives in rural Pennsylvania and loves to spend time in nature.

REBECCA KERTZ

&

JACKIE STEF

An Amish Country Sweetheart

2 Uplifting Stories

In Love with the Amish Nanny and
Their Make-Believe Match

LOVE INSPIRED
INSPIRATIONAL ROMANCE

LOVE INSPIRED®

INSPIRATIONAL ROMANCE

ISBN-13: 978-1-335-47601-2

An Amish Country Sweetheart

Copyright © 2023 by Harlequin Enterprises ULC

In Love with the Amish Nanny
First published in 2022. This edition published in 2023.
Copyright © 2022 by Rebecca Kertz

Their Make-Believe Match
First published in 2022. This edition published in 2023.
Copyright © 2022 by Jacqueline Stefanowicz

For questions and comments about the quality of this book, please contact us at CustomerService@Harlequin.com.

Harlequin Enterprises ULC
22 Adelaide St. West, 41st Floor
Toronto, Ontario M5H 4E3, Canada
www.LoveInspired.com

Printed in U.S.A.

Recycling programs for this product may not exist in your area.

CONTENTS

IN LOVE WITH THE AMISH NANNY

Rebecca Kertz

For Colleen, with love.

Whoso findeth a wife findeth a good thing,
and obtaineth favour of the Lord.
— *Proverbs* 18:22

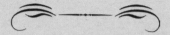

Chapter One

Early August, Lancaster County, Pennsylvania

She thought she saw him this morning. Again. The wagon had passed, and she caught sight of the back of his head with his straw hat tugged forward, giving her a glimpse of his light brown hair. His royal blue short-sleeved shirt stretched over his wide shoulders, and she saw the cross of his dark suspenders in the center of his back. She would have known that familiar form anywhere. Except it was impossible. Because Jacob, her betrothed, was dead. He'd died in a farming accident a month before they were to marry nearly a year ago.

Katie Mast stared down at the vegetable garden in her parents' backyard. Weeds had sprung up after the last two days of rain, and it was her job to pull them. She knelt on the edge of the garden and coaxed out the first weed near a zucchini plant. Placing it in a bucket, she tilted her head up and allowed the warm summer breeze to caress her face. The sunshine felt good, but it didn't stop her tears as she thought of the man she'd loved and lost. She'd kept herself together for months now and thought her grief was finally easing, but seeing someone who looked a lot like Jacob brought back the pain.

She continued to pull weeds, being careful not to tug on the roots of the vegetable plants, placing each plant in a bucket. Would she ever be able to fully get over her loss? Jacob had been the love of her life and now he was dead. She would never be married to him, never have a home with him. Never have his children.

She'd always wanted a husband and children, but it wasn't meant to be. She was devastated by the loss of the only man she'd ever loved, her soulmate.

She frowned. Katie knew her parents worried about her. They constantly urged to go to a youth singing to find someone new, but she couldn't do it. It didn't seem right. How could she when the memory of the day she'd learned Jacob had been run over by farm equipment while harvesting a field still made her heart ache like it had happened only yesterday?

Why? Why did he have to die? What was Jacob doing that day working alone on his family's farm field? No one in his family knew the reason. Jacob didn't like farming. He'd wanted to be a farrier, and he'd been excited to work as an apprentice under Peter Troyer, the best farrier in New Berne. Jacob should never have been working in that field alone. None of the details of his death and the time leading up to it made any sense.

It was his time to go.
He's in a better place now.
He's with Gott.

How often had she heard members of her Amish community say those words to her? None of them had brought her comfort. Katie jerked on a weed a little too aggressively, nearly uprooting a tomato plant before she pulled it from the damp soil. Breathing deeply to calm herself, she offered up a silent prayer that the Lord would give her the strength to continue her life alone. For she would never marry. She could never marry a man she didn't love, and the man she loved no longer existed on this earth.

A harsh sob burst from her throat. "Please, Lord, help me."

"Katie! *Katie!*" Her mother's call broke through the haze of grief that was starting to overwhelm her.

Katie took a moment to pull herself together, wiped her eyes with the back of her hand and turned to see her *mam*'s face briefly in the kitchen window. "*Ja*, Mam?" she called back.

"Would you please come inside? We have a guest."

"Coming!" Katie frowned. A guest? Who? She stood, glanced down and saw that the bottom edge of her dress was dirty. Not the best way to greet a visitor, but there was nothing she could do about it.

After she washed her hands at the water pump in the backyard, Katie headed toward the house. As she hurried, she prayed that her mother hadn't invited a man for her to meet. Mam had been hinting that she needed a husband, but Katie wasn't interested in meeting anyone new. She'd told her mother that. If she couldn't have Jacob, she wouldn't marry. *Ever.*

Entering the kitchen, she found her mother seated at the table with a younger woman, who wore an Amish head covering on her dark brown hair that was different from those worn here in Lancaster County. The woman had a kind face, and Katie found herself relaxing as their visitor smiled at her.

"There you are," Mam said. "Naomi, this is my *dochter* Katie. Katie, meet Naomi Hostetler. She is visiting from Michigan."

"Hallo," Katie greeted with a small smile as she moved farther into the room.

Her mother caught sight of Katie's dress hem and frowned. *"Katie."*

Her face heating with embarrassment, Katie brushed down the length of her skirt as if she somehow could remove the thin wet soil stain. "I was gardening, Mam."

"A hard worker," the other woman said with an approving twinkle in her warm brown eyes. "It's nice to meet you, Katie."

She nodded then felt a prickle of unease as the woman and Mam exchanged secretive glances. Her mother gestured to a chair. "Have a seat."

Katie obeyed and sat down, feeling more than a little self-conscious.

"Would you like some tea?" Mam asked, starting to rise to wait on her. "The water is still hot."

She gestured to keep her mother seated. *"Ja*, I'd like a cup, but I'll get it. Would either of you like more?"

"Nay, we still have some," Mam said.

Katie made herself tea before returning to the table and taking the seat across from their visitor. "Do you have family in the area?" she asked, wondering why a woman would come all the way from Michigan to visit New Berne.

"My *schweschter* Berta lives here," Naomi said pleasantly. "I'm considering a move to the area permanently." She smiled. "I'll be staying a few months with Berta until I can decide."

Katie nodded then took a sip of tea. The warmth of

the brew felt good sliding down her throat. She wondered why her mother wanted her to come inside. "Do you need someone to show you around town?" Was that why Mam asked Katie in to meet the woman?

Naomi shook her head. "I came to talk with you."

She frowned. "You did?"

"*Ja*, I have someone I'd like you to meet. A widower with three children."

"Excuse me?"

"Naomi is a matchmaker, *dochter*," her mother said.

Katie jumped up from her seat. "I don't want to be matched!" she cried, her eyes suddenly filling with tears. "You know that."

"Sit down, Katie." Her mother's voice was gentle, but firm. "There will be no forcing you to do anything you don't want to do."

Relieved, Katie sat back down, her intertwined fingers clenched tightly on the table. "I'm sorry, but I—"

Naomi placed her hand over Katie's. "I understand what you've been through. It's a terrible thing. I don't blame you for not wanting to move on with your life. It's hard without the man you love, *ja*?"

Katie nodded, her tears overflowing. She quickly wiped them away.

"But what are you going to do without a husband and family?" the woman asked softly. "You have to be practical. How will you provide for yourself in the coming years?"

Katie had already thought about this. "I can sew well. I plan to support myself as a seamstress."

"Commendable," Naomi said with compassion in her gaze. "Will you live with your parents forever?"

Katie blinked. "*Nay*. I'll find a place of my own."

"Will you be able to afford to live on your own with the money you make as a seamstress?"

"I think so. I'll work for Englishers as well as anyone who needs my services in our community," she said. But Katie wondered if she could do it. *I have to.* There was no other choice for her since she would be living the rest of her life as a spinster.

"May I make a suggestion?" Naomi asked as she absently stirred the tea in her cup with a spoon.

Eyeing her warily, Katie nodded and gripped her teacup.

"The widower? He is a man who has suffered a great loss. His three children are young, and he recently moved to the area to get help from his family. He finds it hard to work to support his children when he has no one to babysit them. His mother is watching his children. Unfortunately, Micah's parents also have his younger siblings to care for at home. His father works long hours away from the farm, which leaves his *mam* to handle everything at home. They love and want to help their *soohn*, which is why he asked me to find him a wife."

Katie listened and couldn't help feeling sad for the man who had lost his wife and the mother of his children. "I'm sorry for his loss, but I don't plan to wed. Ever."

"Why?" Naomi asked. "There are different types of marriage within our communities and not all are love matches. There are unions of two people who are deeply in love, and there are marriages born of two people who become companions to help each other because circumstances make it better for them to be together rather than alone." She watched Katie carefully as she sipped from her tea. "Will you at least meet him? If nothing else, if you are comfortable doing so, you can offer to watch his children while he works. Temporarily until he remarries."

Katie's gaze went to her mother, who appeared worried. *About me*, she realized. She'd caused her parents nothing but worry since learning of Jacob's fatal accident. She wanted to ease her mother's concern, and if she could help the man who needed a babysitter while simultaneously lessening her parents' burden, she'd do it. She'd offer to watch this Micah's children for him.

"If I meet with him and it suits us both that I babysit his *kinner*, will you continue to look for a wife for him? That's what he wants, *ja*?"

"Ja," Naomi said. "He needs one. I'm not sure if he has a choice of not marrying again."

"Mam?" Katie wanted her mother's advice.

"It's up to you, Katie, but I think watching his little ones if nothing else will be *gut* for you. You always wanted a family of your own. Helping Micah will allow you to spend time with *kinner* who don't have a *mudder*, especially since you don't plan to have any of your own."

Blinking rapidly against tears, she could only nod. "Sometimes *Gott* has other plans for us," Katie said. "But I will meet him and watch his children if he is agreeable."

"Gut." Naomi finished her tea and stood. "Can you be ready to meet him tomorrow afternoon? Say at two? I'll double-check with him and get back with you if there is a change."

Feeling a sudden attack of nerves, Katie hesitated.

"It will be *oll recht*, Katie," Naomi assured her. "He is a *gut* man. I know that you understand the pain of his loss. He'll appreciate that you want to help in his time of need."

Katie nodded. "I can be ready at two."

"*Gut*. If you don't hear from me again today, then expect me tomorrow. It's best if I take you so that I can introduce you to each other," the woman said.

Standing in his side yard, Micah Bontrager gazed with satisfaction at the house he was renovating. Soon to be his new home for him and his children. Although he had a lot of work left inside, he was pleased with how much he'd accomplished today in the kitchen. Fortunately, the man who'd sold him the property had replaced the roof and siding before he'd put the house on the market. The farmhouse had come with eighty acres of rich farmland. Fixing the interior of the residence was necessary first, as it was too late in the season for planting anything new. However, there were ten acres of hay already planted by the previous owner, ensuring Micah would be harvesting hay before the end of September. By late October he'd be picking fruit from the five fall apple trees on his property not far from the house.

Micah climbed into his market wagon and headed home to his parents' farm. It was a sunny day in August, and the warm breeze filtering in through the open side windows of his buggy felt good on his face. He thought about how much his life had changed in the past year. After his beloved wife Anna's passing, he'd found it difficult to work and care for his three children at their home in Michigan. Members of his community there had helped him with childcare, but he'd felt it wasn't right for him to keep accepting their aid. With Anna gone and none of her family—or his—in the area, there had been no reason for him to stay in Centreville. And he'd thought his parents deserved the opportunity to spend time with their grandchildren, with the distance between Michigan and Pennsylvania making it difficult for him to see his family. He missed his father, mother and siblings, and he knew they would pitch in when he needed them until he could make other arrangements for his children's care. So, he'd sold his property in Centreville, Michigan, and moved his young family to New Berne in Lancaster County, Pennsylvania, where his parents had moved two years previously.

Micah was grateful for his family's love and support. His heart hurt from his loss of Anna, and although he didn't want to marry again, he realized he had to for his children's sake. Jacob, Rebecca and Eliza needed a mother. He couldn't be both mother and father to them while working to support them. He needed someone to take care of his children and make his house a home while he provided for them. So, he'd asked a matchmaker, Naomi Hostetler back in Michigan, to help him find a wife. She'd been the one who had introduced him to Anna, and it hadn't taken long for the love between them to grow into something special. To his surprise, when he'd moved away, Naomi had followed. Naomi had told him that she had a sister in New Berne she'd been wanting to visit and she could continue her search for his wife there. The thought of another woman in his life, another wife, upset him, but the choice had been stolen from him the moment Anna had died from double pneumonia, a complication after contracting the flu. He'd no idea that Anna had suffered from asthma as a child—or that asthma never went away as an adult, although she'd seemed fine when they'd met and after they'd married. He needed a spouse but he didn't want love. He'd loved and lost Anna, and he didn't want to suffer another loss.

Another few weeks of work and the house would be livable, he thought as he drove down the road toward his parents' farm. Today he'd replaced the kitchen floor and installed wall cabinets. Tomorrow he'd install the base cabinets and the countertop. Fortunately, he'd made enough from the sale of his farm in Centreville to finance the trip and the farm property here in New Berne with enough money left over for renovations and other expenses. Micah had known the trip from Centreville to New Berne would take nearly ten hours by car. He couldn't drive a buggy that great distance, and the cost of having his moved was too much considering the age of the vehicle. So, before he'd left, he had sold his family buggy and had purchased a used one in excellent condition within a day of arriving in New Berne. The carriage was a lot like the one he'd had in Michigan, but the color was gray instead of black. It was a formerly owned buggy in great shape and still a long while from having to be rebuilt for continued use. It was in much better condition than his old one. And it was big enough for a growing family. It was possible that after he remarried, his new wife would want more children. Micah closed his eyes as he reminded himself that taking a second spouse was necessary because he needed a mother for his children. Although it wouldn't be a love match, he wouldn't deny her if she wanted to give birth.

Micah pulled onto his father's property and parked near the barn. He sat a minute, willing to admit that he felt bad for bringing his family to his parents' door.

While his mother was happy to have her grandchildren close, he knew it was still a burden for him to be here. He thought of his middle brother. Anna had been sick at the time of his death and he'd been unable to leave and attend his brother's funeral. Anna's death occurred within a week of his sibling's. Afterward, Micah should have gone home to check on his family, but the deep pain of his loss and his struggles to manage without his wife had made traveling impossible.

After inhaling then releasing a deep breath, Micah climbed down from the wagon he'd borrowed from his father, pulled by one of the horses he'd had trailered in from Michigan. A buggy entered the yard as he started toward the house. He paused as the vehicle pulled up next to him and stopped. He immediately recognized Naomi Hostetler in the driver's seat. His stomach felt as if suddenly filled with lead. He'd hired the matchmaker because he'd had to. At least his parents had thought it a good idea at the time they'd met her. They'd managed to convince him after he'd moved to New Berne to allow Naomi to continue to find a match for him.

"Micah," the woman greeted through the open window. "Just the man I'd wanted to see."

"Ja?" He moved closer to the vehicle, his stomach churning.

"I've got news for you."

Everything in him wanted to pull back from remarrying. "Naomi…"

"Now, Micah, you need a wife. You know it's best for the little ones."

He swallowed hard and nodded, as visions of his sick wife filled his mind, compounded with the guilt of being forced to move on. "Will you come inside?"

The matchmaker grinned. "*Ja*, I'll be right in."

Micah headed toward the house. He entered the kitchen, took off his hat and hung it on a wall hook. His mother was at the stove, putting the kettle on.

"*Soohn*, did you have a *gut* day?" she asked, turning to face him with a smile.

"*Ja*, I got the floor done in the kitchen."

Mam looked pleased. "The heart of a home. Good choice to finish that room first, Micah."

Micah shifted uncomfortably. "Naomi Hostetler is here."

"Is she now?" She smirked.

He nodded. "*Ja*, said that she has news for me."

His mother approached him, placed a gentle hand on his arm. "I know it isn't easy."

"*Nay*, it's not." He saw a batch of cookies cooling on the kitchen counter. "Where are my little ones?"

"Your eldest, Jacob, is upstairs playing with Emma." Mam untied her quilted apron and removed it from around her waist. "Your two *bubbel* are napping. Your *schweschter* is *wunderbor* at keeping children entertained. They are *gut kinner, soohn*."

"It was their *mudder*'s influence."

His *mam* shook her head. "*Nay*, she has been gone ten months now. You've had a hand in how well-behaved they are."

Micah glanced away, unwilling to take credit for his children's good behavior.

"I should get washed up before Naomi settles in to talk with us." He went toward the bathroom at the back of the house and washed his hands and then his face. After drying himself, he reentered the kitchen and found the matchmaker seated at the kitchen table with his mother, drinking tea.

"Micah," Naomi greeted with a smile. "Join us."

He approached, his heart beating wildly. How could he marry another after losing the love of his life? Micah took the seat at the end of the table between the two women. There was a cup of coffee instead of tea waiting for him, fixed just the way he liked it. He cracked a smile for the woman who'd raised him. "You have some news?" he said to Naomi.

"Ja." The matchmaker nodded. "There is a young woman who has agreed to meet you."

Micah raised an eyebrow. Naomi knew, though, that he wanted a wife not a love match. "How old is she?"

"Twenty-one." A flicker of concern crossed Naomi's face. "She lost the man she loved a month before they were to be married."

"So young," he murmured, sympathetic. "I'm sorry to hear that."

"I have to tell you, Micah, that she doesn't want to marry. *Ever.* Her parents worry about her, and they wish nothing more than to see her with a husband and children, but she has had a difficult time. She has agreed to meet you so that she can help you with your *kinner.* I don't know if anything will come of your meeting except that you may have a potential temporary babysitter."

"She doesn't ever want to marry?" He frowned. "Why do I need her help?"

"Because your parents have enough on their plate, and Katie will handle your three well. She loves *kinner.*"

He wasn't sure what to say. She'd suffered a loss like he had. He hated the thought that a twenty-one-year-old had endured such awful pain. "It would be nice to have someone help me with them," he admitted. "Mam and Dat have enough to do."

Naomi nodded. "Exactly." She sighed. "It's a shame. Katie is meant to be a wife and *mudder* even if she doesn't believe it. It's possible she will change her mind, but I doubt it."

"Katie," he murmured thoughtfully.

"Katie Mast."

His gaze went to his mother. "Do you know this young woman?"

Mam's expression was grave as she nodded. "What happened to her was tragic. She is a lovely young woman who deserves to be happy." To his surprise, he saw tears fill his mother's eyes.

"I would like to meet her," he said. A grieving single woman should not be forced to wed, he thought. Still, if it suited her, he could use her aid. Maybe they could help each other. "When?"

Naomi sat up straighter in her seat. "I thought I'd bring her by your *haus* tomorrow. I hear you've been working hard to make it a home for you and your *kinner*."

"What time?" he asked after a nod.

"About two?" The matchmaker watched him closely, making him suddenly aware of her intense scrutiny. "I'll continue to look for a wife for you, Micah. In the meantime, you'll find Katie a big help with your children."

Micah nodded. "I'll be ready to meet her tomorrow at the *haus* at two." At least, he hoped he'd be ready. He wasn't eager to have any new woman in his life, even one who would be watching his children temporarily.

Chapter Two

Katie washed up after a morning of baking. She dressed carefully in her light blue dress, white cape with apron and a white prayer *kapp* pinned to her rolled blond hair.

She was nervous about meeting Micah regarding his children and she had no idea why. It wasn't like she'd agreed to marry him.

"Katie!" her mother called from downstairs. "Naomi's here."

"I'll be right there!" Drawing a calming breath, Katie ran a hand over her head covering to make sure it and her hair were still neatly in place.

Vanity was a sin, but that wasn't why she fussed over her appearance. She wanted to make sure that the man, Micah, liked what he saw so he would trust her. The prospect of spending time with children other than her own younger siblings excited her. Maybe he would even allow her to mend or make the children's clothes. She would do it for the cost of the fabric and nothing more. A good way to hone her sewing skills and have others see what she could do for them so that word would spread about her services as a seamstress.

A funny flutter stirred in her belly as Katie slowly descended the stairs. Naomi greeted her with a smile when she entered the kitchen.

"Are you ready to go?" the woman asked.

Katie nodded and grabbed the pound cake she'd made for Micah to make a good impression, before she turned toward her mother. "Mam, I don't know if I should do this."

"Why not?" Naomi's expression filled with compassion. "You're planning to babysit not marry him, *ja*?"

"Ja," Katie admitted softly.

"Then why are you worried?"

"I guess I shouldn't be." Katie followed Naomi out to the woman's vehicle, a boxy gray buggy like the others used in Lancaster County. She climbed into the passenger side and watched Naomi get comfortable. "What can you tell me about... Micah, is it?"

"Ja. Micah. He's a kind man and *gut vadder*, but he suffered a terrible blow after his wife died while battling the flu. With the help of his community in Centreville—that's the community in Michigan where I'm from, in case you're wondering—Micah managed to work and take care of his *soohn* and two *dechter*, but he missed his family and wanted them to be able to spend time with his *kinner*. He moved here to be closer to his parents and siblings who have been living in Lancaster County for the last two years."

"I'm sorry to hear of his wife's death."

"Ja, it was sad thing, and to be truthful, I don't think he is done grieving for her. It's hard to tell with him. He

seems strong, but no one knows how he is when alone after such a loss. Micah is *gut* at hiding his feelings."

"I understand grief."

"Ach ja. You know what it's like, don't you, Katie?"

"I know what it's like to lose someone you love beyond any other. But we never got to marry or have children." A sudden thought startled her. "I think it is worse for Micah."

"That's kind of you to say, but loss is loss no matter the circumstances. Both are unbearable for those suffering from it."

Katie blinked back tears. *"Ja."*

About fifteen minutes after they'd left her father's property, Naomi rolled her buggy into the barnyard where a house had been built far enough from the road to have a measure of privacy. Katie glanced up at the large farmhouse and thought it had been built in mind for a family with several children. "It looks nice," she said.

Naomi smiled at her before she opened her door and climbed down. Katie followed suit and joined the matchmaker on the walkway leading up to a back door

"The roof and siding were new when Micah bought it. The last owners never finished fixing the inside. Micah is in the middle of renovating."

Katie gazed up at the house, picturing what it might have been like for her and Jacob to share such a home if he'd lived and they'd married.

The back screen door was open. "Micah! It's Naomi."

"It's two o'clock already?" a deep voice called back, rumbling pleasantly in Katie's ears. "Come in."

The door squeaked as she followed Naomi inside.

"I'll just be a minute," the man said.

The interior of the house was dark compared to the bright sunshine outside. It took a moment for Katie's eyes to adjust and for her to realize that they were in the fellow's kitchen. His back was to them as he set a piece of countertop on the base cabinets that formed an L shape. Katie might have considered it fancy but she realized that the larger cabinet and counter space would be necessary for a man with a growing family.

Katie's gaze took in the rest of the room before it returned to take in the man as he worked. She froze as she studied the back of his head and the breadth of his shoulders. The back of him looked familiar. Then Micah turned, and she reeled in shock when she locked gazes with him. "Jacob?" she whispered, feeling as if she'd spiraled back in time. She suddenly felt woozy and struggled to grab hold of the edge of the doorway to keep from falling. The pound cake she held threatened to topple onto the floor.

The man hurried to her side, and she felt the warm, firm grip of his fingers on her arm. While still holding on to her, he used his free hand to rescue the cake and set it carefully on the kitchen counter. "Is she ill?" Katie heard him ask Naomi.

"*Nay*, she's surprised, because she was startled by your appearance."

Frown lines appeared on his brow. "I don't understand."

Katie blinked rapidly as the fogginess passed. "I'm sorry," she whispered, fighting tears. "You look so much like..."

Ignoring her apology, he continued to watch her intently, gentling the hand that held on to her arm. "Naomi?"

"She expected to meet you, but…" Naomi's voice trailed off. "Micah, this is Katie Mast."

"I'm fine," Katie said as she straightened, pulling away from him, determined to prove that she was more than fine.

"Katie, this is Micah Bontrager," Naomi said as Micah released his hold.

"Bontrager," Katie murmured. Micah must be Jacob's brother, which explained why he looked like her deceased betrothed. He and Jacob shared similar facial features and build and the same shade of light brown hair. Micah was clearly older with tiny lines at the outer corners of eyes that were a brighter shade of blue than Jacob's. The soft brown beard that outlined his outer jaw from ear to ear, leaving the rest of his handsome face shaven in the Amish way, proclaimed him as having married.

Katie released a shuddering breath and said a name no one had mentioned since his death. "Jacob's older *bruder*?"

Micah stiffened. "You knew my *bruder*?"

"Katie was betrothed to him when he died," Naomi said.

She heard Micah draw a sharp breath. He saw his pain mirrored in her pretty blue eyes. "I'm sorry," he told her. "I didn't know. My wife… I couldn't come back for his funeral."

Her heart ached, making it difficult for her to gaze at him, but Katie didn't—couldn't—look away. Her pain changed suddenly into anger. She glared at Naomi. "What is this? You knew about my relationship with his *bruder*! How could you do this? You set me up!" She turned her ire on Micah. "I don't know what to say!"

"I didn't know!" he breathed, shock in his blue eyes.

Katie closed her eyes and breathed to calm herself. Micah Bontrager had lost someone he loved like she had. And he too suffered from the loss of Jacob, his brother. It wasn't his fault that they had been forced to meet this way. He'd been set up, too. By whom? Did Naomi or her parents have something to do with this? She shook her head and stared at him. "I don't understand. Why didn't he ever mention you?" She'd known he had an older brother who'd stayed in Michigan. Naomi was visiting from Michigan. She bit her lip as she studied him. "Wait! Are you M.T.?"

He looked devastated by the turn of events. He nodded. "A nickname. No one uses it anymore." His expression turned hard as he glared at Naomi. "Did my *eldra* put you up to this?" His jaw was tight as he mentioned his parents.

Naomi shook her head. "I heard about Katie from a woman I met in Kings General Store. I didn't know Katie was the girl who was going to marry him. I only found out yesterday while talking with her *mudder*. Since Katie is just offering to watch your *kinner*, I thought meeting each other might be *gut* for the both of you." She looked shaken by their reactions as she glanced back and forth from Katie to Micah. "I wasn't trying to hurt either one of you."

Firmly in control again, Katie nodded. "I did offer to babysit," she admitted grudgingly. "I still am. I was just—"

"Startled," Micah said, his eyes softening.

"Ja." Katie recovered enough to pick up the cake she'd baked for Micah and give it to him. "I made this for you. I hope you like pound cake."

His continued scrutiny of her was unsettling, as he looked so much like Jacob it was uncanny. "I do. *Danki*." He accepted the cake and moved it to the corner of the countertop he'd just installed where the two base cabinets met.

Katie couldn't take her gaze off him. Now that she could see him more clearly, she realized that he was more muscular than her late twenty-one-year-old fiancé. And she noticed other differences about him. His hair was a lighter shade of brown than Jacob's was, and his eyes were bigger, the lashes much thicker than his deceased brother's.

How old is Micah? Jacob had talked about having family out of state come for their wedding, but he never elaborated on any of them. She and Jacob had known each other less than a year, but it was love at first sight for her—and it seemed so for him too since he'd asked her to marry him within six months of courting her.

With a wide-eyed look, Micah searched the kitchen, his brow furrowing. "I've been so intent on the work that I didn't think to bring chairs."

"That's *oll recht*," Katie murmured shyly. "We don't have to sit. We won't be staying long, as I don't want to keep you from your day."

Micah couldn't get over the fact that Katie Mast was the woman his brother Jacob was to marry. She was a beautiful young woman with blue eyes and golden blond hair. Her light blue dress highlighted the color of her eyes, making them bluer and brighter. Her nose was slightly red from the sun, telling him that she frequently spent time outdoors. "Do you garden?" he asked suddenly.

Katie blinked. *"Ja.* Why do you ask?"

He shook his head. "It looks like you've spent time outside."

Looking horrified, she glanced down as if to check her clothing.

"It's on your nose and a bit of your cheeks, Katie," he said. When she met his gaze, he smiled. "Sunburn."

"Ach." She blushed, further brightening her cheeks.

"Naomi said that you'd be willing to watch my children while I'm at work," he observed.

Her expression softening, Katie nodded. *"Ja,* I love children, but…" She paused, her expression sad. *"Ja,* I'd be happy to watch them for you until…" Her features burned hotter, causing red from her neck up.

He glanced at Naomi, saw approval in her gaze. He would have to talk with the matchmaker later. "Can you come to my parents' *haus* to meet my *kinner*? I have three—two girls and a boy."

"How old are they?"

"My *soohn*, Jacob, is my oldest at three, nearly four, years old. My *dochter* Rebecca is two. My youngest, Eliza, is almost a year old." He studied her, noting the way her expression changed when he mentioned his son's name. He had named Jacob after his younger brother, one of the nicest people he'd ever known. He saw the way her eyes softened as he told her about his children. He'd known that Jacob was to get married, but with harvesting to be done and then Anna's sudden illness, by necessity all their plans had shifted. He'd been thrown into a tizzy and barely able to recall the names of his offspring, never mind what was happening in New Berne. Then he'd learned Jacob had died and shortly afterward Anna was gone. He'd become exhausted and unable to think straight. The men in his Centreville community had stepped in to help with the harvest while the women had pitched in with his children. Weeks turned into months until he realized something had to change. That was when he'd decided to start somewhere new where there was family, and he'd moved to New Berne.

To his delight, Katie had cracked a smile as he'd told her about his son and daughters. "I see why you might need help with three of them." She bit her lip. "Will you want me to watch them at Evan and Betty's?"

Of course, she would know his parents, he realized. "*Nay*, my *eldra* will watch them until I move us into this house. The rooms still need a bit of work, but I should be finished in three weeks."

"I'll start in three weeks then, if you want me to."

Micah nodded. "I do." He saw Katie taking stock of her surroundings.

"It's a *wunderbor* kitchen," she said, looking impressed. "I assume I'll be cooking for you and your *kinner*?"

"You want to cook for us?"

Katie inclined her head. "I love to cook and bake."

His gaze went to the pound cake on the countertop. "I'd appreciate that." He hesitated. "I can pay you."

She gasped as if insulted. "*Nay*, I could never take your money. Let me help you, *ja*? I have the time to babysit. You're a Bontrager. You're like family."

"*Danki*," he murmured, unable to take his eyes off her flawless complexion and pretty face.

"Naomi said that you'll be marrying again soon."

He frowned as he nodded. "My *kinner* need a *mudder*."

"I'll watch your little ones until you take a wife."

Katie shifted her attention to the matchmaker. "I should get home," she told her.

Naomi nodded. "*Ja*. It's getting late, and I know you like to help your *mam* with supper."

Katie started toward the door, pausing once to glance back at him. "Will you send word when you want me to come?" she asked him.

"*Ja*, I'll let you know."

"*Gut*. Please give my regards to your family."

"I will." Micah watched her open the screen door and exit the house. Something about Katie Mast tugged at something deep inside him. *Because she is the woman my* bruder *loved.*

"Don't worry, Micah," Naomi said. She had stayed behind after Katie had gone outside. "You'll have your wife. I'll find a *gut* match for you. Just like you want." She peered through the screened door as Katie climbed into the matchmaker's buggy and settled in for the ride.

"Naomi—"

"I'll not force you to wed someone you don't want, Micah."

Micah looked at her without a word. Still, he gave her a nod. He didn't want to marry anyone but he had to, so what the matchmaker said seemed pointless. "Would you tell Katie to stop by the house in the morning so that she can meet my *kinner*," he said as Naomi headed toward to the door. "We didn't set a time."

"I will. Is nine okay?"

"*Ja*." He followed her toward the door. "Katie seems nice."

The matchmaker halted and faced him. "She is a lovely young woman who believes she'll never be happy again. I think watching your *kinner* for you while I search for your new wife will be *gut* for her."

Micah watched Naomi as she crossed the yard and climbed into the driver's seat of her vehicle. He'd never imagined that the woman willing to watch his children was the woman Jacob had loved and planned to wed. She was only twenty-one. She'd barely lived, and she was so heartbroken over his brother's death that she decided she'd never marry or have a family of her own.

"What a tragic loss," Micah murmured as the buggy pulled away and he turned back to the work at hand. He was twenty-six, and he'd been fortunate enough to have had five years with Anna before the Lord had called her home. His throat tightened as he thought of his late spouse. She'd been a beautiful soul and a wonderful wife and mother.

Forcing away the pain, he concentrated instead on finishing the home for himself and his children…and wondering about his new wife, whoever she might eventually be.

Riding silently home in Naomi's buggy, Katie thought about meeting the widower. Her parents and his apparently had had nothing to do with the matchmaker's decision to bring them together. Coincidence? She didn't know. The fact that Micah was Jacob's older brother made her wonder what plan *Gott* had for putting them in each other's path.

Naomi shifted on the bench seat beside her. "Katie, do you have any questions now that you've met Micah?"

"Jacob mentioned an older *bruder*, M.T., who lived out of state. I had no idea his name was actually Micah."

"And now you know," Naomi said with a small smile in her direction.

"Ja." She stared out the open side window, watching the passing scenery. It was early August and corn grew in farm fields, the tall stalks green against the azure blue backdrop of the sky. The warmth of summer blew in through the window, but still she felt a chill from deep inside. "Do Evan and Betty know about my offer to watch their *kinskinner?*"

"Ach ja. They know." The matchmaker's voice was soft. "They love you and they love their *soohn.* They know you will take *gut* care of the *kinner.*" Naomi paused briefly to glance her way. "They want both of you to be happy."

"Did they set us up?"

"Nay, I told the truth," Naomi said. "Although I only learned about the connection between your families after I spoke with your *mam,* and then it didn't seem to matter since you only offered to babysit."

Katie rolled those words around in her mind. "I… am I doing the right thing?"

"You don't think it's a *gut* idea to help a young father in need?"

"Nay, it's not that."

"Then what?" Naomi turned to stare at her briefly before turning her attention back on the road. Her expression was tense, as if filled with disappointment.

"I…he looks so much like Jacob. When I saw him, it seemed as if he were Jacob years from now."

"Micah is nothing like him, Katie," the woman said. "He can't be. His life took a different path than his family. He experienced things that his younger *bruder* never did."

"I know that, but their similar looks startled me. Do you know I thought I'd seen Jacob a few times around town during the past week? I was alarmed. I believed I was finally getting over losing him until I imagined him as I went out to get the mail after he'd driven by in his wagon. But it wasn't Jacob. It must have been Micah. He and Micah look so much alike that it…hurts." When Naomi didn't say anything, Katie went on. "He could have been my *schwayger*." She could tell by the matchmaker's expression that she understood that under other circumstances Micah would have been her brother-in-law.

Katie recalled the man's thick arms. "Micah seems to know what he's doing with the *haus*. He must work in construction." Whatever he did, it certainly had to involve using muscle.

"Micah is a farmer."

"What?" Katie stiffened. Jacob had died while working on his parents' farm. Why would Micah farm when farming had killed his brother?

Naomi sighed. "Katie, Micah is an experienced farmer. He's been farming all his life. He owned a farm in Centreville, where he and his *frau* settled. The land he'd lived and worked on in Michigan was vaster than the eighty acres he purchased here in New Berne. He knows what he is doing."

Katie felt a tightness in her chest. "Does he have help working the land?"

"I'm sure his *bruders* will help him."

Her fear eased a bit. His brothers Matt, Jonathan and Vernon were now old enough to help their father, Evan, with farming. Perhaps Evan would pitch in before or after his own farm work was done. "*Ja*, you're right.

He has three *bruders* to help him." And three sisters, she thought, smiling as she recalled Emma, Sarie and Adel, the Bontrager sisters between the ages of twelve and fifteen with Emma the eldest at fifteen.

"Have you seen Evan and Betty lately?" Naomi asked.

"Last Sunday after church. I see them every church Sunday and occasionally on Visiting Days, but I haven't spent much time with them." Which pained her and made her feel bad that she hadn't visited with them sooner. She loved her one-time future in-laws, but after losing Jacob it had hurt too much to spend the day with them, as they were a reminder of Jacob, whom they'd loved.

"I think you should visit them," the matchmaker said. "You can do it tomorrow. Micah asked if you would stop by in the morning at nine to meet the *kinner*. I'm sure Betty if not Evan will be there."

Katie closed her eyes. Naomi was right about visiting Betty and Evan, but with the past distance between them, it wouldn't make the time at their house any easier. *It's been almost ten months since Jacob has passed. I should be able to see and visit his family without feeling awful or sad.*

"What are they expecting between Micah and me?" Katie asked quietly.

"They want for you to be more than a babysitter for their grandchildren, Katie. But don't let that stop you from helping Micah. They just want Micah to be happy. Once I find him a wife, their expectations will go away in the joy of seeing him married again with a *mudder* for his *kinner.*"

Katie knew she should take comfort from Naomi's

words but she didn't. Her thoughts filled with Micah and another woman, and she experienced a painful pang near her heart. *Because he looks like Jacob.*

Chapter Three

After being awake for most of the night worrying about his children's first meeting with Katie, Micah woke up before the crack of dawn to help his brothers with the farm animals while his son and daughters still slept.

He noticed some new animals in the barn, ones that hadn't been there yesterday. "Dat starting a dairy farm? Looks like he bought a few new cows."

Vernon grinned. "He's thinking about it. It was my idea."

Micah arched his eyebrow. "You?"

Matt chuckled. "*Ja*, he's got cows on the brain."

Snorting, Vern filled a water trough. "And you don't like fresh milk?"

"You can get milk from a goat, too, *bruder*," Matt said with a snort, "but you don't see me asking our *dat* to buy more goats."

"Because they chew everything in sight!" Vern exclaimed. "We've got more than enough of the critters."

Micah shook his head as he regarded his younger brothers with exasperation tempered with affection.

"Seems as if nothing's changed much around here. You two still argue about every little thing."

"Nay," the two brothers said together and then burst out laughing before they grinned at each other.

Their brother, Jonathan, entered the barn as the three of them were getting ready to leave.

"Nothing like coming early for a little work," Matt said sarcastically.

"I was helping Dat with Joe," Jonathan said.

Joe was one of the two horses the family relied on to pull their vehicles. "What's wrong with Joe?" Micah asked with concern.

"Dat said he's been limping a bit," Jonathan said. "I took a look at his rear right hoof, and I think he's suffering from a stone bruise." He rubbed his forehead. "Thought I'd ask Peter to come by and confirm it. Joe will have to settle in the barn for a time so he can recover if it is a bruise." Jonathan was apprenticing under Peter Troyer, a farrier with a solid reputation in New Berne.

Micah had learned that Jacob was working under Peter before he'd died, which made him wonder, now and again, why Jacob had decided to get a jump on harvesting when no one else was around to help. He had complete faith in Jonathan's diagnosis. "Dat can use one of my horses while Joe heals."

Hungry and wondering if his children were up yet, Micah returned to the house with his brothers for breakfast. His mother had the table set, and he inhaled with gratitude the smell of coffee mingled with the scent of freshly baked muffins.

"Why didn't you tell me Katie and Jacob were to be married?" Micah asked his mother after he and his brothers were seated at the table. He brought his coffee cup to his lips and sipped, enjoying the taste of brew.

Mam pulled a fresh tin of muffins out of the oven and set them on a hot mat on the counter. Sorrow filled her expression as she faced him. "I didn't know at first who Naomi had in mind for you. Once I found out, I didn't want you to make the connection between her and us ahead of time. I thought it best if you met her without prejudice."

"Katie is great," his young brother Matt said. "But ever since…" He looked away, unable to continue.

"How did you meet Katie?" Jonathan asked.

"The matchmaker introduced him," Vernon said.

Matt blinked. "Wait. *What?* Katie is your match?"

"Nay," Micah assured them. "She offered to help with my *kinner* until I can marry again."

Jonathan reached for a muffin from the plate at his end of the table. "Katie would make a *gut* wife."

"She's still grieving." Vernon got up and poured himself another cup of coffee from the pot on the stove. He faced them, leaning back against the counter. "Which is why she hasn't been around us since the funeral."

Micah felt terrible. "Why was Jacob working the farm alone?" His gaze settled on each brother, who appeared stricken.

"We don't know why," Jonathan said. "He never liked farming, but he knew how to farm. The work didn't need to be done immediately."

"Vernon and I were working on a construction job site," Matt said, staring down at his plate.

"Your *mudder* and I had gone into town for supplies," their *dat* said as he entered the room.

Mam gazed at each of her boys. "I don't know if we'll ever know or understand what happened."

His sister Emma entered the room. "I heard what you've been saying." She took a seat at the table and poured herself a glass of orange juice. "I think there was something wrong with him."

Micah narrowed his eyes. "What do you mean?"

Emma met his gaze. "I…he seemed off, like he wasn't feeling well."

"Why didn't he tell any of us?" Mam asked, upset.

"I asked him if he was *oll recht*, and he said he was fine." Jonathan handed her the plate of muffins, and Emma took one filled with chocolate chips.

"Was he unhappy?" Dat asked. "With the wedding the next month and his recent apprenticeship with Peter?" He took a seat at the table and grabbed for a muffin. He smiled at Mam when she handed him a cup of coffee.

"Nay," Emma said, spreading butter over her muffin. "He was happy to marry Katie." She set down her knife and looked at their father. "He liked working with Pete, too. I think it was something else that worried him." She took a bite of her muffin, chewed then swallowed. "I saw him sway and grab the doorframe to keep himself steady. When I asked him about it, he just grinned and said he hadn't slept well and was tired. I believed him." She looked upset that she had.

Watching his sister, Micah thought about what she'd told him. Jacob always had been the one person with the ever-present smile. It didn't surprise him to learn that he might not have been feeling well when he decided to start harvesting one of the back fields on their father's land.

The family got quiet for a minute as they continued to eat breakfast. Micah's youngest sisters Sarie and Adel entered the room. Sarie held Micah's baby daughter Eliza while Addie carried his middle child, Rebecca. His son Jacob walked closely beside Addie, holding on to the back of her skirt.

Young Jacob saw him. "Dat," he greeted with a sloppy smile as he moved up to him.

Micah's heart melted as it usually did whenever he saw children. "You're awake. Are you hungry?" His son bobbed his head. Micah turned to smile at his sisters. "*Gut* morning. Thanks for getting them up and dressed."

Sarie beamed at him and set Eliza into a high chair. "I enjoy your little ones." She stood back, held his gaze. "I'm glad you moved here, Micah," she said softly.

Addie sat down with Rebecca in her lap. "*Hallo*, everyone," his sister said, holding Rebecca easily as she reached for a muffin and broke it into bite-size pieces. She gave a piece to Rebecca who chewed and swallowed.

Matt finished his breakfast and stood. "Time to go, Vernon," he said. "We've got a lot to do on the job site today."

Micah nodded. Matt and Vernon worked for a local construction company when they weren't helping at the farm.

The brothers grabbed their hats and started out the door. Matt stilled then turned toward Micah. "Katie's here," he said.

Soon, the family was scrambling to give Micah and his offspring privacy so that the children could meet Katie for the first time alone. His father moved to leave.

"Dat, take one of my horses until Joe recovers," he said.

"Danki, soohn," he said before he escaped into another room of the house. Addie, Sarie and Emma fled the room with the intention of cleaning the upstairs bedrooms.

He spoke to his mother before she could exit. "Mam, stay," Micah said gently. "When was the last time you spent any time with Katie?"

"Months ago," his mother said with a sad smile. "She hasn't visited since…"

Since his brother Jacob's death. Micah squeezed his *mam's* shoulder. "Then stay a moment, at least, to say *hallo.*"

Mam gazed at him thoughtfully then nodded. "I'll heat up the water for tea."

Katie parked her family's buggy on Evan Bontrager's property and sat quietly, needing a moment before she could get out and face Jacob's family. She was nervous and felt awful that she hadn't spent any time with her betrothed's family in the months since Jacob's funeral. They'd seen each other at church functions, but other than a wave or a quick hello, she'd kept her distance. Seeing them at first had brought back the pain of her loss. *I loved his family. I should have stopped by for a visit.*

She glanced at the cherry pie on the bench seat behind her. Katie thought that Micah would appreciate another baked item besides a pound cake. If he didn't like it, other members within the family would eat it.

A knock on the back then the side of the buggy startled her. She turned as a man popped up in her open

side window. Matt Bontrager. She couldn't help returning his grin.

"Katie!" He popped the door and reached in to grab
her. She could see the difference one year had made
in the teenager. Matt seemed to be more handsome at
eighteen than he was at seventeen. He'd always been
a charmer, but now his muscled arms, sparkling eyes
and wide smile would soon be breaking hearts all over
the county.

He easily picked her up and set her on her feet next
to the buggy. "It's *gut* to see you, *schweschter.*" His
dark eyes so different than Jacob's or Micah's studied
her intently. "You've lost weight." He took stock of her
from head to toe. "We've missed you, Katie."

Katie opened her mouth, closed it. She cracked a
smile. "I missed you—all of you," she admitted. And
she had. More than she'd realized.

"Katie?" Vernon, the youngest Bontrager brother, approached more shyly. He wasn't as welcoming as Matt.

"Vern," she murmured. "You've grown at least six
inches in the last year."

One side of his mouth tipped upward. "Time has a
way of changing us," he said, his gaze warming.

She studied Vernon, noting that the sixteen-year-old
looked more like a full-grown man than the boy she'd
first met. Like his brothers, he was handsome. Her gaze
went to the house, and Katie experienced a nervous
flutter in her belly.

"Go on in, Katie," Vern said. "Micah is waiting for
you with my nephew and nieces."

Katie nodded then reached in for the pie on the front
passenger side. She straightened while holding the plate
carefully.

"You baked for us, Katie?" Matt asked.

"*Nay*, she baked for Micah," Vern grumbled. "Just like the pound cake he'd barely allowed us a taste of."

Katie gazed at the pie then looked up to zero her gaze in on Vern. "He liked the pound cake?"

"I'll say." Matt made a face. "We each got a thin slice, but he and his *kinner* ate the rest of it." He smiled. "It was delicious!"

Unable to help herself, Katie chuckled.

"What kind of pie did you make?" Vern asked.

"Cherry." With pie in hand, she stepped away from the buggy to close the door.

"We'll not get any of that," Matt complained. "It's Micah's favorite."

Warmth filled Katie's chest. "I'm glad I made something to be enjoyed."

"Why don't you give us each a taste now?" Matt reached for the dessert but Katie kept it away from him.

The slam of the screened door had Katie's gaze shooting toward the house. She smiled as twenty-year-old Jonathan, a year younger than Jacob had been when he'd courted her, approached, his eyebrows raising as he saw his brothers standing on either side of Katie.

Unlike Vern and Matt who had dark hair but brown eyes, Jonathan had blond hair and eyes the same color as Jacob, whose eyes were a paler blue than Micah's. As Jonathan approached, Katie closed her eyes and breathed in to calm herself while shutting out thoughts of her deceased fiancé.

"Katie," Jonathan greeted, not as open as the other brothers.

"*Hallo*, Jonathan. I hear you're working with Peter Troyer. How is that going?"

The man's expression softened. "It's going well. I enjoy working with him."

"I'm glad." She sensed someone on the back stoop and glanced over. As if waiting for her, Micah stood with a baby in his arms. "I…it's *wunderbor* to see you," she said to the three brothers. "I'm glad to know that you are all doing well."

She heard them telling her that they would see her later as she started toward the house where Micah waited. She suddenly felt shaky inside and prayed that she wouldn't trip and make a fool of herself. As she drew near, she saw that there was no smile of welcome. Her heart started to beat rapidly, and her hands holding the pie felt damp and clammy.

Katie continued right up to the back stoop where she halted and looked up at him. "*Hallo*, Micah." Today he was dressed in a spring-green shirt and navy pants with matching suspenders. He wore no hat since he'd come from inside the house.

Micah nodded, then stepped aside and opened the door for her, allowing her to precede him inside. She immediately detected the clean scent of soap and another fragrance that must belong only to him. His light brown hair was nicely combed and covered just the tips of his ears. His beard was clean, neatly groomed and not as long as the older married men with their gray beards. He had an attractive face with a nose that was like Jacob's but not. His brown lashes were long for a man, framing eyes of a blue that was startling in its intensity.

She waited for him to close the door behind him before she handed him the pie. "I hope you like cherry pie."

Micah stared at the pie before his gaze settled on

her face. She couldn't tell what he was thinking as the two locked gazes. "How did you know that cherry is my favorite?"

Katie relaxed and smiled when she saw the sudden stunned, pleased look on his face. "I didn't know. I like cherry pie so I hoped you did, too."

"I do. *Danki.*" A small smile curved Micah's lips and she felt the impact of his softening expression. He shifted the little girl in his arms.

"Who do we have here?" Katie asked, beaming at the sweet face of a child who looked no older than a year, if she was even that.

Micah gazed at his daughter with a smile. "This is Eliza."

The bubbel. She moved closer to catch the child's eye. When beautiful blue eyes encountered hers, Katie smiled and held out her arms. To her delight, Eliza leaned forward as if eager to be held by her. Katie immediately cuddled the baby girl. The child smelled clean and sweet, and Katie was happy to have the privilege of holding her. Eliza made a coo of delight when Katie turned her to face her, and the child grinned at her. "You're a delight, Eliza Bontrager."

Conscious of Micah's gaze, Katie glanced up at him with a smile on her lips that quickly died when she saw his expression. Was he unhappy that Eliza was quick to accept her?

Katie ran her hand down the child's back. "How old is she again?"

"One." Micah placed a hand on his son's shoulder. "Jacob is three."

She stilled as she studied the little boy. He didn't

look at all like her Jacob, and she relaxed with a smile for him. "*Hallo*, Jacob. I'm Katie."

The boy's father frowned when Jacob didn't immediately say anything. "Jacob? Say *hallo* to Katie. She's a friend of the family."

Jacob looked up at his father before he left Micah's side to stand in front of Katie. "*Gut* morning, Katie," he said politely.

Katie smiled, and to her amazement, the boy smiled back at her. She returned her attention to Micah. "You have three *kinner*. Where is your other *dochter*?"

"Kat-ie," a little voice said, and Katie turned, only just then noticing the little girl seated in a high chair in the far corner.

She approached the child. "You must be Rebecca," she said softly, studying the girl with warmth. "Are you eating a muffin?" The young one nodded. It wasn't hard to see that she was since there were muffin crumbs and pieces all over the tray in front of her. "Hmmm, what kind?" Katie leaned closer. "Chocolate chip?"

Rebecca hit the high chair tray with her two hands, scattering and smearing crumbs onto the flat surface. *"Chip, chip, chip."*

Katie felt Micah close behind her. She turned and watched as he went to the kitchen drawer, pulled out a washcloth, then used it to wipe Rebecca's face and hands. He pulled the tray out enough to lift his daughter from the high chair. Katie saw the mess on the tray, grabbed the cloth and cleaned it up before she used a tea towel to dry it.

The kettle on the stove whistled. Movement in the doorway to the great room drew Katie's attention to Betty, who stood uncertainly at the edge of the kitchen before she moved to the stove and turned off the flame. Katie smiled and, still with Eliza in her arms, moved to greet her properly.

"Betty," she breathed, fighting tears. She had always loved Jacob's mother and now she felt bad for not spending time with her sooner.

Betty blinked and her eyes glistened with emotion. "Katie."

Katie drew the woman close with her free hand. "It's been too long," she said softly. "I'm sorry."

"I've missed you," Betty said.

"I've missed you, too. I saw Matt, Vern and Jonathan outside. I've seen them all from a distance, but they have matured into fine young men."

A snort of derision drew her attention to Micah, who eyed her with good humor. "You obviously haven't seen them misbehave at the table. Or act like children when they fight over a dessert."

Katie stared at him. "Like pound cake?"

To her surprise, she saw his cheeks turn bright red. "That and other things. And no matter what they told you, I did share the cake with them. We each had an equal-sized piece."

The laughter that came unbidden from her mouth startled her as much as it did Micah and Betty. "I'll make two next time." She smiled at Micah. "You can keep one for yourself over at the *haus*."

Micah's smile hit her like a ton of bricks. "Would you like some hot tea?"

Katie nodded. "I'd love one." Betty pulled cups out of the cabinet. "Why don't you sit down and I'll take care of it."

"You were always a sweet girl," Betty said.

She chuckled. "I'm not sure my brothers and sisters will agree with you."

Micah put Rebecca back in her chair then reached for Eliza and placed her in a second high chair that was behind the table, leaving Katie free to fix their tea. She turned and watched as he then lifted Jacob onto a kitchen chair and pushed it under the table before handing him sheets of paper and crayons so that his son could draw pictures.

Micah locked gazes with Katie as she turned with the tea she'd made. She blushed then looked away and set the cups carefully on the table.

"Do you still take sugar without milk in your tea?" she asked Mam.

"*Ja.*" His mother smiled. "You remembered."

She is a lovely woman, and someone who most likely knows my family better than I do. He'd stayed behind after his family had left Michigan for Pennsylvania two years ago. He'd known he couldn't ask Anna to leave her family and friends because of his parents' choice to move. So he, Anna and their little ones had stayed in Centreville. Since their departure, his parents had visited him and Anna once right after Rebecca was born.

"How are your *mudder* and *vadder*?" Mam asked Katie.

"They are *gut*. They keep busy. My siblings are a handful for Mam." Katie took a drink from her tea then gave her attention to Micah. "Would you like a piece of your cherry pie?"

"You made him a cherry pie?" Mam said with a smile.

"She did." He narrowed his gaze on his mother. "You didn't tell her it's my favorite, did you?" He saw Katie stiffen. She'd already told him that she didn't know cherry pies were his favorite when she'd given it to him. "I believe you didn't know, but that doesn't mean Mam didn't put a bug in your *mudder*'s ear."

Her expression tight, she looked at him. "My *mam* wasn't home when I made the pie earlier."

"I apologize. I didn't mean..." Micah felt flustered in a woman's presence for the first time. He hadn't experienced such strange feelings when he'd first met his late wife.

Katie tilted her head as she studied him. They locked gazes, and she must have read regret in his expression as she suddenly smiled. "I'm glad you like it," she said. "Do you want a piece? Or would you rather wait until after lunch?"

He shifted his eyes to his mother, who was watching with a small smile of amusement on her lips. "You're a grown man and a father. If you want some, eat it," Mam said.

Turning back to Katie, he nodded. "I would love a piece of pie."

She rose, found two plates in a wall cabinet easily, which showed him how at home she had been when Jacob had been alive. "Betty, would you like a piece?"

Betty was silent for a moment. "Why not? Let's taste your cherry pie. If it's anything like your other baked goods, it will be delicious."

Micah watched Katie cut two slices before giving one to him and one to his mother. "Aren't you having a piece?" he asked.

"*Nay*. It's your pie."

"Actually, it's yours. You made it." Micah said with a twinkle in his blue eyes. "Have a slice if you want it."

"*Nay. Danki.* I'm not certain it's safe to eat," she said as he took a big bite and began to chew. He froze instantly and stared at her with horror. She laughed out loud, and he was enchanted with the joy and good humor on her beautiful features.

Mam gazed at Katie, looking pleased. "It's *gut* to hear your laughter, *dochter*."

"I'm sorry," she began, becoming subdued.

"*Nay*, I love seeing you enjoy life again," Mam said. "'Tis been too long."

As he went back to eating his pie, which tasted delicious, he knew he'd have to hide it from his brothers if he was to enjoy a second piece. She felt his gaze on her and looked up. Katie's eyes crinkled as she grinned at him.

"So now that you've met these little ones," Betty said, "are you still willing to watch them for Micah?"

"*Ja*, I would be happy to watch them." Katie smiled as she looked at his daughters in their high chairs, each sharing a small serving of pie from their grandmother's plate. Then she focused her attention on his son. "Jacob, would you like a little cherry pie?"

Jacob, who had been bent over his drawing with his tongue between his lips, lifted his head and looked up at her. "Can I have another muffin instead?"

"What kind would you like?" Mam rose to grab the muffins that had been wrapped up and left on the kitchen counter.

"Cimmamim?"

"Cinnamon," Micah corrected.

His son nodded. "*Ja*, cimmamim," he said with a grin.

Micah laughed. He couldn't help himself. He caught Katie's glance and saw her warm expression and the approval in her blue eyes. And he experienced a sensation of warmth inside his chest as he held her gaze.

He understood what had drawn Jacob's attention. There was something riveting about Katie Mast. She'd told him that she would never marry again, which was a shame. He could envision her as a wife and mother of many children. She was different from Anna. Like Katie, he didn't want to marry again, but unlike her, he had no choice. Although this was only the second time he'd spent any time with her, he got the feeling that he could trust her. *With his children.*

And maybe—just maybe—they could be friends.

Chapter Four

Katie woke up, gasping, heart racing. She'd dreamt of the accident again with Jacob lying in the farm field prone and bloody. Katie never saw Jacob after the accident. No one would let her see him, so since learning what had happened to her beloved betrothed, her mind had filled with horrific images of how Jacob must have suffered, how awful the accident must have been.

Throwing off the top sheet, she got out of bed then quickly made it. Still shaky after the nightmare, she dressed, pinned her hair and put on her head covering. "Jacob," she murmured, blinking back tears. "I miss you."

Was she dreaming of Jacob again because she'd met Micah, his older brother? Someone who looked so much like the man she'd loved and lost that she'd nearly fainted when she'd first set eyes on him? A father with three children. A widower. *A Bontrager.*

She paused a moment to close her eyes and breathe deeply. Jacob was gone. She had no other choice but to go on. Katie waited until she felt composed again and then headed downstairs to help her mother with breakfast for her father and five siblings. Her younger sisters Abigail, seventeen, and Ruthann, fifteen, were already in the kitchen when Katie entered the room. They had set the long trestle table large enough for her family. Her mother stood near the stove, cooking eggs and bacon.

"*Gut* morning!" Ruthann greeted, seeing Katie first.

"*Gut* morning, Ruthann. Everyone," Katie said. "I'm sorry I'm late."

"Didn't you sleep well?" Mam asked as she flipped the bacon in the cast-iron frying pan.

"I slept." Katie went to the refrigerator to pull out butter and jam then placed them on the table. As she started to slice a loaf of bread, she could feel her mother's gaze. She tried to smile at her.

"You *oll recht*?" Mam stirred the eggs then turned off the heat.

"I'm fine." Katie placed the slices of bread into a cloth-covered basket and set them on the table near the butter and jam. "Where are our *bruders*?"

"Outside taking care of the animals," Ruthann said. "At least Abe is."

Katie could control a grin despite still feeling the aftereffects of her bad dream. Her youngest brother, Abraham, was responsible and kind at twelve years old. "What about Joseph and Uri?"

"Joseph is with Dat," Abigail told her. "Uri hasn't come downstairs yet, but I know he's awake as I heard him in his room earlier."

She eyed her sister thoughtfully as she considered her eighteen-year-old brother. Uri was the oldest son and three years younger than her. Was he well? She'd sensed that something had been bothering him lately. *But what?* She, as the most senior of her parents' children, should try to have a talk with him later, when the opportunity presented itself.

Mam dumped the eggs onto a plate and placed the crispy strips of bacon onto a platter. She covered the plates to keep them warm and started to cook more of both. "Katie, would you pour coffee for your father and Uri?" she asked as she finished up the eggs and bacon.

"*Ja*, Mam." Katie took four mugs out of the cabinet, one each for her father, her brothers Uri and Joseph and herself. "Would you like tea?" she asked her mother.

"I think I'll just have juice," Mam said as she set the food in the center of the table. As if the scent of breakfast drew everyone from outside, Dat, Joseph and Abraham entered through the back door.

"Smells *gut* in here," Dat said, eyeing the food.

Uri entered from the great room and quietly took a seat.

"*Gut* morning, Uri," Katie said softly as she made up a plate and set it in front of him.

Uri met her gaze. "*Danki,*" he murmured.

"You didn't come out to help with the animals," Abe accused with a look at his eldest brother.

"Abraham," Mam said quietly. "I need Uri's help with a plumbing problem upstairs."

Katie hid a smile as she saw the quick, surprised look on Uri's face.

"I could have done it for you, Sarah," her father chimed in.

"Merv," her mother said softly, "you have enough to keep you busy."

Dat nodded. "*Soohn,*" he addressed Uri, "if you want help, just let me know. *Ja?*"

Uri nodded.

There was a knock on the back door, and everyone turned as Abe opened it to reveal Betty and Evan Bontrager. The first thing that captured Katie's attention as the couple entered the house was Micah's resemblance to his father with his brown hair and bright blue eyes. Jacob's coloring had been similar, but his blue eyes were a lighter shade than Evan and Micah's bright blue.

"Hallo!" Mam said with a smile as she got up from the table. "Breakfast? Joseph, can you pull a few chairs in from the other room?" She had made enough to feed more than her family.

"No need. We already ate." Evan grinned with warmth. "Betty made biscuits and gravy."

"Ja, we can't stay long," Betty said. "We wanted to invite you for Visiting Day this Sunday. You'll come, *ja?"* Her gaze fell on Katie briefly then slipped over to Mam. "Sarah?"

"We will be there," Dat said before Mam could answer.

Katie's heart stuttered in her chest. She wouldn't mind going. The thought of seeing Micah again made her nervous, but if she was going to watch his children while he worked then she needed to learn to interact with him.

"Coffee? Tea?" she asked Jacob's parents.

"Danki, but *nay.* We have a few errands to run," Betty said. Her blond hair and hazel eyes made an unusual combination in the Bontrager family. Her spring dress was a shade lighter than her husband's short-sleeved shirt.

"Micah working on the *haus* today?" Katie asked casually, the mention of his name causing a flutter in her stomach.

"*Ja*, he is. Emma and Addie are with the children, so I don't want to be gone long," Betty said.

"The children seemed content with your *dechter*," Katie said.

"They are *gut* with them," Betty agreed with a nod. She exchanged glances with her husband, before turning back to address Katie's family. "We'll see you on Sunday then."

"What would you like me to bring?" Mam said.

"I can bake some desserts," Katie offered.

Betty smiled. "That sounds wonderful."

Mam glanced at Katie before turning back to Betty. "*I'll* make potato salad and coleslaw, if that's *oll recht*," she said.

Jacob and Micah's mother grinned. "We'll look forward to it."

Dat followed them outside and talked for a bit with Evan before he returned to his seat to finish breakfast. "It will be *gut* to spend time with them again."

Katie immediately felt guilty for keeping the families apart. "I'm sorry," she said, meeting her father's then her mother's gazes.

"You have nothing to feel sorry about, *dochter*," Dat said.

"It's my fault that you haven't spent enough time with them."

"Katie," Mam said, "I've had tea with Betty a couple of times this past month. We know you've been grieving and have every right to be. Knowing that you're willing to take care of Micah's children makes things easier for us all to get together." Her gaze softened as she studied Katie. "We hated to see you hurting, but I truly understand why you couldn't see Jacob's family."

"Mam…"

"We'll not be pressing you, *dochter.*"

Katie released a powerful breath. "Anyone want more coffee or juice?"

Uri held his mug to her. She smiled at him and filled it. "Dat?" she asked.

Her father shook his head. "Had enough this morning. This wasn't my first cup." His blue eyes focused on her until her brother Abraham drew his attention.

"Are we going into town today?" Abe asked.

"Ja," Dat said. "We need feed." His gaze found another brother. "Joseph, you going to come with us?"

"Ja, why not?"

"Uri?"

He stared at his plate before meeting his father's eyes. "I've got plumbing to fix for Mam."

As her family made plans around the table, Katie thought of what she needed to do today. She had sewing items to deliver to Kings General Store. Over the last two days, she'd made cooking aprons, a baby quilt and a number of prayer *kapps.* Visiting Day was in three days. As she sipped the last of her coffee, she thought about what type of desserts she would make Saturday morning for Sunday to enjoy after the midday meal. *Cherry pie and pound cake.* She recalled how much the Bontrager family, especially Micah, had enjoyed both treats. She wanted to make a third dessert but wasn't sure what to take yet. A coffee cake? Shoo-fly pie? She had a little time to think about it. Whatever she made, she hoped that everyone would enjoy it.

Saturday morning dawned clear and bright. Katie stepped outside to think for a few moments before she returned to the kitchen to check on the cake and pie she'd put in the oven, the desserts she'd promised to take to the Evan Bontragers the next day.

She drew in a breath as she stood in the barnyard, enjoying a quick fresh inhale of late summer air. The squeak of the door behind her drew her attention as Uri stepped outside. "Uri."

He nodded. "Katie."

She studied him intently, noting the lackluster look in his brown eyes. "What's going on with you, *bruder*?" It was the first opportunity she had to speak with her brother alone. "You can talk to me. I won't tell anyone. I'm your *schweschter*, and I can tell when something is wrong."

Uri met her gaze with a sigh. "You won't tell anyone?"

"You have my word," Katie told him.

"Emma."

"Emma Bontrager? Micah's little sister? She is about fifteen, *ja*?"

He nodded. "Almost sixteen. She'll be sixteen next month."

Katie watched the myriad of expressions cross her brother's face. "You like her."

He ran a hand across his nape. He wore no hat, and his dark hair looked as if he'd run his fingers through it multiple times in the last hour. "*Ja*, I like her."

"What is the problem then?"

"She doesn't like me."

She frowned. "How do you know that?"

"By the way she's acting." He scowled. "And now we're going over to the Bontragers on Sunday. I know she'll ignore me. She's acted odd at church singings every time I approached so I just walked away. And whenever our paths cross, she refuses to look at me. The other day I went to the store for Mam and I saw her. She pretended she didn't see me, but I know she did. Our gazes found each other before she turned away."

She laughed. "She likes you, Uri. If she didn't, she'd meet your gaze and say *hallo* then move on. She wouldn't do her best to avoid you. I have a feeling that she is nervous around you because she likes you, too."

Uri's brown eyes brightened. "You think so?"

"I do."

He grinned before the good humor left his expression. "So what should I do?"

"You can ignore her and see what she does. Maybe she'll hate that. Maybe she'll seek you out to talk with you."

"*Danki*, Katie."

"I don't know if she'll do that, Uri, even if she does like you." She eyed her brother affectionately. "You're *willkomm, bruder*." She faced him fully. "Let me know how it turns out, *ja*?"

"*Oll recht*."

An hour later, Katie took the golden-brown pound cake from the oven and set it on top of the stove. She then reached in for the cherry pie. The crumb topping covering the fruit looked perfect. The rich smell of cooked cherries filled the air as she set the pie carefully on a hot mat on the kitchen counter. She made a fresh peach cobbler as well, as she wasn't sure how many families would be at the Bontragers visiting. The cobbler wouldn't be as good tomorrow as eating it fresh from the oven, but she figured it would be delicious anyway since she'd bought peaches from a local orchard.

It was quiet in the house. Her sisters had gone out for the day. Two of her brothers were in the barn cleaning the stables. Her father was visiting a friend on the other side of New Berne. Her mother was at the store with her youngest brother, Abraham. Mam had decided to make more salads for Visiting Day than what she'd told Betty.

Katie finished the desserts and put them on a shelf in the mud room to cool. She'd have to watch to ensure her siblings didn't get into the sweets before tomorrow. Anticipating the visit made her think of Micah and his children. She looked forward to babysitting Jacob, Rebecca and Eliza. She loved young ones and now that she wasn't going to have any of her own…

She thought of her betrothed. Jacob had treated her well, wonderfully in fact. His smile frequently had lit up his expression, especially when he'd set eyes on her. Katie felt a pang in the region of her heart. *Why did you work in the fields alone that day, Jacob?*

"I guess I'll never know why," she murmured as she removed her apron and put it in the laundry. She cleaned up the kitchen then went up to her room. Suddenly, the house felt too quiet. The silence left her with thoughts she longed to forget but knew she never would. Not when it came to Jacob Bontrager. The man she'd loved and wanted a future with. *Why, Jacob? Why?*

Sunday morning Dat drove the family to the Bontrager residence. Katie held the cake and pie on her lap while her sister Abigail held on to the cobbler. The Bontragers lived less than fifteen minutes away. Katie felt butterflies in her stomach as her father drove past farms close to the Bontragers' property. When Dat pulled into the lot, the butterflies became more active, almost painful, as she grew increasingly nervous. It wasn't the family that made feel her way. It was the thought of seeing Micah again. She was convinced that seeing Micah look like a much older version of Jacob had triggered the accident nightmare.

The screen door on the side entrance flew open, and Vernon and Matthew burst out of the house. *"Hallo!"* Matthew called with a grin.

Katie waited for her parents to get out of the buggy first before she got out carefully, holding the two desserts. "Matthew, how are you?"

"Fine, fine!" His dark eyes gleamed as he studied her. "It's *gut* to see you again, Katie."

"Hallo, Katie. Ruthann." Vernon said, blushing when her sister said *hallo*. Ruthann was just a year younger than him. He transferred his attention to Katie and reached to take the cake and pie from her. "I'll take these into the house."

"Danki, Vern," she said with a smile.

Jonathan came out to join his brothers. He approached Abigail with a small smile. *"Hallo*, Abigail. May I take that from you?" he asked, referring to the peach cobbler.

"I don't know," she teased. "Are you going to eat it or wait until after the midday meal when everyone gets to have a taste?"

"You can trust me," he said, blue eyes twinkling, pale unlike Micah's and his father's.

Abigail nodded and handed it over. Jonathan grinned at her and raced toward the house. "I've got peach cobbler!" he shouted with a look over his shoulder at her. Abbie laughed and walked toward the house with Ruthann and Abraham.

Katie waited until Uri approached more slowly. She

placed a hand on his arm without a word, and Uri smiled slightly as they walked together toward the house.

They hadn't gotten far when the door opened again, and Micah stood in the opening with his baby daughter Eliza on his hip. Katie halted briefly as her heartbeat spiked, drawing Uri's attention. When she saw the welcome on Micah's handsome features, she pulled herself together, nodded at Uri, and then brother and sister continued the rest of the way to the house. Micah stepped back to allow them entry.

"*Hallo*, Micah," Katie said pleasantly as she brushed by him.

"Katie. We're glad that you could visit today."

"I'm glad, too." She swallowed against a suddenly tight throat. "I've missed your family." Looking away from him, she experienced a moment of sadness and guilt. "I shouldn't have stayed away so long." She could feel Micah's gaze on her.

"I understand," he said sincerely, and Katie shot him a glance as she realized that he most likely did. He tragically had lost his wife. Had he avoided his wife's family because it'd been too painful after she'd passed away?

"Katie!" Emma Bontrager looked happy to see her.

"Emma, it's *gut* to see you!" Just then Uri entered the house, and Katie saw a change in Emma's demeanor.

"*Gut* morning, Emma," Uri said softly.

"Uri," she said stiffly.

Katie looked at each one's expression and wondered what she could do, if anything, to ease the tension between them. She glanced toward Micah to see if he noticed the exchange between Uri and his sister Emma, but Micah's attention had been drawn away by his father. Katie saw him walk into the other room with his daughter, and she relaxed.

Soon, she and Uri were surrounded by their own family members as well as numerous Bontrager siblings. Emma was pleased to see Ruthann. The two girls were the same age.

Katie blew out a breath. By the end of the day, things would be fine, she told herself. She would get used to being around Micah and his family. She saw Micah's son Jacob run up to his uncle Matthew. Matt hefted him high into the air, and the little boy's giggles made Katie's heart light up. She loved children. She might not have any of her own, but her siblings would no doubt marry, and she would be a good aunt to them. But until then she'd have to be content to enjoy Micah's children once they moved into the renovated house and she spent her days watching them while Micah worked.

Chapter Five

Katie stood at the kitchen window, peering out into the backyard as she unwrapped two large bowls of cold salads for the midday meal. She'd been glad to learn that her family were the only ones visiting. Despite her initial nervousness, she enjoyed catching up with the Bontragers who had come to mean so much to her after Jacob had brought her home to get to know them. She smiled. Today she even felt a new easiness around Micah.

Her brothers and the Bontrager brothers, except for Micah, were playing baseball on the back lawn. The women and girls were in the kitchen getting the food ready. Micah watched from his chair with Eliza and Rebecca on his lap, far enough away from the game to be safe from fly balls. Young Jacob sat on a patchwork quilt next to his father. It was a sunny summer's day with clear blue skies—wonderful weather for enjoying a lovely outing. Katie's father and Evan Bontrager had worked together to construct eating tables from wooden sawhorses and plywood. A long white plastic folding table had been set up in the backyard for the food.

Katie reached in a kitchen drawer for serving utensils and pulled out two large spoons. She put a spoon in each bowl and glanced outside again, grinning as she listened to her brothers' enthusiasm for playing ball.

"Micah!" her brother Abraham shouted. "Why don't you come play with us?"

"*Danki*, but I can't right now," Micah said, and she saw the tiny smile he gave to his children.

"Boys," Betty called through the screen door leading to the kitchen. "You can go back to your ball game after we eat."

"Food!" Matthew Bontrager shouted, appearing eager as he tossed the baseball up in the air and caught it as he headed toward the food table. "I'm hungry!"

"You're always hungry," his brother Jonathan teased with a laugh.

"You're all always hungry," his sister Emma said, sticking her head out the door to see where their fathers had set the tables, which Betty and Sarah, Katie's mother, had covered with sheets as tablecloths.

Everyone laughed at Emma's comment, even Micah. Katie settled her gaze on him with his children and felt a little tug on her heartstrings. If things had been different, the man would have been her brother-in-law and his children her nephew and nieces. She quickly blinked back tears and turned away from the window. "I'm going to take these outside," she said of the two salads in her arms. "I'll be back to help carry out the rest."

"Wait up," Emma said, "and I'll walk out with you." The fifteen-year-old held a platter of cold roast beef.

Katie smiled as the girl joined her, and they went outside together. "It's *gut* to spend time with you, Emma," she said as they headed toward the food table. "I can't believe how much you've changed since…"

"I know," Emma said softly. "Things—people—change."

"I'm sorry I didn't come by sooner. It was just too—"

"Painful," the girl said. "I understand. But, Katie, we missed you. Our *bruder* loved you and we do, too. After you were gone, we felt as if we also lost you."

Fighting tears, Katie nodded. "I'm sorry," she whispered. "I promise to be better about visiting. *Oll recht?*"

Emma grinned. "I would like that."

Katie set the bowls of macaroni salad and potato salad at one end of the food table and watched Emma place the platter of meat in the center. Ruthann left the house carrying a platter of cold ham. Emma stayed to chat with Katie's sister as Katie headed back to the house. She was conscious of Micah's eyes on her as she passed him to climb the porch steps. Emma headed inside with Ruthann after allowing Betty to pass with a plate of cheese and crackers.

"I'll take that," Katie offered, reaching for snacks.

"*Danki*, Katie." Betty smiled as she gave Katie the plate then headed into the house.

After setting it down outside, Katie turned to find Micah watching her intently. On impulse, she stopped before him. "If you'd like to play baseball with our *bruders* later, I'll be happy to watch your little ones," she said.

The little uptick of his lips made her heart beat faster. "That's kind of you."

"It will be *gut* experience," she managed. "With you being here while I… Ah, then you'll see you can trust me with them."

"I already do." His blue eyes watched her carefully as if trying to gauge her reaction. A tiny smile blossomed on his face. "I accept your offer," he said, "and not because I need to see the way you handle my *kinner*. I could tell immediately the first time I saw you with them that you are *gut* with *kinner*." He stood with his two youngest cradled within his arms. She saw the flex of his forearm muscles as he shifted to allow Eliza, his sleepy baby, to become more comfortable.

Katie felt her lips curve. *"Danki,"* she said softly. Her gaze fell softly on Eliza. "Do you want me to put her down for a nap?"

"I think I should get her to eat first."

She nodded in understanding. The way Micah continued to study her made her wonder if she had a few stray hairs. She started to reach up to her *kapp* to check when he grinned.

"You look perfect," he whispered. "Not a hair out of place."

She could feel her cheeks heat as she glanced away. "I should go inside and help bring out the rest of food so we can eat." She took a few steps toward the house.

"Katie?"

She spun, stunned to hear him calling her. *"Ja?"*

"Danki for your offer," he said. "To watch my *kinner*."

Flustered by the intensity of his gaze, Katie needed a minute to answer. When his gaze softened, she relaxed. "You're *willkomm*," she murmured then hurried into the house.

Within minutes, the women had the food set up on the table outside. Her *dat*, Evan and their sons got up first to fill their plates.

"Mervin, I can fill a plate for you," *Mam* said, drawing Katie's attention.

"*Nay*, Sarah," *Dat* replied with a smile for his wife. "Get yourself a plate and enjoy your meal. You don't need to wait on me."

Listening to her parents' exchange, Katie experienced a warmth. She knew they loved each other but hearing the affection in their voices touched her deeply. Not every couple who married had the kind of relationship they did. *I would have enjoyed it with Jacob.* Sighing, she grabbed a plate and got at the end of the food line.

"You made cherry pie and pound cake," a familiar masculine voice murmured suddenly from behind her.

Spine tingling, Katie turned and met Micah's gaze. "Your family seemed to enjoy them so I thought they would be a *gut* choice to bring," she told him. "I enjoy baking and can make other things as well."

"What's next to the pound cake on the left?" he asked, gesturing toward a square baking dish at the other end of the table.

"Peach cobbler," she told him, following his gaze toward dish in question. "It tastes better warm, but the peaches are fresh."

"Miller's Orchard?" he asked.

She nodded.

"Their peaches are delicious," he said. "I think I'll have a taste of your cobbler." He shifted behind her, making her overly aware of him.

He stood alone, and she wondered where his children were. Then she saw that Emma had Rebecca on her lap while Addie held Eliza. Her sister Abigail was giving young Jacob tidbits of food from her plate.

"Have you gotten a lot done on the *haus*?" she asked, meeting his gaze again.

"Well…" he replied, sounding pleased. "I finished the kitchen and laundry areas, and now I've switched to renovations to the upstairs bedrooms and bathroom."

"What do you have to do?" she asked as she moved down the line, adding a small spoonful of each salad to her plate.

"I need to paint and replace the floors," he said, taking salad as Katie added a helping of chowchow, a pickled mixture of garden vegetables, to her plate.

"Wood floors or vinyl?"

"Vinyl," he said. "At least in Jacob's and the girls' rooms. Easier to maintain when dealing with children's messes. I haven't decided about the main bedroom yet."

Katie nodded. Sheet vinyl was a common choice for floors in Amish houses because they were easy to keep clean. She wondered what pattern he'd chosen or if he'd yet to choose one. She forked a piece of roast beef onto her plate then handed the serving fork to Micah.

"Danki," he murmured. He added two slices of roast beef to his plate and continued along the line behind Katie.

Katie eyed the ham and decided that she had enough on her plate. She turned to head back to her table when she accidentally brushed against Micah's arm as he moved down the line. "Sorry," she mumbled, moving out of his way.

He grinned at her. "Enjoy your lunch, Katie." Then he continued down the table to finish loading his plate with food.

Katie sat with her sisters, her brothers and Addie Bontrager, who came over to eat with them. There were two tables, set up short end to short end, creating a large family eating area. Matthew and Vernon had joined them at their end, and they chatted about events happening in their lives. While she ate slowly, listening to the others talk, she was conscious of Micah's gaze. She looked over but he'd turned his attention to his mother beside him. Mam and Dat sat close to Betty and Evan with Jonathan next to his father and his sisters Emma and Sarie seated across the table from them.

"I'm going to get some dessert before it's all gone," Katie said as she stood. "Anyone want anything?"

"Will you see if there is any pound cake left?" Matt asked.

"*Ja*, I'll be happy to."

His sister Addie rose to her feet. "I'll go with you." She glanced toward Katie's brother Uri. "Would you like a piece of cake or pie?" she asked him casually, but Katie recognized something in her expression that made her think that Addie was sweet on Uri.

Uri met the girl's gaze and shook his head. "*Nay*, I had plenty."

Katie sighed. If only her brother liked Addie instead of Emma, he would be much happier.

Soon the meal was over, and Katie helped the women clean up. When she was finished, she hurried outside to see if Micah wanted her to watch the children while he played ball. As she approached, she heard Micah and his sister Emma talking.

"I'll put them down for their naps," Emma said, and Katie saw that the children looked sleepy.

Micah saw Katie's approach. "Let Katie help you with them," he said.

Emma spun, saw Katie and smiled. "*Ja*. Katie? Would

you mind helping me to get these little ones upstairs to bed?"

"My pleasure." She met Micah's gaze to see him watching her thoughtfully.

Emma reached for Rebecca, and Micah carefully slipped little Eliza into Katie's arms. "We'll come back for Jacob, *bruder*," Emma said.

"Jacob, go with Katie upstairs," Micah told his son, surprising her.

"*Dat*, I'm not tired."

Micah studied him. "*Ja*, you are. Lie down like a *gut boo*, and I'll make sure you get a special treat when you wake up."

"Some more pound cake?"

"If there is any left."

"Jacob," Katie said softly. "I'll make you another one if you take a nap for me."

"You will?" He narrowed his eyes as he gazed up at her.

"*Ja*, I made this one and the one you had the other day."

He blinked, smiled then held out his hand to her. "*Oke.*"

With the baby cradled in one arm, Katie took Jacob by the hand and, with a last quick look at the boy's father, led him toward the house behind Emma. The boy's fingers was small and warm clasped within her own. She felt a wave of affection for the child, her Jacob's namesake. Katie thought of the children she would have had with her deceased betrothed and experienced a moment of sadness, which she dispelled as they continued toward the stairs.

Emma led her to a second-story bedroom where

there was a crib and a toddler bed. Emma laid Rebecca down carefully and smiled when the little girl continued to sleep.

Katie released Jacob's hand and was impressed when he waited quietly for her to place baby Eliza in her crib. She loved how Eliza curled up on her side and kept snoozing. When she turned, she found Jacob watching her thoughtfully. "Now it's your turn," she said.

Emma grinned at her as they left the room. "Want me to help?" she asked.

Shaking her head, Katie glanced at Jacob. "*Nay*, it's fine. I'll be down soon." She turned to Jacob. "Will you show me where you sleep?"

Jacob nodded, released Katie's hand and led the way to another room where there was a large bed and a smaller one. "I sleep here with *Dat*," he told her.

"It's a nice room," she said, feeling strange as she eyed its contents. A blue shirt and black felt wide-brimmed hat hung on wall hooks next to a dresser on the other side of the room.

"Did you really make the pound cake we had today?" he asked, watching her.

"I did. I made the cherry pie and peach cobbler, too."

"I like pound cake." He continued to study her with innocent blue eyes.

"Me, too. I'll make you one tomorrow then ensure you get some, *ja*?"

He bobbed his head. Jacob then climbed onto his bed.

"Do you want the shade drawn?" Katie asked. "The sun is bright."

Jacob shook his head. "Can we leave it up?"

"*Ja*." She took off his shoes, watched as he settled in, then straightened. "Sleep well, Jacob."

"*Danki*, Katie, for the pound cake."

"You're *willkomm*, little one." Katie slipped out of the room and went downstairs.

The children were still sleeping when Katie and her family said their goodbyes. Micah pulled her aside as she started toward the buggy.

"I'll let you know when we move into the *haus*," he told her, his deep voice having a strange effect on her.

She nodded. "*Oll recht*. You've done well with your little ones. They are kind and precious."

Micah blinked, seeming surprised by her comment. "*Danki*. They are everything to me."

"I understand why." His comment reminded her why he needed a wife. "I told Jacob I would make him a pound cake tomorrow. I'll bring it over or send it with one of my *bruders*."

He continued to study her as he inclined his head. "Have a *gut* night, Katie."

"Same to you, Micah."

Katie and her family arrived home by three in the afternoon. They weren't home a full hour when she heard a buggy pull into the yard. She peered through the window in time to see Jonathan Bontrager step from the vehicle and approach the house. He looked solemn, and she got the feeling that something was seriously wrong. She hurried downstairs to find out.

"Katie," Jonathan gasped as she opened the door. "We just received word that my *grossdaddi*—my *mudder*'s *dat*—fell and got hurt. We will be heading to Indiana, tomorrow. Micah wondered if you would watch the children for him."

"*Ja*, of course. I'll help in any way I can. Where are you going and when do you leave?"

"Middlebury, Indiana," Jonathan said. "First thing in the morning. We don't know what to expect. Dat wants us to come, as he may need our help with Grossdaddi's farm and my sisters with the household chores."

"I'm sorry to hear to learn of your *grossdaddi*'s accident. Please tell Micah that I'll take *gut* care of his *kinner*. I can come in the morning and bring them back here."

"I'll let Micah know."

"What time will you be leaving tomorrow? I can be there as early as you need me."

"Can you come at six?"

Katie nodded. "I'll be there." Jonathan started toward his buggy. "Please tell Betty and Evan that we are thinking of them and your *grossdaddi*."

"I will. *Danki*." Then Jonathan left.

Katie's mother appeared behind her as she turned. "Was that Jonathan Bontrager?"

"*Ja*," Katie confirmed. Then she proceeded to tell her about Betty's father and the family's plans to go to Michigan. "I'll bring the children here, if it's *oll recht*."

"*Ja*. Of course." Her mother gazed out the window with concern.

"It will be fine," Katie assured her. "We will pray and everything will turn out fine."

She sent up a silent prayer that Micah's grandfather wasn't seriously hurt and for the Bontrager family.

Chapter Six

At six the next morning, Katie drove to the Evan Bontrager residence with her sister Abigail. She had planned to go by herself but wondered how she'd manage to drive home with three young children. She wasn't worried about Jacob. He was old enough to sit in the middle bench seat, but two-year-old Rebecca and one-year-old Eliza would be more of a challenge.

She glanced fondly toward her sister beside her in the front seat. Fortunately, Abigail had gotten up and finished her chores early. In fact, she and Abigail had worked together to ensure they finished everything they needed to get done. Her parents were upset to hear that Betty's father was ill, and they were more than happy to have Micah's children stay.

"I hope everything turns out *oll recht* with Betty's *dat*," Abigail said.

"*Ja*, I hope so, too." Katie worried about the family, could only imagine what they were going through. Micah must be beside himself with worrying about his grandfather and leaving his children behind to go with his parents.

The trip to Evan's property didn't take long. Katie drove onto the dirt road leading toward the residence and parked close to the barn. She and Abigail got out and started toward the house. The inside door was open, leaving only the wooden screen door to keep out bugs.

As they approached, Katie heard Micah's deep voice from inside the house as they got closer to the back door. He was having a conversation with his mother and father. She froze, unwilling to move closer, and felt her sister halt beside her.

"You don't have to come with us, Micah," Betty said. "You have a *haus* to finish and *kinner* who need you."

"Mam…"

"*Nay*, Micah," Katie heard Evan say. "We have enough help should we need it once we get to Middlebury. You stay here with your *kinner*."

"What about Katie?" Micah asked.

"She can still watch the children. How else will you be able to work on your *haus*?"

Katie exchanged concerned looks with her sister, who appeared as uncomfortable as she was.

"Hallo!" Katie called, after moving farther back in the yard after signaling her sister to do the same.

Betty came to the door, appearing glad to see her. "Come in, Katie. And Abigail? Come in! Come in!"

Katie moved first, eager to find out what everyone wanted her to do. If Micah insisted that he travel with his family to see his grandfather in Indiana, then she would continue with plans to take the children home. But what if Micah wanted to take Jacob, Rebecca and Eliza with him? *Nay*, he wouldn't do that. He was a wonderful *vadder*, and she knew it would be hard on the children to travel that far.

As soon as she stepped inside the house, she could feel the intensity of Micah's gaze. She focused her attention on Betty. "I'm sorry to hear about your *vadder*."

"*Danki*, Katie." Betty moved to the pantry and pulled out a plate of muffins, which she set on the table. "I'm glad you're here."

"*Ja*, there's been a change of plans," Micah interjected. "I'll be staying behind so rather than taking my *kinner* back to stay with you, I hope that you will feel comfortable enough to watch them here each day. Just until I get home in the afternoon after working on the *haus* renovations."

Meeting his gaze, she nodded. "I can come here. It's not a problem."

He looked relieved. *"Danki."*

"You're *willkomm*." Katie heard a vehicle pull up outside. She saw through the screened door that it was a white van, large enough to carry a big family and their belongings.

"Our ride is here," Evan said before Katie could comment. He looked at Micah. "*Soohn*, would you help us with our things?"

"*Ja*, Dat." He grabbed his parents' valises and carried them outside.

Betty and Evan left the room, and Katie could hear their footsteps on the stairs to the second floor. While Micah was absent, Emma and Addie entered the kitchen carrying small suitcases.

"Katie! Abigail!" Addie exclaimed.

"Hallo," Katie said. "I'm sorry about what happened. I'll pray for your *grossdaddi*."

"Danki." Emma blinked back tears.

Micah entered the house and reached for his sisters' suitcases.

"I can carry mine," Emma said.

"I know you can, *schweschter*. Since I can't go with you, please let me help you."

Emma nodded, handing him her suitcase, and his sister Addie gave him hers. Micah carried their cases out to the vehicle. Jonathan, Matthew and Vernon came downstairs with their belongings.

"Katie, Abigail," Jonathan greeted with a nod before he continued outside with his suitcase.

"Matthew, Vernon, is there anything I can do to help?" Katie asked softly, noting their solemn expressions.

"*Danki*, Katie, but we'll be fine."

"Safe travels," Abigail said. "Katie and I will pray for your *grossdaddi*."

Emma reentered the house. "Where are Micah's little ones?" Katie asked.

"They're still sleeping," Addie told her.

Soon everyone but the children were outside near the vehicle. Betty approached Katie where she stood with Abigail and Micah.

"Katie, *danki* for everything," she said.

"I'm glad I can help," Katie said with a soft smile. "If there is anything else I can do..."

"You're doing more than you'll ever know." Betty turned toward Micah. "We'll send word to let you know how *dei grossdaddi* is faring."

Micah nodded. His blue eyes became cloudy with worry. "Are you sure you don't want me to go?"

Evan joined his wife. "We are certain, Micah. Take

care of your *kinner* and finish your *haus*. We'll look forward to seeing your progress once we get home."

The couple turned toward the large passenger van. "Mam, Dat," Micah called, drawing their attention. "Have a safe trip."

"It's in *Gott*'s hands, *soohn*," Evan said before he climbed into the vehicle after his wife and children.

Katie heard Micah huff out a breath after his family was seated in the van. As the driver drove off, Katie glanced at Micah and was immediately worried about him.

Once they were gone, Micah faced her and her sister.

"Micah," Abigail said, "would you drop me off at home?"

"Take your buggy. I'll make sure that Katie gets home safely this afternoon."

"Abigail, it would be best if you came back for me. Micah, you may be too tired to bring me when you get home." Katie looked questioningly at him. "Four thirty?" She wasn't sure it was a good idea for her to be watching the children without a vehicle should she need one. And it wouldn't be the best idea for him to take the children with him to bring her home. After Abigail had left, Katie told him about her concerns.

"I doubt after you've been working all day that you'd want the children with you when you take me home," she said. "But I don't like the idea of being without a vehicle while I'm babysitting."

Micah nodded. "Feel free to take *meim dat*'s family buggy if you need to go anywhere." His bright blue eyes gazed at her with intensity. "Do you have somewhere special you have to be?"

Katie blinked. "*Nay*, but just in case of an emergency…"

"There are other vehicles in the barn. With a family like ours, we need several carriages to get where we're going, but I'll be taking two of them to the carriage-maker's to see if any need repairs or replacement parts."

"*Oll recht. Gut* to know. I'll drive myself over tomorrow morning." She returned to the house, and he followed her inside. "What do the children like to eat for breakfast?"

Micah took her to the pantry. "This cereal is fine for all of them. Jacob will want a bowlful with milk. You can give Rebecca and Eliza some on their trays to eat with their fingers."

Katie nodded. "What about lunch?"

"There is leftover macaroni and cheese in the refrigerator. They love that, especially Jacob. But feel free to give them whatever you think is best."

The mention of Jacob made her remember her promise to him to make a pound cake. "Do you have the ingredients for a pound cake?"

His smile made her heart beat harder. "*Ja*, I'm sure my *mudder* has what you need. Help yourself. I know whatever you make will be *gut*." He ran his fingers through his hair. "I'm going to check on Jacob and then my *dechter*. I'll let you know if they are awake. I doubt they are, or we would have heard them by now, and Jacob would have come downstairs on his own."

She relaxed after Micah left the room. Why was she so uncomfortable, so nervous suddenly? Katie looked in the pantry and pulled out the dry ingredients for a pound cake. She started to search for loaf pans in a kitchen cabinet but then stopped, debating whether it was a good time to make the cake batter.

"Nay," she murmured, "I'd better not. If the children are awake, I'll be busy feeding them." She wondered how she was going to bake with three little ones to watch over. Maybe she could find a way to entertain Jacob and the girls in the kitchen so that she could keep an eye on them while she worked.

Micah entered the room a few minutes later, carrying his sleepy son in his arms. "Jacob woke up and saw me," he explained with a soft smile for his little boy.

Katie observed, warmed by Micah's affection for his little boy. She reached for Jacob, who had been dressed by his father, but he simply burrowed against Micah's chest. She tried not to let it upset her. Jacob didn't know her well yet. Maybe once he did, he'd feel comfortable enough to let her hold him.

"I told you I'd make pound cake for you today, *ja*?"

Jacob lifted his head from his father and regarded her with bright blue eyes. He looked adorable in his little maroon short-sleeved shirt with black suspenders and navy triblend pants. His feet were bare, and she noted with a smile the boy's little toes. His father must have combed his hair, too, because his brown locks looked smooth and shiny. "You'll make pound cake?"

"Ja, I said I would, and I will. Pound cake takes time to make and then bake, but it will be ready to enjoy after lunch or supper."

Jacob struggled to get down, and Micah set his son carefully on his feet. "Why don't you sit at the table, and Katie will get you something for breakfast." He met Katie's gaze. "I'll get the girls up and dressed."

"Are you sure I can't help? Don't you need to be over to the *haus*?"

Micah nodded toward his son. "Take care of him, and I'll bring the girls down so you can have all of them within sight before I leave. All three should sleep for you around ten until eleven or twelve."

Katie nodded. "I imagine after a busy morning they'll be tired by then."

Lips curving upward, he agreed. "I'll be right back." He left the room, leaving her a lingering awareness of him.

"Your *dat* told me that you like cereal with milk," Katie said to Jacob as she helped him into his seat by the kitchen table. She went to the pantry and pulled out a cereal box. "These?"

Jacob bobbed his head. "*Ja*, I like them. Becca and Liza does, too."

Katie took out a bowl, filled it with cereal and poured a little milk on it. "How's this?"

He smiled. "It looks *gut*."

Micah entered the room, carrying his two daughters. Both still wore their little white nightgowns. "I changed them, but as you can see, I haven't dressed them yet."

Grinning, Katie gazed at the large handsome father holding his little girls, and her heart melted. Whomever he married would be a lucky woman. Suddenly, she didn't want to envision him married to someone else.

"I'll dress them after they eat," she told him.

"*Danki.*" He settled Eliza and Rebecca into their high chairs. "Be *gut* for Katie, *ja*?"

"We will, Dat," Jacob said.

Micah grinned at his son. "*Gut boo.* Help Katie if she needs it."

"*Ja*, Dat," he said before he spooned cereal with milk into his mouth then grinned as he chewed and swallowed it.

"I have to work on the new *haus*," Micah told his son. "I'll be home later. Katie is here to take care of you."

"Where is *grossmammi* and *grossdaddi*?" the boy asked.

"They went on a trip with my *schweschters* and *bruders*."

"Why didn't we get to go?"

"Because that would make too many people in the van." He smiled at Jacob with affection. "And it's a long journey, *soohn*. Like when we moved here."

Jacob seemed to give it some thought and nodded, as if he understood. "It took too long to get here," he said.

His daughters seemed content to wait patiently for breakfast while Micah and Jacob talked.

"I'll be back this afternoon between three thirty and four. Four thirty at the latest." Micah ran a hand over his son's hair. "Will that be *oll recht*?" He reached for a glass on the table and drank the rest of his iced tea. "*Ja?*"

"*Ja*. Take as long as you need, Micah. Abigail will be back for me at four thirty. If you want to work longer, feel free. Abigail will wait until I'm ready to go." She studied him a moment as he checked on his children one last time before leaving. "Did you eat breakfast?" she asked.

"*Ja*, I had one of *meim mam*'s muffins."

"May I make you a sandwich for lunch?" she asked, concerned that he would skip a meal after not having much of a breakfast.

"I'll pick up something on the way," he told her,

and Katie decided that from now on she would make sure that he had breakfast and lunch each day. And she would fix him supper before she headed home late this afternoon.

Micah left, and the children happily ate their cereal. Katie poured each of them a glass of milk, using sippy cups for Eliza and Rebecca so that they wouldn't spill it.

"Where's Dat?" Jacob said when he was finished breakfast.

"He is working on your new *haus*. Remember?" Katie said as she cleaned up his face and hands with a damp dish towel.

"Where's *grossmammi*?" he asked.

"She is on her way to Indiana where her *dat* lives."

Jacob blinked rapidly as if he was holding back tears. "Where's Ind-ana? I want to see them."

"Jacob, you can't right now. They will be gone for a while, but your *vadder* will be home later today." Katie watched as Jacob pushed back his chair to get down. She hurriedly helped him.

"I want Emma! I want Addie!"

"They are with your *grosseldra*."

"Why?" he wailed, his eyes filling with tears.

"Because your *grossmudder*'s *dat* is sick, and they need to help him," Katie said softly, soothingly. "But they will come home and you will see them."

He gazed up at her with eyes brimming with tears. "When?"

"I don't know. It won't be today, maybe next week, but we can have a *gut* time until they do, *ja*?"

"I want Dat!" he cried as he gazed up at her. She longed to hold and comfort him.

"He'll be home later, *oll recht*?"

Seeing their brother upset, his sisters started to cry. Katie listened to the three upset children, and she tried to think of a way to soothe them. If she could convince Jacob to calm down, maybe the girls would, too.

"Jacob, do you want to help me make pound cake?" she asked.

Sniffling, with tears on his cheeks, he looked at her with interest. "Pound cake?"

"*Ja*, with chocolate chips if you like them."

"*Ja!* I like chocolate chips!"

"Shall we go upstairs to dress your *schweschters* before we start?"

"I can help make cake?"

Katie ruffled the boy's hair. "*Ja*, you can help."

He nodded then smiled as he wiped his eyes. His sisters continued to cry. "We're going to have cake," he told them.

"Will you come upstairs with me to show me where they sleep and where their clothes are?"

He grinned. "I'm a *gut* helper. Dat says so."

"I'm sure you are."

Jacob moved toward his sisters' high chairs and began to make faces at them.

Rebecca and Eliza looked at him and they stopped crying. Their brother's antics made them laugh.

Problem solved for now! "You *are* a *gut* helper," Katie murmured with a grin. She cleaned Rebecca's face and hands then took her out of her high chair. Jacob took his sister's hand and kept her close while Katie wiped up Eliza before she picked her up. Cradling Eliza in one arm, she met Jacob's gaze. "Ready to go upstairs?" The little boy nodded. "Do you want me to carry her?" she asked, referring to Rebecca.

"I can help her," Jacob said. "I've done it before."

"*Oll recht*, let's go then."

To Katie's amazement, young Jacob was careful and considerate of his two-year-old sister as he helped her slowly up the steps to the second story. Katie had gestured for him to go ahead so that she could be close behind the two in case there was an accident and Jacob tripped and fell, pulling Rebecca with him. She was grateful that she'd had nothing to really worry about when they reached the top landing with no incident. She felt a surge of affection for Micah's children as she followed Jacob into the girls' room. Her feelings for the little ones overwhelmed her, stealing her heart. Jacob kept hold of Rebecca's hand, and Katie saw that the little girl didn't seem to mind her brother's grip.

What am I doing? These children weren't hers. She shouldn't get too attached, but how could she not? They were wonderful. She'd never have children of her own, so why not enjoy these three young ones and hope until Micah finally married and found them a new mother. Then she would have to accept the change and get over the heartbreak that was surely to come when she was no longer in their lives.

Chapter Seven

Micah stared at the existing floor in the main bedroom and debated what to install in its place. He'd had
trouble concentrating since his arrival this morning. He
was worried about his grandparents and concerned for
his parents and siblings. And he couldn't stop thinking about Katie back at his parents' house taking care
of his children.

He should be in Middlebury with his family but the
trip would be too hard for Jacob, Rebecca and Eliza…
and with his house… His parents had been right; it was
best that he'd stayed home. He said a silent prayer for
his grandfather.

He bent over to take a closer look at the wood floor.
Maybe he could sand and refinish it. He'd ripped up the
old vinyl in the great room downstairs and replaced it
with hardwood. He loved the look of wood, especially
the wider planks. The master bedroom's floor already
had wide planks but it was scratched and scuffed and
the finish had worn off in several places.

"*Ja*, I think I'll keep this floor and refinish it myself," he murmured. "A *gut* sanding and coat of polyurethane will make it look brand new."

His stomach growled, and he realized that he'd never picked up anything for lunch and the muffin he'd eaten for breakfast at five this morning wasn't cutting it. He glanced at his watch. It was 11:10. His children should be napping.

He wondered how Katie was making out with them. He experienced a sudden strong urge to go home for lunch. On the way back he could pick up a new battery for his power sander and sandpaper. A little "scuff" sanding to the floor would be necessary for the new finish to hold.

Once downstairs, Micah locked up the house before he climbed into his buggy and headed home. Would Katie mind if he stopped by for a quick sandwich? He surely hoped not. It wasn't a question of trusting her with his children. Because he did, as he'd told her previously. Katie was caring and warm whenever she was with them. A natural mother, he thought, and it was a shame that she had no intention of marrying and having a family.

Katie had been his late brother Jacob's betrothed. His parents had told him that Katie had grieved so much since his death that she hadn't been able to bear spending time with his family.

Micah knew what it was like after losing someone special. It had been difficult seeing his late wife's family after Anna had passed. But he'd had no choice since his children were their grandchildren. Anna's parents hadn't lived in Centreville for years. Her parents and siblings had moved during the early years of their marriage to a very small Amish community in Idaho, outside of the town of Salmon. Apparently, the family who had first settled there were relatives of Jeb and Marcie Miller, Anna's parents. They had returned for Anna's funeral, and it had been an emotional time for everyone. Later when they'd suggested they should move back to help with the children, Micah had assured them that he and his offspring would be fine and that he was seriously contemplating a move to where his family lived in New Berne, Lancaster County, Pennsylvania. Jeb and Marcie, who were happy in Idaho at the time, had accepted his decision to move. Micah had been grateful for their support, he understood their concern about seeing their grandchildren again. Micah invited them to come for an extended visit in New Berne once he and his children were settled in their new home.

His thoughts returned to Katie. Naomi, too, seemed to think that Katie was still hurting. The matchmaker had promised him that she'd keep looking for a wife for him since Katie wasn't open to the idea. Katie was only twenty-one. Losing Jacob had devastated her, but he thought she was too young to know for certain that she was done with the idea of marriage and children. Which was why he was concerned for her.

Micah frowned as he pictured her blue eyes and sweet face. When the Mervin Mast family had come for Visiting Day, he'd enjoyed seeing Katie's ease and familiarity with everyone in his family. Everyone except himself since he hadn't known her for long. It was obvious that his parents and siblings loved Katie and had missed having her in their lives.

His father's farm was ahead on the left. Micah turned on the battery-operated blinker on his buggy and pulled onto the property. Suddenly, he wanted to see Katie more than his need to fill his empty stomach. To ensure she was fine.

"Let's wait until your sisters are asleep before we make the cake," Katie said with a smile for Jacob. She had just put the girls down for their morning nap. "You don't need to lie down yet. You're their big *bruder*."

Jacob looked pleased. "We can make the cake while they sleep?"

Katie nodded. "We can stir all the ingredients together. Once the cake is ready for the oven, then you should lie down, too. *Ja?*"

He seemed to give it some thought. *"Oke."*

"Gut boo." She ruffled his hair. "Let's check on Rebecca and Eliza. If they are asleep, we can start on the cake."

Jacob grinned then followed her upstairs.

"You must be very quiet," Katie whispered.

He bobbed his head. *"Ja,"* he whispered back. "We can't wake 'em if they're asleep."

The girls were snoozing. Jacob was quiet as Katie tiptoed toward their beds to check on them. She smiled at Jacob as she waved him out of the room.

Once near the stairs, he said, "We can make cake now?"

Katie grinned at him. *"Ja.* Right now."

The little boy's eyes brightened. He looked so much like his father that Katie could picture a young Micah with his bright blue eyes and mop of brown hair at Jacob's age. She thought of Micah with his blue eyes, handsome face and light brown beard that grew along his chin in the Amish way that married men wore them, and sighed. Micah was a good-looking man. He was kind and thoughtful, and the woman who married him would be grateful to have such a man in her life.

Back in the kitchen, Katie allowed Jacob to help her gather the main ingredients for the pound cake— flour, sugar, butter, eggs, baking powder, salt and vanilla extract. She found Betty's hand-crank mixer with its large bowl to stir everything together. Jacob showed her where his grandmother's loaf pans were and carried them carefully for her to the kitchen table, a flat surface he could reach easily from a chair.

Katie turned on the gas oven. While it preheated, she showed Jacob how to grease and flour the loaf pans. She carefully measured each ingredient so that he could dump them into the mixing bowl, starting with the softened butter then adding all the other ingredients. She'd decided earlier that they would make enough for two cakes—one to eat now and another to freeze for later.

Jacob grinned at her when Katie allowed him to crank the mixer.

"Carefully," Katie instructed when the little boy got a little too ambitious with his cranking. "Hold on." She scraped the sides of the bowl. "*Oll recht*, go ahead."

When the little boy got tired of turning the crank, Katie took over. Next, Katie stirred in chocolate chips by hand. Soon the cake batter was ready to be poured into the pans. Jacob watched as she tipped the bowl easily, filling each loaf pan before she placed them side by side in the preheated oven. She turned a timer on for an hour.

She turned to Jacob. "Time for a nap."

Jacob nodded. "It will be ready when I wake up?"

"It might," Katie told him. "It depends on how long

you sleep. If you take a *gut* nap, it will be." She cleaned his hands and face then went with him upstairs to his room. "Sleep well, Jacob," she said as she took off his shoes. She then sat on the edge of the bed and tenderly brushed the hair off his forehead. "You were a *gut* helper today."

He grinned at her. She knew that soon at nearly four years old, Jacob would be too old for naps but not yet, as he went in for his nap willingly.

"I'll come up and check on you a little later," she told him as she stood.

"*Danki*, Katie," he murmured sleepily.

"You're *willkomm*, Jacob."

With a smile on her face, Katie went downstairs to clean up the mess from their cake making. She washed the dishes and put them away. When she finished, she decided she'd enjoy the quiet with a hot cup of tea. She put the kettle on the stove to boil then found tea bags in the cupboard. Minutes later, after settling in a kitchen chair, Katie enjoyed her first sip of the steaming brew. The morning had begun with somewhat of a rocky start, but everything had righted itself once the children had stopped crying.

Three sips into her tea, she was startled when she heard movement at the kitchen door and watched it open. Micah walked in, hung his hat on a wall hook then saw her at the table and smiled. "I hope it's *oll recht* that I'm back. I forgot to pick up something for lunch. I thought I could make a sandwich and eat here before I head back."

Katie rose, feeling her cheeks heat under his direct gaze. "I'll be happy to make you sandwich."

"No need," he said, his blue eyes crinkling at the corners as he studied her.

"Please. It will be my pleasure." She pulled her gaze from Micah, who, she realized, was far too handsome for her peace of mind. Opening the refrigerator door, she viewed its contents. "There is leftover roast beef and ham. Which one would you like?" She spoke without turning.

"Roast beef is fine," he said softly over her shoulder, making her gasp at his sudden nearness. Her heart thudded until he stepped back, giving her room.

Katie closed her eyes, drew in a calming breath and faced him. "Macaroni or potato salad with your sandwich?" she asked before she pulled out both salads from the refrigerator and set them on the countertop. Alone with him without the children, she was more aware of Micah than ever before.

"Potato salad." He reached over her head for a plate then set it on the countertop next to the salads. "I'd like a little mayonnaise on my sandwich, too, please."

Katie nodded and grabbed bread out of the pantry. She quickly made his sandwich the way he liked it, aware that he'd taken a seat at the kitchen table. After cutting the sandwich in half, she added a dollop of potato salad and set the plate with a fork on the table before him.

"What's that delicious smell?" Micah asked as he studied her.

"Pound cake. Jacob helped me make it before he went up for his nap."

He took a bite of his sandwich. Katie saw his Adam's apple bob as he swallowed. "Did you have any trouble with the children?"

"*Nay.* They were upset, at first, that you and your *grosseldra* weren't there, but they calmed down. I kept them busy during the morning, and they gave me no trouble with naptime." She checked the cake in the oven, and the wonderful scent filled the kitchen. "I'm sorry. I didn't ask. What would you like to drink? Iced tea? Lemonade?"

"Iced tea would be *gut.*"

Katie poured him cold tea from a pitcher in the refrigerator, adding two ice cubes into the glass for good measure. She then took a seat across from him to finish her hot tea. The children would be up soon, and she wanted a few quiet moments before her afternoon became busy with them. She relaxed as she cupped her tea mug and brought it to her lips. Having Micah seated across from her felt...amazingly right.

"That's probably cold by now," he said, eyeing her tea.

"It's fine." She smiled before she sipped from her tea.

He didn't say anything more for several seconds. "I appreciate your help, Katie."

"I like your *kinner.* I enjoy spending time with them." Katie thought he might say something more but then he went back to eating without a word.

Minutes went by without conversation. Strangely, she didn't feel flustered like she had earlier.

"How are the *haus* renovations coming along?" Katie asked, breaking the comfortable silence. "Did you get a lot done?"

He sighed. "I finished painting and now I'm trying to make a decision about the floors. I'll put vinyl in the children's rooms, but for the great room and master bedroom I would like to keep the wooden floors. The wood is in fine shape. I don't have much to do to it. I may use a fresh coat of a varnish or something to put some shine back. But the main bedroom's wood floor needs work. I'm thinking I'll need to sand and refinish it."

Katie got up and brought him the cookie jar filled with chocolate chip bars. She opened it and held it out to him. "Sounds nice but a lot of work."

"Ja." He grabbed a treat then took a bite. "Sanding will take a lot of time, but it will be worth it."

"My *bruder* Uri is *gut* with construction work. Maybe he can help you. Shall I ask him? Would you consider it?" Katie waited patiently for his response. She was sure her brother would agree to help Micah.

"I could use the help but..."

"Let me talk with him. I'll casually tell him about the work you're doing. If he offers to help, I'll let you know, and we can arrange to have him meet you at the *haus*." Katie took the last sip of tea, which had cooled until it was almost cold. Still, it tasted good to her.

"Katie..." Micah looked uncertain.

"I won't press him, Micah, if that's what you're afraid of." She stood and brought her mug to the sink where she filled up a dish basin with soapy water and placed it in the suds. When she turned back, he was watching her. "Is something wrong?"

"Nay," he said with a shake of his head. He finished the last cookie then stood. "I should get back to work."

"Will you still be back at 4:30?" she asked.

"Ja." He got up and brought his plate and glass to the sink. Katie reached for them, and he handed them over with a look of gratitude. "I appreciate everything you're doing for me...for us."

"It's my pleasure," Katie said, knowing that it was true. She was beginning to like Micah. A lot. It was as if she'd known him forever. He seemed more serious than his younger brother Jacob, yet she was comfortable with him after only a short time.

He grabbed his hat off the wall hook and opened the door, turning to meet her gaze. "The sandwich was delicious. *Danki*, Katie."

"You're *willkomm*, Micah." And she watched him leave with her heart pounding hard in her chest and a strange feeling enveloping her as he climbed into his buggy and, with a wave, rode off. She went back inside to the sound of the timer and pulled the two pound cakes from the oven. Katie placed them carefully on the cake racks she found earlier. She stood back and eyed them with satisfaction. The cakes were browned to perfection.

Micah wasn't gone fifteen minutes when she heard the children stirring. Jacob was talking with his sisters. As she approached the staircase, she could make out what he was saying.

"And me and Katie made chocolate chip pound cakes," he said. "It will taste so *gut*. We have to eat lunch first but then maybe each of us can have a piece."

Katie hid a smile as she climbed the stairs and entered the girls' room. "Do I hear three young *kinner* awake in here?" she said.

Jacob spun and looked up at her. "*Ja*, and we're hungry!"

"Let me change Rebecca and Eliza," Katie said, "then we'll go downstairs and eat lunch."

"And pound cake?"

She grinned at him. "*Ja*, and pound cake."

His blue eyes lit up his little face. Katie reached for Eliza first and changed her diaper before she did the same for Rebecca.

"I don't need that," Jacob said.

"Because you're a big *boo*," Katie agreed.

Carrying Micah's two young daughters, she followed Jacob down the steps. "Hold on to the bannister, Jacob," she told him.

The boy obeyed, grabbing on to the rail as he went down the stairs carefully.

Katie made the children lunch and then they each enjoyed a small piece of chocolate chip pound cake. She debated about whether she should allow Eliza a piece of cake and then decided that she would break it into bite-size pieces and see how the child did. The youngest of Micah's children loved it. By the time all of them were done eating cake, they had crumbs around their mouths and a bit of chocolate on their hands. She cleaned them up then set them down to play. By three o'clock, Eliza and Rebecca were getting sleepy so with little Jacob's help, Katie put the girls down for their afternoon nap.

It was quiet in the house after that. Katie gave Jacob a pencil and some paper. She watched as he made squiggles, which he explained were some of the animals who lived on the farm. One was a cow, another a goat and the larger one was a horse. Katie smiled at him when she heard his explanation. Jacob grinned, creating tiny dimples in his cheeks that she'd never noticed earlier. Micah's son was adorable and sweet, and she loved her time with him.

When the back kitchen doorknob rattled before opening, Katie realized how late it had gotten as Micah entered the house. She glanced at the clock. It was three forty-five. The afternoon had flown by.

"Dat!" Jacob climbed down from his chair and ran to his father.

Micah scooped up his son, making Jacob laugh and hug his father. "Have you been a *gut boo*?" he asked, meeting Katie's gaze over his son's head.

"He was a *gut* boy and a big helper today," Katie assured him.

Jacob smiled at her over his shoulder. "Katie and me made chocolate chip pound cake!"

"You did?" Lips tilting upward, Micah eyed her with approval.

"*Ja*, Dat, and it tastes delicious!" Jacob struggled to get down from his father's arms. "Come mere! I'll show you." He grabbed Micah's hand and tugged him to the pantry where Katie had stored the cake. "Look!"

Micah's expression held affection as he smiled at his son. "It looks delicious."

Jacob bobbed his head repeatedly. "It is!"

"Is this yours? Or are you going to share?"

"There's some for you, Dat. Katie made two cakes. She put one in the freezer for later."

Micah's glance immediately focused on Katie. He silently mouthed *"danki,"* and Katie could only nod and grin back at him. "Are the girls sleeping?"

"*Ja*, they were exhausted." Katie left the pantry to reenter the main kitchen area. Micah's presence made her stomach fluttery and caused a strange sensation to run the length of her spine. She sensed that he followed her closely. "Your *kinner* are *wunderbor*, Micah. It's a pleasure to spend time with them."

"I appreciate your time and patience with them." His expression warmed as he held her gaze. "You are a sweet and caring young woman."

Katie blushed, unused to such effusive compliments. "Have you heard from your *eldra*?"

"*Nay*, I don't expect to hear from them until tomorrow. It's nearly a ten-hour drive, and my *dat* wanted the driver to stop at a hotel and rest for the night."

"I hope everything is *oke* with your *grossvadder*," she said.

"I do, too." Sounds from upstairs signaled that the girls were awake. Katie moved to get them. "I'll bring them down," Micah said. "Abigail will be here for you before you know it. I don't want to keep her waiting."

"May I make you supper? Abigail won't be here for forty-five minutes yet. I'll make something simple, an easy dish that can stay warm in the oven until you're ready to eat it."

"Katie, I don't expect you to cook for us."

"I don't mind," she said as she tied on an apron. "I enjoy cooking."

Micah grinned. "If your cooking is anything like your baking, we're all in for a treat."

Heart beating hard, Katie watched as he left the room with Jacob. Seconds later, she heard father and son go up the steps. What was easy to make that they might like? Something quick but tasty.

After digging through the refrigerator's contents, she decided to make a breakfast that was also great, in a pinch, for a supper. Made with eggs, bread, leftover ham, melted butter, milk and some cheese plus a few other minor ingredients, Katie thought Micah and his children would appreciate the hearty dish that was both filling and nutritious.

Katie quickly set the oven to 325 degrees. She assembled the ingredients then placed the mixture into an oblong pan. When he appeared with a daughter in each arm ten minutes later, he was surprised to see her slide the casserole into the oven and set a timer for forty-five minutes.

"I made a breakfast casserole," she explained. "I'll be happy to have something else ready when you get home tomorrow, but this was quick and easy and..." She blushed. "I hope you like breakfast casserole. I used the leftover ham."

"I love breakfast casserole and so do my *kinner*," he said, appearing stunned yet pleased that she'd gone to the trouble.

"When the timer goes off, just turn down the heat and leave the dish in the oven to keep warm until you're ready to eat it." The sound of buggy wheels filtered in through the screened door. "That must be my *schweschter*. She's a little early." She quickly set the table for them for later. "What time should I be back in the morning? Six?"

"No need to come then. Eight is fine. Or you can come at nine if you'd like." He put down Rebecca. "Katie, I can set a table."

She looked at him. "I know." Was he upset with her? *Nay*, he wouldn't be smiling if he was. She returned his smile. "I'll be here at eight tomorrow. Have a nice night, Micah." Katie turned her attention to his son. "I'll see you tomorrow, Jacob." She picked up Rebecca and gave the child a hug before setting her down again. Eliza reached for Katie from her father's arms. Instead of taking her, she gently caught the child's hand and smiled at her. "See you soon," she whispered.

With a nod in Micah's direction, Katie left, aware that he had followed her into the yard, holding both daughters again. She waved, pleased when he waved back at her.

"Looks like you had a *wunderbor* day," Abigail said as she pulled the vehicle onto the road in the direction of home.

"I enjoyed myself," Katie admitted. "The children were so *gut*, and… I…liked spending time with them."

"So, you don't mind going back tomorrow?"

"*Nay*, not at all." Katie thought of Micah and knew her eagerness to return was due not only to her enjoyment of the children, but because she'd get to see their father again.

Chapter Eight

The next morning Katie steered the horse-drawn buggy toward the Bontrager residence, her thoughts on her conversation with her mother the night before.

How was it? Mam had asked as they'd worked side by side, preparing a light meal for the family.

Gut. *The children are* wunderbor. *I enjoyed watching them. Jacob helped me make chocolate chip pound cake. I let him add all the measured ingredients, and he loved it. His blue eyes lit up when I allowed him to take a turn stirring.*

Her mother had smiled. *That's nice that you included him.*

It was fun, and Jacob is easy to please. Katie had fried bacon in a cast-iron pan as they chatted. *They're having breakfast casserole*, she said with a grin. *I made it for Micah and the children before I left.*

Mam had paused in the act of taking out dinner plates. *You cooked for them*, she said, nodding in approval. She set the plates on the table and returned to pull out two oblong baking dishes. *Katie, you don't have to be home in time to prepare supper with me. Your sis-*

ters can help. If Micah and the children need a meal, do what you can for them. If Micah happens to invite you to eat with them, stay.

"Mam…"

Katie, I'm not asking you to marry the man. I'm simply saying it's gut that you help him whenever you can. I saw Naomi earlier today and she's actively looking for a wife for him. Until then, he needs someone to watch his children and cook his meals if he doesn't have time.

As a car passed her on her way to the Bontrager farm, Katie continued to think about her mother's words. Her involvement in their lives was a temporary situation. *Mam is right. I should help Micah and the children whenever I can.*

"Naomi *is* actively seeking a wife for him," she murmured as she tried not to visualize Micah with another woman. Why did the fact that he would eventually marry someone else bother her? *Because I'm worried about his kinner.* She knew instinctively that it wasn't the only reason she was upset. She shouldn't be since she'd already decided not to marry or have a family. She should be happy for Micah when Naomi finally found him a wife and mother for his children. Katie thought of Jacob with his adorable smile and Rebecca who grinned at her as she ate whatever Katie put in front of her. And little Eliza… She would miss her tiny hugs, the way her body would curl against her in sleep or when she held on. Micah's new wife would feed his children, put them down for their naps…and be with Micah after the sun went down and the children were in bed.

Katie felt her throat tighten as the Bontrager property loomed ahead. She parked near the barn and headed toward the house. The door opened at her approach.

Micah stood there, looking too handsome for her tranquility of mind in a royal blue short-sleeved shirt and navy triblend trousers held up by dark suspenders. As she closed the distance between them, the man flashed her a smile.

"*Gut* morning, Katie," he murmured, the sound of his deep, pleasant voice vibrating down her spine.

"*Hallo*, Micah. Is that your wagon?" she said, jerking her head toward the vehicle and noticing the family buggy parked beside the barn. She hoped the wagon didn't belong to Naomi because it meant the matchmaker had come with news of a potential match for him.

"*Nay, meim vadder*'s. I need it to pick up vinyl flooring this morning for the children's rooms."

Relieved, Katie nodded. "Did you eat breakfast?"

"I did. *Danki*. I reheated some of the tasty breakfast casserole you made us for last night's supper." He held the door open for her, and she was aware of his clean masculine scent—of soap and time spent outdoors in the fresh air—as she passed by him to enter the house. Every one of her senses buzzed with awareness.

"I'm glad you enjoyed it," she said, stunned by her reaction.

"The children loved it. I warmed it in the oven for ten minutes. Eliza's messy fingers as she popped bite-size pieces into her mouth told me how much she enjoyed it."

Katie laughed. "That's *gut*." She saw that his daughters were happy in their high chairs. "Why don't you let me make you lunch?"

When she met his gaze, she found that he watched her intently.

"You don't have to—"

"Micah, I'm happy to do that for you. I see that you

already dressed the children. I don't mind dressing them each morning. I'm sure you have enough to do to get ready for work. Let me see what's in the refrigerator for your lunch." She noticed the coffeepot on the stove as she moved to check on the food. She paused. "Would you like a cup of coffee while you wait?"

"*Ja*, I would. *Danki*. It should still be hot."

Katie poured him a cup of coffee and set it before him with sugar. She reached into the refrigerator for a jug of milk and placed it on the table within his reach.

She made him a sandwich of cold roast beef and cheddar cheese, put the sandwich in a paper lunch bag and added a wrapped piece of pound cake. When she turned around, Micah was sipping from his coffee mug, watching her. "A sandwich and cake," she said. "Would you like iced tea in a thermos?"

He nodded. *"Danki."*

Katie found the thermos she'd seen the day before in a cabinet when she was looking for loaf pans. She filled it to the brim with the tea, sealed it and added the outer cup lid. "Here you go," she said with a smile, placing it on the table near him.

"I appreciate this." He stood then grabbed the thermos and bag. "I'll be home between four and four thirty."

"Take your time. I'll fix supper for you."

"Katie, that doesn't seem fair."

"I like to cook, Micah. Is there anything you don't like?"

He shook his head. "I can't think of anything." He grabbed his hat, opened the door and settled the hat on his head. Once outside, he faced her. "I'll see you later. Maybe tomorrow we can arrange for you to come with the children to the *haus*. I'd like your opinion about the interior."

Katie nodded. *"Oll recht.* Just let me know when." She watched him put his lunch in the back before he climbed onto the seat. "Have a nice day!"

He smiled and waved, and Katie quickly turned back to the children who were eagerly waiting to get down from their high chairs and the table. She cleaned up their hands and faces and helped them from their chairs. "Would you like to play outside for a while?" she asked Micah's son.

"Ja!" Jacob exclaimed. "Can we eat a picnic outside?"

"We can, but not today," Katie said, grinning. "Maybe tomorrow. It is important that you stay in the backyard and near me. *Ja?"*

The little boy bobbed his head eagerly.

"Wait here a moment so I can see what's in the freezer for supper. Your *dat* can't be here for a midday meal so I'll make something *gut* for all of you for dinner." She looked in the freezer and saw a pack of chicken. She could make fried chicken and mashed potatoes, she thought as she pulled out the chicken and placed it in the refrigerator. She'd place it in warm water to thaw it later while the children napped.

Katie searched in a chest of drawers in the great room and found a quilt that looked as if it had been used outside in the past as a picnic blanket. *I'll wash it once we are done outside.* Throwing the quilt over her arm, she went into the kitchen to see Jacob standing near the back door with a wide grin on his face.

She eyed Jacob's hands. "Are your hands clean?"

The boy bobbed his head. "I wiped them *gut.*"

"*Wunderbor.* Let's bring out paper and a pencil. You can find things in the backyard to draw."

She found paper and pencil where she'd put it yesterday. She gave them to Jacob and grabbed a kitchen cutting board for him to use as a lap desk.

Katie turned her attention to Micah's daughters. She wiped their faces and hands then lifted Rebecca down from her chair before reaching for Eliza. After picking up the little girl, she held the child close to her and reached for Rebecca's hand.

It was a beautiful day. The sun shone on the dew-covered lawn. Katie debated where to put the quilt because of the dampness on the ground but decided it didn't matter. The quilt was thick enough to keep them dry. With Jacob's help, she managed to spread out the quilt then ensured that each child stayed close to her. It was nice for them all to get some fresh air.

The morning went quickly. Jacob was content to draw, and Katie was able to keep the two younger children entertained. Before she knew it, it was time for Rebecca and Eliza to nap. To her amusement, the fresh air had made Jacob quiet.

"Let's go inside, Jacob." She stood up, reached for the two little girls. Jacob got up silently with his pencil and papers.

The interior house was dark compared to the bright outside, but her eyes adjusted quickly. Within minutes, she had them upstairs in their beds. Their eyes closed immediately, and it didn't take long for the three of them to fall asleep. Katie made bread while they slept. Once she had put two loaves in the oven, she placed the frozen chicken in warm water to thaw then fixed herself a cup of tea and sat down to relax.

When she pulled the bread out of the oven an hour later, she realized it was lunchtime. She searched in the pantry for something to make the children to eat after they woke up. There were jars of homemade jams and jellies in several flavors. Katie checked the refrigerator and found a few flavors already open. She'd make them jam sandwiches—or peanut butter and jelly. Most children, including her siblings when they were young, loved peanut butter and jelly. She smiled as she left the kitchen and headed toward the stairs to check on the children.

The house held the aroma of fresh bread as she climbed the steps. She heard noise from Jacob's room and entered to find him awake, sitting on the floor with a marble roller. She watched him place a marble on the wooden track and smiled at his delight as it rolled from the top to the bottom.

"Jacob."

He blinked as he looked up at her. "I woke up."

She nodded, hiding her amusement. "I see that." She paused as he scrambled to his feet. "Please pick up your toy and put it where no one can trip over it."

Katie smiled in approval as he quickly obeyed. "Shall we check on your sisters?"

"*Ja.* I'm sure they're hungry, too," he said as he followed her out of the room.

"Would you like a peanut butter and jelly sandwich for lunch?"

His grin melted her heart. "I like peanut butter and jelly."

They entered the girls' room just as Eliza stirred. Rebecca was already awake. She carried the girls downstairs and fixed them lunch. All three of the children were in good spirits. The afternoon went quickly with the girls napping. Jacob sat at the kitchen playing with the marble roller she'd retrieved from his room while Katie took the chicken out of the refrigerator where she'd put it after it thawed. It was close to four in the afternoon. Micah would be home at any time.

Satisfied that Jacob was happily occupied, she breaded the chicken and set it aside until it was time to fry it. By the time that Micah came home, his dinner of fried chicken, mashed potatoes and chowchow would be ready for him. She looked forward to seeing his enjoyment of the meal. The thought of seeing him made her smile, and she felt the tiny twinge of excitement in knowing that he could walk in the door at any time.

Micah moved his tools into the master bedroom before leaving and locking the house. As he drove his wagon home, he wondered what Katie was making for dinner. She'd been a lifeline for him. Her kindness, compassion and warmth when dealing with his children made him appreciate her even more. He knew that Naomi was looking for a wife for him, but he found that he wasn't in any hurry to meet someone new, not with Katie there ready to step in and help. But was it fair for him to expect her to take care of his children? Of him?

It was a short trip home. As soon as he entered the house, he was hit with the tantalizing aroma of food. Fresh bread. Fried chicken. He hung up his hat and looked for her.

Katie was at the stove flipping chicken over in a fry pan. She turned at the sound of the door. Her smile warmed him. "You're home."

Jacob looked up from his drawing. "Dat!" He pushed

back his chair, got down and ran to him. Micah felt overwhelming love for his son as Jacob hugged him with his little arms around Micah's legs. As he held the boy against him, he spied his two daughters who were content in their high chairs.

"How were they?" he asked Katie.

"*Gut.* We had a nice day."

Jacob pulled back to gaze up at his father. "I was a *gut boo*. I had two naps and I helped Katie."

Micah settled his gaze on the young woman, who nodded with a look of affection for Jacob. He liked seeing Katie in his parents' home. Her face was flushed from the heat of the stove. A tiny strand of blond hair had come undone at the right side of her forehead. Her blue eyes sparkled with pleasure until something in her expression changed as their gazes continued to stay locked, and she looked suddenly guarded.

He moved farther into the room. "Something smells delicious."

"Fried chicken, mashed potatoes and fresh bread. I looked for fresh green beans in your *mudder*'s garden but couldn't find any left. I found a jar of chowchow in the refrigerator I thought you might enjoy instead." She seemed to relax a little as she discussed supper. "The chicken will be done in a minute or two." She flipped the pieces of chicken in the skillet as she spoke. "Do you think that Eliza will be able to eat any of this food? If not, I can cook something else for her."

"She'll be fine with everything you made."

Katie grinned. "I'm happy to hear that."

Micah saw that she had set the table earlier, but several plates had been pushed to one side so that Jacob had a place to draw. He addressed his son. "Want to show me what you drew?"

He watched the child run to the table and pick up a several sheets of paper, which he brought back to show him.

"This one is a tree, like the one out back."

He eyed Jacob's pencil drawing and smiled. "That's a *gut* drawing, *soohn*."

"And this one is us." There were five stick figures without faces. "This one is you, Dat. These are me, Becca and Eliza. And that one is Katie."

Micah froze. "Nice," he said, but inside his heart was hammering hard. Why would he draw Katie with the rest of them?

"Katie is with us, because she is like family 'cuz she helps us," Jacob explained with a young child's innocence.

"I see." He glanced toward Katie and was grateful that she hadn't heard what Jacob had said. At least, he didn't think she had. She was intent on cooking, and he saw no change in her demeanor, no tension in her shoulders.

He watched her take the chicken out of the skillet and place it on a plate with paper towels to drain the pieces. She lifted the lid of a pot and stirred its contents. *Mashed potatoes.*

Within minutes, Katie had them all seated at the table before she brought over their food. A loaf of bread came first, sliced into mouthwatering pieces, followed by the butter dish. She put out a bowl of his mother's sweet chow-chow. Next, she set out a platter of fried chicken that smelled wonderful and looked even better along with a bowl of mashed potatoes, and the meal was complete.

"I hope you enjoy it," she said as she untied her apron as if to get ready to leave.

"Katie, stay. Sit down and eat with us." He could see indecision on her pretty features. *"Sigh so gude."* Please.

"If you're sure you don't mind…" she began.

"Eat with us, Katie!" Jacob urged.

She looked at Jacob before meeting Micah's gaze. "Micah."

"I won't force you to eat with us, but we'd like you to stay. *Ja, soohn?*"

"*Ja*, Dat!"

Micah was rewarded with her smile.

"Danki." She pulled out a chair and sat down. *"Ach nay!* Drinks! What would you like to drink?" She started to rise, but Micah placed his hand on her arm, stopping her.

"I'll get the drinks." She looked stunned by his offer and he hid a smile. "Jacob, milk? Katie? Iced tea or would you like something else?"

She blinked. "Iced tea is fine."

He nodded. Micah poured milk for the children and iced tea for Katie and himself. When he sat back in his seat, he saw Katie eye him curiously but with a softness in her expression that made him inhale sharply.

He realized that he enjoyed spending time with Katie Mast way too much. *We are friends. Nothing more.* It was only natural for Katie to eat with them since she'd worked so hard to prepare a delicious meal.

The image of his wife Anna's face slipped into his mind, but he forced it away. It wasn't wrong to eat dinner with Katie, who cared for his children while he worked. It wasn't wrong. Memories of his life with Anna rose to haunt him. Guilt hit him hard, but he refused to allow it to ruin their lovely meal—or his friendship with Katie Mast.

Chapter Nine

Micah couldn't stop thinking about Katie. She'd been taking care of his children daily for four days, and something about her lingered in his mind. It felt wrong to develop feelings for her. He had loved his wife, Anna, and it didn't seem right to care for another woman with Anna not in her grave a full year, but his feelings for Katie were complicated and constantly growing.

I need to fight feeling for Katie the way I do. I know I must marry again, and I thought I wanted a wife who will be happy with simply caring for my children. Like a marriage of convenience or a business arrangement. Whenever he thought of marrying again, he pictured Katie in his life, in his home, as a mother to his children. And there was nothing convenient about that.

He and Katie enjoyed a friendship. Katie had loved Jacob and still did. He realized he must find a way to distance himself mentally and physically to fight his growing feelings for her. And he needed to do it now, because he knew she wasn't ready, may never be ready to move on.

Micah got down on his knees and scuff-sanded the

bedroom floor, smoothing out the scratches and nicks with the sandpaper. He worked vigorously, spurred on by his dilemma because of Katie and his confusing thoughts.

Each night Katie continued to cook for him, and they enjoyed supper together with the children like a family. Micah had realized he was in big trouble when he found himself frequently heading home for lunch so that he could spend more time with her. He couldn't continue this way. Something had to change before he said something to Katie that he'd regret.

Naomi, his matchmaker, needed to find a wife for him and soon. Katie was off-limits, because she was having a hard time forgetting his deceased brother, the man she'd loved.

He sanded the floor harder, running it from one side of the room to the other. He shouldn't be working so hard to get the house done, because if the matchmaker hadn't found him a spouse once he finished, Katie would be here in his house, watching his children, while he worked on building a new outbuilding on his farm. Seeing Katie in his house would be difficult, giving him ideas of a happily ever with her that would never come true. He had loved Anna. It felt disloyal to think of Katie as anything other than his brother Jacob's girl, but Micah couldn't help himself. He knew that if she ever learned how he felt, she'd avoid him. Could he deal with her rejection? *Nay*, so he would have to keep his feelings private, pretend that every moment in her company wasn't hurting his heart.

Micah rose, surveyed his handiwork and winced. Lost in thought, he'd gotten a little too ambitious in one part of the room. He would have to figure out a way to make the uneven sanded surfaces of the wood flow together with the finish. The idea of going home for lunch pleased him, but he knew it wouldn't be wise, given his current feelings. He decided that he would stay and work until noon then run over to Kings for a sandwich. And he'd eat lunch here in the house and force himself to concentrate on what he needed to do next rather than ponder his growing affection for Katie.

Katie fed the children and tried her best to smile at the little ones who had no idea that she was upset Micah hadn't come home for lunch. He and she had enjoyed sharing both lunch and dinner these last two days. But he seemed different this morning. Quieter.

Was he worried about the house renovations? He hadn't confided in her. He'd seemed distant—a distance that bothered her more than it should.

As she continued with her day, Katie fought to convince herself that Micah's behavior didn't concern her. After all, she wasn't marrying the man. *Nay,* he'd be marrying someone else, a woman Naomi found for him, and she had no right to feel slighted. She was just the babysitter. With the firm reminder of her position, Katie washed the clothes she gathered from the upstairs bedrooms earlier as Rebecca and Eliza slept. Next, she planned supper while Jacob played quietly at the kitchen table until, bored, he climbed down and stood by her side.

"What'cha doing?" he asked.

"Making macaroni and cheese for your supper."

The little boy beamed at her. "I love mac'roni and cheese!"

She gave him an affectionate smile. "Why don't you play in the great room until your sisters wake up, *ja*?"

"Oke." He obeyed and left the room. She looked in on him a few minutes later and found his attention occupied by two wooden toys: a horse with wheels and what looked like a farm tractor.

"Jacob? Let me know if you hear your sisters, *ja*? Or you can come and play in the kitchen, and we'll check on them in a little while."

"I'll play here," he told her, preoccupied with his toys. "If I hear them, I'll tell you."

Katie smiled and thanked him before she returned to the kitchen.

The macaroni and cheese casserole was a simple and easy meal to make. The girls woke up shortly after she'd placed the casserole to keep in the refrigerator until it was time to put it in the oven. She brought Rebecca and Eliza downstairs.

"Feel like a snack?" she asked Jacob as she stopped with a sister in each arm.

"Cake?" He looked hopeful.

"How about crackers with cheese?"

"Oke."

The rested girls were in good humor as she took them into the kitchen where she set each one in her high chair. Jacob followed them and took his seat at the table. Katie gave each of them a small cup of milk and a light snack of cheese and crackers to hold them over until supper.

Two hours later Katie pulled the hot, bubbling cheese dish out of the oven as Micah entered the house. "Something smells *gut*," he said pleasantly.

She set the hot dish on top of the stove before she faced him. He offered her a smile that was less than his usual good-humored one, and it struck Katie again that something was bothering him.

"It's just macaroni and cheese," she told him as she busied herself pulling out plates, utensils and napkins. "Supper will be but a minute," she said, setting the table for him and Jacob.

She would make sure everything was ready, then she would leave. If he asked her to stay, then she would know she wasn't the reason he was so distant, that whatever was bothering him wasn't because of something she'd done. She shot him a glance, caught his frown as he eyed the table. He was so handsome that he stole her breath. He was Jacob's older brother, and she'd never expected to feel this strongly for him.

"I'll get your drinks ready," she said, "and then I'll leave you to eat." She managed a smile for him. "I know it's not much of a meal. I took the other pound cake out of the freezer. I saw vanilla ice cream in there if you'd like to have it with your cake." She knew she was babbling. "Iced tea?" She saw him nod. She pulled out a tall glass for him and small plastic cups for the children. "I thought the children should have milk again. Unless you'd like them to have something else to drink." When he didn't respond, she found herself blinking back tears. *I will not cry.* She composed herself as she fixed their drinks and placed them within easy reach of Micah's family. "Do you need anything else?"

"Katie." Micah's deep voice drew her attention to him.

"Ja?" She gazed up at him with a suddenly tight throat.

"Why aren't you staying to eat with us?"

"I don't know if that's a *gut* idea," she whispered, looking away.

He was silent, but she could feel him watching her. "Katie—"

His tone drew her gaze to him. *"Ja?"* Her heart beat hard. Something in his expression alerted her that she wasn't going to like what he had to say.

"I was finally able to talk with my *dat* on the phone this morning. My *grossvadder* is doing much better. My *eldra* are hoping to head home any day now. I'm taking tomorrow off, so I won't need you to watch my *kinner*." He averted his eyes.

"Oll recht," she said softly, her heart hurting. "There are leftovers in the refrigerator. You should have enough to eat for the next day or so. If you need anything, send word and I'll see what I can do to help." She untied her apron. "Enjoy your supper, Micah."

Katie turned quickly away to hang up the apron. She didn't want him to see that she was upset that he was fine with her leaving. It was always a given that her time with them would end. Katie just hadn't expected it to be this soon. Nor had she expected to feel this heartache.

She smiled at him and then headed toward the door.

"Katie?"

Katie spun to face him.

"Danki," he said softly.

She nodded. "You're *willkomm*, Micah." Feeling the oncoming threat of tears, she quickly opened the door and left.

Katie allowed herself to cry as she drove home. Spending time with Micah and his children made her realize what she would never have. *Jacob, why did you have to die?* She sent up a silent prayer for help. *Gott, help me be content with my decision to stay single.* After caring for the family, she suddenly was having a hard time with her choice.

Once home, she headed inside to help her mother with supper. She'd spent only a few days with Micah and his young ones but that short time with them had changed her forever.

"Katie!" Her mother's eyes widened as Katie entered the house. "I thought you'd be eating with Micah and the children."

She managed a smile. "*Nay*, I fixed their supper and left. Micah won't be working tomorrow so I'll be able to get back to sewing. I still have Lucy Fisher's mending to do."

Katie could feel her mother's concerned gaze on her as she set the table.

"Is something wrong?" Mam asked.

She shook her head, dismissing her mother's worry. "What could be wrong?"

"*Dochter...*"

"I'm fine, Mam. Micah doesn't need me now, and it's fine."

Her mother studied her a long moment. "Would you peel the potatoes?"

Nodding, Katie went right to work. She would keep busy and wait until, or if, Micah needed her again. If he didn't, that would be fine. She had a sewing business to get off the ground. Besides Lucy's mending to do, she needed to make aprons, prayer *kapps* and items that visiting Englishers might like for her to sell at Kings General Store.

The next morning Katie arose early and it occurred to her with a start that there was no reason for her to head toward the Bontrager residence to take care of Micah's children. Disappointment overwhelmed her as she went downstairs to help her mother and sisters with breakfast. After she ate with her family, she returned to her bedroom, where she pulled fabric out of a dresser drawer. She then got to work on the sewing machine that was set up in her room. She concentrated on sewing, only taking a break for the midday meal and later for supper before she went back to work.

That night Katie fell into bed, tired from all the hours of work she'd done. She was too exhausted to think about Micah and the children until she woke up in the middle of the night and thoughts of them returned, causing her to worry about what she'd done so terribly wrong that Micah no longer wanted her around.

By the time the morning sunshine filtered in through her curtains, Katie had slept only a few hours, and she felt groggy with sleep. After coffee with breakfast, she started her day as she had begun yesterday with sewing and mending until late afternoon when she was finally finished with the work she'd wanted done.

She'd make her deliveries tomorrow morning, Katie decided. That night when she went to bed, she had trouble falling asleep. She was plagued with images of Micah— and Jacob, her late betrothed. She stared at the ceiling and blinked back tears. She missed Micah and the children. The knowledge that she missed Micah made her feel guilty, as if she was betraying Jacob's memory. But she couldn't stop caring about Micah and his little ones.

It was best that Micah no longer needed her, she thought the next morning as she packed up items to be delivered to the store and to Lucy Fisher. *I miss Micah's*

children, because I won't be having any of my own.
Katie had always wanted to be a wife and mother, but
God had planned another life for her when He'd called
Jacob home.

As she carried her delivery items to her pony cart,
Katie saw that the day was a little overcast with the
sun peeking in and out from behind the clouds. Good
weather for being out and about making deliveries.

She drove to Kings General Store and dropped off
the items for sale she'd promised Rachel King during
the last church service day.

Rachel greeted her with a smile as Katie entered the
shop, stirring the bells on the door. "Our customers are
going to love these," she said as she held up an apron
from the box of items that Katie had brought. Her eyes
widened as she saw the white organza Amish prayer
kapps. "You did a *wunderbor* job with the head cover-
ings. Not everyone can make them. These *kapps* will
sell out in no time."

"*Danki*, Rachel. I'm happy that you're willing to help
me out this way," Katie told her. "If anyone mentions
they need someone to do mending, would you give out
my name?"

"*Ja*, of course! Do you have a cell phone?" Rachel
asked.

"*Nay*, I…my *vadder* doesn't think they are necessary."

"I'm sure the church elders will approve one for business use. Explain to your *dat* and see what he says first."

Katie nodded. She glanced outside and saw dark
clouds gathering in the distance. "Is it supposed to
rain?"

"*Ja*. There is a chance of a severe thunderstorm but

not until this afternoon," Rachel said. "Would you like some tea?"

"*Nay*, but *danki*. I have one last delivery for Lucy Fisher. Another day?"

Rachel smiled. "*Ja*. You are always *willkomm*. Tell Lucy *hallo* from me." Her expression was soft. "Her first baby with Gabriel. The two of them must be thrilled. Gabriel loves her first two like his own. Still, I love to see them so happy as they extend their family."

Katie nodded. "*Ja*. They are *wunderbor eldra*. Is it *oke* if I bring more items in a few weeks?"

"*Ja*. Anything you make we'll take." Rachel laughed. "I'll let you know what sells the quickest, although I'm sure everything you brought in will sell. You are truly a skilled seamstress." She picked up the box that Katie had brought in. "Enjoy your day, Katie. Stop by anytime."

With a wave and smile, Katie left for Gabriel Fisher's house with the basket of finished mending that Lucy had hired her to do.

Lucy opened the door as Katie stepped down from her vehicle. She grabbed Lucy's basket and headed toward the house. "*Gut mariga*, Lucy!" she called out with a wave. She could see Lucy's wide smile as Katie drew closer.

"*Gut* morning to you, Katie! Want to stay awhile and chat?" Lucy said as Katie carried the basket into the house.

After a quick glance at her wristwatch, Katie saw that there was time. She smiled. "I'd like that."

"Coffee or tea?"

"What would you prefer?" Katie asked, unwilling to have Lucy wait on her.

"Iced tea."

"Do you have enough made?" When Lucy nodded, Katie insisted on waiting on Lucy. "How are you feeling?" she asked.

"I'm feeling *gut*." Lucy took a sip of the iced tea. "You stopped by at the perfect time. Susie is with Gabriel in his workshop. Our *soohn* is napping."

"I'm glad I came at the right time," Katie said.

The two women drank iced tea and caught up.

"I heard you were helping Micah Bontrager with the children." Lucy settled a hand on her pregnant belly.

"*Ja.* It's been a pleasure to spend time with his little ones. Betty's *vadder* is ill, and the family left for Indiana to see what they could do to help. Micah stayed home—at his *dat*'s insistence—to be there for his children when he's not working on the *haus*. The journey would have been too much for them anyway."

Katie didn't want to talk about Micah or the children, but Lucy's gentle manner made it easier to discuss the subject. She was relieved that Lucy didn't ask any uncomfortable questions about Micah, perhaps because Lucy knew how devastated Katie was by Jacob's death.

They discussed many things including Lucy's pregnancy and her husband, Gabriel. They talked about Katie's sewing, about recipes they liked, which they shared, until Katie realized how late it was.

"*Danki,*" Katie said as she picked up their glasses and washed them at the sink.

"You don't have to do that!" Lucy moved to help, grabbing a dishtowel to dry the glasses.

"Take the help when you can get it," Katie teased.

"Gabriel helps me a lot."

Katie softened her expression. "I know he does. You married a *gut* man, Lucy Fisher."

"*Ja*, I'm extremely fortunate to have him."

The sky had darkened by the time Katie climbed into her buggy to return home. She realized that she had stayed at Lucy's too long, but it was nice to spend time with her friend. Lucy was fortunate in her second marriage. She'd found a new love in Gabriel Fisher, a man much more generous and loving than Lucy's first husband, Harley, who hadn't been interested in his new spouse after the death of his beloved first wife. *Which is why people who have loved and lost should not marry if they aren't able to accept them as they should.*

Thunder rumbled in the distance as she drove toward home. The darkened sky was expanding, and a streak of lightening lit up the clouds startling her, making her cry out. The initial rain became a downpour as the storm roared in with a vengeance. Katie knew she needed to find shelter in the worsening storm. She steered her buggy, keeping to the side of the road, concerned with her horse which she feared would spook if she didn't get her inside soon.

It was too far for her to go home. A property loomed ahead in the near distance, and Katie recognized it as the Evan Bontrager residence. *I can't stop there.* She hadn't seen Micah in two days. It would be awkward, and she didn't want to come across as needy.

The next lightning flash followed by a horrendous boom of thunder had her rethinking her decision to keep going until she found another place to get out of the rain. She steered her vehicle onto the Bontrager property and parked near the barn. There were no other buggies in the barnyard. It was entirely possible that Micah and the children weren't home. She ran to the rear door first and knocked hard but no one answered.

Katie raced back to the barn and opened it. If she could find an empty stall…

There was one close to the door. She unhitched her mare from the cart and brought the animal inside to the dry, empty stable. Satisfied that her horse would settle and be safe, she walked the length of the outbuilding as she searched for another place for her to sit. There were no other stalls available. She went back to her horse and sat outside the stall door. When the storm raged loudly, making her scared more than nervous, she slipped inside the stall and took refuge in a back corner. Hugging herself with her arms, Katie prayed that the storm would be over soon so that she could go home and take comfort in the company of her family.

Chapter Ten

❧

"Jacob, stay by my side," Micah said as he walked down an aisle in Kings General Store. His youngest daughter, Eliza, sat in the seat of the shopping cart. Rebecca was being entertained by Rachel King behind the counter in the back of the store. She'd offered to take Eliza, too, but he thought he could manage Eliza and find the grocery items he needed for the next couple of days. Meals he could fix easily.

"Dat, can I have a cookie?"

"We have cookies at home," Micah said.

"A cupcake?" Jacob looked up at him, his eyes filled with hope and innocence.

"*Ja*, maybe a cupcake, but only if you help me shop like the *gut boo* you are."

His son beamed up at him with excitement. "What do we need next, Dat?"

Micah ruffled Jacob's hair as he regarded him with affection. He loved his children. They were his world. Which was why he was willing to marry again—not because he needed a wife but because his children needed a mother.

The image of Katie filled his mind, creating an ache in his heart, as he pushed the cart down the aisle. There had been something about her from the first moment they'd met that captured his attention. But then when he learned that she'd been his younger brother's betrothed...

She will never marry. He could see her married and with children. *With me.* His own thoughts shocked him, because he'd loved Anna and he never thought he'd feel that way about any woman again.

Which was why he put distance between them. Katie would never be his.

He glanced outside and saw the sky had turned dark. He had filled his cart with nonperishables. He grabbed a few snacks before he headed to the register area to pay.

Rachel's husband, Jed, grinned as Micah approached. He was manning the cash register in front while Rachel was in the back where she made sandwiches and other food items.

"Did you find everything you need?" Jed asked with a smile.

"I hope so." Micah glanced out the window. "Looks like a storm is on its way."

"*Ja*, I hope it's a quick one."

"Me, too. I'm worried about our farm animals outside." He needed to get home to ensure their safety, but it would be difficult with the children.

His concern must have been apparent, because with a thoughtful, smiling look at Eliza and Jacob, Jed offered, "Why don't you head home to check on them? We can keep the children here until you get back. No need to hurry. With this storm, the store wouldn't be busy for a while."

"I don't want to impose." Micah had come to know the King family well since moving to New Berne. It wasn't that he didn't trust them with his son and daughters because he did. He wished that Katie was here. His children were afraid of thunderstorms, and Katie would soothe them and make them feel safe.

Rachel approached from the back of the store, holding Rebecca. "What's wrong?" she said as if feeling Micah's concern, just as thunder rumbled in the distance.

"Storm," Jed told her. "Micah needs to get to the farm to get his livestock inside. I suggested it's better if he leaves the children here with us, but he worries that he'll be imposing."

The woman laughed. "Micah, I assure you that I will enjoy every moment with your little ones. Mine are with my in-laws. Now that they are getting older, I miss having young children."

"Micah, leave them here. Please! I like to see my wife happy." Jed grabbed Jacob's hat from the shopping cart and settled it on his little head. He grinned when Jacob took off his hat and put it carefully back inside the cart. "To tell you the truth, I enjoy little ones as much as Rachel does. And we promise not to get them all sugared up so they're a handful when you come for them."

Micah widened his eyes at the thought of having rambunctious children due to sweets. "I'd appreciate it." He lowered his voice so that they wouldn't hear. "They're afraid of thunderstorms." He turned toward his son and bent down to explain the situation with Jacob. "You'll stay with Rachel and Jed. I have to take care of your *grossdaddi*'s livestock."

Jacob met the other man's gaze, and Jed smiled at him in reassurance. "We'll fix you a *gut* lunch," he said.

"And if your *vadder* says it's fine, we'll have cake or cookies afterward." His gaze met Micah's. "Just enough for a boy of Jacob's size," he said.

Micah nodded. "They usually go in for a nap by now, but I don't know if they will sleep as long as they can hear the storm. They've been amazingly *gut* all morning, but I can't guarantee they will stay that way."

"We have a storage room in the back that is quiet and private. We can put them down to nap on some quilts that we store there."

"But don't you usually sell them?"

"Nay," Rachel said. "These belong to our family."

"They were for our children when we had to work late," Jed explained. "Now they're too old for naps."

Micah said goodbye to his little ones and then a few minutes later, he was on his way back to his parents' farm, convinced that the children would be fine with Jed and Rachel. The storm picked up in intensity as he steered the buggy along the road. He kept on the blacktop, afraid that if he went too far off the side that his vehicle would get stuck in a water-filled ditch or, worse, tip over.

The downpour was nearly blinding as he parked the buggy close to the barn on his family's property. He hurriedly got out and raced to check the pasture where the animals were situated. To his immense relief, he saw that the cows and goats had congregated under a lean-to within the fence. They would be fine there.

Rain dripped off his hat and soaked his clothes. Micah ran back to the barn where he untied his horse, opened the door and led the animal inside. Thunder crashed overhead. Lightning flashed through the loft window. He headed toward the front stall where he usually kept his mare Jenny and was surprised to find it already occupied, with a strange horse's head peeking at him over the stable door. With a frown, he looked back outside and saw a pony cart, which, in his haste to check on the animals, he hadn't noticed until now. After closing the barn door, he looked in the stall door currently housing the unfamiliar horse, and that was when he saw her huddled in one corner, eyes closed, shivering, her hair and clothes wet. *Katie Mast.* His breath caught when he realized that she was here. He moved his horse down the main barn corridor and tied him to a support post.

When he returned to Katie, she stirred and gasped with alarm as he opened the stall door.

"Katie, it's me—Micah," he said as he entered the stall. He reached down to help her stand.

"I'm so sorry, Micah!" Her blue eyes were filled with remorse. "I was driving home when it started to rain. I didn't want to bother you...so I took shelter here."

"Katie, it's fine. I wouldn't want you out in this storm. It's getting much worse." As if to prove him right, lightning lit up the barn interior, followed by a deafening huge thunder boom.

Micah saw Katie jump and fought the strongest urge to pull her into his arms. He watched her wrap her arms around herself, and he left the stall to find a blanket.

"Where are you going?" she asked, clearly nervous about the storm.

He softened his gaze. "Not far. You're wet and cold." He saw her swallow hard. "Come here," he said as he grabbed a bale of straw. "Have a seat." He helped her to sit. "I'll be right back." He started to leave.

"Micah!" she called. He faced her. "Where are the children?"

He smiled. "Safe. They're with Rachel and Jed King at the store."

She nodded, looking relieved until a crack of thunder frightened her, and she hugged herself with her arms.

When he returned quickly, as promised, Micah felt her relax. He'd retrieved a large quilt and a flashlight from a shelf along one wall of the barn.

"Found this," he said, unfolding it. He turned on the flashlight and set it down, then he wrapped her up in the quilt. "This should keep you warm."

"Micah, I'm soaked."

"*Ja*, which is why you need this." He worked to make sure she was fully covered. "Hold on to the ends to keep it closed."

Katie obeyed. "What about you? You're just as wet."

"I'm fine." He picked up the flashlight and sat on the barn floor beside her. She was beautiful. She looked vulnerable with her wet hair and her prayer *kapp* slightly askew. He could see her glistening blue eyes in the lamplight. Softening, Micah fought the strongest urge to remove her head covering so that she would be more comfortable. "Are you *oll recht*?"

She nodded. Katie felt safe whenever Micah was nearby. What was she doing? She shouldn't be feeling this way about him. Jacob had been the one meant to be her husband and when he died… Shivering, she stared at the ground and away from the one man she couldn't seem to forget.

Micah began to engage her in conversation. "I warned Rachel that my *kinner* usually nap at this time…"

"They will be fine," she said with a soft smile. "Rachel can handle them. She is an experienced mother with children of her own." Because of Micah, Katie was starting to relax despite the intensity of the storm raging outside. Fortunately, the barn roof was solid without a single leak.

"Tell me about your family." Micah shifted closer as if trying to gain warmth from her quilt-wrapped body. Katie was tempted to open the quilt and offer him space but she didn't. Because she knew it would be wrong.

"What do you want to know?"

"I understand you have three *bruders* and two *schweschters*. Who is the oldest? Uri?"

She shook her head, amused. "I am."

"*Nay*, impossible," he said, and she frowned at him. He arched an eyebrow. "You are too pretty and young to be the oldest child in the Mervin Mast family."

"Micah…" She loved what he'd said, but this situation, their proximity with the storm outside creating a cozy and odd sense of intimacy, an intimacy that made her feel things she had no right to feel, made her breath catch as every one of her senses grew active and aware. She gazed at him, comparing his features to her deceased betrothed, but the only face she could see now was Micah's. Somehow, she'd lost the memory of Jacob. Which made her feel more than a little guilty. And sad.

Upset with herself, she looked away.

"Katie, what's wrong?"

She shook her head, unwilling to confess the truth.

"Tell me," he urged with a look of concern.

Katie briefly held his gaze before she looked down, anywhere but at him. He was so handsome that he stole her breath every time she saw him. The case of their conversation had only brought home to her how much she wished things were different, that he wasn't a widower who only wanted a mother for his children. That he was seeking a wife he could love.

"I'm fine, Micah." Warmer now, Katie unwrapped the quilt and offered it to him.

His blue gaze seemed to regard her thoughtfully "I don't need it, but *danki*."

She nodded and stood. She felt anxious suddenly, and she wished that the storm would pass so that she could be on her way home—and away from Micah. Not that she wanted to leave him, but considering the way she was feeling right now, she thought it would be best if she could put distance between them.

Following her lead, Micah rose. "The storm doesn't look like it will be ending soon," he said after they'd heard another reverberating rumble of thunder.

The horses inside the barn shifted slightly but didn't seem overly bothered.

Katie wished that *Gott* had chosen a different path for her. One that didn't include a dead fiancé and an older brother who had loved his wife too much to fall in love again.

She faced him, studying him, wanting to preserve these last moments to take out as memories later when Micah married and her remembrances would be all that she had left of their time together.

A sharp, loud crack from above startled her, making her cry out. Micah reached for her, pulling her close, as the scent of smoke assaulted her nose. She glanced up to see bright flames along the barn ceiling, smelled the burning wood.

"Micah!" she cried. "Look! The barn is on fire!"

Micah released her and focused his gaze on the ceiling, where a small fire from a lightning strike grew quickly along the barn roof, fed by the wind.

"Katie!" He caught her by the shoulders, turning her to fully face him. "We need to free the animals," he said calmly. "Help me open the back door so we can release them into the pasture."

Micah's unruffled demeanor gave Katie a sense of purpose and worked to settle her fears of the storm. She couldn't allow innocent livestock to be injured or killed. She raced to help Micah with the rear barn door, then she pushed and prodded each horse until they were out of the burning building and into the field. Micah ran ahead and opened a gate that led to another pasture far from the flames. With a wild cry, he herded the horses through the open gate then returned to the barn.

Smoke filled the interior of the structure until Katie could barely see. There was one horse left, and she hurried to set it free. Micah appeared at her side. "That's Joe. My *dat*'s gelding," he said as he took the reins from her to help the animal outside. "He's injured. I'll bring him out. Katie, we've done what we could. Please get out of the barn now."

"Just let me take one last look to see if we missed any," she cried. Unable to leave until she knew for certain that every animal was safe, Katie ignored his concern and ran through the smoke to search for livestock she might have missed. She coughed as she found a mother and baby goats still inside. She urged them outside, then took one last look and realized that every animal that was inside had been evacuated.

"Micah," she cried. "Our vehicles! They're too close to the barn!"

Together, Micah and Katie worked to alternately push and pull three vehicles away from the burning structure.

Moments later, from a safe distance, Katie stood in the pouring rain with Micah, watching with horror as the Bontragers' barn crumbled on itself, destroyed by fire. The pouring rain did little to nothing to fight the flames and heat. "I'm going next door to call the fire department!" she cried, suddenly spurred into action.

"Katie!" Micah called out. "Be careful!"

She nodded. She then raced across the street and banged on the neighboring Englisher's door. A young male answered and stared at her, his eyes widening as he looked at her with mounting horror. "Are you all right?" he asked.

"*Ja.* I'm fine. We got the animals out. I'd hoped to use your phone."

"I already called the fire department," he told her. "They're on their way."

"*Danki!*" she cried before she raced back across the street, grateful that there were no oncoming vehicles to stop from hurrying to Micah.

Micah stared with dismay at the flame-ridden out-building as Katie reached his side. "Micah," she murmured, briefly running a hand along his arm soothingly.

He didn't immediately acknowledge her presence. His masculine face was layered with soot, and she realized that she, too, must be covered.

The rain slowed to a drizzle as the storm started to move on. Black rivulets, resembling dark tears, cascaded down Micah's face. His hat was gone, no doubt left and destroyed in the barn, and black dust clung to his brown hair, along his neck and over his clothes to his muddy boots. He seemed lost, and Katie wanted to comfort him.

"Micah," she said softly.

Without meeting her gaze, he reached out and clasped her hand, interlocking their fingers. He stood quietly for a moment, keeping her close. She gave his fingers a gentle squeeze to show that she was here for him.

"*Danki*, Katie," he said, his voice raspy.

Sirens screamed in the distance and strengthened as the fire trucks drew near. Two vehicles pulled onto the property with flashing red lights. Ten firefighters climbed out of the vehicles. A water truck drove in and parked next to the other trucks. Two firemen unrolled the hose away from the water truck, and three others helped the hose along while two firefighters raced toward the burning barn, one with the hose nozzle in his hand.

"Miss. Sir," an older fireman said from behind them, "please step out of this immediate area so we can do our job."

Micah nodded and, still clasping Katie's hand, drew her away from the barn and toward the house. Fortunately, the downpour had wet the main residence enough to keep it safe from sparks that could set the house on fire. Micah continued to pull her with him to the front of the house and closer to the street, a safe distance from the men from the fire department. Katie watched helplessly as the firefighters fought to put out the raging fire. The fire was put out, but it was too late to save the old barn.

Katie didn't care if she was wet and sooty. Micah held her hand, and she was glad she could be there for him; he needed someone. Needed her.

Having heard the sirens while some had caught sight of the flames, the Bontragers' neighbors and fellow church members arrived within the hour with offers of assistance. The fire had been put out, but smoke from the smoldering embers hung heavily in the damp air. Gabriel Fisher approached, and Micah quickly released her hand. Katie felt the loss of his grip as he left her to greet him and the others who had come to help.

"Micah, I can take your goats to shelter," Gabriel Fisher said. He'd been burned in a house fire years ago, and Katie knew that Gabriel had firsthand experience with the devastation caused by fire. "We don't have a large farm like you do, but we certainly have room in an outbuilding on our property." He smiled. "Lucy wants to get goats, but I suggested she wait until after she gives birth to make a decision. This will give her an opportunity to feed and care for them."

Katie, standing next to Micah, smiled at him. "A wise suggestion," she agreed.

"*Danki*, Gabriel," Micah said. "My family will appreciate this."

Levi Yost stepped up to him next. He had come with Gabriel, which shouldn't have surprised Katie, but it did, since Levi's wife was Lucy's deceased first husband Harley Schwartz's sister. "We'll take your cows," the man offered pleasantly. "I've got me plenty of room for the whole lot of them until after the barn raising."

Aaron Hostetler, an experienced construction worker, approached next. "I'll order the material for the new barn. I'm thinking we can have everything here in a week or so."

"*Danki*, Aaron," Micah said, his voice gravelly from the smoke.

Katie could tell that Micah was deeply moved by the concern and offers of assistance. She knew the animals could probably stay temporarily in the lean-tos on Evan's property, but then Micah would have to worry about caring for them alone until his family returned—and with three children to tend to, it would be difficult.

She joined a group of women who had congregated in a gathering away from their men. She heard Mary King speak as she approached.

"We need to figure out the food for the barn raising," Mary said. "Kings will donate several large containers of salad and a platter of roast beef."

"I'll bring vegetables and some ham," Nancy Yost, Lucy Fisher's former sister in law, said. "I'm sure Lucy will want to contribute. I'll do what I can to help her since she tires more easily these days."

"I'll make desserts," Katie said with a smile. "I love to bake, and Mam and I will also bring sweet and sour green beans."

She glanced toward Micah and wished she could go up to him and give him a hug. She could tell he was overwhelmed by what had happened. He looked lost as he stood among the men who were deep in discussion about their plans to hold a barn raising for the Bontrager family as soon as the material was on-site. After excusing herself, Katie left the women and headed in Micah's direction. The men dispersed, passing by her as they joined their wives then proceeded to their vehicles.

"Micah?" she said softly, alarmed by the look of

devastation in his blue eyes. "Micah, everything will be *oll recht*."

He turned toward her with a pained expression. "Will it?"

She blinked, stunned by the change in him. "It will. How can I help?" She knew he was a kind man, but the disastrous fire and its damage, while his family was away, was apparently way more than he could handle.

"What am I going to tell my *vadder* and *mudder*?" he asked, his jaw tight, his blue eyes filled with concern.

"Have you spoken with them recently?"

"The other day. They decided to stay with my *grosseldra* another few days." He sighed. "What can I say to them?"

"The truth, Micah. You tell them what happened. That a storm caused a barn fire and their animals were saved—and no one was hurt."

His expression softened as he gazed at her. "*Danki*, Katie."

"Your *kinner*?" Katie basked under the comforting glow of his blue gaze. "I'm sure they are waiting for you to bring them home."

A car pulled into the driveway, and a man stepped out. Katie recognized Bert Hadden, an Englisher who frequently gave rides to members of her Amish community. "I thought I might be able to help."

Katie stepped up to him. "You can. Will you give Micah and me a ride after we get cleaned up a little? His children are at Kings General Store." Hoping that her presence offered comfort, she decided that she would stay with Micah while he picked up his children. She wondered, though, if it wouldn't be better for Micah if Jacob and the girls spent the night with the Kings. But that was up to Micah and the Kings. She and Micah were both too tired to round up their horses and hitch them to their vehicles. That task would be held for tomorrow.

Chapter Eleven

It was midmorning the day after the fire, and his children were still asleep. Worried about his family's reaction to the loss of their barn, Micah had lain awake all night. He was so tired, but there was too much to do to think about resting. He studied the charred structure from inside the house, through the screened door. The sounds of bird song filtered in, reminding him that life continued as it always did. The scent of smoke hung heavily in the air, reminding him of the horror of the fire. Still, he was grateful that no one was hurt. Katie was fine, and he was fine. *Thanks be to Gott.*

The site needed to be cleared before the new structure was built. He hadn't been able to get a hold of his parents to tell them the bad news. Micah didn't want to worry them or have them come home early. His grandparents needed them, and he could take care of things here. A barn raising was scheduled, and he wanted to assure them that everything would be fine. But for them not to know? It didn't feel right, which was why yesterday afternoon, while in Kings General Store, he'd called and left a message at Smith's Market, the business closest to his grandparents' Indiana home.

Yesterday, after Bert had driven him with Katie to pick up his children, Micah had walked inside the store, after taking the time to clean up and change clothes, and he tried not to show his concern about what had happened. Having Katie with him had helped greatly. She too had cleaned up at his parents' house, and Micah had found a spare dress that belonged to his sister Emma.

Something about Katie soothed and settled him. He'd been grateful for her company as they rode to Kings, even more so as they entered the building. Jacob and his girls had been happy to see him, but when his little ones saw Katie, they'd cried out with joy and reached for her. Amazing, he thought as the memory hit him of Katie holding his daughters, one in each arm.

Rachel and Jed had offered to keep his children overnight, but Micah had wanted them home with him. As Bert drove them home after dropping off Katie, he feared his children's reactions to the ruined barn.

Dat! Jacob had cried, his eyes wide, when he saw the charred remains in the car's headlights after they had climbed out of the vehicle.

The roof caught on fire, he explained.

But how?

It happened during the storm, but don't worry. Our neighbors are holding a barn raising for us, and there will be a new barn in its place soon.

Where are all of grossdaddi's *animals?*

They're safe, soohn, he assured him. *Our friends and neighbors took them until the new barn is ready.*

Thankfully, his explanation had satisfied his son, a fact that surprised Micah whenever he thought about it.

He expected Jacob to be upset more over the fire, but then who knew what was in the mind of a nearly four-year-old? His worry eased. *The resilience of young, innocent children.* After supper, his little ones had crashed and gone to bed early, leaving Micah concerned about speaking with his father.

He smiled as he thought of Katie. They had both looked a mess after the fire with their hair and faces blackened and their clothes covered with soot, which was why he'd offered her his sister's dress. She'd been reluctant at first, but then she finally agreed.

The soft rumble of a car engine from the road, getting louder by the second, drew him back to the present. Micah opened the door and stepped outside just as a white van pulled close to the house and parked. When he saw his parents and his siblings climb down from the vehicle, he felt his stomach turn. He stepped out onto the porch and watched his family gaze at the ruins left by the fire.

"Dat. Mam," Micah said, drawing their attention as he approached them.

His father turned first, and Micah was shocked that his parent was surprisingly calm. Dat met him halfway. "What happened, *soohn*?"

"Lightning strike during yesterday's thunderstorm." Micah ran a hand across the back of his neck. "Katie and I were in the barn when it hit. We were able to get the livestock out safely. Our neighbors are housing them until the new barn is built."

Evan shook his head. "You and Katie were in the barn? Are you *oll recht*? Is Katie?"

Micah nodded. "*Ja*, we're fine. We were able to save the animals before the roof collapsed." He saw his mother approach. "The barn raising will be quick, thanks to your neighbors and friends. Jed King said that we can make it happen by a week from Tuesday—and possibly sooner." It was Saturday, and the charred wood and debris had to be taken away before they prepared the site for the new structure. "I'll work on clearing the ground. Dat, you, Mam and everyone can head inside to rest. You must be weary after your trip." He was too but he'd never admit it.

"Mam," he greeted as his mother joined him and Dat. He felt terrible that his parents had come home to the mess. "I called Smith's and left a message yesterday for you to call. I had no idea that you were already on your way home."

"We left yesterday morning. My *vadder* is doing well enough to travel," his mother said. "We decided that Mam and Dat should move to New Berne, and your *grosseldra* agreed. Your *vadder* wants to build a *dawdi haus* for them here on the farm." She glanced toward the barn. "But seeing this now… I don't know…"

"We'll get their *haus* built, Mam," Micah assured them. "*Grossdaddi and grossmudder* need to live close to us. The new barn won't take long with our church community's help. Jonathan, Vern and Matt will build their *dawdi haus* with me."

"But what of your own *haus*, Micah?" his *vadder* asked. His face was drawn from the ordeal of the trip and his father-in-law's illness. For the first time, Micah thought his *dat* looked much older than his forty-eight years.

"I'm not worried about my *haus*, Dat. It's nearly done. I've been working on the floors in the bedrooms. The downstairs is move-in ready." Micah ran a hand raggedly through his hair. "I'm sorry you had to come home to this."

"*Soohn,*" his father said. "*Gott* gives us only what we can handle. You saved our animals and everyone is *oll recht.* What more can we ask for?" He frowned. "Where are my *kinskinner?*"

"In their rooms, sleeping. They stayed with Rachel and Jed King during the storm yesterday while I came back to check on the animals. They didn't nap for long and were tired when they came home. I need to check on them."

"May I?" Mam said.

Micah smiled at his mother. "*Ja,* of course, Mam. They're your *kinskinner.* They'll be excited to see you."

His sister Addie joined him and their father. "Micah…"

"Lightning," his *dat* said before Micah had a chance to explain.

"*Ach nay!*" Addie said. "That must have been terrible for you! When did it happen?"

"Yesterday," Micah said. "Katie and I were able to save our livestock. Except for the horses, Gabriel Fisher and Levi Yost are sheltering the animals until we replace the barn." He frowned. "Where's Emma?"

"She and Matthew stayed behind to help your *grosseldra,*" Dat said.

Addie studied the barn with a frown. "That was kind of our neighbors to help." She paused. "So, Katie was here?"

"*Ja.* She was on her way home from Lucy Fisher's when the storm hit. When I came home to check on the animals, I discovered Katie had sought shelter in our barn. No sooner had I brought Jenny in out of the bad weather when lightning set fire to the roof." He smiled as he thought of the amazing young woman who had sprung into action to assist him. "Without Katie's help, we would have lost a lot of them."

"Thank the Lord that you came home and she was there to help," Dat said.

"Ja," Micah agreed. *Ja. Thank Gott for Katie Mast.*

Katie held a casserole on her lap as she rode with her family to the Bontrager farm. After they'd heard about the barn fire, her parents and siblings wanted to see what they could do to help.

"Ach nay!" her mother exclaimed when she saw the black remains of the barn.

"Ja, it was bad."

"We can clear away the charred debris," Uri suggested as he leaned forward as their father pulled their vehicle onto the property.

A van passed by them on its way back to the road. Katie saw Evan with some of his children staring at the barn. As her father drove closer to the house, Micah turned, his gaze immediately catching hold of hers through the buggy's open side window.

"I'm sorry to see this, Evan," Dat said sincerely when he joined his friend in the yard. "Gabriel Fisher let us know what happened before Katie got home. There is much to be done before the material for the new barn is delivered next week." Her father raised his straw hat and settled it back onto his head. "Best to get it cleaned up before one of the children wanders over and gets hurt."

Katie agreed. She stared at the ruined barn and recalled how frightened she'd been when she'd seen the fire caused by lightning. Yet, when it came time, she'd jumped to help Micah, no longer afraid of anything in her quest to save livestock. Micah had that effect on her.

The sound of wagon wheels had them turning as vehicles belonging to their fellow church members came onto the property. Katie saw the Hostetler brothers drive in followed by Gabriel and Lucy Fisher with their children. David Bontrager, the preacher, had brought his neighbors, the Yoders. The young male Englisher who had called the fire department crossed the street after seeing all the activity, wanting to help.

Men stepped out of their buggies with their sons. Two wives, who accompanied their husbands, brought food like Katie and her mother.

Rachel King wore a grim look as she stared at the barn before she approached Katie who still stood in the yard. "Katie," she breathed, "I had no idea. When I think of what could have happened to you and Micah... Weren't you afraid?"

Katie nodded. "*Ja*, terrified, but then Micah remained calm as he and I ran to save the animals, and I was too busy to be afraid. In fact, Micah told me to leave at one point, but I just couldn't—not until I knew for certain that every one of them was out of danger."

"Thank the Lord that you're *oll recht*."

Ja, praise the Lord, Katie thought as Rachel left to put food in the house. She shuddered when she thought about how things could have turned out differently. If something had happened to Micah... She offered up a prayer of thanks that Micah and she were fine.

It was ten in the morning, and the yard filled with activity as the men moved around the burnt wreckage, discussing the best way to clear the site before they dove into the job. Katie watched, pleased, as her brothers quickly went to work, followed by Micah and his brothers—and both of their fathers.

"You two start on the back side of the building," Uri directed to Joseph and Abraham, easily taking charge. "*Bruders,* be careful. I'd doubt there still are hot embers, but it doesn't hurt to be cautious. Just hover your hand over the area you want to work on. If you don't feel any heat, go for it!"

"Uri, where should we pile everything?" Joseph asked.

The oldest of her younger brothers looked around. "Let's stack it over there."

Katie watched as they moved the garbage to a cleared area away to the far left of the barn. *A good choice.*

The volunteers' faces, hands and clothing became filthy with soot as they toiled to get the job done. It was well past noon when the women convinced them to break for a meal.

"You need sustenance to finish," Betty said.

Katie watched the workers wash up at the water pump before they headed to the food table outside, where they grabbed and loaded up their plates. Her attention was drawn to Micah, who was covered in soot, his head bare, as he ate. As if sensing her regard, he turned and locked gazes with her. She gave him a little smile and nod, but to her dismay, he watched her without expression a few seconds before he threw out his paper plate and went back to work.

An engine roared as a massive dump truck pulled onto the dirt driveway and entered the yard. Bert Hadden, the English friend of their community, parked the truck and got out. "Load 'er up," he said.

Soon, the garbage was gone and the site of the old barn clear of all rubble.

Katie helped pack up leftover food and clean dishes. When the work was done, she, her mother and sisters went out to the buggy to wait for her father and brothers to join them.

Betty approached them. "*Danki*, Katie," she said. "You have truly been a blessing."

At a loss, Katie could only gape at her. "Betty, I haven't done anything."

"That's not what Micah said."

Katie felt a rush of pleasure as she wondered what Micah had told her.

Her mother placed a hand on her shoulder. "She has always been a *gut dochter*. I don't know what I would have done without her all these years."

Katie looked at her with surprise. "Mam…"

"It's true, *dochter*. When I was sick right after Abraham was born, you took care of your siblings, including Abraham, and you were just a child."

She blushed. "I… I should see what's taking Dat and my *bruders so long*." Katie was eager to escape. She didn't like being the center of attention. She hadn't done anything any daughter or friend wouldn't have done for someone who needed them.

Escaping the females, Katie approached the men conversing in a group near the barn site. She heard them talking as she drew closer to them.

"We'll come back early Monday to finish up," she heard her father say.

"Not necessary," Micah said, his voice pleasant. "My *bruders* and I can handle it."

Dat looked as if he wanted to argue, but it was Evan's

barn and land, and if this was what his friend wanted, she knew her father would respect his wishes.

"*Ja*, we'll be fine, Merv," Evan said. "We appreciate your help today."

Her father nodded. "Who's ordering the lumber?"

"Jed King and Aaron Hostetler." Micah ran a hand along the back of his neck, unknowingly spreading black across his nape.

"That's *gut*," Dat said. "Both have construction experience."

Their faces and clothes were black with soot. Mud caked their shoes, and Katie saw patches of it on their elbows and knees where they must have knelt while working.

Katie stepped back to wait patiently for her father's attention.

Micah saw her outside the fringe of the men's gathering. "Katie."

She blushed. She didn't want them to think she was eavesdropping.

Her father turned to her with a frown. *"Dochter..."*

She pulled her gaze from Micah to meet her father's. "I didn't mean to interrupt you. We weren't sure if you were ready to leave." She turned to go. "You're busy. I'll tell Mam and we'll wait inside with Betty."

"Nay," he replied, drawing her attention. "I'm ready." Dat addressed his friends. "I'll see you at service tomorrow."

Evan smiled at him. *"Danki*, Merv."

"No need to thank me," her father replied. "You'd do the same for me if our positions were reversed."

"Ja, I would," his friend agreed.

Katie started to turn when she felt Micah's intense

gaze on her. She started across the yard. She wasn't there to listen in. Did Micah think she was?

"Wait up, Katie," her father called. She watched him signal to her brothers to follow before he hurriedly reached her side.

She shifted uncomfortably, expecting a reprimand from him. "I wasn't eavesdropping, Dat."

Her father looked at her with surprise. "I didn't think you were." His warm smile eased the nervous butter-flies in her stomach. "You did a *gut* thing yesterday when you helped Micah. It scares me to think about what might have happened to the both of you. I believe *Gott* was watching over you, so I will think only of the positive and not what could have been."

"Dat, I shuddered to think about what could have happened," she told him as she reached the area where her mother and sisters waited. Her brothers walked past and arrived at the buggy before the two of them.

"But it didn't." Her father eyed her thoughtfully. "You did a fine thing, Katie."

"I just did what anyone would do."

Dat smiled. "I don't think that's true, *dochter*. I doubt another woman would have stayed in a burning barn to help. It was a noble thing you did, and Micah had nothing but *gut* things to say about your role in saving their animals. Now let's go home." He waved her to go ahead of him and Katie obeyed, climbing inside the ve-hicle to sit beside her sisters.

As her father drove their buggy toward home, Katie marveled that Micah had mentioned her at all. He hadn't seemed happy to see her this morning. In fact, every time their gazes collided, he looked away. He seemed distant…his expression stoic…as if she wasn't worth his time.

It had been three days since he'd told her he wouldn't be needing her to babysit. And now that Betty and Evan were home, Katie knew that her time with his little ones was most definitely over. She stared out the window at the passing scenery. Would Micah ask her to watch the children once he moved them into his newly renovated house? Or would she no longer be needed—or wanted?

Katie felt an ache in her chest, a pain that reminded her that she had begun to regard Micah as more than a friend. Her throat tightened and she had difficulty swallowing,

Micah needs a wife, and I… I can't marry, she reminded herself. She couldn't take the chance of losing someone she loved again.

Loved? Nay, she didn't love Micah. *I can't possibly love him.* Katie closed her eyes, upset with the painful direction of her thoughts. It would be best for Micah—and her, she assured herself—if Naomi found him a wife soon.

It would be best for all of them. She sighed. And she would learn to get by with her sewing business and the memory of Jacob, the man she'd loved and lost.

Chapter Twelve

Everyone attended Sunday service at the Jed King residence. Katie knew the second Micah and his family arrived that morning for church. She felt the air change and thicken inside the house at the exact moment she saw Micah enter with his family. She couldn't seem to take her gaze off him. Micah looked extremely handsome in his white shirt, black vest and black pants. He had taken off his wide-brimmed black felt hat, his Sunday best, and his light brown hair looked clean and soft. His blue eyes were bright in a face that was masculine and riveting. She saw him smile at the preacher's wife, his teeth a flash of white above his beard. Katie willed him to look in her direction, but he didn't. He made his way through the Kings' great room and took a seat with his father and brothers.

The space was filled with men and their older sons in one section and women with young children in another. When his gaze swept over the women's section, he didn't pause to acknowledge her. It was almost as if he was distancing himself from her again. She drew a painful breath. The time they'd spent together working side by side to evacuate the animals during the fire might never have happened.

Betty and her daughter Addie sat directly in front of Katie and her mother. Addie held little Jacob on her lap while Betty was attempting to hold both of her squirming granddaughters. Seeing Betty struggle, Katie tapped her on the shoulder. "May I help?" she asked with a smile for the girls.

"I'd appreciate it," Betty said with a grin before she allowed Katie to pull Micah's youngest into her arms.

"That was a nice thing to do, *dochter*," her mother whispered as the little girl snuggled against Katie.

She smiled at her *mam* who eyed her with approval. "Betty needed help."

The service began with a hymn and everyone stood. Katie held Eliza on her hip and sang along with the congregation. As she sat down again, she sensed someone staring at her. She was surprised to see it was Micah. His gaze dropped for a moment to his daughter in her arms, and she noted a softening of his expression... until his face became unreadable as his attention returned to Katie.

Hurt, she averted her eyes. She thought they'd become friends but she was wrong. Sick to her stomach, she had trouble concentrating on the preacher's sermon. She tried to focus on what the man was saying, but her mind kept drifting to Jacob, her deceased betrothed... and Micah, his older brother, who was very much alive.

Three hours after it started, the service ended, and Katie was relieved. She wanted to go home to avoid any interaction with Micah. She loved the Bontragers. They were like a second family to her, but Micah apparently didn't much care for her. She had no idea why. They had gotten along fine when she first watched his children. Until three days later when the man told her he wouldn't have use of her babysitting services the following day because he was taking a break from his house renovations and would be home with his children. It had been five days since he'd told her not to come. Apparently, he no longer needed her.

Katie helped in the kitchen with food and even managed to smile when she saw the fresh homemade bread and peanut butter provided by Rachel and Jed. Peanut butter on fresh bread was a traditional meal to share with the church community after service, although members of her congregation enjoyed adding other dishes to the meal, especially desserts. Theirs was a small district. Katie and her family used to belong to a much larger church district of about 59 families north of New Berne. It had taken over an hour to get to service, and traveling time meant leaving home early and getting back late. Then Bishop Amos Miller in his wisdom had decided that it would be better to start another district right in New Berne.

Two long tables were placed up along one wall in Jed and Rachel's great room for food, and the men had set up folding tables for eating. Katie carried dishes to the food table until she finally found her mother in the kitchen alone.

"Mam, I'd like to ask Uri to take me home."

Her mother's expression immediately filled with concern. "What's wrong?"

"I feel sick. I thought I'd lie down for a while this afternoon."

"Would it help to eat?"

"Nay," she whispered, upset. "I can't eat anything right now." She placed a hand over her churning stomach.

Mam's face softened. *"Ja,* of course, you may go home. It won't take long for your *bruder* to eat. Ask him when he's finished."

The burning sensation in her belly had gotten worse. She knew it had something to do with Micah's stoic expression and lack of smile whenever their gazes met.

Despite feeling unwell, Katie served food to the men and then stepped away to wait until her brother finished his meal. She'd avoided Micah. His distance since telling her that he no longer needed her to watch his children hurt and she felt…unwanted.

Uri finished eating and stood, chatting with a group of young men, including their brothers, Abraham and Joseph, and Lucy Fisher's brother Seth. Katie approached him before he became involved with a baseball game with his friends. The others had stepped away and only Seth remained with her brother.

"Uri," she called. *"Bruder,* may I talk with you for a second?"

"Ja, Katie," he replied with a frown. "Seth, I'll see you outside."

Seth nodded. In her estimate, Seth Graber was a wonderful young man, and Katie knew that his sister Lucy felt the same way.

"What do you need?" Uri asked her, eyeing her with curiosity.

She sighed, closed her eyes briefly. "Would you please take me home? I'm not feeling well."

"Ja, of course, I will. Is there anything else I can do? Does Mam know?"

"She does." Katie glanced toward the window to see

a group of young men assemble out in the yard. "Baseball?" She placed a hand over her churning stomach.

"*Ja*, but it's not important. I can take you home then come back, if you'll be all right by yourself at the *haus*." He studied her with concern.

"I'll be fine. I just want to lie down for a while."

Uri continued to eye her with worry. "Katie…"

"*Danki, bruder.* I just want this afternoon to rest and recover. I'm sure I'll be fine tomorrow."

"I'll meet you at our buggy," he said.

Katie nodded. "I'll let Mam know you're taking me home." She watched Uri walk away and was aware that he was concerned, but she couldn't confide in him—or anyone—about why she was feeling ill. She shouldn't feel this way. She would be fine. She'd loved Jacob with everything inside her. Now, after realizing she felt similar—but more powerful—feelings for Micah she felt terribly guilty. How could she forget Jacob so quickly?

"I'm sorry, Jacob," she whispered. "You're all that I ever wanted, but… I didn't mean to fall for him. I'm so, so sorry."

Katie told her mother where she was going and headed to meet Uri in the family buggy. As she walked up to the vehicle, a man stepped out in front of her. Micah.

"I'm sorry you don't feel well, Katie," Micah said. "I told Uri that I'll take you home."

She shook her head. "You don't have to do that."

"I want to," he said. "I'd like to talk with you." Micah held her gaze until she had to look away.

"Fine." Uncomfortable with the situation, she couldn't do anything about it without calling attention to the problem between them. She didn't want her—or his—family to know.

* * *

Micah could feel the tension coming off Katie in waves. Uri had told him that she wasn't well. Concerned, he'd offered to be the one to take her home, and Katie's brother had agreed. As they reached his wagon, he held out a hand to help her climb up. He noted her hesitation before she accepted his assistance. Her small hand felt warm and fragile within his grasp. He heard her gasp when he lifted her up onto the wooden seat.

Katie didn't look at him but stared straight ahead as he climbed up into the wagon to sit next to her. He grabbed hold of the leathers. "You haven't eaten," he said softly.

She shot him a quick look. "I'm not hungry."

He nodded, and then with a flick of the reins, he eased forward out from the row of parked vehicles and steered his wagon toward the road.

Katie didn't say a word to him as he drove onto the street and toward the Mervin Mast property. He needed to clear the air between them. Micah knew that he hadn't sought her out for a conversation since the fire. Soon the lumber for the new barn would arrive, and he had so much to think about and do. He'd learned this morning that the lumber would arrive this Tuesday, not the following Tuesday as anticipated.

"Katie," he murmured, finally drawing her attention. "Can I get you something that will help you feel better?"

She shook her head. "*Nay*, I just need to lie down for a while. I'll be fine."

"I hope it helps." He gave her a soft smile.

She blinked as if taken aback.

"What?" he asked.

"You…" She sighed and looked away.

"I what?"

"You told me you didn't need me to babysit because your family would be home soon. But then they stayed longer and you didn't ask me to come back."

"I know." He felt awful for making her feel unwanted. His feelings were more than he should have for her, which was why he'd made the decision to keep his distance. Something he was afraid he was no longer able to do. Like today he'd been unable to stay away from her.

Silence reigned as he drove closer to her father's farm. He steered his horse onto the Mast property, upset that he didn't know what to say to ease the tension between them. He parked close to the house. Katie turned to climb down.

He touched her arm to stop her. "Katie." She stiffened but met his gaze. "I'm sorry. I've had a lot to deal with, and I didn't mean to keep you from watching and spending time with my *kinner*. It's clear that they love you." Although he wasn't sure that was a good thing. "Once we move into the new house, I'd like you to watch them again." He felt her relax a little, and her eyes held on to his.

"Micah, if you don't want me to babysit for you, all you have to do is say so. *Oke?*"

He nodded and thought how pretty she looked in her Sunday best dress of royal blue. The cape and apron over her dress were white while her head covering was black, a color that unmarried women frequently wore to church.

"I understand this is a temporary arrangement," she continued, "because you won't need my help once you marry again."

"I know." But, if the situation had been different and he could have had his choice of wife, he would have wanted Katie. "But until then, will you help me? Take care of my children?"

She gave him a genuine smile. "*Ja*, I will watch them. Just let me know when." She turned to get out.

"Katie, hold up."

Eyes filled with curiosity, she regarded him over her shoulder.

"Wait, *sigh so gude*," he said. *Please*. "Let me help you."

Katie opened her mouth as if to object but then she surprised him by nodding without a word.

Micah hopped down and rounded his vehicle. He reached up for Katie, caught her by the waist before he gently lifted her down. He studied her and felt a longing for something that would never be. "Lie down and feel better, Katie." His tone was gentle.

She smiled at him. "*Danki* for the ride home, Micah." Then she turned and started toward the house.

He couldn't stop himself from calling her name. "Katie!"

Katie paused and faced him. "*Ja?*"

"I'll let you know when we move into the house. It may be longer than I'd hoped now that we must build the barn. My *grosseldra* will be moving here to New Berne, and my *vadder*, *bruders* and I have a *dawdi haus* to build."

She grinned at him. "Just let me know when you need me and I'll be here." She turned back to the house, halted and faced him again. "I'll see you at the barn raising on Tuesday."

Unable to help himself, he grinned back at her. "See

you then." He watched her enter the house before he climbed into his wagon for the drive back to Jed's place. He felt a little better after talking with Katie. Micah hoped she was all right. He didn't like that she was feeling poorly.

He was eager to see her on Tuesday for the barn raising. He hoped that she felt well enough to attend.

His brother Jacob would have married Katie if he'd lived. Yet, he couldn't help liking her for himself... wishing for something more with the lovely woman whose allegiance was to a man who was no longer alive to marry her.

Her heart was racing as Katie entered the house. She was surprised—and pleased—by her conversation with Micah before he'd left. She went upstairs to lie down but she already felt better. His apology and the way he regarded her warmed her heart. She knew that he would marry someday, but she hoped they would still be friends, even though she wished they could be more. But Micah wouldn't be marrying for love, and she would never marry for anything else.

She entered her room and lay down on the bed. Katie felt the pinprick of tears as she thought of not being able to spend time with him, with his children. She closed her eyes and tried to conjure up Jacob's face, yet all she could see was Micah's. Guilt hit her hard, but there was nothing she could do about her feelings for Micah.

She would take each day as it came. Tomorrow she'd make food for the barn raising to ensure that the workers were well fed. And she would talk with Uri about helping Micah with the *dawdi haus* and Micah's.

She tried not to think about Naomi and the match

she'd make for Micah. It hurt too much. Sleep eluded her, and her stomach burn came back with a vengeance.

Whatever happened would be *Gott's* will, and she must accept the fact that her life hadn't turned out as she'd hoped it would.

Please, Lord, keep me strong in the days ahead. Days when everything between Micah and me will change.

Chapter Thirteen

"That's going up faster than I thought," Betty said as she eyed the nearly completed new barn.

Katie's mother put a plate of brownies on the table for the men to enjoy when they took their break. "Everyone turned out to help. Members of our community are always there for each other."

Katie didn't comment. She was too busy watching and worrying about Micah who knelt high up on the roof trusses, setting plywood and nailing it. If he fell from that height... Her heart stopped when his brothers Jonathan and Vernon climbed up on two ladders, carrying a plywood sheet between them. Micah reached for it and helped his brothers slide it into place before he hammered it down. She watched nervously for a time then had to turn away.

"Katie." She spun to find her mother studying her thoughtfully.

She managed to smile. "*Ja*, Mam?" A brisk breeze blew in, making her hug herself as she shot another nervous glance toward the roof.

"They'll be fine. They're about finished with the plywood."

Katie nodded. "I don't like them up there. The wind has picked up." She felt her mother's touch on her shoulder. The framework was done. Her brothers Uri and Joseph along with her father had installed metal siding across one side of the structure. Would it hold in this wind? Her gaze returned to Micah. She wanted him—and his brothers—to get down safely before there was a terrible accident.

"Dochter." Her *mam* pointed toward the barn. "See! They're coming down now. Looks like the only thing left to be done is the metal roof and the rest of the siding. I'm sure they'll wait until the weather is more cooperative before they finish it."

"I hope you're right," Katie murmured, her gaze fixated on Micah, the one man she'd been unable to put out of her mind. The wind had calmed a bit, but she didn't trust that it wouldn't return.

"Let's finish putting out the food," Mam said. "I'm sure the workers will want a snack to hold them over until supper."

"Do you think we should keep the food inside?" Katie asked.

"Nay, I doubt Betty will want them traipsing through the house, trailing sawdust and who knows what else on her floor." She glanced at the food table, apparently satisfied by what she saw. She gestured toward a five-gallon water jug. "Katie, will you check to see if that is full?"

"I will, Mam." Katie checked the jug and saw that there was plenty of water. She wished she'd thought to make enough iced tea or lemonade to fill it, but water was probably best for thirsty men.

She brought out the two dried apple pies she'd made yesterday then placed them on the table. She had baked all Monday morning so that she could bring a huge pan of brownies, two apple pies and two chocolate cakes that the men had snapped up earlier with pleased expressions on their faces. She hid a smile. At least Micah had grinned as he'd enjoyed a piece of the chocolate cake earlier. He'd sat on one of the chairs that she had carried outside for whenever the workers took breaks.

A gust rose, catching hold of a stack of paper plates and sending them soaring across the yard. Katie grabbed what she could, but then she had to chase after the rest as they skittered across the lawn. Several times as she stretched for one, the breeze moved it out of reach. She managed to step on one and caught another. As she picked up the one under her foot, she sensed someone kneel down close by to snag those she couldn't capture. She glanced up to thank the person and inhaled sharply when she saw it was Micah. With several plates in one hand, he grinned at her as he stood and helped her to her feet.

"Here you go," he said, his voice husky and warm. "I don't know if you should use these."

She nodded. "We can't. *Danki*." Katie felt her face heat as she accepted the paper plates he'd collected for her. A strong blast of air grabbed her *kapp*, stripping it from her head. *"Ach nay! Meim kapp!"* She gasped and pressed a hand to her head as the continuing wind tugged on her hair, freeing numerous strands from their pins. Alarmed, she met his gaze. His lips twitched before he chased down her head covering and returned it to her.

"Danki," she murmured, feeling shy under the intensity of his gaze.

Another gust blew, taking Katie by surprise, making her stumble. Micah reached out to steady her. "We can't control the weather, Katie," he said with a touch of humor.

She blinked. Was he flirting with her? "I know."

He released her with a smirk. She gaped at him, startled, as he caught her hand and tugged her to the food table. "What treats do we have here?"

Buzzing from his grasp, she pulled away. Katie didn't care for his expression as he studied her with gleaming blue eyes and an odd little smile on his very masculine lips. Was he mocking her? Or teasing her?

She studied him. Teasing her, she thought with amusement. Micah wouldn't willingly hurt her feelings. Their discussion and his understanding when he drove her home after church service assured her of what type of man he was. *A gut man.*

A blast of high wind threatened the table. "Maybe get everything inside," Micah suggested as he reached for the pie that had slid to the edge of the table.

"Ja." She picked up the brownies and the remainder of the chocolate cake. "Betty! Mam!" she called. "We're going to get these desserts inside out of the wind!"

Katie started toward the house, then paused to look back. Micah was right behind her, carrying her two dried apple pies. "Mam didn't think your *mudder* would want the workers inside," she said.

"My *mam* raised five strapping sons. A little dirt or

sawdust doesn't bother her." He rubbed a hand across the back of his neck.

Katie nodded, sadly aware that Jacob had been one of them. "You're not going back up on the roof today, are you?"

"*Nay.* We'll wait until the weather is better suited."

Relieved, she smiled at him before she continued into the house.

A burst of wind rattled the installed metal siding. She glanced back toward the barn. "Is the siding going to hold?"

Micah narrowed his gaze as he checked the integrity of the siding. "Hope so. If not, I guess we'll have to redo it. I don't want anyone or anything hurt if it goes."

As they climbed the two steps, Micah's sister Addie opened the door for them and took the pies from her brother. Micah went back outside. Katie placed the desserts on the kitchen table and looked through the window to see that Betty and her mother had picked up the rest of the food while the men, including Micah, were grabbing chairs and tables to store out of the wind. She saw her brother Uri coming out of the structure with a hammer and boxes of nails.

Several minutes later, Uri entered the house, grinning. "Stuck the tools on the front porch in the corner," he told Micah as they walked in together.

Micah smiled. "*Danki.* Just have to finish the siding and the metal roof and then we'll be done."

Uri nodded. His brown eyes flickered to his sister. "Katie, Dat said we'll be heading home in about an hour."

"*Oll recht,*" she said without meeting Micah's gaze. Katie enjoyed spending time with him. More than she should. He'd been helpful today, and she couldn't seem to get him—and this sweet side of him—out of her mind. Soon, she'd be babysitting at his new house. She loved his little ones, and it didn't hurt that she might be able to spend more time with their father.

Micah's fifteen-year-old sister approached. Emma had returned to New Berne yesterday afternoon with her brother and grandparents, who now lived in the main house until a *dawdi haus* could be built on the property. The teenager had spent most of the day inside with Micah's children. "Katie, Micah's *kinner* and I loved your chocolate cake," Emma gushed. "It was so moist and delicious. Chocolate is my favorite."

Katie smiled. "I'm glad you all enjoyed it. Are the little ones asleep?"

"*Ja*, I just put them down."

"Emma, you didn't eat all of the dessert, *schweschter*, did you?" Micah teased.

His sister grinned. "And what if I did?"

Micah moved to go after her, and Emma shrieked and laughingly scooted out of reach. Watching them, Katie chuckled.

She was setting out plates when her mother approached. "Katie, your *kapp*," she murmured for her ears alone.

"*Ach nay!* Sorry, Mam," she exclaimed, but her mother only smiled and gestured toward the great room with a nod of her head. Embarrassed, Katie hurried and did the best she could putting her head covering back on. It wasn't easy, given the state of her wind-tousled hair. She felt self-conscious as she rejoined the others until she saw the men smiling and heard them chatting as they filled the Bontragers' family dinner plates with the desserts she'd made.

After everyone had eaten, her mother washed the dishes while Katie dried them. Micah's mother and sisters put away the leftover food and wiped down the kitchen table and counters.

Soon, with the kitchen cleaned and dishes put away, Katie was on her way home with her family, empty plates on her lap. Reflecting, she decided it had been a good day. Micah had teased and flirted with her, which made her giddy. And for the first time in a long time, she realized that she hadn't been so consumed with Jacob's memory that she couldn't enjoy the day…or her interactions with his older brother.

A week had passed since the barn raising. Katie hadn't been back to the Bontragers, but she knew the barn was complete. She'd heard the news from Uri, who had helped Micah and his brothers with the metal roof and siding. It hadn't been the type of day that involved feeding the community so there'd been no reason for Katie to go, except to see Micah, which would be awkward given their circumstances.

"Gabriel and Levi brought back Evan's livestock," Uri said conversationally as the family ate lunch together. "The new barn is bigger than the old one. There's plenty of room for more animals if Evan wants them." He grinned. "We ordered the lumber for the *dawdi haus* for Betty's *eldra*. I'm going to build it with Micah and his *bruders*. Betty insists Micah finish his *haus* renovations first. Micah agreed, said it would be best for his family if he moved into his own home with his *kinner*."

Katie felt a flutter in her chest as she anticipated Micah's move. She'd be babysitting again once they lived in the new house, and she looked forward to spending time with Jacob, Rebecca and Eliza…and their father. "Are you going to help him with the renovations?"

"*Ja*, I'm going to refinish his wood floors." Uri took a bite of fried chicken. "Micah wants to install vinyl in the children's rooms. I'm going to help him with that, too."

"*Gut*," Dat said. "I'm sure he'll appreciate it."

Katie regarded her brother with affection. "I'm sure he'll be pleased for your help, *bruder*."

She longed to see the progress Micah made on his house, but she knew it would seem odd if she showed up unannounced when she had no reason to be in the area.

"The outbuilding is too small on Micah's property." Uri forked up a mouthful of mashed potatoes. "Micah told me that there is no hurry with a barn, as he only has his two horses. He plans to purchase livestock in the spring."

"I know he's worried about making sure his *grossel-dra* have enough room." Mam passed her husband the bowl of buttered corn. "Betty told me Micah is sharing a room with all of his *kinner*."

Katie could only imagine how tight the quarters were in Micah's room with himself and his three little ones. "I'm sure everything will work out in the end," she said, and her family agreed.

"How is Betty's *vadder*?" Dat asked.

Mam handed a bowl of peas to her youngest son. "Weak, Betty said. He's been having problems with his legs since he fell. Betty is going to take him to a doctor here in New Berne."

"That's wise." Katie watched Abraham spoon the green vegetable onto his plate.

The family spoke of other things as they ate their lunch. Her father wanted to buy a new plow, but it would have to wait. He'd need to use the old one until money was available for the purchase. Katie thought about the money she'd been putting aside from her sewing work. She had given some of it to her *mam* to contribute to the household. She could afford to give Dat money toward the new plow and could make do without savings for a while. It wasn't as if she had to move out of the house next month. Katie would keep enough for any sewing supplies she'd need to continue with her business.

When lunch was done, Katie cleaned up with her mother and sisters and then went to her room. She'd sewed each day since the barn raising and was thrilled after learning that several customers had requested her services through Kings General Store. Two days ago she'd picked up several more bags of items that needed mending. Katie decided to make Emma a new dress to replace the one she'd borrowed on the day of the fire.

She smiled. Emma was the Bontrager sibling who looked most like her oldest brother. With bright blue eyes like Micah's and features much the same, Emma could be considered the feminine version of him. The only other difference was her hair color, which was a much darker shade than Micah's light brown.

She had finished her mending work that morning and was nearly done with Emma's dress. Katie decided to make deliveries to her customers' homes this afternoon before returning to the house to complete the last bit of stitching on Emma's clothing.

As she made the trip toward her last stop, Katie realized that she would have to pass by Micah's house.

She recalled the first day she'd met him. She'd been so shocked to see someone who looked so much like Jacob, her late fiancé, that she had almost passed out. Fortunately, she had come to know Micah and was well over the shock now. His personality was nothing like Jacob's. The brothers' features and mannerisms might be similar, but Micah was taller, his presence more commanding and it was clear that he was the older of the two.

She was eager to see the house. It would be all right if she stopped, wouldn't it? It wasn't as if she had driven over just to see the progress. She was making deliveries and she still had one left. No one would think anything of it if she stopped to say *hallo* and to see what he'd done.

It was a beautiful day for a ride in her pony cart. Fall had come upon them, and bright red-and-green apples hung on trees in Beiler's Orchard as she rode past. She considered buying some fresh apples, but then decided she would come back to shop another day. Apple season had just begun, and there was plenty of time.

Micah's house was ahead and to the right. She waited for a car to pass from behind her before she made the turn onto Micah's driveway. She parked, eager to see his house—and him. There was another vehicle in the driveway so she stopped close to the road. It didn't look like Uri's, but maybe one of Micah's own brothers had come over to help him.

Katie got out and started toward the house when the side door opened and two women stepped out—one older and a much younger woman with auburn hair and lovely features. Katie recognized the older woman as the matchmaker, Naomi Hostetler. She froze as she realized Naomi must have found a match for Micah. While Katie watched with a sinking feeling in her chest, the women climbed into a buggy. Micah came out of the house and waved at them from the steps as they left.

Heart pumping hard, stomach burning with pain, Katie could only gaze at Micah, the man, she suddenly realized, she had fallen for hard, despite her attempts to convince herself that she only wanted to be his friend. If he were just her friend, she wouldn't be feeling this heartbreak. She spun and climbed into her pony cart, eager to get away before he saw her.

"Katie!" he called out.

She inhaled sharply and kept going. Ignoring Micah calling her name, she drove away from the house and the man she loved. She was hurt and angry. Apparently, he planned to be married soon; yet, he hadn't told her he no longer needed her.

Struggling against tears, Katie made her last delivery but didn't stay to chat. When she got home, she ran up to her room where she lay on the bed and allowed herself to cry. Finally dry eyed, she got up and went to work adding the final touches to Emma's dress with a painful lump in her throat.

"Katie." Her mother entered her room.

Katie didn't immediately respond. She pressed on the sewing machine pedal and ran stitches down one seam.

"Dochter." Mam's tone was firm.

She blinked up at her. *"Ja, Mam?"*

"What's wrong?"

"Nothing, Mam. I'm fine." She started sewing again. "Just busy trying to get this dress done and one other order that came in through Kings."

Her mother didn't say anything, but she didn't leave either. When Katie stayed silent, Mam sighed then left.

Katie stopped the sewing machine and hung her head, trying not to cry. Micah was getting married and she'd lost something special. She loved the man and he would wed that other young, pretty woman, leaving Katie to continue with her plans to make a living from her sewing.

Micah watched Katie climb into her vehicle and leave. She wouldn't look at him. He didn't understand why she stopped but didn't stay to visit. And then suddenly he realized that she must have seen Naomi and Iris as they left.

She's upset because she believes I no longer need her to babysit.

He would have to explain to Katie that it wasn't the case. He had planned to tell her about the finished house later this afternoon and that he would be moving in by the end of the next week. He needed—and wanted—her to watch his children for him again. He'd been excited at the prospect of seeing Katie in his newly renovated house.

He frowned. Did she have so little faith in him that she was quick to believe he wouldn't talk with her first to tell her he was marrying?

Closing his eyes, Micah tried not to be angry with her. He cared for her, more than he should since the only thing Katie was willing to give him was her babysitting services—and her friendship.

Nay, he couldn't be angry. Katie had looked distraught, and it bothered him to see her so upset. He would have to find out why she seemed hurt so that he could repair their friendship...

And if he had anything to do with it—he would seek to find out if there was a possibility of something more with her.

Chapter Fourteen

Emma Bontrager visited Katie two days after she saw Naomi leaving Micah's house with the young woman. "Mam wants you to come for tea. She would have extended the invitation herself," the teenager said, "but she doesn't want to leave my *grosseldra*."

Katie knew that Betty worried about her parents, especially her father. "How is your *grossdaddi*?"

Emma toyed with her *kapp* string. "He doesn't have good use of his legs which frustrates him, but otherwise he seems *oll recht*. He eats and sleeps well."

"I hope they find the answer to his problem soon."

"*Ja*, I do, too," Emma said. "So, will you come over for tea? I know you're probably busy, but Mam would love it if you could."

Katie didn't want to visit the Bontragers because of Micah, the last person she wanted to see. But she couldn't deny his mother, who'd been nothing but kind and loving toward her since the day her new beau Jacob had brought her home to meet his parents and share a meal. At the time, the Bontragers were recent additions to New Berne and her Amish community. Katie had met Jacob after he'd come to a singing at the invitation of their neighbor, a young man close to Jacob's age.

"*Ja*, Emma. I'll be there. What time?"

Emma blushed. "Can you come now?"

"*Oll recht.*" Katie managed to smile. "But can you wait a moment? I have something I want to get for you. Let me just run upstairs, then I'll follow you to your *haus*."

Katie hurried up the stairs to retrieve Emma's new dress from her bedroom. She'd chosen a beautiful shade of purple, a color that went well with Emma's pretty blue eyes. And she knew the teenager would love the cheerfully bright color.

When she returned to the kitchen, she saw that her brother Uri had come in from outside. He and Emma stood in the kitchen in silence. Uri appeared uncomfortable but couldn't take his eyes off the lovely girl. Emma barely looked at him and apparently had nothing to say to him. The tension between them seemed thick and painful. Katie hesitated in the doorway before making herself known as she entered the room.

"Here we are, Emma!" Katie announced loudly, breaking the awkward silence. She pretended to be surprised to see her brother. "Uri! I'm so glad you're home, *bruder*! I'm running low on baking supplies, and I wondered if you'd do me a big favor and pick them up for me."

She saw Uri reluctantly drag his gaze from Emma to focus on his sister. Katie glimpsed a sadness in his lovesick brown eyes, and she wished she could do something to ease his pain. "*Ja*. What do you need?"

After fetching a list of items she'd wanted for baking

from a kitchen drawer, she handed it to him. She smiled when he took it from her. *"Danki, bruder."*

His eyes fell on Micah's sister. "Emma," he murmured with a nod and then he left.

The girl's expression as she followed Uri longingly with her eyes as he left the house was telling. Katie hid a smile. The teenager clearly liked Uri but didn't know how to interact with him. "Emma."

The girl blinked. *"Ja?"*

Katie gave her a soft smile. "I borrowed your dress after the fire. Mine was ruined...and well... I'm afraid yours is too since I did a quick washup and couldn't take a shower. I'm sorry but I haven't been able to clean it for you. So, I made this. I know it isn't the same color as the one I borrowed..." She held up the new dress to show Emma.

"Purple!" Emma exclaimed as she reached to finger the fabric. "I love it!" She frowned as if something suddenly occurred to her. "Katie, you didn't have to go to all this trouble. I don't care if my dress is ruined. You didn't have to replace it." She smiled and her expression was soft as she studied her new garment with glistening blue eyes. "It's such a beautiful dress," she said with reverence. "I've never had one like it." She sniffed as she met Katie's gaze. *"Danki,* Katie. I can't wait to wear it. When I do, I'm going to tell everyone that you made it for me."

Katie shifted uncomfortably. "You don't have to do that."

Emma bobbed her head. *"Ja,* I do." She accepted the dress from Katie. "Mam said that you're a seamstress. If I wear this and tell them about you, you may get new customers."

Nodding, Katie realized that the girl had a point. She hadn't done it because she wanted recognition but simply because she owed Emma a dress. If someone wanted her to make a dress for them, she'd be happy to do so. After all, she wanted to sew for living. Didn't she?

Emma insisted that Katie ride with her when it was time to leave. "You don't need to drive over, Katie. I have to run an errand later, and I'll be heading past your house when I do."

Katie decided not to argue and agreed. How could she fault Emma's logic? She said a silent prayer that Micah wouldn't be home while she was there.

Ten minutes later, Emma pulled close to the Bontrager house. Betty opened the door as the girls got out of the pony cart and approached. "Katie!" Micah's mother greeted. "It is *gut* to see you! It seems too long since we chatted."

Katie smiled. She wondered why Betty was so eager to have her to tea.

"Mam, look at this dress!" Grinning, Emma held up the new garment. "Katie made it for me!"

"She did?" Betty was clearly surprised. "That was kind of you, Katie."

"I borrowed one of hers after the fire. Emma's size was the closest to mine." She blushed, remembering how Micah had grabbed a dress out of Emma's room for her so she could wash up a bit and then change before they rode with Bert to pick up his children. "Mine is ruined," she explained, feeling awkward.

"I'm sorry to hear that." The older woman eyed her with affection.

"I tried to clean Emma's, but I can't get all of the soot and mud out."

Betty shuddered, no doubt thinking of the fire. "Every time I think of you and Micah in that barn…"

"It was frightening," Katie said as she thought about what it would have been like if Micah hadn't arrived when he had. She would have been alone in a burning barn. Would she have been able to save Evan's livestock?

With Micah's name coming into their conversation, she wanted to ask Betty about the woman who was with the matchmaker, the one her son planned to marry. But she didn't. She knew it would hurt too much to learn about Micah's future wife—and the family's pleasure in their son's upcoming wedding.

"Please, Katie. Sit down," Betty invited.

Katie pulled out a kitchen chair and took a seat as Emma poured each of them tea.

"Cookies?" Emma asked, and her mother nodded. "I hope you like chocolate chip."

Katie smiled. "I do."

"How is your *mudder*?" Betty asked.

"She's doing fine. Been busy. She bought apples to put up. Abigail and Ruthann are going to help her when she's ready." Katie took a sip of tea. "How are your *eldra*, Betty? Emma said that your *vadder* is eating and sleeping well. Is he any better?"

"*Nay*." The older woman sighed. "He's still the same. I made an appointment for him to get his legs checked. We have no idea why he's still having trouble with them. I can only hope and pray that the doctor will shed some light on his problem. And that something can be done."

"I have faith that you'll find an answer soon," she said softly.

"My parents are managing by sleeping downstairs,

but it will be *gut* for them to have their own *haus*. Their place in Indiana is up for sale. The Realtor thinks it will sell quickly."

"That would be a blessing," Katie agreed.

Unable to help herself, Katie wondered about the progress on Micah's house. Was it finished? Uri hadn't been home much lately and she hadn't wanted to ask when he didn't offer the information.

"I will continue to have faith that Dat will get better and my *eldra* will be happy here in New Berne."

"I'm sure they will." Katie sipped her tea. "They have you and your family, and our community will do everything we can to help."

"They will, Mam," Emma said. "*Grossdaddi* and *grossmammi* wanted to move here."

Betty smiled at her daughter. Then the woman focused her gaze on Katie with a thoughtful expression that made Katie slightly uncomfortable. "I have a favor to ask."

"Ja?" She hoped the favor had nothing to do with Micah.

"I have a great deal of mending to be done, and since my parents moved here, I haven't had the time."

"Mam, I can do it for you," Emma offered.

"Nay, Emma. You've seen Katie's ability to sew in your new dress," Betty said with a glance toward the garment. "I'd like Katie to do this for me, if she will." She gave Emma an affectionate smile to soften the sting before she returned her attention to Katie. "I'll pay you the going rate."

"Betty, I'll do it, but you don't have to pay me—"

"Ja, I do. Please. Just knowing that you're willing to do this for me is such a blessing."

Katie nodded. *"Oll recht."* She watched as Betty stood up and left the room. Micah's mother returned within minutes carrying a large wicker basket of clothing. Katie stood and took it from her. "You didn't have to invite me to tea to ask for my help. Emma could have just dropped it off."

"I wanted to visit with you, Katie. I feel as if we don't see enough of you these days."

"I'm sorry, Betty. I don't mean to keep *meim* distance."

"Will you be going to the preacher's *haus* for Visiting Day?" Betty asked a half hour later when Katie got up to leave after Emma said she was ready to run her errand and take Katie home. It had been a lovely afternoon. Except for a short conversation about the fire, the subject of Micah hadn't been discussed.

"Mam mentioned spending time with her *schweschter* on Sunday."

"Ah well, then have a *wunderbor* time. Don't be a stranger."

"I won't," Katie promised. *"Danki* for the tea and cookies." Emma had plated delicious homemade chocolate chip cookies for Katie to take home.

"You're *willkomm*." The woman smiled as she walked Katie to the door.

As she followed Emma outside, Katie heard metal buggy wheels on the driveway.

"Micah," Emma greeted.

"Schweschter," he said, sounding amused.

Alarmed, Katie stole a quick glance in his direction and encountered the intensity of his bright blue gaze. She quickly averted her eyes. Katie tried to act as if she wasn't affected by Micah's presence as she prayed silently that he wouldn't address her directly. Since the day she'd seen Naomi and the pretty young woman leave his house, she'd felt vulnerable—and hurt. She knew she had no reason to feel that way. It wasn't as if they were in a relationship. She only wished they were.

Since then, however, she'd managed to avoid him. He would marry the young woman Naomi had found for him, and he'd marry not for love but to provide a new mother for his children. *But what if he falls in love with her?* She swallowed against a painful lump. Micah had captured her heart, but given the circumstances, there was nothing for her to do except try to get past her feelings for him.

"How is the *haus* coming along?" she heard Emma ask.

Micah smiled. "*Gut.* It won't be long before we can move."

"We love having you all here with us," his sister said with a frown.

"You know it's better for everyone if we move. It's not far. You can visit whenever you like."

Her heart picked up the pace as she attempted to slip by unnoticed toward Emma's vehicle with the wicker basket in her arms. When it was silent, Katie paused to check whether Emma was following, but there was no sign of the girl.

"If you're looking for my sister, she apparently forgot something in the house." Micah had approached, and he was so close she could smell his soap and a pleasant outdoorsy scent that only belonged to him. "Let me help you with that."

Katie met his gaze, and the warmth in his blue eyes made her catch her breath. "Your *mudder* asked me to tea," she said, feeling suddenly shy as she allowed him to take the basket.

He carried it and set it on the ground next to the cart before he extended his hand to her. Katie hesitated. She wanted to clasp that strong hand, feel the warmth of his fingers surrounding hers. But she knew that the moment their hands touched, she'd be lost.

Ignoring his outstretched hand, Katie reached up to grab hold of the side to hoist herself in. With a growl of frustration, Micah startled her when he grabbed her waist from behind and lifted her into the vehicle. He picked up the basket and handed it to her.

"Danki," she murmured, meeting his gaze, but it was as if a shutter had closed over his features, effectively shielding his thoughts. Without another word, he started to walk away. "Micah!"

He froze and then faced her.

"I wish you every happiness," she said softly, fighting tears.

His expression softened. "Katie, we need to talk—"

"Ready to go?" Emma exclaimed, interrupting.

"I'm ready when you are," Katie said, tearing her gaze from the man who was constantly in her thoughts.

"Bruder, tell Mam I won't be long," his sister said happily. "After I take Katie home, I have a quick errand to run."

"Be careful," Micah said, his deep voice drawing Katie's attention. He had spoken to his sister but his gaze was locked on Katie. The concern in his eyes for her warmed her heart.

Katie rewarded him with a genuine smile. "Take care of yourself, Micah," she said as Emma climbed onto the side and picked up the leathers. "Give your *kinner* a hug from me."

Emma drove the cart away, leaving Katie wishing things were different, that he wanted her—not as simply a woman as a mother for his children, but as the woman he wanted to marry because he loved her.

Micah couldn't stop thinking about Katie. It seemed like forever since he'd seen her. Today was Visiting Day at the preacher's house. David Bontrager was a distant cousin on his father's side of the family. Would Katie and her family be visiting there today? He hoped so. He wanted to talk with her, find out what had upset her, see if he could help in any way. Did it have something to do with Naomi and Iris's visit? He frowned. Surely, she didn't believe that Naomi had found him a wife. *Nay.* Katie must know that he would tell her if his circumstances changed.

He pulled his suspenders over his shoulders and clipped them in place. He had dressed Jacob, and with his sisters' help, Eliza and Rebecca were ready for the outing as well. Micah ran a comb through his hair before he went downstairs. He really hoped he'd get to see Katie today.

"Are you ready to go?" his father asked.

"Ja." Micah looked around. "Where are my youngsters?"

"Outside with your sisters," his brother Jonathan said as he entered the house.

"It would be nice seeing everyone, but I think I should stay home with my *eldra*," Mam said.

"Why can't they come with us?" Micah asked. "They traveled by car here from Indiana, and they did fine, *ja*?"

"*Ja*," his mother conceded. "They did."

"Why don't I take *Grossdaddi* and *Grossmammi* and you take Eliza and Rebecca?"

"That sounds like a fine plan," his grandmother said as she moved into the room. "Betty, your *dat* will be right here. He may have trouble with his legs, but he wants to go. He is tired of being cooped up inside."

"Truth," his grandfather said as Matthew and Vernon helped him into a kitchen chair. "I may have not *gut* use of my legs, but I have my faculties. With my *grosssoohn*'s help, I'll get to visit. You can put me in a chair there and go about your business. I'm sure I'll find someone to talk to."

His mother looked apologetic. "Dat, I don't mean to keep you from everyone." She moved closer to touch her father's shoulder. "I just worry about you, but if you want to go, we'll make sure you get there." She glanced toward her oldest son.

"*Ja*, I'll make sure you get there safely," Micah said with a smile.

Less than an hour later, the Bontrager and Yoder families were on their way to David Bontrager's house. Micah's grandfather, Elmer Yoder, sat beside his grandson in Micah's family buggy. Elmer's wife, Mae, Micah's grandmother, was in the backseat with little Jacob and Matthew, Micah's brother.

His grandfather seemed comfortable and lighter in spirit since they'd left the house. It wasn't far to the preacher's property, and before long Micah made the turn and pulled onto David's driveway. There were already buggies parked along the left side of the barn. Micah parked on the end closest to the road so that he could leave if his grandfather got too tired to stay.

Micah climbed down from the buggy then skirted the vehicle to help Matthew with their grandfather. "*Gross-daddi*, do you think we should get you a wheelchair?" Matt asked.

"*Nay!* I can walk," Elmer said. "I haven't seen the doctor yet, and I'll not be giving up anytime soon."

Micah's father drove into the lot with the rest of the family. He parked on the farthest side of the line of buggies, no doubt understanding why Micah parked where he did.

After Matt took care of their grandfather, Micah helped his grandmother from the carriage. Jacob hopped out behind her and held on to Grandmother Mae's hand. Micah couldn't help smiling at his son. He turned to his brother.

"Matt, can you find a chair for him?"

His brother nodded and took off, running toward the house and the gathering of men outside. Micah saw him talking with the preacher, who glanced briefly in their direction. David nodded and then retrieved a chair from the front porch, setting it close to the circle of men who were more than happy to include Elmer in their conversation as soon as he was situated.

Naomi Hostetler arrived with Iris, the young woman who had come to visit from his former Amish village in Michigan. Micah helped his mother and sisters carry the food toward the house. After he'd relinquished the dishes into his sister Emma's capable hands, he turned to see where Naomi and Iris had gone. He'd known Iris for many years. He was surprised and pleased to see her.

Another vehicle pulled onto the property. Micah was stunned to see Mervin Mast and his family, as his mother had mentioned that the Masts wouldn't be visiting the preacher today. A few minutes later, he became alert as Katie came into view, carrying a large metal pan. Wondering what delicious dessert she'd made, he smiled. It was good to see her. He'd have to find time to talk with her. He would be moving soon, and he needed to know if she was still willing to watch his son and daughters for him.

"Micah!" Uri called out to him as he followed with his brothers behind his sisters.

Micah saw Katie stiffen and briefly glance his way. She was clearly unhappy to see him. He frowned. The question was why? As he moved to speak with her brother, he decided he would find out exactly why she was avoiding him when he thought they'd become, at least, friends.

Micah was here. Katie struggled to take deep, calming breaths as she walked toward the house, knowing that he watched her. She'd thought they were going to visit her mother's sister for Visiting Day, but she found out only this morning that her parents had changed their minds and decided they would visit Preacher David today instead. Fortunately, Katie had baked a huge pan of bread pudding to bring to her aunt's and a batch of whoopie pies for the family to enjoy during the week. Now she carried the bread pudding while her sister Abigail carried the large tray of whoopie pies.

She entered the house with Abigail behind her.

"Katie!" Betty exclaimed, the first to see her. "You're here!"

Katie smiled. "*Ja*, Mam and Dat decided to come here instead of Mam's *schweschter*'s."

"I'm glad you could make it."

"I am nearly finished with your mending. I can drop everything by next week. Will that be soon enough?"

"*Ja*, of course, Katie," Betty said, looking pleased. "I'm surprised you can get through it so quickly."

Katie's mother entered the house with a bowl of cold baked beans. "Betty," she greeted with a smile.

"Sarah, I'm glad to see you," her mother's friend, Micah's mother, said. "It's been a while since we last visited."

"Wasn't it only two weeks ago when they came to our *haus* for Visiting Day?" Betty's son Vernon said with dry humor as he heard the last of the conversation when he entered the house.

"*Ja*, but we used to get together more during the week." Betty flashed Vernon a look that scolded. "What do you need, *soohn*?"

"Some iced tea for Grossvadder. He said he's thirsty."

"I'll be happy to get it for him," Arleta Bontrager, the preacher's wife, offered as she approached.

"*Danki,*" Vernon and his mother said simultaneously and then they chuckled. Amused, Katie joined in, grinning and laughing softly.

Katie's sister Abigail entered the house. "Naomi Hostetler's here and she asked me to bring this in." She carried a large foil-covered tray.

Katie stiffened. "What is it?"

"Cream puffs," Abigail said. "I took a peek and they looked *wunderbor.*"

"I'm surprised that Naomi went to all that trouble."

"I don't think she did," Katie's sister said. "Apparently, Iris made them."

Betty smiled and nodded. "*Ja*, Iris is a *gut* cook."

Her spirits plummeting fast, Katie excused herself

and went outside. So that girl Iris—was she the one she saw with Naomi at Micah's? Her eyes felt scratchy as she left the house and headed toward the barn. She thought of her and Micah trapped together during the storm in his father's barn, when he'd brought her a blanket because she was shivering. She couldn't forget the way he tenderly wrapped it around her shoulders. When they'd worked together to get the livestock out of the burning building, Katie recalled his concern for her safety. He'd sounded worried, frantic. But she couldn't leave any of the animals inside to die, so had kept going until she'd felt Micah grab hold of her hand and pull her from the building. Memories of that day sent image after image into her mind. The horror of the fire was real. But being there with Micah…she'd realized that she wanted a second chance at love. With Micah. But it was too late for that. Micah had someone else now.

Katie fought tears as she entered the preacher's barn for a few moments alone. She walked slowly down its length, stopping every so often to say *hallo* to the animals that remained in their stalls. No one knew where she'd gone, but that was fine. No one would miss her. *He* wouldn't miss her.

She slid open the back barn door and exited the building. She saw a small patch of grass and sat, uncaring of possible grass stains on her sky-blue dress.

Katie wiped her eyes. She should be happy. It was a glorious sunny day, and she was finally finding peace over the loss of Jacob, her betrothed. Closing her eyes, she prayed for strength. Katie would always miss Jacob, but she knew he was happy in the house of the Lord. *Ja*, he had died too soon, but *Gott* must have had a reason to bring him home.

She didn't know how long she sat there. It hurt to realize that Micah had found a wife, but she would go on living as she had always done. Katie stood, brushed off the back of her dress and reentered the barn. She went back the way she came until she was out in the yard.

Mam and the other women were putting out food. Katie felt guilty for not returning sooner to help them. She approached her mother. "Where have you been, *dochter*?"

"I was looking in the barn, visiting with the animals. I'm sorry I'm late. What can I do to help?"

"You can help by bringing out the desserts," Mam said quietly as if disappointed with her as she set a huge container of potato salad on the food table.

"Mam—"

"You can bring out whatever is left," Mam said firmly as she rearranged things on the table to make more room.

"*Ja*, Mam," Katie said sadly, feeling chastised. She turned to obey.

"Katie."

Katie stopped and looked back. Her mother took a long time to study her, and whatever she saw on her daughter's face softened her expression. "Are you *oll recht*?"

Katie shrugged. "I'll be fine," she said as she continued toward the house.

The screen door opened as Katie climbed the steps. The young woman she'd seen with Naomi at Micah's place came out of the house, carrying Katie's whoopie pies. Micah's future wife smiled at her. She had auburn hair and green eyes. And she was extremely pretty. Katie could only imagine the beautiful children they'd have together. Excusing herself quickly, Katie entered the house and took a moment to just breathe. Once she'd regained her composure, she grabbed a basket of cookies and fruit, the only items left in the house, and returned outside. She saw Micah talking with Uri. The two men got along well together. Katie watched Emma approach them, and with a few words for Micah, she pulled Uri away.

Katie grinned. Judging from the interaction between the couple, she realized that Uri must have told the girl that he had feelings for her. Emma smiled up at him, and Uri returned her grin. Katie's gaze settled on the man she loved just as Iris headed in his direction with a big smile on her face. Micah spied her and flashed her a grin. Katie set the desserts on the table and walked away.

She couldn't live this way. Every time she saw Micah, she would regret that she hadn't accepted Naomi's decision to match her with him. *But I wasn't ready.*

Katie realized that she would have to move on and find a life of her own. Single and alone while sewing for a living no longer seemed enough for her. She drew a sharp breath then released it.

If I can't have a life with Micah Bontrager, maybe I can have one with someone else.

Chapter Fifteen

The men were seated at tables. Katie made her way down the length of each one with an iced tea pitcher in hand, pouring refills. Iris was offering her tray of cream puffs to each of the men. At the next table, Katie watched her offer the tray to Micah and his smile as he grabbed one of the desserts.

"These look delicious," she heard him tell Iris. "I may have to go back for more."

"Why don't you take some now?" Iris suggested with what Katie considered a flirty grin.

Micah shook his head. "*Danki*, but there are other desserts I need to have."

"Are you offering a refill?" a young handsome man asked Katie from the far end of the table. He didn't look much older than she was.

"*Ja*, sorry." Katie reached for his cup and poured him iced tea. "Did you get any dessert?"

"I did. The cream puffs were delicious, but I'm partial to whoopie pies, and I saw some on the dessert table." The young man's dark eyes warmed as he smiled at her. "I'm going for one of them next."

Katie found herself smiling back. "I can bring you one if you'd like." She lowered her voice. "I made them."

"Then I definitely want one," he said with a grin, "but you don't have to serve me. I'll go grab one for myself."

Katie arched her eyebrows. "Who are you and where did you come from?" she murmured softly as she left the table, wondering why this man was unlike many other men who expected to be waited on. *Except for Micah, who is often sweet and thoughtful.* And her father.

She left the young man's table to refill the pitcher from a huge jug near the food then continued to the next dining table, the one where Micah sat. After a quick glance toward the dessert table, she saw the young man with a whoopie pie. Katie returned her focus to refilling cups with iced tea, smiling as she made her way down the table until she came to Micah.

"Micah," she mumbled, suddenly tongue-tied, as she met his gaze.

"May I have some iced tea?" he asked softly.

Nodding, she reached for his cup, and their fingers brushed as they tried for it at the same time. Katie caught her breath as she withdrew and he handed it to her. Her fingers gripping the pitcher shook a little, making it awkward as she poured his iced tea. She hoped he didn't notice. When she gave his cup back to him, he captured her attention with his warm smile. She couldn't help but smile before she started to move away.

"Katie." Micah's voice drew her back to him.

"Ja?"

"Did you make the whoopie pies?"

She nodded.

"What about the bread pudding? Do you know who made it?"

She shifted under the intensity of his bright blue gaze. "I did."

He chuckled. "I knew it."

"Is there something wrong with them?"

"*Nay*, they were both delicious," he said. "I could tell they were yours because everything you make always tastes so *gut*."

Oh. "I'm glad you liked them."

Micah inclined his head, a tender smile for her teasing at his lips. *"Ja."*

She was confused. Should she thank him? Let it go? He was to marry another, but she couldn't help but be drawn to him time and again. Because Micah was a kind man. An honest man. The type of man who would make a fine husband for some fortunate woman. The moment had become suddenly awkward. "*Danki*, Micah," she said simply and continued down the table.

"Katie," Micah's voice stopped her a second time. She looked at him with confusion. His lips twitched as if he found something about her amusing. "Meet me by the barn? I need to talk with you."

"I don't know, Micah…"

"It's a *gut* thing, I promise." The look is his eyes drew her like a bear to honey.

"*Oll recht*. When?"

"Now?"

"I have to finish the refills."

"Emma!" Micah stood and waved to his sister.

"What are you doing?" Katie hissed.

Emma approached and smiled at Katie. She was

wearing her new purple dress, and Katie saw that the teenager felt confident wearing it.

"*Schweschter*, would you mind helping Katie by taking over iced tea refills?"

His sister smiled. "I'll be happy to."

And Katie was forced to hand the pitcher to Emma. Once the girl left to pour tea, Micah said, "Now you can meet me by the barn."

Katie sighed dramatically. "You are a confounding man—do you know that?"

His eyes seemed to laugh at her. "I'll go first." He held up his iced tea. "I'll be there as soon as I finish this."

She didn't feel comfortable meeting Micah near the barn. Why not just have the discussion here in the yard? Still, she went to find a spot to wait for him, because Micah had asked her to—and she couldn't help herself.

He arrived a few seconds after she found a place in the rear of the barn near the preacher's pastures, eyeing the view. She sensed him immediately. He would marry another woman and she didn't have the right to spend time with him alone.

"What do you have to tell me?" He stood close, gazing down at her with a small smile on his lips.

"Ask you actually," he said. "I'll be moving into my *haus* with my *kinner* the day after tomorrow, and I was wondering if you would mind coming over to babysit for them during the day."

"You want me to watch Jacob and your girls?" she asked, surprised.

"*Ja.*" He looked confused. "Wasn't that our arrangement?"

"*Ja*, but that was until you married."

"And have I married yet?"

She averted her gaze. "*Nay*, but didn't Naomi find you a wife?"

He didn't say anything at first. Sensing his hesitation, she stared up at him. "She did," he admitted softly, "but she hasn't agreed to marry me yet."

Katie felt a drop in her stomach. "I see." She cleared her throat. "You will tell me when she agrees?"

Micah held her gaze. "You'll be the first to know."

"Oke."

He sighed in apparent relief. *"Gut. Danki."*

She shrugged. "I enjoy spending time with your *soohn* and *dechter*. It's no hardship for me. They are *wunderbor kinner*." It was a pleasure to babysit for Jacob, Rebecca and Eliza, but she knew she shouldn't have gotten attached to them. But she *had* become attached.

Soon they would have a new mother to care for them, and she would no longer be needed…or be able to spend time with them. Katie turned to head to the gathering. "I should get back. I need to help with the cleanup."

Micah fell into step with her as they left the side area of the barn and approached their families and friends.

"Micah!" A big smile accompanied the feminine call as Iris beelined toward Micah.

Katie froze and she felt her face drain of color. "Micah," she said, "I'm afraid that I won't be able to watch Jacob and the girls this week."

Micah looked disappointed. "What about the following week?"

Wanting only to leave, she shook her head. "I have a lot of sewing that I almost forgot about." She managed a small smile for him. "I wish you happiness in your new *haus*, Micah." *And your new bride.*

With a sinking feeling in her chest, Katie quickly excused herself and left. She grabbed dishes along with the other women who were cleaning up and brought them into the house. She stayed inside to wrap up leftover food. Betty entered the building with Naomi. Unwilling to listen to how wonderful it was that the matchmaker had found Micah a wife, Katie put a wrapped dish in the refrigerator then left for the quiet peace of the preacher's empty great room.

"Katie." To her shock, Naomi had followed her, looking concerned. "What's wrong? How can I help?"

"Naomi, congratulations on finding a match for Micah. I'm sure he'll be very happy with her."

The matchmaker frowned. "Who?"

Katie was confused. "Micah's future wife. Iris."

The older woman smiled. "I am *gut* at making matches," she admitted. "In fact, I know someone who I think would be a good match for you, if you're interested."

Katie's immediate instinct was to say no. She meandered to a window and gazed at the gathering in the backyard. "Naomi," she said, shaking her head. Then she saw Micah talking with Iris in the yard. They stood away from the thick of the gathering, both clearly enjoying each other's company. And she made her decision. "*Oll recht.* I'll meet the man you think will be *gut* for me."

Naomi clapped her hands with excitement. "*Gut! Gut!* Come outside and I'll introduce you."

"He's here?"

"*Ja*, he's new to the area so David invited him so he

would get to know members of our community. He is a *wunderbor* man. So handsome and kind!"

She followed Naomi outside. She looked at her friends and family, anywhere but where Micah and Iris stood.

"Katie, I'd like you to meet Samuel Stoltzfus. He recently moved here from New Holland."

Katie spun and was pleasantly surprised. It was the handsome man she'd served iced tea to, the man who wanted a whoopie pie.

"Samuel, this is Katie Mast."

"Ah, the woman who made the delicious whoopie pies and bread pudding," he said with a warm smile and sparkling green eyes. "It's nice to be formally introduced." He looked at Naomi. "*Danki* for this," he told her.

Naomi nodded. "Go, take a walk together. That is, if Katie is willing."

The look in Samuel's expression pleaded with her to agree.

"*Oll recht.* I'll walk with you," Katie said, "but we can't go far. I have to be ready when my *dat* says it's time to leave."

He grinned, and she couldn't help staring. Samuel truly was a handsome man. The only person who was more attractive than him was... Micah.

They started their walk toward the front yard of the preacher's house. "What made you move to New Berne?" she asked.

A long moment of silence made Katie glance up at him. There was a hint of pain in his eyes, and Katie was afraid to hear why.

"I lost *meim frau*," he admitted.

Katie closed her eyes. He'd lost his wife. *Nay*, not him, too. "I'm sorry."

"I'm fine. It was a few years ago. And just recently I made the decision to move closer to *meim bruders*, who live in New Berne."

She had so many questions and struggled to decide what to ask first. "Do you have children?"

"*Nay*, we weren't married long enough." They walked along the flower garden that Altera, David's wife, must have planted last spring. "Do you like *kinner*?"

Her soft smile. "I do."

They continued around the front of the house to the side yard. Samuel gestured toward the side entrance to a large porch that ran the full front length of the house. "Would you like to sit for a bit?"

"Sure." Katie climbed onto the porch and took a seat in a white rocker. "It's peaceful here, away from everyone." She began to rock back and forth in the chair.

"*Ja*." She could feel this direct gaze on her. "Tell me about you," he said. "Why aren't you married and with children?"

She looked away. "I should have been," she said softly, "but I lost my betrothed last year. Farm accident. It happened the month before we were to marry."

"Less than a year then." Samuel got quiet.

His green eyes were enhanced by his light spring-green shirt. She couldn't help but notice the thickness of the man's arms. A man who, no doubt, did physical work for a living, she thought. "Are you in construction?" she asked.

He seemed surprised by her question. "*Ja*, I am. Why do you ask?"

She blushed. "The thought just occurred that maybe you were."

"I worked for a construction company in New Holland. Not sure what I'll be doing here, though."

"Hmm. Maybe you can check with Jed King at the general store or Aaron Hostetler. They both have worked in construction. If you want to continue with that line of work, then I'd talk with them. They may be able to help you."

"That's nice of you, Katie. I'll do that."

Katie liked Samuel, but Micah was the only one for her. While she'd never have Micah, she realized that she wasn't ready to spend time with any other man except as a friend. "Samuel, I don't know what Naomi told you about me…or if you're looking for a sweetheart or wife, but I… I can be your friend but I can't be anything else."

Samuel grinned. "To be honest, I'm not looking for anything serious. But a friend I can use."

Katie grinned and stood. "We should get back to everyone. My *dat* will be about ready to go home."

Samuel went down the stairs ahead of her and then offered his hand to help her descend the steps. As they returned to the backyard, he excused himself as Naomi made her way to Katie's side.

"How was it?" the matchmaker asked.

"Samuel is a nice man. Kind and handsome just as you said…"

"But?"

"I'm sorry, Naomi, but it isn't going to work between us. Samuel and I will be *gut* friends but nothing more."

To Katie's surprise, Naomi wasn't the least bit upset. "Tell me…how do you feel about Micah Bontrager?"

"We're neighbors. His family and mine are close friends."

The matchmaker's gaze turned shrewd. "How do *you* feel about him?" She paused. "Not as a family man but as an attractive man?"

"Naomi…"

"I know you have feelings for Micah, Katie," the older woman said.

Katie gasped and felt her face flush with heat. She knew that Naomi would see the telltale sign of Katie's bright red skin and realize that she was right. Katie did find Micah attractive, and she had fallen in love with him. "I know he'll be marrying Iris," she said.

"*Nay*, he doesn't want nor love Iris," Naomi assured her. "Iris is a friend of mine and… Micah's late wife's cousin. She is like a *schweschter* to him."

As if hearing her name, Iris approached. "Have you seen Betty?"

"I believe she's near her family's buggy." Naomi gestured toward the buggy in question. "Iris, I'd like you to meet Katie Mast. Katie, this is Iris. She is visiting from Centreville. She is friends with Micah because of a family connection with…" She stopped before she said the name, but Katie knew it was Anna, Micah's late wife.

Iris eyed her with a smile. "Katie, it's lovely to meet you."

Katie smiled back. Now that she knew Micah wasn't marrying the woman, she was happy to be friendly with her.

Iris left in search of Micah's mother, and Naomi faced Katie. The matchmaker's expression softened. "You love him. You love Micah."

Katie released a sharp breath. "I do. I know I shouldn't. It doesn't seem right after losing Jacob—"

"What if you and Jacob weren't meant to be? Maybe the losses that you and Micah suffered are because *Gott* had a plan to bring you and Micah together."

Katie could only stare at her. "Micah doesn't feel that way about me."

Naomi grinned and gave a nod to someone behind Katie. She turned to find Micah, the man she loved, standing some distance behind her with a smile and a warm look in his bright blue eyes.

"Katie, may I have a minute? There is something I need to tell you."

"Micah," Katie rushed on, hoping that he hadn't overheard her conversation with Naomi.

"Sigh so gude." Please. "It won't take but a minute." His brow furrowed as he waited patiently for her consent.

"Oll recht."

He captured her hand and pulled her gently back toward a cleared area next to the preacher's barn. Once there, he gazed at her without a word.

"Micah, what do you need? If it's to watch your *kinner*, I thought about it and I've changed my mind. I'll be happy to babysit for you."

"Katie," he said huskily, "I don't need you for a babysitter. What I need is you. In my life." He took her other hand so that he was holding both her hands, one in each of his. "I never expected to fall in love again, and I know that you lost someone you loved." His voice broke at the last word. "You're still grieving for…" He looked concerned. "I know what it's like to lose someone. It's hard to move on, but, Katie, I want to move on with you." He paused and gazed at her with love. "I'll wait until you're ready. If you're ever ready." He drew a sharp breath before releasing it. "I hope someday you'll be ready. I love you, Katie."

She gaped at him. "You love me?"

He nodded and she started to laugh, overcome with joy. Stiffening, Micah released her and stepped back. Katie quickly rushed to capture his hands. "You don't have to wait for me to love you, Micah Bontrager," she admitted with a soft smile. "I already do. By allowing me into your life to watch your children, you gave me hope." She softened her gaze as she looked into his eyes—eyes full of love and sudden understanding. "I love you, Micah, so much it hurt when I thought you would be marrying Iris. Then Naomi told me who Iris is to you."

Micah's smile was like bright sunshine after a rainy day. He laughed and pulled her close to him. "I want to marry you, Katie, not because I need a mother for my children. But because I love and need you in my life. Will you be my wife—and a mother to my *kinner*?"

Katie beamed. "*Ja*, Micah! *Ja!* Of course, I will!"

"I want us to marry soon," he said, his features making him more attractive with his happiness on full display. "No long engagements. We can be married this November."

"*Oke.*" She couldn't stop grinning. Katie was eager to tell her parents.

Micah caressed her cheek then took her hand. She was conscious of the warmth of his grip as they walked back to the gathering, holding hands. "I guess Naomi was right. You are my match, Katie. I felt something for you from the first moment she introduced us, but... I was afraid to love again. And I knew you were grieving for… I'm not afraid anymore. You're it for me, Katie." He grinned. "And just so you know, Naomi's match for me was you. It was you who hadn't agreed to marry me yet."

Katie beamed at him. "It was?"

He nodded.

They approached their parents who stood talking in the yard. Her father was clearly ready to leave.

"Mam. Dat," Micah called out.

Both sets of parents turned and saw their son and daughter holding hands.

"Katie?" Mam said, looking hopeful.

"Micah?" Betty gazed at the couple through a film of tears. "Does this mean…"

"*Ja*, Mam. Katie and I are in love and plan to marry as soon as possible."

"Praise the Lord," Micah's and Katie's fathers said with great feeling at the exact same moment. "It's about time."

Katie looked at Micah, and he gazed at her with love—a love that warmed her inside and out. Then they both laughed joyfully.

Their desire to wed was welcomed by their families. It would be a new beginning and a second chance at happiness for them.

Epilogue

Three years later

"Dat, where's Mam?" Jacob asked as he approached his father, who stood, leaning against the kitchen counter, sipping coffee.

Micah eyed his seven-year-old son with affection. "Out in the back hanging clothes." He saw Jacob cast a glance out the window. "What do you need?"

"Should she be doing that?" Jacob looked worried. "Isn't the clothes basket heavy?"

Stifling a smile, Micah nodded as he set down his coffee mug. "*Ja,* but I carried it out for her. Your *endie* Emma would help, but your *mudder* wants to do things herself."

His son looked concerned. "She can't keep working so hard, Dat. Not with the *bubbel* coming."

Micah grew thoughtful. "*Hmm.* I see what you mean." He patted his son on the back. "You and I—we'll just have to help out more." He paused. "Why don't you go outside and see if she needs your assistance."

Jacob bobbed his head. "I'll do that. Where's James?" he asked of his little brother.

"Napping."

"And Eliza and Rebecca?"

"At *Grossmudder* Sarah's."

"Gut." The boy appeared pleased. He put his hands on his hips and rocked back and forth on his heels. "Dat?"

"Ja, soohn?"

"How many more *bruders* and *schweschters* am I going to have?"

Micah started to choke but got himself quickly under control. "As many as *Gott* wants us to have, Jake."

He sighed. *"Oll recht."* He opened the door to head outside then halted to pierce his father with his blue gaze. "You know, Dat, being a big *bruder* can be hard work."

"Ja, I know, *soohn*. I'm a big *bruder."*

Jacob blinked. *"Ja*, that's right!" He grinned as if pleased that he and his father were both big brothers.

The door opened and Micah saw his wife step in, looking lovely in a pale blue maternity dress. "What's going on with *meim* boys?" Katie said as she smiled at Jacob then looked at Micah with eyes filled with love.

"I was coming outside to help you," Jacob said, drawing her attention.

"You were? That was sweet of you," she said. Micah could tell that she hid a smile. He knew his beautiful wife like the back of his hand. She was the love and light of his life. He'd never thought he'd be this happy, and it was all because of Katie Mast Bontrager.

They heard a baby crying from upstairs. Their son James.

"I'll get him," Jacob said.

Micah opened his mouth to object. Katie touched his arm and shook her head, and he relaxed.

"Danki, soohn," Katie said with a smile.

Jacob was big for his age, and Micah knew he was always good with his siblings, patient and kind, a wonderful trait in a big brother. But as a father, he couldn't help worrying about all his children.

Katie gazed at Micah and her heart melted. He looked so handsome in his dark blue shirt that brightened his striking blue eyes. The man held the most special place in her life. She had not expected to be this happy. They hadn't waited long to marry after discovering their love for each other, choosing to wed that November, the month of weddings. It had been a lovely ceremony before their families and the entire church community with Micah's sister Emma and Katie's brother Uri as their attendants.

Micah and she had added to their family a year and a half ago with James. Now they would soon be adding a fifth child. She didn't know if it would be a boy or girl, but it didn't matter. She and Micah simply wanted the baby to be healthy.

Katie thanked the Lord every day for the life she'd been given with her husband and children. "Do you think Jacob and Anna would be happy for us?" she asked Micah as she thought about their first loves.

"*Ja*, I do," Micah replied and flashed her a loving look as he pulled her to his side. "I'd like to think that if they had lived, Anna and I would have moved here to be closer to Mam and Dat. I believe we all would have been close. I think you would have liked Anna and she would have liked you. But—" He stepped back and gazed deeply into her eyes. "I truly believe that *Gott* meant for us to be together. I have never been happier since I took you as my wife."

Eyes glistening with emotion, Katie beamed at him. "And I have never been happier since you became my husband."

They heard footsteps on the stairs. Jacob must be coming down with his baby brother.

"Want to know what Jacob told me before you came inside?" Micah asked with a smile.

Katie shook her head. "He wanted to know how many more children we'd be having. He told me it's a hard job being a big *bruder*."

Delighted, Katie laughed softly. "How precious! I'm surprised, though, because he clearly enjoys his younger siblings."

Micah chuckled. "He does. I think it's his way of discovering how much larger our family will grow."

She reached out and touched her husband's beard, loving the texture of it, loving his features, his temperament and his smile. "Well, *Gott* willing, there will be, at least, one more precious child in our family," she said, rubbing her baby bump. Using her finger, she traced the outline of his mouth when he smiled. "After that, only *Gott* knows the future." She sighed and leaned her head against his chest. "I love you, Micah Bontrager," she breathed.

"I love you, *meim* wife, *meim* heart, *meim* everything."

"Mam, I changed James's diaper before I brought him downstairs," Jacob told them as he carried his baby brother into the room.

"*Gut* job, *soohn*! You're a *wunderbor bruder* and your *mudder*'s special helper," Katie said as she exchanged glances with her husband. The first time Jacob had called her Mam, she'd worried that Micah would be upset, but instead he'd been grinning from ear to ear.

With a nod of approval for Jacob, Micah took James from Jacob's arms and settled him in his high chair. Jacob immediately went into the pantry and returned with a box of the dried cereal that his baby brother was partial to, before he dumped some of the cereal onto James's high chair tray. James instantly began to stuff bits of cereal into his mouth with his little fingers.

With a glimmer of amusement, Micah studied his sons then, eyes twinkling, he caught Katie's gaze. "I love you," he mouthed.

Katie grinned and was filled with warmth and happiness. She never got tired of his confirming his love for her. "I love you, too," she whispered. And she thanked *Gott* every day for the blessings she received and the life she'd been given that fulfilled her like nothing else could.

* * * * *

THEIR MAKE-BELIEVE MATCH

Jackie Stef

This book is dedicated to my wonderful parents,
Diane and Mark Stefanowicz, who have always
supported my dream of becoming an author.

Thank you to Angel Milazzo and Mekaelah Moray,
two of my close friends who encouraged me and
helped me brainstorm when writer's block hit.
(And it hits quite often!)

A special thank-you also to
Tamela Hancock Murray, my literary agent,
and Melissa Endlich, my editor—
thank you for believing in me!

Trust in the Lord with all thine heart; and lean not unto thine own understanding. In all thy ways acknowledge him, and he shall direct thy paths.

—*Proverbs* 3:5–6

Chapter One

~~~

Bird-in-Hand,
Lancaster County, Pennsylvania

Look at those lovebirds!

Sadie Stolzfus jumped when she felt a stream of cool water rush over her toes. She dropped the garden hose, realizing that she'd overwatered the plants she was tending to while watching a young couple that had entered the popular greenhouse in the quaint village of Bird-in-Hand, Pennsylvania. The two were obviously enamored with each other, lovingly glancing at one another more than at the various vibrant flowers and plants offered for sale.

I hope that will be me one day. Sadie, who had been plagued by chronic singleness ever since her peers began courting, forced herself to turn away and focus on the task at hand. Her shift was nearly over and she wanted to be as productive as possible. Allowing herself to daydream about something that would likely never happen wouldn't help her finish her work.

As she hosed the dirty water off her feet and flip-flops, Sadie's heart warmed at the sound of the flirtatious laughter of the couple while they circled the entirety of the greenhouse. Sadie grinned, knowing that she couldn't judge them for doing such a thing. She also took time to stop and smell the roses, more often than not.

I imagine some would say that's why I've been passed over for courting, Sadie mused as she coiled the hose around the crook of her arm and then placed it on its holder. She fought off the notion of inadequacy as a woman and mentally pushed past her longing for love and a family of her own.

Perhaps it was her direct social nature, but more than likely it was her fierce independence and almost childlike zest for life that seemed to have scared away the young men in her community. Even her parents occasionally reminded her not to be stubborn and immature. They'd recently threatened to fix her up with an eligible bachelor if she couldn't find a husband of her own. Absolutely appalled by the idea of matchmaking, Sadie knew that time was running out for her to find a suitor on her own. But finding a man who understood her outlook on life seemed about as unlikely as cats and dogs literally raining from above.

No reason to fret, she reminded herself half-heartedly. *If the Lord wills me to find someone special, He'll pave the way.* Still, the notion that the eligible men in her community found her to be too much to handle threatened to shout at Sadie more loudly than the heavy drumming of the rain on the greenhouse roof.

By the time Sadie swept up the loose soil around the self-serve potting station and assisted a few customers at the cash register, her workday had come to an end.

She bid goodbye to her coworkers before making her way to the exit. She thoroughly enjoyed tending to the plants and assisting the patrons, but briefly thinking about what she was missing in her life had knocked the wind out of her sails. The vision of Rhoda's horse and buggy waiting for her in the parking lot would be a sight for sore eyes. Hitching a ride home with soft-spoken Rhoda, her dearest friend since childhood, was often the highlight of Sadie's day. Time spent with her closest companion was always cherished, as were the day-old pastries Rhoda shared from her work at the nearby bakery.

Sadie exited the greenhouse and her eyes widened with surprise. She knew it had been raining throughout the day and had often paused to marvel at the seeming millions of droplets racing down the sides of the greenhouse's windowpanes, but she hadn't realized that the steady rain had morphed into a downright deluge. Squinting into the spray of water that seemed to be blowing sideways, she dashed through the downpour and made a beeline toward Rhoda's waiting buggy. *Thank goodness she's here on time.* Sadie grinned to herself as raindrops pelted her face.

With gusto, Sadie's running start had her jumping over a puddle and launching herself into Rhoda's buggy. When she'd situated herself in the passenger's seat, Sadie glanced at her reflection in the side mirror. "Well, don't I look like a wet noodle." She poked at her sheer, heart-shaped head covering, which now lay limply on top of her blond head. "Doesn't that look like a dead fish?" She flicked the *kapp* to make it jiggle and then burst into a fit of hearty laughter.

When Rhoda didn't laugh, Sadie turned to face her

friend and let out a gasp. Instead of the familiar female face, she was shocked to see a startled young Amish man staring at her with a curious expression. She had mistakenly entered a stranger's buggy!

Sadie's hand flew to her chest to still her racing heart as she studied the handsome fellow, who was clearly just as surprised as she was. The style of his straw hat differed from the kind Amish men in Lancaster wore. *He must be from out of town.* His drenched sky blue shirt clung to his muscular frame, hard evidence that he, too, had been caught in the rain. A bit of sadness hid behind his bewildered expression, and something within Sadie's heart longed to see this stranger smile.

"Well, you certainly aren't Rhoda," Sadie declared with a playful smirk.

A small grin crossed the fellow's lips. "*Nee*, I'm definitely not Rhoda."

"Didn't think so." Sadie chuckled as she leaned against the seat. "You don't mind if I keep you company, do you?"

The stunned stranger stared at her in obvious confusion. "What?"

Sadie reworded her request. "Do you mind if I sit here while I wait for my friend to show up? My shift at the greenhouse is over, so I ran out here thinking that this was her buggy." She peeked into the parking lot and scanned their surroundings. "Yours is the only buggy parked out here, ain't so?"

"I don't mind at all," the man replied with a slight shake of his tilted head, as if curious as to why a young lady would so willingly sit alone with a stranger.

Truth be told, Sadie felt safe with a fellow Amish person, regardless of whether they had previously met or not. Sadie glanced at the young man, who seemed so down that she wondered if she'd been led to seek shelter in his buggy. *He looks like he needs a friend.*

"We should introduce ourselves. I can't seem to place your face," Sadie suggested, eager to learn more about the good-looking stranger.

The man smiled, seemingly amused by her direct-ness. "I'm Isaac Hostettler. My *mamm* and I moved here from Indiana just yesterday."

Sadie leaned forward, causing rain droplets from the top of her head to run down to the tip of her nose. "That's quite the journey, *jah*? What made you choose to move to Bird-in-Hand?"

Isaac's cute smile vanished as he reached for the horse's reins, perhaps out of nervousness. "My *mamm* hasn't been feelin' so good lately, so we came to live with my aunt, Miriam Fisher, in hopes that it would lift *Mamm*'s spirits." One of his shoulders shrugged as if he didn't have the enthusiasm to move both. "The change of scenery, you know?"

Sadie let out a pained sigh, her heart aching for her new acquaintance. "I'm so sorry to hear your *mamm* is sick. That must be awful hard on both of you."

"Oh, she's not sick," Isaac corrected Sadie, his tanned face rapidly turning pale. "Someone we loved passed away, and it was…very hard for all of us and—"

"I understand," Sadie mercifully interrupted, "you don't have to say any more." She reached for his hand and gave it a reassuring pat. She sensed that a comfort-ing gesture was just what Isaac needed. The brief touch of her hand against his gave her butterflies in her stom-ach that she did her best to ignore.

Isaac shook his head, letting out a sigh that sounded

more like a laugh. "You speak to me like we're old friends." A weak but genuine smile spread across his lips. "I'm glad you clambered into my buggy."

"Well, we are friends now, aren't we?" Sadie asked with a quirked eyebrow.

"*Jah*, and I'm glad." Isaac nodded, studying her as if she were the most compelling creature he'd ever laid eyes on.

Sadie was unsure of what to say or do next as silence settled between them. Without thinking, she puffed out her rosy cheeks and crossed her emerald eyes as Isaac continued to stare at her.

Obviously taken aback by Sadie's unexpected silliness, Isaac squinted at her for a moment, then laughed until he could barely catch his breath. Sadie couldn't help but join in, so much so that she snorted. They continued to cackle until they gasped for air and tears ran down their cheeks.

The sound of horse hooves clip-clopping and buggy wheels rumbling into the parking lot caught Sadie's attention as her sides ached from all of the laughter. She craned her neck and peered through the downpour to get a better look at the approaching buggy. "There's Rhoda." Sadie motioned with a quick head movement, recognizing Rhoda's horse by the distinctive white heart-shaped patch on the muzzle. Pretty, red-haired Rhoda guided her horse up to the hitching rail beside Isaac's rig, then stared into the neighboring buggy with a visibly perplexed smile.

Sadie guffawed and waved at her friend. "One second," she called over the roar of the rain as she reached for her purse. She moved to bid farewell to Isaac but her heart caught in her throat when she turned to see him gazing intently at her. Isaac's chocolate-brown eyes had brightened significantly in just a few minutes and a warm smile decorated his chiseled face. Heat crept up the back of Sadie's neck and spread to her cheeks. Refusing to give in to excitement, she cleared her throat and returned a friendly smile. "*Denki* for letting me sit with you," she chirped. Then, in one swift motion, Sadie bounced from Isaac's buggy into Rhoda's, doing her best to ignore Rhoda's inquisitive glance.

"Who is your friend?" Rhoda questioned just above a whisper as she guided the horse away from the hitching post.

"His name is Isaac, and he and his mother just moved here from Indiana." Sadie tried to reply casually but her voice was trembling. She cleared her throat and sat taller. "He seems like a nice fellow."

"*Jah*, and handsome too." Rhoda wiggled her auburn eyebrows. "Seems like you two are already friends."

"I think a friend is just what he needs right now," Sadie responded as she settled back into her seat, rejecting Rhoda's gentle teasing,

"If it's a friend that he needs, he couldn't have found a better one," Rhoda complimented Sadie. "Seems like a perfect match."

Sadie scoffed and, about to respond with a witty joke, heard a male voice shout, "Hey, wait!"

Rhoda halted the horse and Sadie spun around in the direction of the voice. She was tickled to see Isaac's hat-absent head sticking out of his buggy. "You didn't tell me your name," he hollered.

Sadie chuckled as she watched the rain soak Isaac's mousy-blond hair, though he seemed unfazed. "Sadie

Stolzfus," she called back, hoping he'd be able to make out what she'd said.

Isaac nodded, his bright, wide smile a brilliant sight amongst the dreary surroundings. "Nice to meet you, Sadie! Hope to see you around!"

"Me too," Sadie replied quietly, more to herself than anyone else.

When he returned to his new, albeit temporary, home, Isaac worked quickly to unhitch his aunt's horse, then made sure that the animal had a long, well-deserved drink. After that, he entered Aunt Miriam's house through the back door, deeply inhaling the delicious aroma of the supper she was whipping up. Hurrying upstairs, he quickly changed out of his rain-soaked clothes and donned dry attire.

Aenti Mim's house seemed far too large for a single older woman, with more spare rooms than anyone could possibly need. When he and his *mamm* had moved in yesterday, Mim had offered her sister the first choice of the available bedrooms, to which she had responded with a shrug. Isaac had hoped that his mother would take the front bedroom, with its many windows, since the extra sunlight would surely help her depressive, withdrawn state. Instead, she'd silently gravitated to the smallest, windowless, cavelike bedroom. But in a way, Isaac couldn't blame her for wanting to hide away from the world.

After the unexpected death of his childhood sweetheart, Isaac's world had promptly shattered. Rebecca King—the only woman he had ever loved and had planned to marry—had tragically passed away in a horrific accident, and Isaac refused to entertain the possibility that he could find love again in his lifetime. The way he saw it, a person only got a single shot at finding their soul mate, and his had been stolen from him far too soon.

After nearly two years of mourning, Isaac had accepted his fate as a permanent bachelor. If he couldn't build a life with Rebecca, he wouldn't build a life with any woman. Instead of worrying about himself, nearly all of his attention was now focused instead on his traumatized mother, who had become mute after witnessing the accident that had taken Rebecca's life. *If* Mamm *can recover, that is the best we can hope for.*

"But now is a time to focus on the future," Isaac declared aloud to himself as the encouraging effect of his encounter with Sadie continued to elevate his spirits. Even if his life was meant to be lived without love, nothing was stopping him from having a positive outlook on the rest of his life.

After tromping down the stairs, Isaac was glad to see Aunt Mim busily cooking up a storm and that his mother, Ruth, was seated at the table. With a warm smile on her face, Mim looked up from stirring the pot she stood over. "Just in time for dinner," she chirped. "How do you like your potatoes?"

"I like 'em mashed, if it's not a bother?" Isaac requested, already knowing that he would enjoy life with jolly Aunt Mim.

"*Gut*, because that's what I've already made!" Mim winked at him, then reached into the cupboard for three plates. "There's a kettle on the stove that your *mamm* just put on for tea. Should be ready any minute now."

"*Denki, Mamm.*" Isaac sincerely smiled, wishing his mother could comprehend just how thankful he was to see her taking this small step toward normalcy. She didn't answer, of course, but it was enough to see her making an effort. Maybe the change of scenery was already starting to help!

Isaac retrieved three mugs from the cupboard and joined his mother at the table. *Mamm* continued to stare blankly, her previously vibrant blue eyes now turned gray, focused on nothing in particular. Filled with pity at the sight of her, Isaac snapped to attention when the kettle began to whistle and dashed to retrieve it.

"I was thinking we should take our plates out to the front porch and eat outside tonight," Mim declared as she shoveled heaps of buttered noodles onto each plate.

Isaac chuckled at the comically large portions Mim had prepared but then stiffened at her suggestion. "But it's raining, *aentie*."

"The porch is covered and it's not blowing sideways like it was earlier," Mim countered as she handed Isaac three tea bags.

Isaac cringed at the suggestion. Rainy days were more difficult than most for him, and he noticed his mother seemed to share that sentiment. Going outside to hear the splashing of raindrops might stir up something that was best forgotten. "I think it'd be better to eat inside," Isaac quietly disagreed, putting a tea bag in each mug and then filling each cup with the scalding water.

"Oh, pfft!" Mim exclaimed, lifting all three plates at once like a seasoned waitress. "Fresh air is good for the lungs, even if it's a little damp. What do you say, *schwester*?"

Isaac waited for a reaction from his mother, feeling every muscle in his body tense with anxiety. Would she have an emotional outburst at the thought of going outdoors in this weather? To his surprise and relief, *Mamm* shrugged in response.

"What are we waiting for? Let's gobble this up before it gets cold," Mim triumphantly declared, pushing the screen door open with her backside. Wordlessly, *Mamm* gathered up the three steaming mugs and gingerly followed her sister out to the covered porch.

Astonished by Mim's convincing nature, Isaac shrugged and headed to the porch as well. He took a seat in the chair next to his mother's, then stared down at his overflowing plate of roasted chicken, mashed potatoes, buttered noodles, carrots and coleslaw. Amish meals were known for lacking in nothing, but it had been quite some time since Isaac had enjoyed such a bountiful feast. With only his younger sisters doing the cooking at home recently, his meals had been disappointing compared to what Mim served up.

"You've outdone yourself, *aentie*," Isaac gushed, grabbing his fork eagerly.

Mim chortled. "With you two here to keep me company, there's no excuse for me to have my usual simple salad or bowl of cereal." Mim sipped her tea and glanced at Ruth with a twinkle in her eye. "Isaac, did you know that when your mother was about four years old, she tried to make her own bowl of cereal? Instead, she spilled an entire gallon of milk all over the kitchen floor and then pulled the area rug over the spill to hide the mess."

Isaac nearly choked on a mouthful of chicken. "Did anyone notice?"

"Not until a few days later when the room began to smell dreadful," Mim blurted, nearly unable to finish her sentence. "Our *mamm* didn't even try to clean the little rug. She took it outside and set it on fire!" Mim dabbed at the corners of her eyes while she continued to laugh.

Isaac joined Mim's rowdy laughter until his sides ached. When he composed himself, he took another bite of his dinner and asked, "Did you really do that, *Mamm*?" No answer. Isaac wondered if she thought they were laughing at her, even though it was all in good fun. He glanced at her to see she was looking down at her plate, though she hadn't yet touched her food. "Aren't you gonna eat?" he questioned, hoping to urge her along. "It's awful tasty." Still no response. Isaac cleared his throat, realizing that he should have known better than to expect an answer from his mute parent.

As he forked some carrots into his mouth, Isaac looked out to Mim's well-kept front yard. Never married, unlike her nine siblings, Mim had lived with her parents in this very house until they'd passed away. She'd then kept up the house and small stable of animals by herself, as well as worked numerous jobs throughout her life. Now in her late fifties, Mim enjoyed quilting and entertaining the local children, both Plain and *Englisch*. Nearly every day, small groups of children came to her home to listen to her stories and eat her freshly baked cookies. Isaac admired his aunt and the life she had made for herself. He wondered if his future would be similar to hers, at least in the choice to live as a single person.

Mim must have seen him squinting through the rain and past the yard, across the quiet lane and to the fields of soybeans, corn and alfalfa that stretched farther than eyes could see. "How's Bird-in-Hand treating you so far?" she questioned, probably sensing that a change in subject was badly needed.

"*Ach*, it's beautiful," Isaac quickly replied, "though the tourists seem much more plentiful here than back home. Once you get to the back roads, it's more peaceful. You sure do live in a nice spot."

Mim nodded. "I wish your *daed* would move his woodworking business from Shipshewana, Indiana, to Lancaster County. The Lord has granted him success, but he'd have even more business here since the tourists always want to get their hands on anything that's Amish-made."

Isaac nodded as he scraped his fork against his plate, gathering up every last morsel of food. "Might be something for him to consider. I'll mention that in the letter I'm planning to send him."

Mim clapped her hands and the apples of her cheeks turned a cute rosy hue. "Wouldn't it be nice to have my whole family back in Lancaster again! I'm getting old, and I wanna spend as much time as I can with each one of you."

Isaac snorted and rolled his eyes. "You're not the least bit old, Mim, but I know what you mean. Life can change in an instant and it's best to spend as much time as you can with those you love."

Suddenly there was a clatter of a plate and utensils as *Mamm* shoved her untouched meal onto the small, wicker side table. Without a word, she rose from her seat, opened the screen door and retreated into the house.

Isaac sighed heavily and placed his hand to his head. "I shouldn't have said that."

Placing her empty plate next to her sister's untouched

dish, Mim stood and then lowered herself into the empty chair next to her nephew. "It's all right. She knows you didn't mean anything by it. And I can see that she isn't the only one with a broken heart."

Isaac groaned. "I just wish I knew of something, anything, that could ease her suffering," he responded, ignoring Mim's comment about the state of his own grief. "I wish there was something that could bring a smile to her face, even if only for a moment!" He was startled when a brief image of Sadie Stolzfus flashed through his mind's eye.

"That's something that might be best left in *Gott*'s hands," Mim softly answered, briefly placing a hand on his shoulder.

Isaac ran his fingers through his thick, dirty-blond hair, still damp from the rain. "Well then, I sure wish He would hurry up."

Mim laughed again and Isaac couldn't help but smile. "Don't rush *Gott*'s timing, or you might just miss the little blessings He's planted for you along the way." Mim took his empty plate, placed it on top of hers, then picked up his mother's full dish in her other hand. She stood. "And besides, one of those blessings might be a nice girl."

Isaac resisted the urge to roll his eyes. He thought he'd escaped pestering from his father, friends and sisters to find himself a new girlfriend. Now, even here in Bird-in-Hand, it seemed like Mim would start pushing him to find a new love, and that was something that he was determined to avoid. When Isaac didn't respond, Mim shrugged and carried the dinner plates back inside the house.

As Isaac downed the last of his tea, he mulled over

Mim's proverb. Another image of pretty, spirited Sadie popped into his mind. He smirked at the memory of the ridiculous face she had made to get him laughing when he'd started to feel down. *Who'd have thought that a complete stranger could turn my day around?* Isaac mused, wondering if his unexpected introduction to Sadie had been orchestrated by *Gott* Himself.

Chapter Two

Sadie perched high in the branches of her favorite maple tree, which grew near the peak of her father's farm. From her seat in the branches, she took in a sea of *Gott*'s colorful creation before her. Whitewashed Amish and red *Englisch* barns dotted the landscape like freckles. Fields of alfalfa, tobacco, corn and soybeans danced together in a patchwork quilt of natural colors. After yesterday's stormy weather, the early August sun had no clouds to compete against. A calm breeze whispered through the leaves of the tree as Sadie inhaled the sweet summery scent of fresh-cut grass.

This is where I belong, Sadie reflected. It wasn't that she minded helping her mother and sister cook and clean. Traditional tasks of sewing, quilting and canning also were boring, but not a bother. Yet Sadie wasn't truly alive unless she could be outdoors, breathing in fresh air, marveling at the fireflies that sparkled at dusk, and watching her sunflowers grow into golden blossoms that sometimes soared feet above her head.

Swinging her legs, which hung over the mighty branch on which she sat, Sadie noticed a bluebird perched a few branches over. The bird hopped toward her, chirping a musical greeting. Sadie gently welcomed the blue-feathered critter, whistling to catch the bird's attention. "Hello, little friend."

"Hello?"

Sadie nearly fell out of the tree in surprise. She'd thought she was alone, except for her feathered companion, and surely the bird hadn't spoken to her. Grabbing the branch to steady herself, she leaned to her left and then to her right in an attempt to see through the foliage. When she found an opening large enough to see out of, she spied her twin, Moses, looking over his shoulder. He seemed to be just as startled as she had been. "Mose!" She called out to catch her brother's attention, using the nickname the entire Amish community had bestowed upon him at birth.

"Who's there?" Mose asked, pulling his dark eyebrows together while continuing to search his surroundings.

"It's Sadie!"

"Where are you?"

"I'm up here! In the tree!"

Mose scurried to the wide trunk of the tree and tipped his head in puzzlement. "I've been looking for you for over a half hour now," he shouted up, shielding his eyes from the sunlight that sprinkled through the leaves.

"Well, here I am," Sadie called back. If anyone but Mose had found her up a tree, a small flame of embarrassment would have burned in her chest. It was most unladylike, if not bizarre, for a grown woman to be climbing in a tree like a squirrel. While she assumed others frowned upon her spontaneous behavior, there was no need to tame her wildfire spirit around Mose. Maybe it was because they shared that special bond of being twins. Sadie called to her brother, "Just a second! I'll be right down."

"No, you stay there. I'll come up." Mose took hold of the lowest branch, pressed his boot against the tree trunk and propelled himself upward. Sadie tried to stifle her laughter. The feats of her tall, lanky brother twisting and scaling his way through the thick foliage was something to watch.

Mose wheezed as he lowered himself beside Sadie on the branch. "That was quite an obstacle course." He took his straw hat off and fanned his face. "At least you picked a strong branch to sit on. Don't want either of us to go tumbling to the ground."

Sadie nodded in agreement. "What brings you all the way up this tree?"

As if he was nervous, Mose plucked a leaf from the tree, then twirled its stem between his fingers. "What are you doing up here?" he asked, avoiding his sister's question.

"Just admiring the Lord's handiwork." Sadie gestured toward the marvelous vantage point she had found. "To tell you the truth, I've probably been up here too long. I'm sure *Mamm* is wondering where I am right about now," she admitted without a hint of shame. She sighed at the thought of her chores, filling her lungs with the pleasant, rural air. "If I didn't have any work, I'd probably stay up here all day."

"Well, you certainly picked a *gut*, if not challenging, place to observe all of creation from." Mose smiled, putting his hat back on and gazing into the distance where the cornstalk-covered hills met the periwinkle afternoon sky. He suddenly cleared his throat. "Today when *Daed* and I were hitching up the mules to go rake the hay, he asked if you were gonna attend the singing over at the Grabers' place next Sunday night."

Sadie raised her eyebrows at Mose's mention of their father's question. "I normally attend every singing, and you know that."

Mose stared at the leaf he was holding, then released it. He watched it float to the ground before speaking again. "*Jah*, I guess so."

Mose's obvious hesitation to explain things further ruined the peaceful atmosphere. He drummed his fingers on their branch seat as if he couldn't sit still. Laid-back Mose was never one to be fidgety, and for him to bring up a conversation he'd had with their father was enough to cause concern. Sadie leaned toward her twin. "I may enjoy sitting like a bird in this tree, but I know you're just itching to get your big feet back on the ground."

Mose grimaced at her words.

"Why did *Daed* ask if I was going to the singing?"

Her twin heaved a heavy sigh and tossed his dark, shaggy brunette hair out of his eyes. "To be truthful, I think he's a bit worried about you."

Sadie recoiled. "What does he have to worry about?"

"*Ach*, Sadie, you sure are making this awful difficult." Mose looked away from her for a moment. "I think our *daed* is concerned for you because he hasn't yet heard any rumors about you, if you catch my drift."

"A *daed* who doesn't hear rumors about his *dochder* should be a proud father," Sadie replied, irked at the direction that their conversation had taken.

"Now hold on, will you? What I'm saying...well, you're twenty-one years old now and—"

"And so are you," Sadie interrupted, wanting to put an end to the discussion before it went any further.

"Could you be serious for just a minute?" Mose pleaded with a grumble. "*Daed* hasn't heard any rumors about who you might be courting." Mose clenched his teeth and stared at her as if bracing for the impact of her response.

Sadie narrowed her eyes, aggravated that her father had brought up her nonexistent love life to Mose. Why wouldn't her father have just spoken directly to her if he had something to say? Why on earth was he trying to meddle?

"Sadie..." Mose cautiously ventured, still anxiously waiting for a reply.

"*Daed* hasn't heard any talk through the grapevine because there isn't anything to talk about," Sadie retorted, crossing her arms over her chest.

"But you're twenty-one." Mose repeated his earlier statement, swatting away a fly that had joined them. "Most girls your age are fixing to get married or are at least being courted by a nice guy. He's just worried that—"

"He has absolutely nothing to worry about," Sadie interrupted again. "I joined the church when I was fifteen. I'm not out running around the world, doing things that a Plain girl has no business doing. Why isn't that enough for him?"

"Listen, Sadie," Mose interjected, "I didn't mean to upset you, and neither does our *daed*. He just doesn't want to see his *dochder* end up...alone."

"I know." Hot tears burned in the back of Sadie's

eyes, but she refused to let them fall. "You can tell *Daed* he needn't worry. If I'm ever spoken for, I'm sure the gossip will get to him soon enough."

"I don't know if that will be enough, Sadie. I overheard him talking to *Mamm* while I was putting my work boots on after breakfast this morning." Mose grimaced, then looked away from her, his shoulders sagging. "They agreed that if you couldn't find yourself a beau by the first of October, they will find someone for you."

A sudden feeling of nausea quivered through Sadie. She knew that her parents were thinking of matchmaking, but never expected that she'd face an ultimatum so soon. October was only two months away, and Sadie had no romantic prospects on the horizon. Of course, her parents would never force her to marry someone, but life in their house would quickly become miserable for her if they started to meddle in her personal life. Sadie simply refused to marry, or even date a fellow, if there wasn't a legitimate connection. What was the point of sharing her life with someone who didn't make her heart soar like an eagle? The problem was that she knew there were no Amish bachelors in her community who seemed to have an interest in her due to her fiery spirit and quirky nature, and she was unwilling to change who *Gott* created her to be.

"Sadie? Are you all right?"

Sadie glanced at her brother. "Of course I'm not all right. How would you feel if you were being forced to court someone just for the sake of courting?" She planted her hands on her hips, her tone sounding almost like a snake's angry hiss. "You're twenty-one and single too. Why aren't *Mamm* and *Daed* forcing this on you as well?"

Mose chewed on his bottom lip. "I understand how you feel, and I agree that you shouldn't date someone just for the sake of courting." He let out a small chuckle but then covered it up with an obviously fake cough. "I suppose it won't hurt to let the cat out of the bag now. I've been letter-writing with Rhoda Zook, and I've asked to give her a ride home in my courting buggy after the Grabers' singing." Mose's mouth contorted oddly as he stifled a grin.

Sadie looked away from her brother to hide her reaction. In her heart, she was overjoyed to hear that her twin brother and dearest friend might be starting a relationship. Still, the sting of the realization that she was the last single girl among her friend group bit at her soul like a horsefly that couldn't be swatted away. Putting on her bravest face, she took several breaths before replying to her brother's news. "That's *wunderbar*, Mose. Rhoda is a really nice *maedel*, and I know for a fact that she's had her eye on you for quite some time."

Mose's pathetically hidden smile burst into a full-on grin before he seemingly regained control of his facial expression. "*Denki*, but what about you? Will you at least pray that a suitable fellow will make his presence known? Finding love will make you happy, and will keep *Mamm* and *Daed* at bay."

Sadie sighed and tried to nod, but the movement was so slight that she wasn't sure if her head had moved at all. "*Jah*, I will," she finally agreed, knowing that prayer never hurt anyone.

Mose gave her a relieved, crooked smile. "That's all I needed to hear. I better get back to work." He leaned forward, looking down at the ground far below, then shivered. "How does one get down from here?"

Sadie chuckled against the sadness that threatened to eat her alive. "Very carefully."

Clearly unamused by her less than helpful reply, Mose rolled his eyes, then gingerly crept down the tree, staying near the sturdy trunk.

Once her brother was out of earshot, Sadie let go of the tears she had been holding back. It wasn't that she didn't want a beau, or to be married with a house full of children to love. Throughout her teenage years, she'd experienced a handful of schoolgirl crushes on her male peers, though they'd all turned out to be unrequited. As a grown woman, her prospects of finding love were even grimmer. What conservative Amish fellow would want a woman who refused to let her childlike delight for life be tamed?

"Is there a man out there who would love me for who I am, lively soul and all?" Sadie wondered out loud. "Oh, Lord, if there is such a man, send him to me!"

After a day or two of settling into his new home, Isaac had insisted on caring for Mim's small barn of animals, which included her horse and two Holstein cows. Isaac enjoyed spending time with the peaceful animals and making small repairs to the old barn, but now he was focusing on the task of morning milking.

Isaac was nearly knocked to his feet when the more ornery of the two cows gave him a good bump. Losing his balance, he swayed unsteadily. "Stubborn," he muttered under his breath. When Isaac calmly inched closer to the cow to begin milking, the animal stepped forward, placing her hoof on top of his foot.

"Yow!" Isaac jumped around on one leg, holding the sore foot with both hands. "You big, dumb thing!"

He heard a woman suddenly burst into laughter. He spun around and was surprised to see a thin, dark-haired young woman entering the barn. She held a basket filled to the brim with treats, and the delicious aroma of baked goods caused Isaac to forget about his throbbing foot.

"I'm so sorry," the woman said between giggles, her face flushed with laughter. "That was a funny little dance you just did." She covered her mouth with her slender hand and failed to suppress another outburst.

Isaac couldn't help but grin when he replayed the scene in his head. "I suppose it was." With the sleeve of his shirt, he wiped at some of the sweat that had beaded on his forehead. "What can I do for you today?"

"I just heard through the grapevine that we had new neighbors who moved in with Miriam. My family runs a roadside stand and I wanted to bring you some of our best sellers as a welcome." The woman held out the basket that contained jars of homemade apple butter and peach jelly, two loaves of friendship bread, and a package of assorted cookies.

Accepting the basket, Isaac smiled in appreciation. "That's real kind of you. *Denki,* uh…"

"Nancy Beiler."

"Nancy." Isaac nodded his head. "I'm Isaac Hostettler."

"I know," she seemed unashamed to admit, though she turned a bright shade of pink.

An uneasy feeling settled in the pit of Isaac's stomach. Was that eagerness he saw in her eyes? Maybe she was lonely and looking to make a new friend. What if she was looking for something more?

A wave of panic crashed into Isaac's chest. No, that was an utterly ridiculous thought.

"Well, Isaac—" Nancy squeaked at the end of his name "—maybe I can make supper for you sometime." She pulled her arms behind her back and twisted in half circles without moving her feet.

Feeling uncomfortable yet not wanting to hurt the poor woman's feelings, Isaac kicked at some loose straw on the barn floor. "That's kind of you, but my *mamm*'s still getting settled in here. I want to make sure she's all right before I stray too far away from home."

"What about Miriam? Doesn't she care for her *schwester* when you can't be by her side?"

Isaac was taken aback, feeling suddenly defensive of his family. "Sure she does, but Mim also looks after some children from time to time, and she has plenty of chores around the house. She can't be with *Mamm* all the time."

Nancy squinted at Isaac as if she wasn't sure that she believed him. He half expected her to invite his mother and aunt to dinner as well, just to be polite. Instead, she smiled pleasantly at him and shrugged in defeat. "Okay then, maybe another time." She glanced at the fresh manure that was just a few feet away and made a sour face. "I guess I'll leave you to your work. It was nice to meet you!" As quickly as she had appeared, Nancy turned on her heels and scurried away.

"Sure," Isaac muttered, wishing he could say the same. He watched as she dashed out of the barn, somehow knowing that this would not be his last strange encounter with Nancy Beiler.

Chapter Three

Later that week, Isaac eagerly approached the Stolzfus barn with a spring in his step. He would need a buggy horse of his own while residing in Bird-in-Hand, and Aunt Mim had recommended Mose Stolzfus as "the very best horse trader around these parts." Besides, having a horse of his own would certainly help him feel more at home in this new community.

Reaching the open barn doors, Isaac politely peered inside before entering. "Hello? Anybody home?"

"Just me and the animals," answered a lanky, dark-haired Amish man. He ran a currycomb through the chestnut coat of a horse that stood proudly beside him. With a welcoming grin, the man stepped away from the horse and extended his hand to Isaac. "Mose Stolzfus."

Isaac took Mose's hand, shaking it firmly. "Nice to meet you, Mose. I'm Isaac Hostettler. My aunt Mim said you'd be expecting me."

Mose nodded enthusiastically. "I sure was. I hear you're in the market for a driving horse."

"That's right. Can't be using my aunt's horse every time I need to go somewhere." Isaac reached out to pet the proud horse's shiny, impeccably groomed coat. "Mim said you're the best person to buy a horse from in Lancaster County."

Mose grinned at the compliment. "That's awful nice of her to say. I try to only buy the horses I would want for myself." He ran his fingers through the horse's ebony mane as if he was hunting for tangles. Clearly, he took excellent care of his animals. "I assume you're looking for someone who's a good trotter, and pretty agile as well?"

"I don't know what I'm looking for." Isaac chuckled as he rubbed the back of his neck. "I suppose I'll know the right horse when I see it, though."

Mose seemed to understand. "I'll be glad to show you each horse I have, and you can tell me if one strikes your fancy." He gestured toward the noble steed beside them. "This is Samson. He's a five-year-old, standard-bred gelding." As if Samson knew he was being critiqued, he stood just so, with his head high in the air. "He's an ex-racehorse who I bought off a trainer in the Poconos just a few weeks ago," Mose said. "Want to take him out for a run?"

Isaac squinted at the horse, and the horse glared back at him. "I better see who else you have first," Isaac declined.

Mose showed Isaac two similar horses he thought could also make a fine match. Still, Isaac hadn't met the right horse for him. When they approached the final stall, Isaac's face lit up like the night sky on the Fourth of July. "Who is this?" he asked, petting the horse's muzzle as it approached.

Mose's face contorted as if he was genuinely shocked by Isaac's interest in the animal. "That's just Shadow. To be up-front with you, he's not the fastest or spunkiest of the bunch." He pulled a sugar cube out of a nearby container and gave it to Shadow. "I wasn't going to bring him home, but my twin sister carried on until I did."

Isaac ran his hand over the horse's gray-and-white-spotted coat. "Is there something wrong with him?"

"Not at all," Mose answered with a prompt shake of his head. "He's as healthy as they come. He's just older and slower. I didn't think anyone would be interested in purchasing him, but Sadie insisted."

As if on cue, there was a commotion in the hayloft overhead. Both men looked up just in time to see Sadie leap from the open second story and grab hold of the old rope swing that hung from the ceiling. Isaac and Mose jumped back as she sailed past at a terrifying speed, her dress and the ties of her *kapp* flying in the breeze behind her.

The rope gradually slowed, but before it came to a complete halt, Sadie let go and landed with a thud on the dusty barn floor. "Sorry to interrupt," she apologized as she shook some loose hay off her apron.

"How could you not interrupt with an entrance like that?" Mose replied with a hearty laugh. "What in the world were you doing up there?" he questioned, still smiling at Sadie.

"Reading the Good Book," Sadie stated, pulling her well-used Bible out from beneath her arm. "*Mamm* has friends visiting and I wanted to give them their privacy." She glanced at Isaac and her face instantly brightened. "Hi, Isaac! Are you here to buy Shadow?"

Isaac's mouth still hung open in disbelief. What a tremendously unexpected surprise to see this lively girl again. "Hi, Sadie. I sure was considering it. I think we'd make a good match."

Sadie bounded up to the horse and wrapped her arms around its strong neck. "*Jah*, he's beautiful. His colorful coat makes him stand out from the rest of the brown buggy horses."

As if worried that Isaac might be swayed by Sadie's fond talk of the animal, Mose stepped forward. "Samson or one of the other two geldings would make for a better buggy horse. Shadow is more of a pet, I think."

Isaac studied Mose, then Sadie, then Shadow. Finally, he proclaimed, "There's something I like about Shadow, and I don't need the fastest horse money can buy. I'd like to take him out for a ride first, but I think I'd like to buy him from you."

Sadie squealed and embraced the horse again. "You hear that, Shadow? You're getting a new home!" Whipping back around, Sadie waltzed out of the barn just as quickly as she had appeared, calling "So long, Isaac" over her shoulder.

Isaac watched Sadie leave, astonished by the experience. He'd never known a grown woman to have such an enthusiastic outlook on the world around her, and it was downright refreshing.

Mose smirked and failed to smother a cackle. "You've met my twin sister before?"

"Just the other day, when we had that severe downpour," Isaac responded, still staring out the barn door, though Sadie was now long gone. "She's very, um…"

"Spirited." Mose finished the sentence when Isaac was at a loss for words. Isaac sheepishly nodded, wondering if he had stepped on any toes. Mose chuckled affectionately while picking up a bridle to put on Shadow.

"I don't know of anyone as spirited as our Sadie. Living with her sure makes life more exciting."

Isaac agreed. The two finished hitching up the horse, then led the gentle animal to Mose's open courting buggy, which was resting just outside the barn door.

Once Shadow was fully hitched up to the carriage, Mose handed the reins to Isaac. "The young people from our district are having a singing next Sunday evening at Pete Graber's farm," Mose stated. "I hope you plan to attend."

Now seated in Mose's courting buggy, Isaac rubbed his knee, milling over the idea. It would be fun to socialize with the other Amish youth in Bird-in-Hand, but would it be fair to attend if he wasn't looking for a mate? "It's been a long time, years in fact, since I've attended a youth gathering," Isaac declared, trying to hide the sadness in his voice. "I don't know if I would fit in."

"Sure you would," Mose cautiously ventured as he leaned against his buggy. "Not having attended a singing in a while is the perfect reason to go and have yourself a *gut* time! Besides, Sadie and I will be there, so there'll be some friendly faces if you decide to join us. And you'll make lots of new friends."

"True," Isaac confessed, staring at Shadow as he swatted away some pesky flies with his granite-colored tail. "Let me talk to Shadow about it while I take him out on the road. He's an old man, so he should have the wisdom of Solomon, *jah*?"

Mose snorted at Isaac's joke while Isaac guided Shadow down the long driveway. As he observed Shadow's gait and personality, his thoughts drifted back to Sadie and the second dramatic entrance she'd made into his life. There was something sweet and silly about her that could make anyone forget their troubles within minutes of meeting her. Maybe he needed a bit more of Sadie's enthusiasm for life.

Sadie closed the lid of her family's mailbox and sorted through the letters in her hand. She had been feeling a bit gloomy ever since Mose had clued her in on their parents' imminent plans to find her a mate, and she'd hoped that today's mail would have included a letter or two from one of her many Amish pen pals. An interesting letter would certainly lift her spirits, but she was disappointed to see that there was no mail for her. She wished something would happen to take her mind off her troubles as she headed back up the long, winding drive.

When she was about halfway to the house, she stopped to wave at Isaac as he passed by with Shadow. To her surprise, he pulled on the reins and brought Mose's courting buggy to a halt. Sadie put a hand to her forehead to shield her eyes from the sun. "Taking Shadow out for a test ride?"

Isaac nodded and adjusted his straw hat. "*Jah*, but it's really only a formality. I'm gonna buy him from Mose once we get back from our ride."

"I'm glad to hear that Shadow will finally have a permanent home, but I sure will miss seeing him around here," Sadie confessed as she reached out to pet the dapple-gray.

"If you're not busy at the moment, you should come for a ride with us. It'll give you a chance to make one more memory with Shadow before I take him home," Isaac suggested, his handsome smile nearly outshining the intense August sun.

"Well, don't mind if I do!" Sadie bounced up into the rig and scooted next to Isaac on the driver's bench. A ride with her new friend through the rolling farmlands of Lancaster County would be the perfect medicine to soothe her spirit. Sadie stuffed the mail into her apron pocket as Isaac gently flicked the reins to get Shadow moving, and soon they were headed onto Stumptown Road.

A few minutes of comfortable silence passed between the pair as Sadie listened to the rhythmic clopping of Shadow's hooves. She closed her eyes for just a moment, deeply inhaling the sweet country air. The earthy scents of growing corn and fresh stream water invigorated her as the buggy traveled past Mill Creek. When she opened her eyes, she peeked over at Isaac, and she couldn't help but stare at the contented smile on his attractive face. There was something that felt natural about being in his presence, though they had only known each other a short time.

Isaac took his eyes off the road for just a second and glanced over at her. "Penny for your thoughts, Sadie."

Sadie felt her heart jump into her throat, realizing that she had been caught staring at him. She scrambled to come up with something to say other than admitting that she had been a bit mesmerized by his company. "I was wondering how your first week has been in Lancaster County. Are you enjoying it here?"

"*Ach*, very much so," Isaac replied as he yanked on the reins to guide Shadow down another road. "I do miss my *daed* and *schwesters*, but *Mamm* and I really needed a change of scenery. Plus, it's nice to spend some time with my Mim. I only met her once when I was a little *buwe* when she traveled to Indiana to visit us."

He glanced again at Sadie with a crooked smile and a twinkle in his eye. "I met some real nice folks recently too." He winked at her and then turned his attention back to the country road before them.

So he enjoys my company as well, Sadie realized as she grinned at Isaac. She sat a little taller in her seat, enjoying the notion that Isaac seemed to appreciate her for who she was. She didn't need to dull her sparkle to feel accepted. "You should come to the singing that's gonna take place at the Graber farm next Sunday."

"Mose mentioned the singing earlier." Isaac let out a sigh. "I didn't want to go at first, but Mose also brought up the possibility of making some more friends, so I decided that I'll attend."

"Why didn't you want to go? Singings are always a good time."

Isaac's cute smile contorted into an awkward expression. As he brought the buggy to a halt at a stop sign, he seemed to be mulling over how he should reply to her question. "After the past two years I've had, I know I'll never go courting ever again."

Sadie took in Isaac's somber words. Not wanting to pry, Sadie nodded understandingly. "I'm real sorry to hear that, Isaac."

His shoulders sagged as he made a clicking sound to get the horse moving again. "*Denki*. I don't want to dwell on the past." He cleared his throat, perhaps to keep his emotions at bay. "Anyway, I'm not interested in finding love ever again, and that's really the point of the singings, *jah*?"

Filled with compassion for her new friend, Sadie quickly thought of a supportive response. "That's true, but you can still go just for some fellowship with the other young people. We will be glad to see you there."

"I know that I'll enjoy myself at the singing, but I just worry that the ladies will think that I'm looking to find someone to court." Even though it was a humid summer day, Sadie thought she saw Isaac shiver. "A *maedel* came to *Aentie* Mim's place a few days ago, and I got the distinct impression that she was on the hunt for a husband. I wouldn't want to lead her on."

"Sounds like you met Nancy Beiler," Sadie ventured.

"*Jah*, that was her!"

Isaac's confirmation caused Sadie to let out a belly laugh—that and the fact that Isaac's eyes had grown as large as dinner plates. Once her chortling ceased, she wiped the tears from her emerald eyes. "I understand your concern, but you can't let what others think dictate how you live your life." The melancholy that she'd felt earlier that day started to creep back up on her. "Folks make fun of me because I'd much rather climb a tree and marvel at all the Lord created for us instead of sewing a quilt. I'd rather be out in the meadow, watching a calf be born instead of baking a pie. It's why I'm still single."

She rubbed her forehead where she felt a headache coming. "A few weeks ago my *daed* told me that I should stop playing in the dirt and quit my part-time job at the greenhouse so I could focus on finding myself a husband. The other day I learned that my parents are planning to match me up with someone if I don't have a steady boyfriend by the first of October."

Isaac shook his head and moved his shoulders in a quick shrug. "That's *baremlich*, Sadie. You shouldn't conform to who someone else wants you to be. I think it's nice that you so thoroughly enjoy the world that the Lord created for us. The right man will come along, and he will love you for the sweet *maedel* that I know you are."

A rush of heat passed over Sadie's cheeks. She hadn't expected such a compliment from Isaac. Her heart stirred, knowing that Isaac seemed like more than a friend; they were kindred spirits. "*Jah*, well, unless you want to court me, it looks like I'll be subject to my parents' meddling come harvesttime." Sadie's heart dropped when the words left her lips, and her hand flew to her chest to still its frenzied beating. "Isaac, I'm so sorry. I didn't mean to imply…"

"Actually—" Isaac cut her off "—that would solve some problems for both of us." He waved at the driver of a passing horse and buggy, then returned his free hand to the reins. "I mean, I need an excuse not to date Nancy Beiler—or anyone, for that matter. You need yourself a beau to stop your *mamm* and *daed* from trying to fix you up with someone against your will."

Sadie's mouth fell open, shocked that he would actually consider faking a courtship. "You're serious about this?"

"Well, I don't want to deceive folks." He grinned at her sheepishly. "But desperate times call for desperate measures, I suppose."

"But how…what…?"

"Look, there's a little restaurant up ahead. Let's stop for lunch and we can figure out the details there." Isaac chuckled, then wiggled his eyebrows at Sadie. "We can consider it our first date."

"*Jah*, that sounds good," Sadie agreed. A strange mixture of relief and disappointment floated around her mind. Isaac did make some good points about the mutual benefits of feigning a courtship, but she'd always imagined that her first date would involve some sort of a love connection. Ignoring the nagging reminder that she was destined to become a spinster, she decided to enjoy her date with Isaac. He was a kind person who didn't pressure her to be someone she wasn't, and that was enough to make her smile.

Chapter Four

When Isaac and Sadie entered the quaint countryside diner, they were immediately greeted by the Mennonite hostess, who led them to their table. Once they slid into opposite sides of the booth, they were each handed a sizeable menu to look over. Isaac perused the menu but was distracted when Sadie suddenly started quietly humming a hymn. He glanced up at her, enjoying the simple melody as she read the menu, perhaps not even realizing that she was singing.

He hoped faking a courtship was truly the best thing for both of them. Isaac worried as he continued to study Sadie. There was a possibility that maintaining a feigned relationship could become complicated. It was a wonder to him that she wasn't spoken for. With her golden hair and grass-green eyes, she was a perfect example of natural beauty. It was a shame that the young men in this community didn't appreciate her unusually enthusiastic nature. So what if she was a bit childlike in her enjoyment of the truly simple things in life? Would the young men rather date a boring girl who had nothing special about her?

If his heart didn't already belong to Rebecca, he might be interested in properly courting Sadie himself. Startled by the thought, Isaac shoved it to the back of his mind. He'd been blessed to experience true love once, and that was enough for him. He refused to put his heart on the line again.

Soon a middle-aged *Englisch* waitress approached the table to take their orders. Sadie asked for a lemonade, a BLT sandwich and a side of applesauce. When the waitress turned to Isaac, he realized that he'd been too busy watching Sadie to decide on what to order. "I'll have the same," he said, handing both menus to the waitress before she scurried back to the kitchen.

"I don't know about you, but I'm mighty hungry. If our food doesn't come soon, I might just eat this place mat," Isaac joked, resting his folded hands on the paper place mat in front of him.

Sadie chuckled, then leaned forward, her face growing more serious than Isaac had ever seen it. "I don't think I can eat a single thing until we iron out the details of this courtship." The waitress returned to the table, dropped off their beverages and two straws, then hustled away once more. Once the woman was out of earshot, Sadie spoke again. "Are you absolutely certain you want to be my beau, Isaac?" Her eyes shone as if she was worried that he might decide to back out of their deal.

"*Jah*, I think that is what's best for both of us," Isaac replied without hesitation.

"All right, for how long?"

Isaac was a bit stunned by Sadie's candid but legitimate question. However, he appreciated her direct nature. "How about we court for a year?"

Sadie shook her head. "I think that's too long. Surely there will come a day when some girl catches your attention, and you may want to be free to court her."

Isaac glanced out the window and frowned, noticing some dark, heavy-looking clouds approaching. "That won't happen."

"Well, you never know."

"Trust me, it won't." Isaac's response came out harsher than he'd intended. And it caused Sadie to shrink back in her seat. He sighed, glancing again at the rain clouds approaching in the distance. "If I were to meet a girl who could teach me to love the rain, I'll know she's the one."

Sadie looked at him in obvious confusion, her lips parting slightly as she studied him. Isaac waited in painful suspense, dreading the required explanation that would follow such an unusual statement. Much to his relief, Sadie didn't pry and instead asked, "How about six months? That will get me far past my parents' October deadline, and that should also be long enough for Nancy to become interested in the next unsuspecting young man."

Isaac grinned at Sadie's colorful description. "Six months it is." He offered his hand to Sadie so they could shake on their agreement. The handshake lasted a bit longer than expected, and Isaac was surprised when neither one of them made the first move to pull their hand away.

However, the handshake abruptly ended when the waitress returned with their sandwiches and applesauce. "Now that that's settled, I'd like to hear more about your job at the greenhouse."

Sadie's face brightened at the mention of her workplace. "I've worked there two or three days a week for the past six years. I just adore all of the different flowers and plants." She took a bite of her sandwich, then went on. "I get to learn a lot about all of the different varieties of plants and how to care for them. Each one is so unique." She looked up from her plate and smiled at Isaac. "*Gott*'s ever so creative, *jah*?"

Isaac bobbed his head in agreement. Sadie's passion for gardening was contagious, and it stirred up an idea in Isaac. "You'll have to show me around the greenhouse someday. Mim has some empty flower beds that could sure use some color."

"That's a *gut* idea," Sadie replied as she used her napkin to wipe her face. "What did you do for work back in Indiana?"

"My *daed* owns a woodworking shop, and I've worked alongside him for as long as I can remember. We make a lot of furniture and some decorations that the tourists really enjoy, but I'm much more keen on farming. I hope to run my own dairy farm someday," Isaac confessed before taking the last bite of his sandwich.

"There's just something special about tending to the Lord's creation, *jah*?"

Sadie's statement warmed Isaac's heart. She understood his love for being outdoors, getting his hands dirty and caring for everything the Lord had created. "*Jah*, there sure is."

As they finished their meal, Isaac couldn't help but notice that he felt more chipper than he had in years. He thoroughly enjoyed Sadie's company, and he was honored to be her beau, even though it was only for a short while.

* * *

Sadie spent the rest of the day with some extra pep in her step. Her surprise outing with Isaac had been the highlight of her morning, and she replayed memories of their conversations in her mind as she spent her afternoon pulling weeds in her vegetable garden, helping her father and Mose with the evening milking chores, and assisting her mother with preparing dinner. She couldn't recall ever having such lively, interesting discussions with anyone before, and she looked forward to her next outing with Isaac, which would be the upcoming singing at the Graber farm.

After the supper dishes were washed and put away, Sadie decided to enjoy the rest of the evening by sitting on the porch swing and doing some journaling. With her journal and pen in hand, she padded across the wrap-around covered porch and took a seat on one of the swings. Before she opened her journal, she took in the familiar beauty that surrounded her family's farm. Her flower beds were fit to burst with vibrant reds, pinks and golds that paired nicely with the cool purplish hue of the dusk sky. Fireflies twinkled like glitter throughout the backyard, and an occasional contented moo could be heard from the pasture where the cows had been set free to graze. Cool evening air filled and refreshed her lungs just as her time spent with Isaac had been a balm to her soul. It had been a marvelous day, and Sadie sent up a quick prayer of thanks for the many blessings that she had received.

Opening her journal to a fresh page, Sadie began to neatly document the day's events. She had only been writing for a few minutes when the sound of familiar footsteps clomped up the porch stairs. She looked up to see Mose and patted the empty spot beside her on the seat. "Care to swing with me a spell?"

"I would, but I'm actually planning to turn in early tonight. I've got a driver coming to pick me up at four thirty tomorrow morning. He's gonna take me to Ohio to buy some horses." He leaned against the porch railing and crossed his arms at his chest. "Speaking of horses, I sold Shadow to that Isaac fellow."

"That's *wunderbar*," Sadie replied, unable to hide a growing smile. "I told you the right person would think he was the perfect horse for them."

"*Jah*, sure did." Mose glanced at one of the barn cats that had wandered onto the porch. The black-and-white feline walked up to him and rubbed against his leg. "So, how did your date go with Isaac?" Mose asked as he reached down to pet the friendly cat.

Sadie's mouth fell open. "H-how did you know?"

"I was standing outside the barn, giving one of the horses a bath, when I saw him returning from his ride with Shadow." A coy smile spread across Mose's face, which reminded Sadie of a cat that had just caught a mouse. "I saw him drop you off at the house before bringing Shadow and my rig back to the barn. He mentioned that you and he had met earlier this week, and I thought maybe he'd asked to take you out and seized the opportunity today."

Before Sadie could respond, the screen door squeaked open and their parents stepped outside. Mose issued Sadie a playfully knowing look, made some small talk with their parents, then retreated into the house.

"Sadie, your *mamm* and I need to have a talk with you about something important," announced her father,

Amos, as he took a seat on the top porch step. "Got a minute to spare for your old *daed* and *mamm*?"

"Of course, I always do," Sadie answered with a small smile that hopefully hid her apprehension. She placed her journal and pen on the ground, then picked up the cat Mose had been petting.

Sadie's mother, Anna, took a seat next to her daughter on the swing. "Sadie, your *daed* and I noticed that sometimes it seems like you're lonely." The middle-aged woman reached out to pet the cat nestled into her daughter's lap, then shot a look of sympathy at her offspring.

"We want you to be a happy *maedel* who lives a fulfilling life," her father added, his concern for her shining like stars in his green eyes, which Sadie had inherited from him.

"I'm already fulfilled," Sadie replied just above a whisper, though she knew that this was only partially true. She longed to fall in love, but at the same time, she wasn't willing to tame her fiery spirit for any man, and she was certain that this was what her parents were getting at. "I have a job at the greenhouse that I love, and every day I get to spend time outdoors. What more could I ask for?"

"*Jah*, but there is more to life than planting flowers and climbing trees," retorted her mother. Though she was nearing fifty years of age, Anna normally didn't look a day over forty. However, the concern etched across her pretty face aged her unusually. "*Daed* and I think it's far past time for you to start courting. If you want to raise a family of your own, you'll need to find a suitable husband soon."

"That's why *Mamm* and I have decided to set you up with one of our friend's unmarried sons if you don't find yourself a beau by October first," Amos stated matter-of-factly, as if this was a perfectly reasonable solution.

Sadie bit her tongue. Though she knew that her parents had her best interests in mind, she couldn't bring herself to look at either of them. "Actually, I have met someone. I went on a lunch date with a nice man today."

Anna and Amos exchanged surprised glances. "Who is this man?" Amos asked, rising from his seat on the steps.

"His name is Isaac Hostettler. He and his *mamm* just moved here from Indiana, and they are living with his aunt, Miriam Fisher." Sadie looked up from petting the cat that had fallen asleep on her lap. "You'll get to meet them at the next church gathering, I'm sure."

Her mother's stunned expression quickly morphed into one of cautious relief. "Is he a baptized member of the Amish church?"

"*Jah*, he is," Sadie confirmed, having gleaned this information during her lunch date with Isaac. "You can ask Mose about him too. He sold Shadow to Isaac earlier today."

"Well, this is real *gut* news, Sadie! Real *gut* indeed," *Daed* congratulated her with a bit of a chuckle. "I knew there was hope for you."

After a few more minutes of conversation, Sadie's parents headed back indoors, leaving her alone with her thoughts. A mix of conflicting emotions swirled together within Sadie as she gingerly lifted the sleeping cat from her lap and snuggled the animal like a teddy bear. She had managed to avoid her parents' meddling in her personal life, but it was a bittersweet mix of relief and disappointment.

Isaac was a kind, genuine, caring man, but Sadie

had always imagined being in love when the day finally came that she would tell her parents about her first courtship. Instead, she was a girlfriend in name only. No feelings were involved, except for the butterflies that Isaac gave her whenever he stared into her eyes or smiled at her like she was a field full of wildflowers.

Lord, Sadie fervently prayed, *bless the time that Isaac and I spend together. Heal Isaac's broken heart, and send the right man to love me.*

Chapter Five

On the following Sunday afternoon, Isaac pulled his newly purchased buggy into the Graber family's driveway, surprised by the number of carriages already parked in the field. He knew he'd been running a few minutes late, but had never expected to see that the volleyball game had already begun.

Shrugging off his late arrival, Isaac stepped out of his buggy and hurried to unhitch Shadow. Then he led the horse to the pasture, releasing the dapple-gray to graze freely. Squatting next to the front right wheel of his rig, he reached up to the buggy's seat and pulled down a blue ribbon that Mim had given him. "Better take this along," she'd suggested when she'd offered the ribbon to him. "You can use this as a marker to tell your buggy apart from the others." Smiling at the reminder of Mim's cleverness, Isaac tied the ribbon on one of the front wheel's wooden spokes. Then he headed toward the gathering.

Isaac's attention was instantly drawn to the volleyball net set up in the middle of the neighboring field. This game seemed to be girls against boys. The young women had gathered on one side of the net, giggling and whispering to each other. The young men stood on the other side, eagerly discussing their game plan. A large folding table with a variety of snacks and beverages had been set up under an enormous oak tree and was drawing a sizeable crowd. Feeling his stomach rumble, Isaac decided that he required something to munch on.

He scanned the trays of baked goods and finally settled on a pumpkin whoopie pie. Turning from the table, he faced the volleyball game, snack in hand. He felt a bit overwhelmed as he watched the group of his peers. There were plenty of young Amish folks milling about the Grabers' fields and backyard. With such a large number of unfamiliar faces surrounding him, Isaac felt like an outsider. Plagued with sudden shyness, he continued to stand near the refreshment table, eating and scanning for a familiar face.

A burst of laughter broke out near the volleyball game. One of the chuckling female voices was considerably louder and more contagious than the others. Recognizing Sadie's voice immediately, Isaac quickly located her among the female players. Her bright smile outshone those around her. As she ran after the volleyball, occasionally scoring a point for her team, her energy was evident. It was obvious that the other young ladies enjoyed Sadie's company, and she frequently encouraged those around her with pats on the back and high fives.

Isaac continued to marvel at Sadie's every move. It wasn't just her friendly and outgoing nature that was special. Her cute button nose and warm green eyes also made her the most attractive woman at the gathering. Once again, Isaac found himself baffled by Sadie's singleness. The other young men must be out of their minds not to take notice of such a passionate, albeit unusual, lovely lady.

"There you are, Isaac! I've been looking for you!" It was Nancy Beiler, heading right for him. Her hurried pace indicated that she was on a mission, and Isaac felt certain that he was the prize.

"Hello, Nancy," Isaac greeted her as she stepped up to him, nearly invading his personal space. "Nice day for a get-together, *jah*?"

"Indeed it is," Nancy replied as she wrung her hands together. "I'm glad to see you're here today. I was worried that you wouldn't come."

Isaac peered over Nancy's shoulder so he could continue watching Sadie. He found her to be much more interesting than Nancy Beiler, or any of the other attendees.

Nancy frowned and looked over her shoulder. Turning back to him, she'd plastered what appeared to be a forced smile on her face. "I heard through the grapevine that you recently bought a horse and buggy." She coyly twirled one of her *kapp* ribbons around her finger like a lovesick schoolgirl. "Now you have everything you need to take a special *maedel* out riding after the singing, *jah*?"

Isaac fought the urge to cringe. Nancy seemed friendly enough, but her forwardness was certainly enough to make any sensible young man think twice about her. Overjoyed that he had a reason to escape her obvious prodding, he said, "*Jah*, I'm seeing Sadie Stolzfus."

Nancy's face suddenly paled. "Oh, I... I didn't know."

A sudden shriek pierced the air, followed by a series of gasps and murmurs. Isaac returned his attention to the volleyball game just in time to see Sadie crumple to the ground after diving for the ball. It seemed like a particularly hard fall, and it was evident that she had injured herself.

Isaac dropped what was left of his snack, rushed past Nancy, sprinted toward the game, then skidded to a halt at Sadie's side. "Are you *oll recht*? Did you hurt yourself?" he asked breathlessly.

"No need to make a fuss. I'm okay," Sadie responded through gritted teeth, clearly trying to minimize her ordeal. "I think I just twisted my ankle." She tried to stand, then promptly lost her balance when she attempted to put weight on her injured foot. Isaac dove to catch her, and he did his best to ignore the rush of heat in his face when she landed perfectly into his protective embrace.

"Careful," Isaac chuckled nervously as he helped Sadie regain her balance. His concern for her remained at the front of his mind, though he found it difficult to ignore the sensation that he'd just been struck by a lightning bolt. Fighting off the strange feeling, he noticed that Sadie was able to stand properly, with most of her weight resting on her uninjured foot.

"I think we've got a crutch you could use, Sadie," Pete Graber called from the other side of the volleyball net. "I'll run to the house right quick and fetch it for you." Placing his hand atop his straw hat, Pete dashed for the house.

"Denki," Isaac replied, knowing that a crutch was just what Sadie needed. Noting a bunch of Adirondack chairs under a nearby maple tree, Isaac pointed to the spot. "We'll be sitting under the tree," he called to Pete, but Pete was already out of earshot.

Turning his attention back to Sadie, Isaac let her

use his arm to steady herself as they gingerly inched toward the chairs. Truth be told, Isaac absolutely didn't want to see Sadie in any sort of pain, but he was glad to have the chance to spend some quiet time with her in the midst of the youth gathering. *A silver lining*, he told himself inwardly, knowing that time spent with Sadie, whatever the circumstances, would be time well spent.

After being seated under the towering maple tree, checked on by a gaggle of well-meaning friends, and given a crutch by the singing's host, Sadie felt worn out. The pain in her ankle was already starting to lessen, and she didn't relish being fussed over like a sickly child. She glanced at Isaac and noticed him staring down at her injured foot. "Why don't you go join the volleyball game or mingle with some of the others? No need to spoil your time here on account of me being clumsy."

Isaac shook his head so quickly that his straw hat's placement on his head became crooked. "No way, I'd rather stay near you."

"Really?" Sadie's pulse quickened as she wondered if she had heard Isaac correctly. Surely he only wanted to keep her company so she wouldn't feel alone in a crowd.

"I know what an obstacle an injured ankle can be," Isaac explained as he pointed to her right foot, which she had elevated on one of the empty chairs. "When I was about ten years old, *Mamm* broke her ankle when she fell off a ladder while washing windows. She was in a cast and had to get around on crutches for nearly four months. Wouldn't want you to have to go through that as well."

While Sadie felt blessed and thankful to have a friend who obviously cared about her, she couldn't help but feel disappointed. There simply wasn't a romantic connection that was drawing Isaac to her, and according to his own statement on matters of the heart, that was something that would likely never happen. Doing her best to ignore these feelings, Sadie decided to keep the topic of conversation focused on Isaac's mother.

"It was nice to meet your mother at church," she stated.

His shoulders sagged severely, as if the weight of the world had just come crashing down on him. "Even though she didn't speak to anyone?"

Sadie nodded enthusiastically. "Of course! She is a part of our community now, as are you." She remembered briefly greeting Ruth, Isaac's mother, earlier that day at the church gathering. Though her figure seemed to be too thin, she didn't look ill. Instead, Sadie could see the anguish hidden behind the woman's eyes. It was as if she could almost feel the immense sadness Ruth radiated. Sadie had promptly sent up a prayer that Isaac's *mamm* would find some joy and peace here in Lancaster County.

Sadie also recalled Isaac mentioning that his mother had become unwell after the death of a loved one, but she hadn't initially realized the extent of Ruth's condition. Although it was never a happy event, losing loved ones was a fact of life. What could have so deeply devastated the dear woman, and how was Isaac able to cope after the same tragedy?

Neither Sadie nor Isaac said anything for a few moments. "Can you think of anything I can do to help your *mamm*?" Sadie finally asked, breaking the somber silence. "Is there anything I can do to help you, Isaac?"

Isaac leaned back against his chair and stared up at

the sea of green leaves hanging above them. "That's awful kind of you, but I can't think of anything at the moment." He closed his eyes and sighed before opening them again. "Nothing has changed in two years, so it might just be time for my family and me to accept that this is who *Mamm* is going to be for the rest of her life. To be honest, it's starting to feel hopeless."

"Nothing is hopeless," Sadie replied, eager to encourage her friend.

Isaac crossed his arms over his chest. "You say that because you haven't been through the trauma that we have. How could you possibly say that something like this isn't hopeless?"

Sadie fought the frown that threatened to spread across her face; knowing that Isaac's harsh words were a product of his pain, she didn't take them to heart. She turned her head upward, allowing the sunshine to warm her face. "I know there is hope because *Gott* allowed the sun to rise today. There's still fresh air to breathe, and the birds haven't stopped singing. *Gott* is still providing, even when it's difficult to see it. Where He provides, there is hope."

Isaac's scowl disappeared. "The Lord does indeed provide. He gave me a *wunderbar* friend when I needed one most, and I'm thankful to have you in my life." He reached for Sadie's hand and held it for a few seconds before letting go.

"I'm thankful to have you in my life too, Isaac," Sadie replied as she wished that he hadn't let go of her hand so soon. She was grateful to be able to call him both her friend and her beau, since their unusual relationship had discouraged her parents' matchmaking ultimatum. But still, something deep within her heart reminded Sadie that she would never be fully satisfied until the unlikely day arrived in which she would be swept off her feet by her first and only love.

Chapter Six

After the sun sank into the horizon and the coolness of evening settled in, the fireflies sparkled their way through the darkness. The mugginess of the day melted away as the fresh night air invigorated the Amish youth who still lingered at the Grabers' farm.

When it came time for everyone to head into the barn to begin singing hymns, Sadie had felt deeply moved by the voices joined together in song. By the time the last tune had been sung, her ankle barely hurt at all. It had turned out to be a downright pleasant day, and she was glad to have attended the gathering.

She reached into the bag of marshmallows beside her. She and Rhoda now sat near one of the campfires, roasting them on sticks. Sadie glanced toward Rhoda, who had been silent for quite some time. Rhoda stared into the fire as the marshmallow on the end of her stick turned completely black and was now beginning to smoke. Sadie nudged her friend, causing Rhoda to nearly jump out of her skin.

"Didn't mean to startle you…" Sadie spoke gently.

"But you've cooked that marshmallow for so long your stick is about to catch fire."

Snapping out of her daydream, Rhoda instantly pulled the stick from the fire, waving it around and blowing on the marshmallow. Once it was cool enough to touch, she tried to pull it off the stick, but the marshmallow disintegrated into a sticky black mess on her hand. They both laughed until their sides ached.

Once Sadie composed herself, she said what had been on her mind for the past few hours. "You've been kinda quiet tonight," she pointed out while handing her friend a plain handkerchief.

Rhoda accepted the cloth and wiped at the gooey, charred mess on her palm. "*Jah*, I guess I have been."

"Is something bothering you?" Sadie gently pressed, filled with concern for her dear friend.

Rhoda shrugged as she handed the soiled handkerchief back to Sadie. "I'm awful nervous. Tonight will be the first time that Mose and I can spend some time alone." She put her hands to her cheeks, pressing on the hollows. "What if I can't think of anything to say and he thinks I'm boring? What if it's awkward between us?"

Sadie scooted closer to Rhoda and wrapped an arm around her friend. "I reckon you could say nothing the whole ride home, and my twin will still be completely giddy just to spend time with you. I don't think my *bruder* could have chosen a better *aldi*."

Rhoda exhaled quickly through her nose, seeming like she was trying to fight off a smile. "You're exaggerating, but hearing that from someone so close to him does make me feel better. Besides, I'm not his *aldi* yet. This is only our first date." Rhoda pierced a fresh marshmallow onto her stick and dangled it above the flames. "Speaking of courting, I noticed you spending quite a lot of time with that cute Isaac." Rhoda wiggled her auburn eyebrows. "Makes me wonder if you might've found yourself a beau."

Before Sadie could reply, Leah Beiler, another one of Sadie's friends, rushed over to them and took a seat next to Sadie on the log. "Daniel's still not here! He told me he'd be here tonight," she said as she fought to catch her breath, worry etched across her round face.

With the evening almost coming to a close, Leah's beau should have arrived at the Graber farm hours ago. Not wanting to alarm the poor girl, Sadie asked, "Are you sure he isn't around here somewhere? Maybe he's just talking with the menfolk."

Leah shook her head vigorously. "No, he would have come to see me first. I just know that something's wrong!" Her hazel eyes grew shiny with unshed tears. "I'm so worried."

"Of course you are!" Rhoda replied sympathetically, moving to sit on Leah's other side.

"Maybe he took a nap this afternoon and slept right through tonight's activities. You know how Daniel is," Sadie reasoned optimistically. "Remember the time he fell asleep during a church meeting and let out a snore so loud that he woke himself up?"

Leah laughed nervously, her tears spilling down her cheeks. "You're right." She dabbed at the wetness on her face. "He's never done anything like this before, so I'm very concerned."

"Leah, really," Nancy Beiler groaned as she lowered herself onto the adjacent log seat. "Pull yourself together. You shouldn't immediately assume the worst."

Sadie's mouth dropped open at Nancy's curtness toward her own sister. Was she attempting to show tough love, or was she brushing off Leah's legitimate alarm? Sadie focused her attention back on Leah. "Nancy is right. Try not to worry too much. If he doesn't show up within the next few minutes, I'm sure we can ask some of the men to go to Daniel's house and find out where he is." She gingerly placed her hand against Leah's clammy cheek. "If there is anything I can do to help, please let me know."

"*Denki*, Sadie," Leah quickly replied, "but please don't ruin your evening on my account. If you had plans to go for a buggy ride tonight with someone special, do that. If my beau doesn't show up, I'll ask my brother to stop by Daniel's place as he takes his date home."

"That's right," Nancy chimed in with a squeak as she leaned closer to the group. "Daniel will be fine. Besides, I heard that single Sadie isn't single anymore, so she will indeed be out riding tonight with her new beau."

Sadie turned her face away from her peers. Nancy's words were sarcastic and cruel. She knew that she was rapidly becoming the topic of whispers and the subject of pity in their district. Quite honestly, she yearned to remind Nancy that though several of the young men had taken her out, none of them had stuck around for more than one date once they'd realized her true colors. Instead, she sniffled quietly, listening to the fire crackle and snap.

"I suppose it's nice that Isaac fancies you over the other single women, but he's new to the area and hasn't realized how…unique you are," Nancy went on, her insincere smile front and center on her face.

"Of course Sadie caught Isaac's eye," Rhoda replied, sticking up for Sadie as her eyes narrowed into thin slits.

"She's sweet as shoofly pie and she's the best friend anyone could ever hope for."

"It sounds like maybe you're a little jealous, *schwester*," added Leah quietly, as if afraid to disagree with her elder sibling.

"I'm not at all jealous," Nancy chuckled as her hand flew to her chest in self-defense. "Isaac just seems like such a mature fellow with a good head on his shoulders, and Sadie is very free-spirited. What normal Amish fellow would be interested in a grown woman who would sooner be found up a tree or picking wildflowers instead of baking a pie or sewing a quilt for her loved ones?"

"I would."

The four women turned to see Isaac emerging from the darkness with a stern frown across his face. He marched right up to Nancy and glared at her. "I would rather court a woman with a wildfire spirit and a heart the size of Lancaster County than one who's pushy and judgmental. Maybe you should take a lesson from Sadie and learn to treat others with kindness." Nancy's mouth dropped open before she sheepishly rose from her seat and scurried away from the group.

Isaac turned toward the other three women, allowing his expression to soften. "Do you know where I could find Leah Beiler? Some guy named Daniel just showed up, and he's looking for her."

"That's me." Leah stood as relief flooded her face. "Where is he?" Isaac told Leah and she promptly took off to find him.

Finally, Isaac turned to Sadie. "It's getting kind of late," he said with a crooked grin as he extended his hand to her. "Could I give you a ride home?"

Feeling as if she had been rescued from the jaws of

a lion, Sadie smiled sweetly up at Isaac. She accepted his hand, stood from her seat next to Rhoda and bid her friend farewell. As they walked slowly toward the Graber barnyard, where Isaac's horse and buggy were already hitched and ready to go, Sadie marveled at how Isaac's sudden appearance at the campfire had instantly removed the negativity and embarrassment that Nancy had shoveled onto her. He'd let it be known that she was worthy of love, just the way that the Lord had created her to be. A feeling of safety enveloped her like a warm blanket, and at that moment, Sadie knew that she and Isaac would be lifelong friends.

With only the moonlight and a battery-powered buggy headlight guiding their way, Isaac trusted that Shadow would know the road to Sadie's home better than he did. This was his first nighttime outing since moving to Lancaster County, and he was disoriented on the silent country roads, surrounded by the shadows of whispering cornstalks. It was his job to ensure that Sadie was returned home safely, and he needed to see it through.

As Shadow pulled the rig down North Weavertown Road at a steady pace, Isaac attempted to shake off the unsettling feeling that he'd allowed to consume him.

After pitifully grieving for what felt like the longest time, Isaac finally came to accept his fiancée's death, deciding that she wouldn't want him to carry on mournfully for the rest of his days. Still, Daniel's talk of the roadside disaster he'd witnessed before arriving at the gathering was enough to stir up the dust of sorrow that never seemed to fully settle.

"*Denki* for standing up for me tonight" came Sadie's

voice from the passenger's side of the buggy. As gentle as it was, her words still managed to startle Isaac. They hadn't spoken much since leaving the youth gathering, and in that time Isaac had gotten lost in thought.

"You're welcome," he replied, though he wasn't in the mood to have a conversation.

"It made me feel a lot better after Nancy was unkind to me," Sadie went on.

"*Jah*, I guess so."

A few seconds of silence passed before Sadie spoke up again. "Is everything all right, Isaac? You seemed to be enjoying yourself most of the day, at least until you came to save me from Nancy." There was a hint of anxious sadness in Sadie's tone. "Are you maybe wishing you didn't have to take me home tonight?"

Sadie's question tugged on Isaac's heartstrings. "*Nee*, of course not," he replied, sincerely hoping that she was reassured of how much he enjoyed her company. "I'm honored to be your beau and see that you get home safely."

Sadie seemed to mull that over for a spell. "Then why are you being so quiet?"

Isaac heaved a heavy sigh, then began to explain. "While you were talking with your friends, some of the other guys and I were shooting the breeze. When that Daniel fellow showed up, he told us that he'd witnessed a car clip the side of a passing buggy, which flipped the rig, so he stayed to help the family inside."

Sadie gasped. "I hope no one was injured!"

"Thankfully, Daniel reported that everyone in the buggy was unharmed."

"And you're feeling down because of this story Daniel told?"

Isaac chewed on his tongue, dreading reliving the memories that he was about to share. "I think it's time I tell you the full story of what caused *Mamm* and me to come to Bird-in-Hand for an extended visit." Even though the night air was pleasantly cool, Isaac shivered as if a bitter winter wind had just whipped through the buggy.

"I was once betrothed. Her name was Rebecca King, and I loved her ever since we were *kinner*. She was smart, beautiful and very kind." A lump formed in Isaac's throat that he could not swallow. "Sorry," he apologized as he choked back a sob. He cleared his throat several times to keep his tears at bay. As Isaac gripped Shadow's reins, he felt Sadie's cool, soft hand remove one of his from his white-knuckled grasp on the leather ropes. Tenderly, she took his strong, callused hand and held it in hers. In the light of the moon, Isaac could see that she was gazing at him with a calm but concerned smile.

Sadie's comforting touch effortlessly pierced through even his strongest barrier, and Isaac could no longer restrain his tears. "Rebecca wasn't just my *aldi*, she was my whole world. She was a part of our family even though we never got the chance to get married." His voice cracked, and he tried to regain his composure. "She was close to *Mamm*, too, and they visited with each other every Friday. They would bake all kinds of different pies, cakes...you name it. Seemed like they found a new recipe every week, and the rest of our household sure did enjoy that." Isaac grinned somberly at the·memory.

Sadie continued to hold his hand as Isaac went on. "One afternoon, Rebecca was already on her way to visit *Mamm* when a severe storm rolled up. I wish... I wish she'd done the sensible thing and turned back to go home when the weather got bad." Briefly letting go of the reins, Isaac wiped his eyes. He took a shaky breath and exhaled through pursed lips. Taking hold of Shadow's reins with his free hand, he sighed and went on.

"*Mamm* saw that it had started to rain, so she ran out to our front porch, where we have our clothesline attached. She was taking the dry laundry off the line before it could get soaked when she saw Rebecca coming up the lane on her scooter, right in the middle of the worst of the storm."

Isaac paused, wondering why he was suddenly spilling his soul to Sadie, who had still not let go of his hand.

He'd lost his place in the story and mentally backtracked to where he'd left off. "A car was coming up the road. The driver was distracted by their phone, or so I was told. They were speeding and ran into Rebecca." Isaac heard Sadie sharply inhale, but she didn't interrupt him. "The impact threw her into our yard. Seeing what happened, *Mamm* ran to help Rebecca."

Isaac was silent for several more minutes, as was Sadie. Without realizing he was doing so, he gripped her hand tighter, needing her support.

"*Daed* and I were in the woodworking shop when we heard *Mamm*'s screams. We found *Mamm* kneeling beside Rebecca, wailing uncontrollably. I took off on foot toward the phone shanty at the end of our lane, and I called for help. An ambulance had already arrived by the time I ran back. The paramedics told us that Rebecca had died on impact." He gulped, swallowing against the bitter bile rising in his throat. "*Mamm* was barely able to tell my *daed* what had happened, but when she did, he later relayed the information to me. After she recounted what she'd seen, *Mamm* stopped speaking, and hasn't said a single word since that day."

"I'm so sorry to hear about all the pain that you and your *mamm* have suffered," Sadie whispered, gently touching the side of Isaac's face and wiping away his tears. "From what you've told me, it sounds like Rebecca was a woman after the Lord's own heart. No wonder you and your *mamm* cared for her so much!"

"*Jah*, she was. So when Daniel told us about the accident he'd witnessed tonight, it reminded me of that awful time in my life, in my family's lives. Rainy days are painful, too, since it stirs up memories of a day that we'd all rather forget."

Sadie squeezed Isaac's hand. "I understand. I can't imagine your loss." As if carrying the weight of their conversation, she took a great breath. "After *Gott* sent the rain to Noah, he put his rainbow in the sky. Don't get caught up in the storm clouds, because there's still hope for something beautiful on the other side of the storm."

Stunned by Sadie's gracious wisdom, Isaac suddenly felt lighter. "I know you're right. The initial sting of grief has lessened over time, and I know Rebecca would be pleased that I'm making a life for myself, and taking care of *Mamm* too."

Sadie seemed to ponder this last point. "So you and your *mamm* moved to Bird-in-Hand to encourage her healing with new surroundings?"

"That's right," Isaac confirmed, turning Shadow down the Stolzfuses' long driveway. He slowed the gelding's pace to a walk, trying to prolong this moment with Sadie. He wasn't ready to say good-night, not when he'd just bared the entirety of his soul to her.

There was something mighty calming about her honest presence, and though he was slightly embarrassed, Isaac didn't regret falling to pieces in front of this lovely, unique woman.

They made pleasant small talk until they neared the white Stolzfus barn, where Sadie requested to be dropped off so the noise of the buggy wouldn't wake the sleeping household.

"Sadie," Isaac called quietly to stop her as she exited the buggy. "I...uh... I'm real glad to have spent time with you today." He felt his heart start to beat a little faster as the moonlight illuminated Sadie's lovely eyes.

A smile bloomed on Sadie's face. "*Jah*, me too. I'll look forward to seeing you again real soon." She thanked Isaac for the ride and scurried toward her father's two-story stone farmhouse.

"Good night," Isaac replied, wondering if the twinkle in Sadie's eyes had been a reflection of the moonlight or perhaps a touch more. He felt something almost magnetic growing between him and Sadie. Maybe she'd felt the same emotional bond. After tonight's conversation, Isaac had to admit that he felt closer to Sadie than anyone else in his life, and he wondered how he'd managed to survive these past two years without her.

Chapter Seven

After the noon meal was eaten and the dishes were washed, Sadie padded down the dirt buggy lane that connected neighboring farms with a plate of freshly baked chocolate chip cookies in hand. On this cloudless day, Sadie was headed to Miriam Fisher's house. She'd baked the cookies for Isaac as a symbol of their friendship, though her true motive was to ensure that Isaac was in better spirits. Sadie was the least talented baker in her family, so the cookies were lumpy. The one she'd sampled had tasted just fine, so she hoped Isaac and his family would enjoy them anyway.

Continuing down the lane, Sadie recalled last night's surprising turn of events. She'd never imagined that she would have a beau to drive her home from the youth gathering. It was equally surprising that Isaac had shed some tears in front of her. The story of his fiancée's death, and how it affected his poor mother, pained Sadie. No wonder he wasn't interested in finding a wife again, Sadie thought as the buggy lane led her to the edge of Orchard Road.

When she arrived at the Fisher house, Sadie noticed

Mim seated on a bench under a weeping willow tree with a small group of children at her feet, both Amish and *Englisch* alike. Children from the area often flocked to Mim as if she were the neighborhood grandmother, and she clearly enjoyed their company as much as the children enjoyed hers. The dear woman was animatedly recounting the Bible story of Jonah and the whale, and the eager listeners watched intently, with some of their little mouths hanging open.

Sadie waved to get her attention. "Sorry to interrupt your story," she greeted Mim and the group of children as she approached. "Sounds like a whale of a tale." Mim chuckled at Sadie's pun.

"*Jah*, Mim's telling us about how the Lord sent a great big fish to swallow up Jonah when he was running away!" Leroy Mast, a child from one of the neighboring farms, keenly reported to Sadie, his miniature straw hat tumbling off his copper-colored hair when he mentioned the whale's size.

Sadie giggled. "That's one of my favorite stories." Smiling at all of the children, she gently tapped the tip of Leroy's freckled nose. "We always get in trouble when we run from *Gott*'s will."

"*Ach*, Sadie." Leroy gleefully squirmed. "That may be so, but I ain't never heard of anyone getting swallowed by a fish 'cause of it!"

This caused a loud burst of laughter to ripple through the group of children. Mim and Sadie also chortled at the honest remark from young Leroy. When things settled down, Sadie explained that she was searching for Isaac.

"He just left for the farm supply store," Mim regretfully informed Sadie. "You can leave it on the kitchen table and I'll let him know you stopped by when he returns."

"*Denki*, Mim. I'll do just that." Sadie bid goodbye to the caring woman and the children gathered at her feet. She bounded up the porch stairs, walked through the front door and entered Mim's tidy kitchen, where the scents of cinnamon and apples filled the air. She sniffed at the enticing aroma as she placed the plate of cookies on the kitchen table. As she turned and headed for the door, in the adjacent sitting room she saw a frail-looking woman seated in a rocking chair that faced a window.

Sadie was startled by someone else's presence in the otherwise empty house. After meeting the woman during a church meeting, Sadie instantly recognized Isaac's mother, Ruth. She longed to visit with her, wishing so desperately to heal her hurting heart, but she reminded herself that only the Lord could truly provide healing. Was it wise to disturb the bereaved woman, even if only to say hello?

Ignoring the initial hesitation she felt, Sadie walked into the room and gently knocked on the light green wall so she wouldn't frighten her. Ruth looked up from her chair, a bit of surprise crossing her face.

"Hello, Ruth." Sadie spoke softly as she approached the deeply grieved woman. "It's me, Sadie Stolzfus. It's nice to see you again." Sadie carefully tempered the cheer in her tone, wanting to avoid overwhelming Isaac's fragile mother.

Ruth's bluish-gray eyes glanced toward Sadie, but she didn't make eye contact. She didn't reply, and Sadie didn't expect her to. The woman's golden hair, similar to Sadie's own, seemed dulled, causing Sadie to wonder if the woman's lackluster locks and thin frame were a side effect of the trauma she'd experienced.

Sadie took a seat on the sofa next to Ruth's rocking chair. When she was settled, Ruth returned her gaze to her folded hands. "We're awful glad to have you and Isaac here in Bird-in-Hand with us," Sadie ventured truthfully. She was tempted to ask how Ruth liked living in this part of the country, but quickly nixed the idea. It was probably better not to ask any questions, she decided, worried that Ruth might feel pressured to respond.

Realizing that she hadn't offered Ruth a cookie, Sadie excused herself to retrieve the plate she'd left in the kitchen. When she returned, she presented the strange-looking cookies to Ruth. "I made these for Isaac." Sadie held the plate closer for Ruth's inspection. "They look a little funny, but they taste all right. Would you like to try one?"

Ruth shook her head ever so slightly. "That's okay," Sadie reassured her. "I'll leave them right here in case you change your mind, but I think I'm going to have one now." Sadie popped a cookie into her mouth as she once again seated herself next to Ruth. As she chewed, Sadie noticed a book about gardening lying against Ruth's chair. "May I have a look at this?" Of course, Ruth didn't respond, but Sadie didn't feel right about picking it up without asking for her permission.

She waited for a few seconds and when Ruth's disposition didn't change, Sadie reached for the hardcover book and thumbed through the glossy pages. "I enjoy gardening too. I've worked at our local greenhouse since I was fifteen." She continued to flip through the book and noticed that the first page of the chapter about perennials was dog-eared. "I love perennials too. They're downright faithful, ain't so? Blooming year after year just as sure as the sun rises each morning."

Sadie noticed when Ruth leaned closer ever so slightly. Her visibly tired eyes settled on the page Sadie had turned to. Seeing this, Sadie scooted over to one side of the couch and patted the cushion next to her. "Come sit by me!"

To Sadie's pleasant surprise, Ruth slowly rose from her chair and took a spot next to her on the sofa. When she was seated, Sadie handed Ruth the left side of the book as she held the right. She chattered on and on, pointing out different plants, describing some as stubborn and others as easy-breezy.

Sadie noticed that Ruth's gaze lingered on a picture of purple asters. She ran her fingers over the picture, and for the slightest moment, her dull eyes looked more blue than gray.

"You like those flowers? Those are one of my favorites too," Sadie exclaimed, taking hold of Ruth's hand, giving it a few light squeezes. "I knew that you and I would be friends."

For the first time since Sadie had introduced herself, Ruth's eyes met hers. They were drained, but Sadie thought maybe they were smiling at her. All anyone really needed was an understanding heart to hold their hand, and Sadie was honored to be that person for Ruth.

The screen door squeaked open as Mim entered her kitchen. She did a double take when she saw Sadie and Ruth sitting on the sofa together as if they were lifelong friends. "Sadie, I didn't know you were still here. I sent the *kinner* home since it looks like it could start making down any minute now."

Sadie's brow furrowed at Mim's mention of rain. She leaned around Ruth to glimpse out the window and saw dark clouds gathering on the horizon. "I guess that's the Lord nudging me to hurry on home."

Mim insisted that she wait until the rain passed, but Sadie declined, informing Mim that it was her duty to prepare an afternoon snack for her younger sister, Susannah, while the girl finished her chores. "There'll be a mighty price to pay if I don't have something on the table for her." Mim's laughter reverberated through the house at Sadie's implication, though the sound caused Ruth to wince.

Sadie stood, feeling a strain on her arm. Ruth was still clutching her hand, like a child who was afraid to be separated from her mother in a crowd. Filled with compassion for the dear woman, Sadie squatted to her eye level. "Thank you for spending some time with me. I'll come back to visit real soon."

Ruth nodded with just the slightest head movement, accepting Sadie's kind words. Sadie squeezed Ruth's hand a few times, then headed for the door, Mim scurrying behind her.

When the two women stepped outside onto the covered porch, Mim closed both the heavy wooden door and the screen door behind her. "*Denki* for taking time out of your day for my *schwester*," Mim sighed. "Poor thing is so gloomy that I fear she scares some folks away."

A puzzled expression swept across Sadie's face. "Why would anyone be afraid of someone who's suffering?"

Mim beamed warmly at Sadie as she gently cradled

her palm against her young friend's cheek. "Because, dear one, not all farmers know how to tend black sheep."

Sadie bobbed her head, understanding the proverb. She looked down at the ground as an idea formed in her mind. "We were looking through her gardening book, and she seemed to enjoy it. Do you think she'd like to plant some flowers with me?"

Mim shook her graying head. "Awful nice of you, but I can't imagine that she'd willingly go anywhere for the sake of socializing. It takes a whole lot of tender coaxing just to get her to attend the biweekly church services."

Sadie mulled that over, twisting one of her *kapp* ribbons around her finger. "She doesn't have to come to my house. What if I brought some flowers from the greenhouse over here? You think she'd be willing to come outside and help me plant them?"

Mim shrugged. "We do have a flower bed that's been empty so far this year. I suspect you know not to get your hopes up when it comes to Ruth, but it can't hurt to give it a try."

That evening, after running some errands, caring for all of Mim's animals and giving Shadow a thorough bath, Isaac entered the fragrant kitchen. Hearing the screen door shut behind him, Mim grinned and pushed her foggy glasses from the tip of her nose to the bridge. "You must have known that supper's almost ready, *jah*?"

"If my brain didn't tell me, my stomach sure would have." Isaac patted his middle like he always had since his boyhood days.

"There's a plate of chocolate chip cookies over on the counter." Mim jerked her head in the direction of the sweet snacks. "Better have a few of those, so you don't bite my hands off when I put the food on the table."

Isaac sarcastically scoffed at his aunt, who threw her head back in laughter. Then he moseyed over to the plate of cookies and was taken aback to see that they looked less than tasty. Some of them were tiny and nearly burnt black. Others were orb-like, and couldn't have possibly been baked thoroughly. One seemed particularly lumpy, and another seemed like it had no chocolate chips at all.

Bewildered, Isaac stared at the plate. "Mim, did you bake these today?"

"No, Sadie Stolzfus came over a few hours ago and brought them for you as a gift." Mim plated a few freshly baked dinner rolls and brought them to the table. "Looks like you may have found yourself a sweetheart here in Bird-in-Hand after all."

"*Jah*, I have been seeing Sadie," Isaac admitted, though he chose not to mention that their courtship was merely one of convenience.

"I thought that might be the case," Mim responded in a singsong voice. "Anyway, your *mamm* and I ate some of them, and we're both still alive."

"Well, I suppose I'll try just one." Isaac selected the largest cookie, sniffed it hesitantly, then took a bite. Instantly he was surprised by the delicious flavor. Once he gobbled down the first cookie, he reached for two more.

"Don't eat so much that you spoil your supper," Mim chided him, flicking her dishcloth against his arm. "Go get your *mamm* and let her know supper's ready, would you?"

Isaac nodded as he finished eating the cookies. "Sure

will, but who knows if she'll actually eat anything. She picks at meals like a bird."

"Well, after Sadie spent some time with her this afternoon, your *mamm* perked up so much that she ate a few of Sadie's cookies. I don't think I've seen her snack since you two moved into this house."

Isaac spun around, feeling his heart rate increase. "Sadie spent time with *Mamm*?"

"*Jah*, I was outside reading to some *kinner* when she stopped by to drop off her cookies. I went inside, oh, about a half hour later. She and your *mamm* were like two peas in a pod, sitting together and looking through that gardening book."

Isaac smiled broadly, his heart warmed at the image that Mim planted in his mind's eye. "*Mamm* didn't seem overwhelmed? Sadie can be…you know…a lot."

Mim stifled a laugh, putting her fingers to her lips. "From what I saw, Sadie's quirks might be the perfect remedy for your *mamm*'s condition."

Both comforted and intrigued by Mim's response, Isaac gazed back down at the plate of Sadie's unusual cookies. Not only had the strange girl comforted him during his painful memories, but she also had some sort of positive effect on his sorrowful mother. With an overwhelming need to see Sadie again, Isaac decided to take a ride over to the Stolzfus place after supper.

"There's a visitor downstairs who's asking to see you."

Sadie opened her eyes when she heard a knock on her bedroom door and her sister's high voice. She'd decided to take a short rest on her bed before it was time for the evening milking, but she hadn't planned on falling asleep. She rubbed her eyes and rose to meet Susannah at the door. "Someone's here for me? Who is it?"

"It's that fellow that we met at church on Sunday," Susannah gushed with rosy cheeks. "The same one who brought you home from the singing. If I didn't know better, I'd say that he's your beau."

Sadie felt a flutter of excitement in her chest that outweighed her annoyance that Susannah had stayed up late last night to spy on her. Knowing she would need to have a talk with her thirteen-year-old sister later, Sadie burst out of her bedroom with Susannah on her heels. "Did Isaac say what he wanted?" Sadie asked, taking the stairs two at a time. She hadn't expected a visit from him today, and as thrilling as his sudden arrival was, she also worried that something might be wrong.

"*Nee*, just asked if you were home."

When the sisters reached the bottom of the stairs, Sadie thought she would faint at the sight of Isaac standing there, right in the middle of the kitchen. When he turned toward her, he smiled warmly. Since he was unmarried, he was always clean-shaven, but a small amount of stubble on the lower half of his face gave him an attractive, masculine appearance. "Hiya, Sadie. Could we chat privately for a spell?"

Sadie glanced at her curious sister and couldn't help but grin. "*Jah*, of course. Follow me." She led Isaac out of the house and to an iron bench between a pair of weeping willows that looked over the small stream that wove through the farm. Though there would be an hour or two of daylight left, the moon was already high in the purplish sky. When they were seated side by side, far away from eavesdropping ears, Sadie finally felt free to speak. "Wasn't expecting to see you today, but I'm glad you're here. Is everything all right?"

Isaac took off his straw hat, hung it on one of his knees, then turned to smile at Sadie. "*Jah*, I wanted to thank you for your cookies."

Sadie smiled back. "You came all the way over here just to say *denki*?"

Isaac's head bobbed. "*Jah*, they were mighty tasty."

Sadie's eyes widened in surprise. "Really? They tasted all right to me, but I was afraid you wouldn't eat them since they were so odd-looking."

"*Mamm*, Mim and I polished them all off. I wish there were more!" After Sadie stopped chuckling at Isaac's enthusiasm, he went on. "I wish you had more faith in your abilities, Sadie. The cookies were delicious, even if they did look a bit strange. I'm sure with some practice they could look as good as they taste."

Sadie shrugged. Others had encouraged her to hone her cooking and baking skills, but since these were of no interest to her, she saw no need. "I don't think so. Besides, folks know I'm somewhat useless in the kitchen, so only the bravest souls would be willing to try anything I make."

Isaac studied her intently, as if he cared very deeply about their conversation. "Different doesn't mean useless. I enjoyed your baking, and I think you should keep practicing."

Sadie knew Isaac's gentle coaxing was only for her benefit. She was a grown woman, and it was about time for her to start putting more care into household duties. Besides, how could she turn Isaac down, especially with the cute way he smiled at her? "I'll think about it," Sadie finally agreed with a wink.

Isaac's smile widened. He leaned forward, then said, "Speaking of *Mamm*, I heard you spent some time with her today."

Sadie nervously chewed on her bottom lip. "*Jah*, I spent some time with her talking about gardening. Did I overstep a boundary?"

"*Nee*, not at all," Isaac replied, much to Sadie's relief. "In fact, *Mamm* perked up and ate more than usual at suppertime. Seems like your visit had a very positive effect on her." He paused, clasping his hands together and staring at the neatly manicured grass beneath their feet. "I was just wondering how you managed to break through to her. I mean, you're practically a stranger to her, yet you were able to get her to eat a decent meal when no one else could."

Sadie grinned, pleased to hear that Isaac's mother was feeling a bit better. "I don't know. I just talked to her." She gazed into the gentle water that babbled over the stones in the stream, thinking of how to best describe what was in her heart. "Maybe she just needed someone who wouldn't expect anything from her. Maybe she needs to just be who she is right now, with no pressure to change."

Isaac nodded, taking in everything Sadie had to say. "Well, you could be right. As her family, we're very anxious to see her get back to her old self. I'll have to try to give her the time and space she needs." He let out a small sigh, then inhaled some of the cool evening air scented by a recently cut and raked hayfield. "Well," he said as he placed his hat back on his head, "I better get going. I just wanted to stop by to say thanks for the cookies and for spending time with my *mudder*."

After Isaac climbed back into his buggy and headed

for home, Sadie lingered outdoors for a while. She took several deep breaths, reminding herself that Isaac valued their unique friendship. And that it was only a friendship, despite his sweet smiles and looks. Despite her growing interest in the handsome newcomer, she forced herself to remember that their courtship was only pretend.

Chapter Eight

Sadie pulled her small wagon behind her as she journeyed to visit with Isaac's mother, glad that she could make use of the favorite childhood toy. The little green wagon, crafted by her father nearly two decades ago, was full of bright red geraniums, gold marigolds and bubblegum-pink petunias. Since it was the middle of August, the stock of summer flowers at the greenhouse was significantly dwindling and being replaced with infant autumnal plants. Since these colorful summer flowers were part of an end-of-the-season sale, she'd purchased them for barely a few dollars after her employee discount was added in.

With the wagon wheels squeaking behind her, Sadie hummed a hymn to herself as she walked down Mim's driveway, then around to the back of the old farmhouse. Ruth was sitting on the covered porch, sheltered from the sweltering noon sun. While most of the Amish women in the area wore dresses made from solid-colored fabric ranging in shades of green, blue and purple, Ruth's dress was a mousy color and seemed two sizes too large for her.

"Hello," Sadie called with a friendly wave, stopping at the base of the porch stairs. "Look what I've brought for you!" She turned and gestured to the wagonload of flowers. "I was hoping that you might want to plant them with me."

Ruth leaned forward slightly, peering through the whitewashed spokes that supported the porch railing. When her gaze reached the plants, her eyes brightened, but she didn't get up.

In respect for Ruth's state, Sadie slowly ascended the steps, then peeked into the open window. "Mim, it's Sadie!"

A few seconds later, Mim came to the window and peered outside, smiling to beat the band. "Hiya, Sadie. Isaac's out in the barn, if you came looking for him." She held a mixing bowl in one hand and a wooden spoon in the other, never stopping her stirring.

Sadie felt her cheeks flush. "I'm here to see Ruth," she replied, though the possibility of running into Isaac was certainly a bonus. "I brought some flowers. Is it all right if we make use of your flower bed today?"

Mim's smile faded slightly upon hearing Sadie's request and she stopped stirring whatever she was whipping up in her mixing bowl. She and Sadie gazed knowingly at each other, both understanding that Ruth would probably refuse to participate. Eventually, Mim bobbed her head and resumed her stirring. "That sounds right nice. I haven't gotten to it this year, and the old patch of dirt could use some prettying up."

Sadie thanked Mim, then bounded over to Ruth, the wooden porch creaking beneath her steps. "C'mon, Ruth, let's go get these flowers planted in their new home." She extended her hand to the seated, troubled woman, patiently wondering if she would accept. Ruth weakly took Sadie's hand and rose from her seat with the slowness of a woman twice her age. Hand in hand, the two women padded down the porch steps and onto the neatly mowed grass. Sadie used her free hand to grasp the wagon handle and led Ruth to the large circular plot of dirt in the house's side yard. Ruth certainly wasn't a large woman, but Sadie still felt heaviness as Ruth linked arms with her. Sadie wondered if perhaps she was feeling the weight of Ruth's depressed spirit, and she hoped that the sight of the new flowers would cheer the woman up.

"Would you like me to bring your chair over here?" Sadie offered, wanting to be absolutely sure that Ruth felt at ease. Ruth didn't reply, of course, but she cautiously lowered herself into the grass at the edge of the flower bed. Much less gracefully, Sadie dropped to her knees and grinned at Ruth. "I'd rather sit in the grass too! There's something good for the soul about being so close to *Gott*'s earth, don't you think?"

Crawling next to her wagon, Sadie retrieved a few of the flowers and her gardening tools. She crawled back to Ruth and placed the tools and flowers between them so Ruth could choose to join in without pressure. Sadie reached for her handheld cultivator and began digging into the hardened dirt, which hadn't been broken since the previous year's spring. She continued loosening the soil, disrupting the cement-like top layer of dirt in front of them. "Seems like the Lord's earth matches His people, ain't so? Sometimes there's a hard exterior that protects all the good stuff hidden away under it." She glanced over her shoulder, watching Ruth's unchanging brooding expression.

Once the dormant flower bed had been fully tilled by hand, Sadie dug her hands into the rich, moist soil, plucking away a few rocks and weeds. "I guess I'm guilty of it myself." She leaned back on her heels, wiping her forehead with her forearm. "People expect certain things of girls my age, things that I don't know if I'll ever live up to." Sadie looked up, closing her eyes and letting the sun's warmth caress her cheeks. When she opened her eyes, she looked toward Ruth, who gazed back at her sympathetically.

Sadie covered Ruth's clammy hand with her dirt-covered one, hoping Isaac's mother wouldn't mind her muddy touch. "Sometimes we get so done in by expectations, or worries, or grief, that our ground hardens right up and not a single flower can grow." At this, Ruth looked away, her hand stirring under Sadie's. "If we allow our Heavenly Father, the ultimate gardener, to till up our hardened hearts, He can plant a whole new garden, one that doesn't turn brown and wither away during difficult seasons. Then life can once again become as vibrant as these flowers."

Ruth sniffled, using her black apron to dab at the corners of her eyes. She looked back to Sadie, her eyes shiny and the corners of her mouth turned slightly upward. She reached out, touching the side of Sadie's face, so gently that Sadie barely felt Ruth's fingertips brush against her cheek. Sadie smiled in return, hoping with all her might that her words were of some encouragement to the woman whose heart wept more than anyone's ever should.

A few moments later, Ruth pushed the sleeves of her dress up to her elbows and plunged her hands into the dirt, letting them sink in. Wrist-deep in the soil,

Ruth worked her fingers into the earth, staring into the brown, soft ground with childlike wonder. Perhaps that soil was the first thing she'd allowed herself to feel, other than sorrow, in a very long time, Sadie thought to herself.

Isaac stood next to the barn's side door with a small can of white paint in one hand and a brush in the other. He took a few steps back to survey the work he had done. The fresh paint job seemed a bit uneven. He reached high to add another coat to an area where the paint seemed too thin. Honestly, he was disappointed that his work wasn't living up to his usual high standards.

What was going on with him today? He glanced over his shoulder to steal another peek at Sadie as she and his mother knelt near a previously barren flower bed, planting a variety of colorful flowers together. He could see that color was returning to his mother's pale face, and a gorgeous smile was blooming on Sadie's face. As he took in the scene, Sadie looked up from the flowers, beaming at him. Caught staring, Isaac sheepishly smiled back, then quickly returned to his painting.

When the second coat of paint had been completed, Isaac decided that he could use a break. He chuckled to himself, knowing that he could normally work much longer before needing a rest, but Sadie's nearby presence beckoned for him to visit with her. He made quick work of rinsing his paintbrush and hammering the paint can's lid back into place, then hurried toward the flower bed.

"Wow, you two really spruced up this old heap of dirt," Isaac declared, planting his hands on his hips. He whistled as he took in the sight of the freshly planted geraniums, marigolds and petunias. "Never seen Mim's yard look so pretty."

Sadie grinned, then looked away, as if his indirect compliment had caught her off guard. She turned to Ruth and patted her hand. "Well, the Lord created these lovely flowers. All your *mamm* and I did was plant them, and we had a real *gut* time doing so!"

Ruth gazed at Sadie lovingly. Though her lips didn't form a full smile, Isaac noticed that the corners of her mouth were turned slightly upward, and her eyes had more life in them than they'd had since Rebecca's passing.

"I agree with my nephew," Mim called as she approached with a jug in one hand and several paper cups in the other. "When it was just me living here alone, I couldn't find time to plant beautiful flowers." She took a moment to catch her breath when she reached the flower bed. "I appreciate you two bringing some color to my yard, as well as all the repairs you are making in the barn, Isaac, though you best clean yourself up before stepping foot back into my house!"

From her seat on the ground, Sadie looked up at Isaac and started to laugh. "Looks like you've gained some freckles since I've seen you last!"

Isaac curiously reached up to touch his face and felt some small, tacky paint drops on his forehead. "I guess I got a bit overzealous with my painting."

"You sure did," Mim replied, "which is why I brought some meadow tea out. I'm sure you could all use a cool drink." She handed a cup to her sister, Sadie and Isaac, then filled each with the refreshing beverage. "Why don't you all come sit on the porch and get out of the sun for a spell?"

Everyone agreed. Isaac was pleased to see that Sadie helped his mother up from her place on the ground and walked at her slow place until they were seated in the shade of the porch. It was clear that she cared a great deal about those around her, and Isaac found that to be a very attractive quality.

"Mim, speaking of the barn, I wonder if you'd ever considered building a larger one," Isaac asked as he gently glided back and forth in one of the white wicker rocking chairs.

Mim's forehead creased as she sipped on what little meadow tea was left in her cup. "What for?"

"The repairs I've been making out there got me thinking that the building is awful small. It's really only a stable. There's just enough room for your two cows, your horse and mine. You have a good-sized parcel of land here. If you decided to farm it, you'd need a lot more barn space."

"*Ach*, definitely not. I'm getting up in years and have no intention of starting to farm now," Mim replied with a wave of her hand.

"I could farm it for you," Isaac offered hopefully. "If we added on to your barn, I could get started next spring." He glanced over at Sadie, who looked back at him with a twinkle in her eye. They'd discussed his dream of making a living as a farmer several times, but with his job at his father's woodworking shop, the chance of that was slim to none.

"I don't think so, Isaac. Who knows how long you and my *schwester* will be staying here with me. It would be a shame to build a big barn only to have you two move back home, and then I would have no use for it."

Isaac wanted nothing more than for his mother to recover from her severe depression, but the thought of heading home to Indiana didn't sit well with him. He glanced over again at Sadie, noticing that Mim's words had also caused her to frown. Was she disappointed that Isaac wouldn't be getting the opportunity to farm as he wanted, or was she also upset by the idea of him eventually returning home? Bird-in-Hand was starting to feel like where he belonged, and Isaac knew that this feeling was a result of the unique bond he had with Sadie.

"Mim—" Sadie suddenly spoke up "—what if you were to just build on to the existing barn? Then you'd have a place for visitors' horses to rest without having to wait outside, still hitched to their buggies. You could also store your buggy in there to keep it out of the elements. We could have a partial barn raising, which would be much less expensive than starting from scratch!"

"Jah," Isaac agreed, excited by Sadie's suggestion. "I'd even be willing to split the cost of the lumber with you. Plus, it would be a nice get-together for the community before harvesttime."

Mim smiled coyly, her eyes darting between Sadie and Isaac. "If I didn't know better, I'd think that you two planned this attack on me." Both Sadie and Isaac opened their mouths to deny her insinuation, but Mim held up her hand to stop them. "Spread the word! In a week or two, we'll have ourselves a partial barn raising."

Sadie and Isaac both let out a celebratory whoop. Mim clapped her hands at their joyful reaction, and even Isaac's mother seemed to be pleased with the idea.

When Mim changed the topic of conversation to a letter she'd received from a cousin, Isaac had trouble focusing on what his aunt was saying. He couldn't help but look at Sadie. He'd never had such an instant connection with someone, not even Rebecca.

Isaac shooed the intimate thoughts from his mind. He wouldn't allow himself to fall for Sadie. His heart loved one woman, Rebecca, and losing her felt like a knife had been stabbed into his chest. He refused to put himself in a position where he might endure heartbreak for a second time in his life. Sadie was a dear friend, though he feared that he'd already started to view her as more.

Chapter Nine

After a vivid sunrise, the grayish-blue haze of a humid August morning draped over Bird-in-Hand, the oppressive sticky air making it difficult for man and beast to rise from slumber. Despite the sticky weather, Isaac and Mim were up and completing their daily chores before the rooster's first crow. The day of the barn raising had arrived, and there was plenty to be done before folks started arriving.

Isaac and his *aentie* had just finished setting up some folding tables to place refreshments on when the first horses and buggies arrived. Isaac helped the male guests unhitch their horses and led them to a nearby fenced-in pasture, while the women followed Mim into the house, where they would work on sewing a quilt until it was time to prepare lunch for the workers. Children played together in several groups, buzzing around Mim's backyard like swarms of honeybees. By nine o'clock, it seemed like every Amish family living in Bird-in-Hand had arrived, but there was one specific family that Isaac was especially eager to see.

The Stolzfus clan was one of the last families to arrive. When Sadie stepped out of her family's buggy, the sight of her nearly took Isaac's breath away. She wore a green dress, which perfectly matched the color of her eyes. Her thick, golden hair was pulled into a low traditional bun and mostly hidden beneath her *kapp*. Even dressed so plainly, she looked downright lovely.

Isaac dashed to greet them all, taking a moment to shake hands with Sadie's father, Amos, and her mother, Anna. He also greeted Mose, who had brought along his toolbox. Susannah, Sadie's younger sister, bid a quick hello to Isaac before hurrying off to join a group of girls who were giggling among themselves in a tight cluster.

Glad to have a moment alone with Sadie, Isaac glanced down and noticed that she was holding a pie. "Is that an apple pie?" he asked.

Sadie glanced at the pie and shrugged. "It is. I'm a bit *naerfich*. I've never baked anything for a large gathering before." Her shoulders sagged as if in premature defeat. "Hope I don't make a fool of myself when this is served."

It hurt Isaac to see Sadie looking so unsure of herself. She was clearly stepping out of her comfort zone, and although pride was a sin, he couldn't help but feel proud of her for putting more time and effort into a task that she didn't particularly enjoy. Wanting to encourage her, Isaac said, "You put love into everything you do, so how could this pie not be as sweet as you are?"

Sadie's eyes widened as she gazed up at him. She was about to say something but someone shouted from the barnyard. "*Kumme*, Isaac! Time's a-wasting!"

Isaac's cheeks flushed pink, feeling embarrassed by his words. "I better get to work. We've got half a barn to build," he replied, rubbing his hands together briskly.

"You better hurry to the tables at lunchtime, since I'm sure lots of folks will be clambering to get a piece of this questionable pie," Sadie called after him, her delightful sarcasm causing Isaac to laugh out loud.

"Sadie, *kumme* work on this quilt with us," Anna beckoned to her daughter, motioning for her to join the group.

"I'll be right there," Sadie sighed, resigned to the fact that her place was at the quilting frame, at least for that day. She stood with her nose nearly pressed against one of the windows, watching the sea of men buzz around the frame of the barn's new addition. Some of the bravest fellows even inched along the wooden beams where the roof would soon be built. Though she had been to several barn raisings during her twenty-one years of life, she never ceased to be dazzled by how quickly a structure could be built. In only a few hours, the shape of the building's addition had been erected, nearly tripling the size of the original barn. The chorus of hammers banging wooden pegs into place reminded Sadie of a herd of stampeding horses, and she found all the construction activity to be fascinating.

"I think my oldest *dochder* would rather have a hammer in her hand than a quilting needle," Anna said to no one in particular as she worked on her portion of the quilt, her needle flying effortlessly in and out of the fabric.

"Could be that Sadie would rather spend her day outside watching a certain young man who's working on that barn," Mim replied, peering over her glasses, which rested on the edge of her nose.

Ruth, who was seated beside her sister, peeked up

at Sadie, then exchanged knowing glances with Anna and Mim. Sadie thought she spotted the start of a grin forming on Ruth's lips, but it quickly faded away. A few muffled chuckles escaped from some of the other ladies seated around the quilting frame.

"I know when I'm being teased, and I don't like it one bit," Sadie declared, planting her hands on her hips. She tried her best to muster a serious face, but she couldn't hide the smile that felt like it was bursting through. Truthfully, she enjoyed the lighthearted banter from the dear women in this community, and she was glad to be part of a church family that cared for her.

"*Ach*, it's a *mamm*'s job to tease her *dochder*, and keep her nose in her *kinner*'s business," Anna replied, looking up from her sewing to give her daughter a wink. "Why don't you sit yourself down and work on this quilt with us?"

Though she could quickly think of dozens of other things that she would rather do instead of quilting, Sadie forced herself over to the quilting frame and took a seat between her mother and Ruth. After Ruth handed her some thread and a needle, and her mother explained the portion of the quilt that they had been assigned to, Sadie set to work, doing her best to sew neat, even stitches.

"Speaking of that special man," Anna continued, "I've noticed some changes in you ever since you and Isaac started courting."

"Like what?" Sadie asked, focusing so much on her stitching that she forgot to blink, causing her eyes to burn.

"You've always been my sweet, happy *maedel*, ever since you were little. But since you've been spending time with Isaac, I've noticed that you've been even more chipper." Anna giggled quietly, looking up from her sewing to grin at her daughter. "Can't remember a time when you've had a constant smile on your face from sunup 'til sundown."

"*Jah*, your *mamm*'s right," Mim agreed as she snipped a piece of thread. "You fairly glow, Sadie. Just between us," she said, lowering her voice as she leaned closer to her young friend, "Isaac's had a real spring in his step lately as well."

Sadie bit the inside of her cheek to keep from squealing. "Really?"

"*Ach*, of course! I mean, I haven't spent this much time with him since I visited my sister's family in Indiana over ten years ago. I can only speak for the time he's been living here in Bird-in-Hand, but he does seem to smile an awful lot on days when he spends time with you. Wouldn't you agree, Ruth?" Isaac's mother bobbed her head enthusiastically, but of course, she made no verbal reply.

The topic of conversation soon changed to a new fabric shop that would soon be opening in the neighboring town of Strasburg, but Sadie had difficulty concentrating on that, or any of the countless conversations happening around the quilting frame. Instead, she found herself tickled pink from hearing Mim's description of the effect she'd had on Isaac. She couldn't deny it: they made a great pair, and a connection like theirs was so rarely found.

A hint of gloominess dimmed the sunshine of this revelation. Eventually, Sadie and Isaac would end their courtship of convenience. That would mean spending a lot less time together, and that was something Sadie didn't want to think about. She shoved the idea out of her mind and focused even more intently on her quilting stitches, determined to enjoy this day of fellowship with her church family, as well as her courtship with Isaac, even if was to be short-lived.

"Would you hand me another board instead of just standing there and smiling?"

Isaac's daydream was interrupted by Mose's request. "*Jah, jah*, sorry about that," he replied, reaching for a board from the pile of planks. He handed the board up to Mose, who was balanced on a nearby ladder.

Mose chuckled as he hammered the plank into place. "I've seen that dopey look on my own face recently." He motioned for Isaac to hand him another plank. "Saw it whenever I looked in the mirror after I started courting Rhoda."

Isaac snickered at Mose's observation, then was startled by its implications. Why would he have a lovestruck grin on his face if he were merely courting Sadie to avoid a proper courtship? Sure, he enjoyed her company and admired her unique personality, but certainly, that was the extent of it. Still, Isaac wondered how Sadie had managed to remain single throughout her courting years, and he voiced that very question to Mose.

"Well," Mose began as he climbed down the ladder, "when we were *kinner*, Sadie was kind of a tomboy. She preferred the rough-and-tumble games we would play during recess at our schoolhouse instead of playing with her faceless doll with the other *maedels*." He picked up his jug of water, which was resting in the shade, and took a long drink. "As she got older, her interests began to include bird-watching, fishing, gardening and really anything else that got her outside. The other *maedels* were busy attending quilting bees and trying to outdo each other's newfound baking skills. I guess folks thought it was odd that Sadie would rather spend time in nature than doing things that the others were doing."

Isaac wiped away some sweat from the back of his neck. The blazing sun was growing hotter by the minute, and he hoped that it would soon be time to have lunch and rest in the shade for an hour or so. "So the fellows around here overlooked her just for being different?"

Mose nodded as he took another swig of water. "*Jah*, but I suppose there might be some men who are intimidated by a strong, independent woman like my twin." His expression hardened as if he was recalling a painful memory. "When we first started attending the young people's gatherings several years ago, one of the more immature fellows sent a letter to Sadie, asking if he could be her date and give her a ride home in his courting buggy. Sadie buzzed with excitement that whole week leading up to the singing, only to watch the fellow leave the event with another *maedel*. It was some sort of cruel practical joke."

Isaac frowned, filling with anger at the thought of someone intentionally hurting someone as sweet as Sadie. "That's *baremlich*!"

"*Jah*, but it caused Sadie to have a revelation about what she wanted in life. After that night, she told me that she couldn't see the point of courting unless she felt a genuine connection with a fellow." Mose smiled and slapped Isaac on the back before ascending the ladder. "That means you must be awful special, or at least my sister thinks so."

Before Isaac could reply, the clanging sound of Mim's supper bell rang out through the air. The dozens of men who had been working on the barn scrambled to put their tools away before making their way toward the long folding tables that held the noon meal. As he made his way toward the feast, Mose's words flitted around Isaac's mind. It did something to his heart to know that Sadie found him to be someone special. What was it about him that made him worthy of such a unique, sweet woman's affection?

When Isaac saw Sadie exiting Mim's house, smiling and laughing with the other women as they brought pitchers of lemonade to the tables, Isaac had to look away from her. What nonsense it was to entertain the idea that Sadie might view him as anything more than a friend. Their courtship was merely a mutually beneficial solution to their temporary problems. He would need to be sure to remind himself of that fact regularly, lest his mind start to wonder about the possibility of finding love for the second time in his life.

Chapter Ten

By the time the sun had set, the exterior of the addition was completed and painted white to match the existing portion of Mim's barn. The majority of the families in attendance had departed once the job was complete, but the Stolzfus family remained, and all but one of them were relaxing on Mim's porch, enjoying some of her famous gingersnap cookies.

After the productive, physically exhausting day, Isaac was glad to finally enjoy some quiet time with Sadie as he gave her a tour of the work that had been completed that day. They ambled around the structure several times, both of them pointing out the fine craftsmanship of the building. As they headed inside the barn's addition, Isaac held the gas lantern out to light their way. "The interior still needs some work, but I'll be able to do that over the winter months. I'm not one to brag, but I think we did a pretty nice job getting this barn expanded."

Sadie looked up toward the rafters and watched as a barn swallow happily assessed its new home. "I agree, and so does that little critter."

Isaac chuckled as he handed Sadie the lantern. He sprinted across the massive room to a bale of hay. He easily lifted the square bale and brought it over to Sadie, then motioned for her to take a seat. "*Jah*, I had a right nice day getting this addition built. How was your day?"

Sadie plopped down onto the hay bale. "It was nice to spend some time with our church family outside of a Sunday service." She paused while Isaac hurried across the vast room and brought over a second hay bale to use as a seat for himself. "We were working on a log cabin wedding quilt to give Leah Beiler as a gift since she and Daniel are getting married in November. It was kind of an inside joke, though, since Leah was also working on the quilt, but she didn't know that someday it will be hers."

Isaac pushed his hay bale next to Sadie's and then took a seat. "I think she'll like that."

Sadie nodded as she leaned forward and placed the lantern on the floor several feet in front of them. "It was Nancy's idea and she organized everything. It was nice of her, even though she chose not to speak to me," Sadie said with a smirk and a wink, showing that she wasn't truly bothered by Nancy's snubbing.

"*Ach*, she always has a bee in her bonnet." Isaac guffawed, glad that Sadie didn't take nonsense like that to heart.

"I think she's jealous that we're courting," Sadie replied, quirking one of her sandy eyebrows.

"Well, she can pout all she wants, because I'm all yours." Isaac grinned, quickly feeling his face flush with heat. Hopefully, Sadie had taken what he'd said as only a joke and not something more. Deciding it was best to change the subject, he declared, "That apple pie you brought was downright tasty."

Sadie's green eyes squinted in the low light of the gas lantern. "There were eggshells in it. I didn't realize I'd accidentally mixed them in with the apples until I cut the first slice to be served."

Isaac shrugged. "So? It was still tasty. A little crunch never hurt anyone."

Sadie stared at Isaac for a few moments, then let loose with a laugh that bounced around the barn. Her giggles caused Isaac to chuckle, and soon the pair were nearly doubled over in laughter. Once they composed themselves, Sadie wiped a tear from her eye and swept her gaze around the empty barn once more. "I'm glad that Mim agreed to add on to her old stable. Now you'll have the space you need to start farming next year."

Isaac rubbed a knot in his sore shoulder, his muscles tired from hours of hammering, lifting and climbing. "I sure would love to farm for Mim, but who knows how long *Mamm* and I will be staying here. Can't set up to farm if I'm just going to abandon it when I return to Indiana."

Sadie's posture slumped a bit. She pulled a piece of hay from the bale and began twirling it between her fingers. "Would you ever consider permanently moving to Bird-in-Hand?"

Isaac let out a long sigh and stood, then started pacing circles around the two hay bales. Moving permanently to Lancaster County and finally dedicating his life to farming felt like a dream that could never be fulfilled. "I wish I could, but if our prayers are answered and *Mamm* recovers, we'll be headed back to Indiana. That's my home, and there's no reason for me to move just to farm when I already have a job at my *daed*'s woodworking shop."

Sadie's eyes grew as wide as a harvest moon. Her mouth fell open slightly as she looked up at him before dropping her gaze to the ground. She released the piece of hay that she had been fiddling with and folded her hands in her lap. "There's nothing for you here in Pennsylvania?"

Thrown off by Sadie's sudden change in disposition, Isaac wondered if he'd said the wrong thing. Had he accidentally insinuated that she meant nothing to him?

Before Isaac could tell her that he'd misspoken, Susannah rushed into the barn, slightly out of breath. "Been looking for you all over, Sadie! *Daed* says it's time to head home."

"*Jah*, okay, I'll be right there," Sadie replied solemnly. Susannah nodded and darted out of the barn just as quickly as she had arrived. Sadie glanced briefly at Isaac, as if she was unwilling to look him in the eye. "I'll see you later." She hurried out of the barn and into the evening's fresh air.

Isaac could have slapped himself in the face. "Me and my big mouth," he muttered, giving one of the hay bales a good kick. He hoped that he hadn't damaged his friendship with Sadie, and now he'd have to wait until another day to find out if he had.

Just after ten o'clock that night, Sadie tiptoed noiselessly around her second-floor bedroom, eager for the day to come to an end. She pulled on her flowing white nightgown, glad to slip into the comfortable attire. Letting down her waist-length locks from her low bun, Sadie sat on the edge of her bed, brushing out the tangles. With each brushstroke came a new memory of the evening's disappointing turn of events, letting Sadie know that a long, sleepless night lay before her.

After escaping her disheartening conversation with Isaac in the newly built barn, Sadie was quiet for the rest of the evening. When questioned by both Susannah and her parents on the short buggy ride home, she had been in no mood to discuss what had made her usually bright smile disappear. "My stomach is awful upset" was the excuse she'd half-heartedly given them. It wasn't a lie. She'd felt queasy ever since Isaac had admitted that their courtship meant nothing to him. It deeply confused and frustrated her as to why this bothered her so intensely. After all, they were only friends who had agreed to court for appearance's sake. So why did she feel her heart sink to the pit of her stomach when Isaac had only stated the obvious?

Once the family buggy arrived home, Sadie had wandered deep into the nearby towering cornstalks. She wept in the privacy of the country skyscrapers, watering the soil with a deluge of tears. When she felt she had no more left to cry, she'd crept back to the house and up the stairs to her bedroom, where she'd spent the next several hours avoiding her family's questioning glances.

As she finished thoroughly brushing her golden hair, Sadie heard a quiet conversation coming from her parents' adjacent bedroom. Out of habit, she'd left her bedroom door ajar, lest the room become too stuffy on that late summer night. She stood to close the door, wanting to avoid unconsciously eavesdropping. However, what she heard her father say next caused her to stop in her tracks.

"I imagine we'll be busy planning a wedding pretty soon."

Sadie's heart skipped a beat at the notion. Mose must have said something to their father to hint that he was planning on marrying Rhoda in November's wedding season. As their parents' only son, Mose was a big help to their father when it came to all the daily farm chores. If Mose mentioned his plans to wed Rhoda in the near future, he was likely doing so to politely prepare their father for the fact that he might soon need to hire some additional help once Mose had moved out of the house.

Although Sadie would miss having her twin nearby, she wondered if she might be asked to help out with the farm chores and outdoor work. "And what a *wunderbar* blessing it will be, to have Rhoda as my sister-in-law," Sadie whispered to herself, instantly forgetting about her sadness. With a joyful wedding on the horizon and the possibility of getting outdoors more often, Sadie felt her spirits start to perk up.

"*Ach*, Amos!" Sadie's mother's sweet voice gently scolded her husband, though she didn't sound truly peeved. "I didn't think we'd be seeing one of our *kinner* leave the nest so soon!"

Her father chuckled. "Nothing to worry yourself over. Our *dochders* will still be here even after Mose becomes a married man."

"*Jah*, though I worry about our Sadie sometimes." *Mamm*'s tone had changed dramatically, now sounding full of concern and pity.

There was a long pause before *Daed* spoke again. "I do too. Until recently, I feared that she'd spend her life alone once her siblings were married and you and I have gone home to glory. But since that Isaac fellow has taken an interest in her, it gives me hope that she'll have a family of her own, whether or not Isaac is the man she chooses in the end."

Her father's implication was as clear as a freshly washed windowpane. He expected that Sadie would remain forever unmarried, never to share her life with someone she loved. The weight of his unintentional blow nearly knocked the wind out of Sadie. She stood motionless, feeling tears roll down her cheeks as her suspicions were once again confirmed. People assumed that she was destined to become an old maid, and even her own parents seemed convinced that her future was to be a lonely one. To make matters worse, Isaac wasn't even her real beau. He was merely a close friend, nothing more.

Sadie lightly walked closer to her bedroom door, holding her breath to ensure that her parents would not hear her sniffles. Once she closed the door, she wandered back to her bed, which was draped with a handmade purple, pink and white quilt, stitched together in a patchwork design. Sadie turned off her lantern, collapsed onto her bed and slipped under her quilt, wishing that the comfortable bed would swallow her up.

As she rolled onto her side and pulled her knees up to her chest, Sadie covered her mouth to muffle her sobs. She had never been able to picture herself falling in love and raising a houseful of children, since that would require finding a mate who would accept her quirkiness, but knowing that even *Mamm* and *Daed* seemed to share those thoughts ripped Sadie's heart to shreds. Was it true? Would she never find love?

Memories of the eve of her sixteenth birthday drifted into Sadie's mind. That special night had been the first time that she had attended a singing. Full of girlish excitement and hope for the future, teenage Sadie had taken it in stride when not one fellow looked her way or offered to give her a ride home. Unfortunately for her, being overlooked while her friends found love soon became a noticeable trend. At the point where Sadie had given up on finding her soul mate, both Isaac and her parents had confirmed her worst fear, that she'd likely spend all of her days without someone to call her own.

Clutching her pillow as if it were her only friend in the world, Sadie continued to cry until her pillowcase was thoroughly damp. Flipping it over to the dry side, Sadie considered spilling her aching heart to the Lord and asking Him to soothe her broken spirit. Emotionally exhausted and deciding all hope was lost, Sadie nixed the idea and cried until she drifted into a fitful sleep.

Chapter Eleven

Isaac sat at the workbench in a sunny corner of Mim's barn, realizing how very quiet the past week had been. Even though the cows were grazing contentedly in a nearby pasture, and Shadow and Mim's mare, Daisy, playfully chased each other back and forth across the meadow, things seemed to be unusually still. Even the barn swallows, who normally swooped in and out of the barn dozens of times each day, were absent from their nests high in the rafters.

"No wonder it seems so dull around here," Isaac muttered to himself as he stared at the tools hung neatly on the wall before him. A week had passed since the barn raising, and since his last conversation with Sadie. Isaac had spent the entire time worrying about the status of their relationship. After he'd mentioned his eventual plans to return to Indiana, Sadie's typically bubbly demeanor had visibly darkened. She'd looked pained, and for the life of him, Isaac couldn't fully understand why. Friends often had to say goodbye to each other when one of them moved away, and that was a fact of life. Their relationship was a bit more complex than a simple friendship, Isaac reminded himself, knowing that he wanted Sadie to be a permanent part of his life.

Should he go over to her house to see if she was truly upset with him? Arriving unannounced at her home might make things worse. Besides, if Sadie had told Mose that Isaac had upset her, her protective twin brother might not be too happy to see him either. Had he ruined their friendship just by being honest about how he saw the future unfolding?

"Isaac?" Mim called out as she rounded the corner with a full pitcher in one hand and a basket handle hanging in the crook of her other arm. "Whatcha doing out here?"

Isaac cleared his throat and faked a smile, unwilling to admit that he'd spent the last few hours moping around, unsure of what to do. "I was just taking a break."

"Perfect timing, then," Mim chirped as she set the basket and pitcher down on the workbench. "Figured I'd bring your lunch out here when you didn't come inside. I rang the supper bell three times, you know."

Now that his aunt had appeared with her picnic basket, Isaac realized that his hunger pains were nearly as intense as his worry over Sadie. He eagerly reached into the basket to see what Mim had brought him, and was pleased to find a turkey and cheese sandwich, homemade potato chips and a red velvet whoopie pie. He thanked her for the meal, then bowed his head in prayer before ravenously biting into the sandwich.

"Your *mamm* has regressed a bit recently," Mim somberly mentioned to Isaac as she watched him devour his sandwich. "Seems like Sadie was the only one able to perk her up." Mim's expression brightened with an unmistakable blush of hope. "She used to come over a few times a week to visit either you or your *mamm*, but she hasn't come around since the barn raising. Will Sadie be visiting again, you think?"

Isaac frowned so hard that his face ached, feeling as if he was being interrogated. "How would I know what Sadie plans to do?"

Mim's brow rose at Isaac's sour tone. "I thought you two were a courting couple, but of course it's none of my business." She reached for a nearby broom and used it to sweep away a large cobweb from the corner. "Your *mamm* isn't the only one in better spirits when Sadie stops by."

Determined to respect his elder, Isaac bit his tongue instead of bickering with his aunt. He sighed and ran a hand through his straw-colored hair, ruffling it up as if he'd just walked through a storm. "Sadie and I had a talk the day of the barn raising, and it didn't go so well."

Mim spun around, leaning the broom against the wall before hurrying back to the workbench, where her nephew sat. "Want to talk about it?" she asked, ignoring the broom when it slowly slid to one side before falling over.

Truthfully, Isaac didn't want to discuss this private matter with anyone. But considering that the Lord might have nudged Mim to ask about Sadie so that she could share some wisdom and advice, Isaac decided to share the concerns that had been plaguing him. "We got to talking about the future, and I mentioned that I would head back to Indiana should *Mamm* recover." He paused, somewhat embarrassed. "I said that there was nothing keeping me here in Bird-in-Hand, so it wouldn't make sense for me to move here permanently."

Mim nodded ever so slightly. "And Sadie got upset with you?"

"Well, she didn't come right out and say that, but it sure seemed like what I said bothered her."

"It's clear that Sadie cares for you, Isaac. Could be that your statement gave her the impression that your connection with her isn't strong enough to keep you in Lancaster County," Mim suggested as she reached down to pick up a friendly gray barn cat that had approached.

Isaac stared at the whoopie pie in the basket, though his appetite had left him. "I didn't mean to imply that I didn't value our friendship, because that's not true at all."

Mim stroked the barn cat as it cuddled close to her chest. "Friendship? Is that all you have with Sadie?"

Isaac's gaze dropped to the floor as Mim's question struck a chord deep within him. "It's complicated," he said so quietly that he barely heard his own reply.

Mim placed the cat back on the ground. "There's nothing complicated about two hearts that belong together." She smiled at the cat, then at her nephew. "Why don't you go pay Sadie a visit, after you finish your lunch, that is." She eyed his half-eaten sandwich and gave him the glare of a strict parent.

While Isaac was sure that Mim was mistaken about the possibility of a romantic future between him and Sadie, he agreed that they needed to have a heart-to-heart conversation. Deciding that he would go to the greenhouse after lunch, Isaac sent up a quick prayer that Sadie would be willing to talk to him.

Sadie hadn't been able to shake the sadness that had loomed over her since her last conversation with Isaac until it was time for her to work at the greenhouse. Being among the flowers and plants felt like a balm to her aching heart. What a blessing it was to know that *Gott* had ordained her to look after some of His artistry, nourishing it and helping it to grow, before passing on His creation to others.

Caring for the colorful mums and asters helped to cheer her up. She sang quietly to herself as she spent her morning watering both the indoor and outdoor plants. She answered the occasional question from customers and also put out some food for the greenhouse cat, Whiskers, who was somewhat of a mascot for the store. Before her lunch break, she swept the cement floor of the greenhouse, creating a small pile of dead leaves, soil and pebbles. She took pride in keeping both the shop and the attached greenhouse spick-and-span, and even the mundane task was something she found joy in doing.

When she bent to sweep the collected rubbish into a dustpan, she heard a man's voice calling her name. Then came the racket of a clumsy clattering, as if a bull had charged into a china cabinet. Startled, Sadie straightened to her full height and was amused to see Isaac steadying the large display of seed packets that he must have collided with. Several packets fluttered to the ground like autumn leaves on a breezy day. Red-faced, Isaac immediately bent to pick them up.

"Well, you've certainly caught my attention," Sadie laughed as she walked toward the calamity. Even though there was some lingering pain caused by their last interaction, Sadie couldn't deny that she was pleased and somewhat relieved to see Isaac. She hadn't felt whole for the past several days, and seeing Isaac now felt like a missing puzzle piece had returned to her life.

"Sorry," Isaac muttered. "I suppose this is the second dumb thing I've done recently."

"*Ach*, don't say that," Sadie said with encouragement as she helped Isaac collect some of the packets. "Maybe you've just invented a new way to plant seeds." She offered him a sympathetic smile, displeased to hear him speak poorly of himself. "What's got you so flustered?"

As if unable to look her in the eye, Isaac stared at the cluster of packets he'd picked up as he handed them to Sadie. "I guess I'm just a bit *naerfich*. I've been thinking a lot about the last conversation we had, and I thought we needed to have a talk about it."

Sadie accepted the seed packets from Isaac, placing each one into its correct slot on the display. "I've been thinking about that night too," she admitted, hoping Isaac hadn't noticed the crack in her voice.

Isaac glanced around the greenhouse before focusing on Sadie. "I'll just come right out and say it." His posture straightened as if he was putting on the bravest front that he could muster. "Saying that I had nothing keeping me in Lancaster County was a poor choice of words. I think you might have taken that to mean that our friendship...our relationship...isn't worth moving for, and that is far from the truth." Isaac reached for Sadie's hand and held it securely, his coffee-colored eyes gazing directly into hers. "You mean the world to me, Sadie. Truly, you do. I'll do my best to show you how much I treasure you."

"*Jah*, you mean an awful lot to me as well," Sadie replied, feeling as if she was nearly floating. Isaac's sentimental words and the touch of his hand holding hers caused Sadie to experience a rush of emotions that she hadn't expected. There was no denying it now. She was developing feelings for the man she was courting for the sake of convenience. Sadie tried to convince herself not to pine over a man who would never be truly hers, even if Isaac was the kindest, most understanding, handsome man she'd ever met.

"Now that this has been put behind us, why don't you show me around the greenhouse?" Isaac suggested as he let go of Sadie's hand. "I've been curious to see this place since you've told me so much about it."

"*Jah*, of course." She bobbed her head, leading the way as they walked through the property. Truly in her element, Sadie beamed as she showed Isaac the hardy plants that would soon be available for the upcoming autumn sale. The vibrant yellow, orange, pink and purple mums were her favorites, and Isaac agreed that he was partial to them as well. She couldn't help but notice Isaac smiling attentively at her as she explained the different varieties of houseplants. As they neared the front of the store, Isaac stopped to look at some bird feeders that were for sale, then decided to purchase one with some seed.

After Isaac paid for his items, he and Sadie walked to the parking lot, where his horse and buggy were tied to the hitching rail. They continued their pleasant conversation while Isaac loaded his purchases into the back of his buggy. "There's gonna be a singing at the Beiler farm next Saturday. Would you like to go?"

"*Jah*, I would," Sadie eagerly replied, glad that things had been worked out between her and Isaac, at least for the time being.

"*Gut*, since there is no one else I'd rather attend with," Isaac responded with a cheesy grin and a comical tip of his hat.

Sadie chuckled as he climbed into his buggy and then waved as the rig pulled out of the greenhouse's parking lot. Once Isaac had safely guided the horse onto the quiet lane, Sadie turned to head back into the greenhouse with some added pep in her step. Though she would need to work hard to keep her growing romantic interest in Isaac at bay, she looked forward to the upcoming gathering. If things continued the way they were going, she and Isaac would certainly grow even closer, and that was something that Sadie desired more than anything else.

Chapter Twelve

When the Saturday of the singing arrived, Isaac could have floated up to the moon with excitement. For the past several days his mind had been filled with thoughts of Sadie, and he knew that this outing would satisfy his growing need to be near her. There was something about her sweet nature, unique personality and lovely smile that drew him to her, and he knew that they were in for a special evening together.

Presently, as he sat at a long folding table in the Beilers' barn with some of his male peers, Isaac glanced nonchalantly in Sadie's direction. As was typical, since courting couples didn't pair off until later in the evening, she'd spent most of the Saturday-night youth gathering socializing with her friends and was now seated at a nearby table, sharing a slice of pie with Rhoda and Leah.

Isaac watched the group of girls as they giggled among themselves. He had spent his time playing cornerball with the other young men, singing fast-paced songs with the large group and eating his fill of baked goods, which provided hours of entertaining fellowship. But now, as things started to wind down, he was faced with a conundrum. Soon the time would come to steal Sadie away from her friends. But then what? Isaac pondered, tuning out the friendly debate between the *youngies* seated at his table.

Normally a young man would take his sweetheart out riding late into the night hours before returning her safely home. Would Sadie expect him to take her out riding? Isaac reached under his hat to scratch his head, realizing that engaging in a courtship for appearance's sake came with unexpected complications. Not that he would mind spending some extra time with Sadie to-night, Isaac pleasantly admitted to himself. She was always good company and a balm for the soul.

Isaac rose from his seat, said a quick goodbye to his friends and headed toward Sadie. Though the singing wasn't over and dusk hadn't yet turned to night, Isaac was eager to check in with her. As he approached the group of smiling ladies, Isaac's confidence suddenly left him. Why was he feeling nervous around Sadie? They were friends, after all. Yet Isaac still felt his pulse increase and heat rush to his face as he neared the table where Sadie was seated.

Full of self-doubt, Isaac stopped when he reached the cluster of girls. They were so absorbed in their conversation that none of them immediately noticed his presence. He reached out to tap Sadie's shoulder, but quickly pulled his hand back. Instead, he quietly cleared his throat in hope of capturing her attention.

Sadie turned, and her already smiling face brightened like sunshine. "Hi, Isaac! Wanna go for a walk with me?"

"*Jah*, s-sure." Isaac stumbled over his words, surprised that Sadie had beaten him to the punch. Could it be that she was eager to spend some one-on-one time with him as well? The possibility warmed his heart. Isaac smiled and nodded at Rhoda and Leah. Sadie's friends returned the gesture and then shot knowing, teasing glances in Sadie's direction. Sadie took the gentle banter in stride as she stood and pushed in her chair, with her nose high in the air. Her haughty attitude was clearly a farce that she couldn't maintain. Sadie giggled, wished her friends a good night and followed Isaac out of the Beilers' barn.

As they stepped into the twilight and away from the crowded barn, Isaac felt free to speak. "Your friends seemed amused when I stole you away. I hope they don't hold that against me, since it's still early in the evening."

Sadie shook her head vehemently. "They're just glad to see that I found myself a nice beau." She smiled up at him before quickly glancing away, her cheeks blushing a pretty shade of rose.

Isaac stared down at the path that led from the barn to the buggy shed, where dozens of open courting rigs stood parked, waiting for their owners to return with their dates. Then he released a concerned sigh. "Did you tell them the truth about our courtship?"

Sadie shook her head again, causing her *kapp*'s ribbons to flutter. "No one knows the truth." As they continued to walk, she wrapped her arms around her middle, as if protecting herself.

They strolled beside the wooden fence that twisted throughout the Beilers' rolling land. As they walked together beneath a soft orange-and-pink sunset, Isaac listened intently as Sadie told him more about her parents and siblings, as well as her adventure-filled girlhood days. Sadie seemed equally intrigued when Isaac shared details about his gaggle of sisters and his father's woodworking shop in Indiana. Isaac shared more about how he hadn't met Aunt Miriam until he was nearly ten years old. That was the year Mim had traveled to Indiana to visit her sister's family. Though he was aware that Mim's storytelling abilities drew the attention of many local children, Isaac found it charming when Sadie fondly recounted her own childhood memories of spending time with his aunt to hear her tales and eat her cookies.

Lost in pleasant conversation, Isaac and Sadie traveled quite a distance and soon wandered into one of the meadows. A strong scent of fresh-cut grass perfumed the air, as it often did when animals had spent time grazing there. The fragrance seemed nearly nostalgic and filled with comfort as Isaac breathed in the scent with contentment. When was the last time he had stopped to smell the proverbial roses? Certainly not since Rebecca had passed away.

Isaac turned to Sadie to comment on this revelation and was surprised to see that she was no longer at his side. He spun around and was stunned to see Sadie on her hands and knees, her nose pressed into the grass. "Sadie! *Was iss letz?*"

Sadie tilted her head up toward Isaac while remaining on the ground. "Nothing's wrong. I'm just smelling the grass. Grass is a plant, too, you know, and I think every plant should be enjoyed." With this explanation, Sadie promptly returned her nose to the earth.

Amused by her odd behavior, Isaac's mouth dropped open. "And you crawl on the ground to do that?"

"Well, sure! That's where the scent is best." Sadie

loudly inhaled through her nose several times, then finally stood. She shook some loose strands of grass from her dress and wiped her palms on her apron. "We have to savor it while we can, ain't so? Autumn will soon be knocking on the door, and then it'll be months before we smell something so fresh again."

Isaac stared at Sadie with his mouth agape as she stared back at him. It was a ridiculous but intelligent, strange but honest, explanation. Sadie's pure outlook on life was enough to light a fire in even the coldest heart.

"What?" Sadie leaned her head to the side as if she genuinely didn't understand Isaac's astonishment.

Isaac grinned from ear to ear, taking in the beautiful sight before him. As the sun set behind her, its vibrant yellow rays lined perfectly behind Sadie's sheer, organdy *kapp*. The glow around her head covering appeared almost like a halo, highlighting both her inner and outer beauty.

"What are you staring at?"

Sadie's voice interrupted Isaac's growing admiration for her. He grinned, deciding to tell her exactly what was on his mind. "I was just thinking that you're as lovely as a field full of wildflowers."

"Puh," Sadie exclaimed with a wave of her hand. "I don't know about that, but I might have inhaled a flower or two," she replied as she rubbed the tip of her nose.

Isaac burst into a fit of laughter at Sadie's objection.

Sadie gawked at him as if he'd lost his mind, which made him whoop and roar all the more. Eventually, Sadie joined in the uproar with a few cackles of her own.

"Speaking of funny things," Isaac managed to say

once he'd regained his composure, "was it kinda awkward being here tonight?"

Sadie sprinted forward to catch up with Isaac, and the pair began walking side by side once again. "What do you mean?"

Isaac felt a strong, thick weed snap beneath his boot. "I guess it just felt weird being in Nancy's territory with my *aldi*." Referring to Sadie as his girlfriend sounded strangely natural, which alarmed Isaac a bit. Pushing the sensation out of his mind, he continued, "I'm thrilled to have avoided getting tangled up with Nancy, but I didn't realize it was a blessing in disguise. It brought me to the dearest friend I've ever had, and I don't know what I'd do without you in my life."

Sadie stopped walking and reached for Isaac's hand, halting his pace as well. "That is the nicest thing anyone has ever said to me." She leaned closer to Isaac and lowered her voice, though not a soul was near enough to hear their conversation. "You have a good heart, Isaac. People see that. I see that, and the Lord does too."

Sadie had a way of looking through a person, past their pain, and their defenses. In the short time that they had known each other, she truly saw Isaac for who he was and had unveiled a secret he was trying to hide from even himself. Losing his only love to a tragic death had been horrendous. His mother's emotional breakdown following the incident was morbid. Two years ago, he'd decided to move on with his life, yet he'd done so without hope. But Sadie's presence in his life had reawakened his hibernating sense of hope. Effortlessly, she had planted a seed in the barren wasteland of Isaac's spirit. As that tiny, hopeful seedling began to sprout, Sadie watered it with wisdom and warmed it with kindness.

Isaac opened his mouth to share his epiphany with Sadie, but before he could utter a word, Sadie darted away. She ran a few steps, gently clapped and stopped. Unsure of what Sadie was up to this time, Isaac watched as she lunged forward again. Then he noticed a tiny flash of neon green, which Sadie delicately captured in cupped hands. She was chasing fireflies.

Now that she had gently trapped the shining bug, Sadie hurried back to Isaac. "Put your hands out," Sadie said softly so as to not startle the living light bulb. Amused, Isaac presented his outstretched palms and stood as still as a frozen creek while the summer insect crept from Sadie's hands into his.

"Look how special this lightning bug is." Sadie leaned in for a closer look as the intermittent green glow illuminated her face. "These little ones are only with us for the summer. These are probably the last ones of the season, with the cooler weather soon coming." She straightened to her full height and continued to watch the firefly. A few seconds passed before the insect flew away, and Sadie's eyes met Isaac's. "We can always count on the Lord to send us a little light. We need only look for it, *jah*?"

"*Jah*, and tonight He certainly sent me two little lights."

"I hope you're not referring to me, because I'm too big to catch!" Sadie threw her head back with a laugh, then scampered off to hunt for more lightning bugs.

Feeling as if he were alive for the first time since Rebecca's death, Isaac dropped the weight of the melancholy that he had carried for the past two years. He shook free from the shackles of hopelessness that he hadn't realized had chained him down, then joined in the firefly hunt. Living fully in the simplicity and delight of the moment, he felt as if several cinder blocks had been removed from his spirit.

Like schoolchildren, Isaac and Sadie romped through the meadows until it was nearly too dark to see. Laughing as they nearly collided several times, they captured lightning bugs on a catch-and-release basis, marveling at their sparkling surroundings. Darkness snuck up on the unlikely pair but wasn't noticed until they stopped their frolicking to catch their breath. Sadie dramatically collapsed into the grass as if she'd just run clear across Lancaster County. When she landed with a thud, puffs of dandelion seedlings flew into the air, along with several additional lightning bugs.

Isaac took a seat on the ground next to Sadie, chuckling at her shenanigans. "I haven't had fun like this in... I don't know how long."

With her back pressed against the ground, Sadie stared up at the bright full moon. "Who would've thought that a tiny lightning bug could've brought that out of you."

"Jah," Isaac responded, knowing in his heart that it wasn't the firefly that had prompted his breakthrough. "I wonder what time it is. Seems like it got dark real fast."

"'September is here. It's harvest at last. Leaves start a-changing and nighttime comes fast.'" Sadie giggled after reciting her limerick. "Well, at least, it will be September soon."

Isaac glanced at Sadie and let out a little laugh. "What's that?"

Sadie sat up, resting on her elbows. "My *gross-*

daddi says that every year when the days start growing shorter. He's chock-full of little poems like that one."

Isaac bobbed his head, hoping that Sadie couldn't see how wide he was smiling. "He sounds like quite a character, but that's not surprising, I guess."

"Why's that?"

"Because he's related to you."

Isaac barely got the sentence out before Sadie mockingly chided him, "Oh, really?" She straightened fully, resting her hands on her hips.

After a few minutes of lighthearted repartee, things quieted down again. Without knowing what time it was, Isaac had no way of knowing just how long they had been walking, chasing lightning bugs and stargazing. Self-doubt stalked him like a barn cat hunting a field mouse. Was Sadie still having a good time? Would she want to head home soon?

Isaac pushed himself up and stretched to his full height. He brushed the grass from the seat of his trousers and sheepishly glanced around the darkness. "I suppose it's time to call it a night." He shrugged one shoulder. "Don't wanna get you home too late."

"Okay." Before he could extend his hand to help her, Sadie launched herself up from the ground. "Thank you for giving me a ride home."

Isaac assured her that it was his pleasure to see that she got home safely.

As they moseyed through the fields and back toward the few remaining courting buggies near the Beiler house, Sadie and Isaac walked in amiable silence. Occasionally they would pass by a drowsy mule that had chosen not to spend the night in the barn. Sadie stopped to soothingly pet each animal, wishing it a *gut* night.

Isaac waited patiently for Sadie while she babied each creature, cherishing her gentle nature. Eventually, Sadie quickened her pace, and when she caught up with Isaac, he noticed her giggling softly.

"Did one of those mules tell you a joke?"

Sadie shook her head. "*Nee*, I was just thinking about how you were chasing lightning bugs with me. I've never seen you gallop like that." A few moments passed before Sadie spoke again, but this time her voice was filled with as much sweetness as one of Mim's strawberry pies. "I've never seen you smile so much either."

"*Jah*, well, chalk it up to the *wunderbar* company that I've had tonight." Even in the darkness, Isaac could make out Sadie's smile as clear as day. "Speaking of good company, let's see if there's still light in the windows when we pass Mim's house. I'd love for you to stop in and have a quick visit with *Mamm*. If you can give her just a smidgen of what you've given me tonight, it'll do her a world of good."

Isaac felt Sadie reach for his hand. She made a small, happy sound before she gave her answer. "I can't think of anything else I'd rather do."

Chapter Thirteen

"Would you mind waiting here in the kitchen, just for a minute?" Isaac's voice was low when he led Sadie through the squeaking screen door and into Mim's house. "I just wanna make sure *Mamm* is...you know..."

Sadie nodded, understanding that Isaac needed to ensure that his mother was well enough to receive a visitor. "Of course. Take your time."

Isaac thanked Sadie, then pointed toward the oak cabinets on the opposite wall. "If you rustle around in there, you'll probably find a snack. Mim constantly bakes treats for the *kinner* who visit her. Help yourself!" With that, he went into the next room.

Though she appreciated Isaac's offer, Sadie didn't feel right about rooting through Mim's cabinets. Instead, she padded across the room to a small plant that decorated Mim's tidy countertop. She wasn't surprised to see that the African violet was in great shape, with the exception of three dead leaves. Sadie gingerly pinched off the few crumbly leaves, being careful not to damage the rest of the plant.

"Sadie, aren't you off the clock? Didn't think I'd see

you gardening tonight, especially in my kitchen!" Sadie turned to see Mim entering the room, her waist-length hair neatly braided and slung over her shoulder. Wearing a floor-length nightgown and a terry cloth white robe, Mim appeared to have been thoroughly settled in for the evening.

Sadie tossed the three dead leaves into a nearby waste bin. "Force of habit. Sorry to just drop in when you're fixing to call it a night!"

"You're always welcome here. And, who am I to put a stop to a good habit?" Mim took a seat at the table and then motioned for Sadie to sit next to her.

Once Sadie was seated, Mim offered to fix her coffee or tea, which Sadie politely declined. "I just wanted to say a quick hello to Ruth. Feels like a long time since I've seen her."

Mim's eyebrows rose. "Came all the way here, at this hour, just to say hello, huh?" Sadie started to respond but bit her tongue instead. Mim was clearly privy to the fact that her nephew had attended the gathering earlier that evening. Surely, she didn't think it strange for him to take a girl home afterward, especially since he and Sadie were a courting couple. Mim quickly changed the subject after her gentle teasing. "Ruth perked up after you started coming around here. I can tell she missed seeing you regularly."

Sadie grimaced at the thought of Ruth's emotional suffering, but what a joy it was to know that Ruth found such significant comfort in their friendship. As she pondered their unlikely kinship, an idea whirred around inside Sadie's mind. "Do you happen to have a spare canning jar that I could borrow?"

Mim's lips parted with a puzzled expression. "Sure I

do. I've got some in my storage room." Mim stood and shuffled across the floor in her worn, plain slippers. "What do you need a jar for?"

"Just thought of a way I could surprise Ruth."

Mim shrugged and disappeared around the corner, muttering to herself that she might turn out to be just as surprised as Ruth. A short time later, she returned with an empty jar and a lid. Sadie thanked Mim, then sprinted out of the kitchen and into the darkness, though she was careful not to slam the screen door behind her. Once she reached Mim's lawn, she unscrewed the jar's lid and placed the items side by side in the grass. Then Sadie scampered beneath the nearest tree and stood perfectly still until a green glow gradually buzzed closer to her. She gently captured the firefly, hurried back to the jar, coaxed the critter inside and tightened the lid. She repeated this about a dozen times until she was satisfied with her hunt.

Sadie took her twinkling jar up the porch stairs, through the screen door and into the kitchen. Mim had returned to her seat at the table and was now joined by her sister and nephew. Ruth appeared bright-eyed and eager, and though she was also dressed for bed, she didn't look the least bit weary. Sadie also noticed that a broad smile decorated Isaac's handsome face. She mentally warned herself that he would never be her real beau, so it would do no good to fancy him. A lump formed in Sadie's throat and she wondered if it was too late to give herself that advice.

"*Ach*, there you are, Sadie!" Isaac stood from the table and hurried to her side. "I didn't want *Mamm* to think I was fibbing after I told her she had a special visitor."

"I'd never want to make you look bad." As soon as the words left her lips, Sadie wished she could pull them out of the air and shove them back down. She gauged the room to see the reactions that her statement had received. Mim pursed her lips and quickly hurried to the stove to retrieve her kettle. She seemed to be forcing back an amused grin. Ruth's expression hadn't changed. Perhaps she hadn't heard. Isaac also didn't seem fazed by her tender words. Instead, he appeared downright giddy in anticipation of her and Ruth's reunion.

Deciding that she was overreacting, Sadie ventured over to Ruth, who surprisingly stood to greet her. Judging by their expressions, Mim and Isaac must have also been pleasantly stunned to see Ruth rise without prompting. When Ruth extended her arms, Sadie placed the jar on the table and gladly accepted Ruth's embrace. "Hi, Ruth. Seems like it's been years since I've seen you!" Sadie held Ruth close until Ruth started to pull away, wanting to give her all of the support she could absorb. When the lengthy hug came to an end, Ruth cradled Sadie's face in the palms of her hands, admiring the girl as if she were her daughter. Though Ruth still didn't smile, her eyes seemed much brighter than Sadie remembered them being.

Sadie encouraged Ruth to sit down so they could chat for a while. Understanding that Ruth wouldn't verbally communicate with her, it was plain to see that she enjoyed the company of her young friend. Sadie talked about a new restaurant that opened recently, her twin brother's new horses and the coming change in seasons. When she mentioned the upcoming cooler, shorter days, Sadie remembered the jar of fireflies.

"*Ach*, that reminds me! These little guys are for you,"

Sadie declared, reaching for the jar. As she handed the container to Ruth, the two women marveled at the little creatures as they crawled around their enclosure. "We're nearly at the end of August, so these might be the last lightning bugs we see this year."

Ruth stared down at the jar, watching intently as the insects explored the container. She glanced at Sadie, then back at the fireflies, as if they were the most unique sight she'd ever beheld.

"Maybe these little ones can brighten up the dark for you," Sadie gently suggested. "See how they light up when the others around them are lit up too?" Ruth reached for Sadie's hand and gave it a gentle squeeze. "*Jah*, all anyone needs is a small, steady light to see in the darkness."

What happened next stirred everyone in the room. The corners of Ruth's lips twitched, and a sound came from her throat as if she was about to cry. Instead, a smile slowly spread across her mouth that illuminated her face and softened her features. The weak grin turned into a sincere, pretty smile that was filled with emotion. Her complexion warmed and she appeared considerably younger, as if she were a brand-new woman.

Sadie's heart felt so full that she feared it would burst. She'd never seen Ruth come this far out of her shell, nor had she seen a smile decorate the dear woman's face. She controlled her reaction so as to not startle Ruth. Out of the corner of her eye, she spied Mim wiping a tear from her cheek. Isaac, next to his aunt, had his hand partially covering his mouth, shielding a grin of his own. They both stood back and whispered between themselves, apparently nervous that even the smallest sound would disturb the moment.

Sadie continued talking quietly to Ruth for several more minutes before Isaac cautiously stepped forward. "Well, it's getting late," he hesitantly interrupted, placing his strong hand atop his mother's shoulder. "I should get our Sadie home before midnight, *jah*?" Ruth still didn't utter a single word, but she didn't stop smiling, and that was worth a thousand words.

As she and Isaac made their way back to the buggy, Isaac's words played over and over in Sadie's mind. *Our Sadie?* Did Isaac think of her as his, or was it simply an expression of everyone's collective fondness for her? She sincerely hoped it was the former.

The next morning, Sadie stood at the kitchen sink, staring out the window, elbow-deep in soapy dishwater. After a big breakfast, she and her younger sister went about tidying up. As Susannah finished wiping the table, she chattered about the first few days of her final year at the local one-room schoolhouse. Sadie cherished talkative Susannah, but she found herself unable to focus on her sister's schoolgirl tales. Instead, Sadie's thoughts drifted to the heartwarming events of the previous night.

Ruth had smiled for the first time since she'd known her, Sadie thought as she plucked a dish from the water and swirled a dishcloth over it. The Lord seemed to be working out things for His children. She grinned at the memories as she scrubbed the dish but was taken aback when a speck of her old, familiar burden floated into her mind. Would the Lord work things out for her too?

"I'll dry the dishes so we can get them put away faster," Susannah chirped as she bounded up to the sink. She gawked at the empty dish rack, looked up at

Sadie and wrinkled her nose. "You've been scrubbing so long, I figured you'd be just about finished."

Sadie chuckled at her sister's direct comment. "Well, many hands make light work. We'll get this done in no time." She lifted the clean dish out of the water, causing a wave of suds to slosh onto Susannah's apron. Susannah scowled, then suggested that they get to work.

Deciding that Susannah could stand to lighten up, Sadie scooped up a handful of suds and rubbed them on her sister's cheek. This caused Susannah to playfully slap Sadie's arm with her dishrag. The tomfoolery went on for a short time but was interrupted by the sound of the back door creaking open.

A male voice interrupted the feminine giggles. "Looks like a war has broken out."

Startled, the sisters spun around simultaneously. There stood Isaac in the kitchen doorway, seeking permission to enter. Sadie placed a hand over her racing heart, endeared by the sight of him and itching to know the reason for his unexpected visit. Maybe he was there to tell her about how Ruth was feeling after last night's visit. Or maybe he was there just to see her, though she made sure to keep her composure in front of her younger sister and her guest.

Susannah let out a playful scoff and planted her hands on her hips. "My *schwester* always seems to find fun in every chore, even if all that fun means she takes twice as long to get things done."

"And here I thought I was brightening your day! See if I ever do that again!" Sadie crossed her arms as if terribly annoyed, but winked to be sure Susannah understood that she wasn't truly upset.

"Maybe it's good that I barged in," Isaac said as he

stepped farther into the Stolzfus kitchen. "Someone should break up this fight." After everyone had a good laugh, Isaac's smiling eyes came to rest on Sadie. "Can I talk to you privately for a few minutes?"

Without hesitation, Susannah promptly exited the room. Even before Susannah was out of earshot, Isaac assumed her post at the sink. "I can help with the dishes since I interrupted your chores."

Sadie's heart was warmed by Isaac's thoughtful gesture. "A visit from a friend is never an interruption." She insisted that the dishes could wait, but Isaac was determined to help. Together they worked through the pile of dirty cookware, utensils and plates, making small talk for several minutes. When she felt her curiosity couldn't stand it any longer, Sadie gently nudged Isaac with her elbow. "Everything all right?"

Isaac pulled a clean plate from the dish rack and began to dry it thoroughly. "Everything's just *wunderbar*, Sadie, and it's all thanks to you." Before she could respond, Isaac continued, his voice wavering slightly as if overcome with emotion. "Last night my *mamm* smiled. She smiled for the first time since the accident that took Rebecca's life."

Sadie dropped the fork she was scrubbing and flung her arms around Isaac's neck, wrapping him up in a tight embrace. "That's *wunderbar* news!" She recalled the previous evening's hushed excitement when Ruth smiled, but she hadn't realized that it had been Ruth's first in years.

Isaac held on to Sadie's embrace for longer than she expected, but she was glad to hold him close to her heart for as long as he needed. When they parted, Isaac seemed to ignore the dampness on his shirt from Sadie's wet hands and forearms. "It's a downright marvel! Somehow you managed to change my outlook on the future and breathe new life into my *mamm*'s spirit." When he reached into the sink to retrieve some clean silverware, his hand grazed Sadie's, causing her heart to flutter.

Sadie was unsure of how to react to Isaac's praise. "I just gave her a jar of lightning bugs, but I'm glad that they cheered her up," she reasoned as she handed the last clean dish to Isaac.

Isaac shook his head as he dried the plate. "A jar of bugs is worth more than money can buy if it makes *Mamm* smile." He glanced down at Sadie, grinning at her with obvious fondness. "I'd like to take you to dinner sometime this week."

Lightheartedly snatching Isaac's dishcloth from him, Sadie dried her hands. "Sounds like a date."

Isaac turned and leaned against the counter, crossing his arms over his middle. "Sure seems that way. We are courting, after all, ain't so?"

"*Jah*, I guess we are." Sadie's heart pounded. Just where was their relationship going? She had agreed to a phony courtship to keep her parents from fixing her up with any random fellow in the county, but the way that Isaac affectionately gazed at her made her question just how phony it was. Was she reading too much into his invitation simply because she so desperately pined to find love?

After Isaac departed, Sadie dashed up the stairs to her bedroom, needing some privacy to sift through the strange mixture of emotions that swirled like a twister through her. Shutting the door behind her, she made a beeline to her hope chest and took a seat on the lid. Unlike her sister's chest, Sadie's chest was mostly empty. She'd never seen a need to fill it with items to use in a home of her own. But soon she would be going on a date with her beau, who was really just a friend.

The giddiness she'd initially felt when Isaac had suggested dinner was alarming. Her first reaction hadn't been one of a friend eager to break bread with another friend. No, her feelings were much more significant. Was her newly realized crush on Isaac developing into stronger feelings? Using her finger to trace small hearts on the lid of the chest, Sadie fought back the urge to cry. She firmly reminded herself that their upcoming dinner was nothing more than time spent with a thankful friend, even though her heart painfully longed for something more.

Chapter Fourteen

On the following Friday night, Isaac and Sadie sat at a small table for two in a local, busy diner, enjoying their date. Isaac couldn't remember the last time he had so thoroughly enjoyed a meal, but he knew that Sadie's excellent company was the main reason behind his satisfaction. Their discussion flowed effortlessly, as usual, and it was filled with genuine laughter. The pair were so engaged in conversation that it took them nearly two hours to eat their meals, and an additional half hour passed as they chatted and finished slices of apple-pear cobbler, served with a scoop of cinnamon ice cream.

Isaac stared down at his half-eaten dessert and leaned back in his chair. "Don't think I can ever remember when I've felt so full or had such a pleasant time," he declared, playfully wiggling his eyebrows to emphasize the second half of his statement.

Sadie giggled as she broke off a piece of cobbler with her fork. "Isn't it funny that we came here tonight? This was the same place where we agreed to feign a courtship."

Isaac spooned some ice cream into his mouth. "*Jah*, it's almost like it was meant to be."

Sadie suddenly dropped her fork on her plate. The clanging sound overpowered the murmur of all the quiet conversations happening in the restaurant. "Meant to be?" Sadie questioned, her eyes widening.

Feeling like all stares were on their table, Isaac cleared his throat nervously. His heart began to pound in his ears, realizing that his previous statement held a lot of weight to it. "*Jah, jah.* I mean…us agreeing to court solved both of our problems, so it's like the plan was meant to be."

Sadie stared at Isaac for several painfully long seconds before she grinned and took the final bite of her cobbler. "*Jah*, you're right!"

As Isaac finished his dessert, a chill swept through him that hadn't been caused by the ice cream. With some quick thinking, he'd avoided another near misunderstanding, though he wondered if his statement had been a peek into his true feelings instead of a mere slip of the tongue.

Sadie felt like the summer zipped by in the blink of an eye. Isaac stole her away for a few hours of companionship once every few days, much to her excitement. They enjoyed eating dinner together at various restaurants in the area, browsing the local farmer's market and occasionally going to the bank of Mill Creek to do some fishing. All of their outings proved delightful, but Sadie most enjoyed her lunch breaks when working at the greenhouse, now that Isaac had made a habit of showing up to share the noon meal with her.

On one overcast afternoon, Sadie stepped out of

the greenhouse and headed for the small picnic grove tucked discreetly behind the building. With her tin lunch pail in hand, Sadie quickly spotted Isaac.

Her beau was seated at the picnic table closest to a cluster of white birch trees. With a paper bag and thermos placed in front of him, he politely waited for Sadie's arrival before he began to eat. *He's so courteous*, Sadie thought with a grin. He would make a good husband someday if he ever allowed a girl to love him again. Wishing she hadn't entertained such thoughts, Sadie shook off the hint of disappointment that poked at her, knowing that she'd never become Mrs. Isaac Hostettler, or married at all, for that matter.

As she approached the table, Isaac turned and smiled at her, then began rummaging through his paper bag. Triumphantly, he pulled out a hefty slice of pie. He turned around and held the pie in Sadie's direction, not realizing that she now stood directly behind him. "Taste this," he demanded, nearly shoving the dessert in her face.

"*Oll recht*, but can I sit down first?" Sadie feigned annoyance, but her rapidly spreading grin betrayed her.

Isaac shook his head. "Nope, you have to try a bite now."

Sadie took a seat next to Isaac. She took the slice of pie from him and unwrapped it. Ignoring the fork Isaac offered her, she bit into the pie as if it was a piece of fruit. Isaac burst into laughter and clapped his hands, but Sadie ignored his amusement. "Wow, this is *appenditlich*!"

Isaac seemed thrilled by Sadie's reaction. "I know! Guess who made it?"

Sadie took another bite of the cinnamon-apple pie,

wondering why her friend was so obviously proud of the pie. "You?"

Isaac chuckled. "The only thing I know how to do in the kitchen is eat the food that comes out of it." He paused for a short time, as if gearing up to a big announcement. "*Mamm* baked it! She hasn't baked since the accident!" His eyes twinkled with excitement, like his greatest wish had come true. "She's putting effort into things again. She's getting out of bed in the morning without someone pushing her to do so." Isaac reached into the paper bag and retrieved another slice of the pie. As he unwrapped it, his smile spread from ear to ear. "This was Rebecca's personal recipe that she shared with *Mamm*. It's awful nice to taste it again."

"I'm so glad! The Lord heard our prayers for her, *jah*?" Sadie scooched closer to Isaac and gave him a quick hug. When he didn't embrace her in return but continued munching on his pie, Sadie slid back to her original spot and continued their conversation. "Ruth's been doing so well lately. Was she all right during the storm yesterday?"

Isaac's mouth twitched at Sadie's mention of rain, but he didn't look as sullen as he used to when damp weather was mentioned. "*Mamm*'s doing a lot better, but she cried for a while when it started to thunder." He glanced toward the sky as if to make sure the clouds above weren't about to let loose. "Rain is never easy."

"For both of you?"

Isaac seemed to consider Sadie's question as he pulled a sandwich out of the paper bag, which Sadie assumed had been prepared by Mim. He gently pulled the crusts off the bread, a surprisingly precious action that warmed Sadie's heart. Then he responded, "I used to hate the rain. I don't hate rainy days anymore, but doubt I'll ever learn to love them."

"I see" was the only reply Sadie could muster.

They ate lunch in silence for a few moments before Isaac spoke up again. "I thought it was gonna rain the night that we went for ice cream with Rhoda and Mose. Damp days can be too cold for ice cream."

Sadie took another bite of Ruth's pie and nodded. "I don't think Rhoda and Mose would have been chilly, though, not with the way my *bruder* looks at her."

Isaac smirked before taking a sip of apple cider from his thermos. "They do seem to fancy each other an awful lot."

"That's an understatement if I've ever heard one," Sadie chuckled. "We'll be having a wedding here before too long."

Isaac's eyes grew as large as dinner plates. "Surely, you're not talking about them getting married this wedding season."

"You never know. They may surprise us."

Isaac popped the last bite of his sandwich into his mouth, then wiped his hands on his trousers. "Well, if they do tie the knot this year, it would be awful fast. They've only been courting for what…about two months?"

Sadie shrugged at Isaac's logic, shaking off a birch leaf that landed on her shoulder. "*Jah*, but they've known each other since childhood." Feeling a sudden rush of bravery, Sadie ventured into dangerous territory. "But either way, I suppose you can't deny that special feeling once it strikes you."

Isaac studied Sadie intently, as if trying to solve a difficult jigsaw puzzle. "I thought you've never been courted, but you sound like you've experienced love before."

Sadie was unable to look him in the eye as she tested the waters. Gathering her courage, she turned to face Isaac. "I haven't, but I can learn."

Sadie and Isaac met each other's gaze. He seemed to take her in, chewing on his tongue and apparently pondering her romantic statement. She waited for him to respond, and her heart longed for him to proclaim that he had feelings for her. Oh, if only this caring, gentle, handsome man would see in her what she saw in him. But, much to her dismay, Isaac said nothing. Instead, he chugged down the last of his cider.

Finally, Isaac sighed. Pressing his palms against the table, he stood and began to pack his rubbish into the paper bag. "Well, I've got to get going. I'm doing some repairs on Mim's buggy and I told her I'd have them done by tonight."

"Okay," Sadie quietly replied, scolding herself for being so bold, and wondering if she'd scared her fake boyfriend away. She bid him farewell, immediately losing her appetite. She stared down at the half-eaten slice of pie, wishing she'd never hinted at her growing, serious interest in him.

The rest of Sadie's afternoon was plagued with regret. As she arranged a display of birdhouses, watered the mums and swept the floor, Sadie pouted over Isaac's sudden departure. She'd been foolish to say something so forward, she thought to herself. Their relationship wasn't real, so she needed to stop treating it like it was.

At the end of her workday, Sadie was stopped by the teenage *Englisch* cashier. "That dude you had lunch with bought something for you." Bending down behind the counter, Madison reappeared with a large pot of yellow mums.

"Isaac bought this for me?" Sadie asked, doubting that she heard her young coworker correctly.

Madison dramatically rolled her eyes, as if explaining things further was a major inconvenience. "Well, I don't know his name. That cute guy who stops by every day to visit you picked this out, paid for it and asked me to give it to you at the end of your shift." She smacked on her chewing gum and blew a large bubble. "I think he likes you."

As Sadie's fingers caressed the delicate yellow petals, she recalled mentioning to Isaac many weeks ago that her favorite color was yellow. How sweet it was for him to have bought her the most beautiful plant that the greenhouse had to offer. Maybe he did care for her as more than a friend?

Imagining where the best spot would be to display the cheerful flowers, a concern interrupted Sadie's sudden burst of excitement. Was she mistaking his kindnesses for interest? Feeling the onset of a headache, Sadie rubbed her temples and sighed. It was all starting to become too much for her; she was suddenly feeling as if she was in over her head.

On the following Saturday, Isaac, Sadie, Rhoda, Mose and a few more of their unmarried friends decided to get together at the local miniature golf course for one last hurrah before the busy start of the harvest season, which would soon be underway. After a round of lighthearted mini golf, the group headed inside to enjoy some ice cream at the concession stand.

As he waited in line to place their order, Isaac turned

to ask Sadie what flavor she'd like. He was surprised to see that she was no longer at his side. He looked around, but wasn't able to locate Sadie's pretty face, which always stood out in a crowd.

"Hey," Isaac whispered as he leaned between Rhoda and Mose, who stood in line in front of him. "Do you know where Sadie went?"

Mose glanced around the room. "Thought she was with you. Maybe she's in the washroom."

Rhoda shook her head as her mouth formed a small, concerned frown. "I was just in the washroom and no one else was in there. Maybe she went outside?"

Isaac stepped out of line and up to the window, then squinted through the sunshine that spilled into the parlor. There was Sadie, scurrying toward a small gazebo, hunched over slightly as she walked against the strengthening breeze. "*Jah*, you're right. She's headed for the gazebo."

Rhoda's usually sweet expression soured further. "By herself? Do you think she seemed a bit down today?"

"*Jah*, I noticed that too," Mose agreed, his concern for his twin evident in his tone. "She's been kinda quiet for the past few days. Wonder what's bugging her?"

Filled with senses of both responsibility and guilt, Isaac declared that he would check on Sadie. *Could she be upset because of me?* Isaac fretted as he hurried out of the concession stand and headed for the gazebo.

Come to think of it, he had abruptly left one of their lunch dates and hadn't returned for another one since. Truth be told, Sadie's insightful comment about the sensation of love had startled him to his very core. Sadie certainly had an unparalleled way with words, but how could she brilliantly articulate something she'd never experienced? How could she know what Isaac had been feeling stirrings of deep in his heart?

Sadie's innocent yet dead-on remark had forced Isaac to confront his attraction to her. Never in his wildest dreams had he imagined that he'd start to develop true feelings for another woman, and yet here he was, nearly unable to speak when Sadie half-heartedly smiled up at him from her seat on the gazebo's bench.

"The wind sure is picking up," Isaac pointed out as he stepped into the gazebo, placing a hand on his hat to keep it from sailing away like a tumbleweed.

"*Jah*, sure is," Sadie replied quietly with a grin that looked more like a grimace.

Isaac leaned against the post that supported the tiny hut's roof. "We all thought maybe you got blown away." When Sadie continued gazing at the golden soybean fields just beyond the parking lot, Isaac's anxiety intensified. It wasn't like her to be so quiet. "Are you gonna come in and have some ice cream with us?"

Sadie shook her head, keeping her stare focused on the fields that would be harvested within the coming weeks.

Isaac rubbed his hands together to release some tension before taking a seat next to his beautiful friend. Something Mim had recently said came to the front of his mind, and he decided to see if her idea would cheer Sadie up. "Mim mentioned that she thought your and Mose's birthday was coming up soon. Is that right?"

Sadie studied Isaac curiously as the wind whipped the ribbons of her head covering around her face. "*Jah*, our birthday is on September 16."

"*Mamm*'s is on September 12, and Mim thought it might be nice to have a joint get-together to celebrate the September birthdays," Isaac told Sadie before his hat blew off his head. He jumped up and sprinted to catch it before it flew out of the gazebo, which caused Sadie to giggle.

"*Jah*, I think that sounds like a nice plan. It was nice of Mim to think of me and Mose," Sadie replied with a small smile and a quick, uneasy glance at Isaac.

"Mim said she remembered your birthdays because you are the only set of twins in this church district, and hearing of your birth was news that she would never forget," Isaac stated as he returned to his seat beside her. He sensed that something was off in their communication, like humid summer air before a thunderstorm rolled in.

"Is everything all right between us?" Sadie asked as concern contorted her lovely face, as if she'd read his mind.

"*Ach*, of course everything is all right," Isaac responded as he placed his arm around Sadie's slight shoulders. "What makes you think something is wrong?"

"You suddenly left in the middle of one of our lunches, and you haven't been back to see me since. Was it something I said?"

Isaac appreciated her directness. "*Nee*, not at all, Sadie." He felt her tremble, perhaps from the cool wind or maybe out of anxiety. Isaac decided to continue cautiously explaining himself. "I'm really enjoying the time we spend together and the unique bond we have." He paused, feeling his heart beat several strong thumps. "I guess I just don't know what to do with myself because I never expected to have such a close connection with someone ever again." He glanced at her nervously, then turned to stare at the same soybean field that Sadie had been focused on earlier. "I'm just…scared."

Sadie moved closer to Isaac and leaned against him, as if she knew that the gesture would comfort both of them. "I understand and feel the same way. Good to know we're on the same page."

Isaac agreed and did his best to remain calm so Sadie wouldn't notice that her nearness affected him. The pair talked for a short time before Isaac suggested they re-join the group.

As he and Sadie headed back to the concession stand to join their friends, Isaac greatly doubted that they truly were on the same page. They had agreed to fake a courtship for a short time to get themselves out of situations that neither one of them had wanted to be in. Yet Isaac now knew that he would not be satisfied with only a pretend, short-lived courtship.

What if he had a real shot at courting Sadie? Without a proper courtship, it would be impossible to fully understand his feelings for her. How was he to know if his attraction to Sadie was just puppy love or something much more? The warm feeling in him might be just infatuation with Sadie's positive, unique outlook. Or maybe he was afraid to love someone again and the static energy that he felt was only fear of the unknown.

And what would Sadie's reaction be if he were to suddenly confess his interest in her? Would she think their entire friendship was a farce? Was it even possible for them to have a real relationship now that things were becoming so complicated?

Isaac had so many questions, and so few answers…

Chapter Fifteen

"What did your *schwester* have to say in her letter?" Mim asked Isaac as she carefully frosted the large chocolate cake that she had baked the night before.

Isaac sat at the kitchen table, reading the note that had arrived in the mail from Judith, one of his five sisters. He glanced over the top of the page before scanning the letter once more. "Judith says that everyone back home is doing well. Our youngest sister, Rachel, just started eighth grade, and she's excited to graduate come next summer. Our eldest sister, Hannah, and her husband, Luke, are expecting a new *boppli* in April. Judith also mentioned that business has slowed down a bit in *Daed*'s woodworking shop. Without me being there to help, he got behind on several orders, so he's still keeping plenty busy." He placed the letter back in its envelope for safekeeping. "She also mentioned that everyone misses me and *Mamm*, and that I should tell you that everyone back home says hello."

"How nice," Mim replied as she spread the chocolate icing on the cake with a spatula. "When the mail came in, I saw several cards for your *mamm* postmarked from Indiana. It's nice that her *mann* and *kinner* want to celebrate her birthday even when she's not home with them." Mim glanced up from her icing and sighed. "Just look at the clouds! What a gloomy day for a party."

Isaac had also noticed the heavy gray clouds that had been rolling in throughout the morning but had chosen to ignore them. Today was a special day to celebrate his mother, Sadie and Mose, and he wouldn't let the threat of wet weather ruin the day. "We'll still enjoy ourselves even though we decided to move the party indoors," he stated confidently, though he knew that getting his mother outdoors would have certainly been preferable.

"*Jah*, and your *mamm* will have those nice cards and notes to read to distract herself from the weather," Mim declared, as if she had just read Isaac's mind.

Before he could respond, Isaac noticed some movement outdoors. There came Sadie, bounding up the porch steps, wearing a navy blue dress and an excited grin. "I think a little sunshine might be coming toward us after all," Isaac stated, knowing that Sadie's vibrant personality would brighten up even the gloomiest day.

Sadie stepped through the screen door and cheerfully greeted them. "Where's the birthday girl?" she asked as she took off her shoes and placed them neatly beside the door.

"Well, one just walked in the door," Isaac answered, causing both Sadie and Mim to chuckle. "The other one is taking a nap before the rest of our guests arrive."

Mim looked up from her work and glanced at the small, plain clock that hung on the wall. "Speaking of guests, I thought I said that the birthday party would be starting at three o'clock. It's only noon."

Sadie shrugged as she moved to the counter, where

Mim finished icing the cake. "I came to lend a hand with setting things up."

"Such a sweet *maedel* you are, Sadie," Mim gushed, giving Sadie a few pats on the shoulder. "Isaac already set up the extra chairs and put out some snacks while I was decorating the cake, so I'm afraid there's not much else left to do."

Though he was sure Sadie wasn't aware of it, her early arrival had given Isaac the perfect opportunity to present her with his birthday gift. It was something quite personal, and he felt that his particular gift would best be given away from curious onlookers. Leaving the letter from his sister on the table, Isaac stood and headed toward the door. "Would you like to go for a walk, Sadie?"

"*Jah*, that sounds nice!" She hurried over to her shoes and slipped them back on, as eager as a fish on land to return to water.

"Take umbrellas with you," Mim called to Isaac right before he stepped onto the porch. "Looks like the sky is going to let loose any minute!"

After he found two plain, black umbrellas in Mim's coat closet, Isaac and Sadie were on their way. Just as Mim had predicted, raindrops began to fall from the gray sky just a few minutes later. As he and Sadie made their way through Mim's barnyard, then into her over-grown fields, Isaac found himself not minding the rain for the first time in years. His lively conversation with Sadie chased away any memories of the painful past, so much so that he barely noticed when the rain shower started to intensify.

"I'm glad Mim had the idea to celebrate all the September birthdays," Sadie said, breaking into Isaac's musings. "The Lord thought that each one of us was needed here on earth, so everyone must take time to celebrate the day they were born." She moved her umbrella to one side so she could see Isaac, seemingly unfazed by the mist that now lapped against her face. "What was your favorite birthday memory?"

"I'd have to say it was the year I turned twelve," Isaac shared. "My birthday is in December, and there had been decent snowfall that day. After *Mamm* cooked up an *appenditlich* birthday supper with all my favorite foods, *Grossdaddi* called all of us *kinner* outside. He'd hitched his old sleigh to one of the draft horses, who was wearing a harness full of bells. By the time we'd all clambered into it, *Grossmammi* came outside with thermoses of hot chocolate for us to pass around. *Grossdaddi* must've driven us around their farm for over an hour while we sang songs and sipped our cocoa. We probably would've stayed out longer if *Mamm* hadn't called us all back indoors." Isaac chuckled at the fond memory. "What was your best birthday?"

"This one is, of course," Sadie answered like she was surprised Isaac didn't already know the answer.

Isaac smirked at Sadie's response, wanting to hear more. "Why's that?"

"Well, because you're here. Having you and your *mamm* here in Lancaster County is the best gift anyone could ever ask for," Sadie stated as they approached a small grove of maple trees in the midst of one of the overgrown fields. "You're the best friend I've ever had."

As the pair ducked beneath the trees to get out of the rain, Isaac turned back and looked toward the barn. He suddenly realized that they had walked at least a half mile through soggy meadows. What would have normally felt like an endless, boring trek through uncomfortable, damp conditions had instead been filled with laughter and warm, meaningful conversations.

"I've got a little birthday present for you," Isaac announced, noticing his hands beginning to tremble when he set the umbrella on the ground. He reached into his pocket and felt around for the item he'd found for Sadie. Feeling his face flame with shame, Isaac stammered over his words. "To be honest, I'm...embarrassed. This is...well, it's such a tiny, dumb thing. I don't know if you could even call it a gift."

Sadie closed her umbrella and leaned it against the trunk of the nearest tree, allowing the canopy of leaves to shield her from the rain. She stepped forward curiously to see what Isaac had for her.

Isaac opened his hand, revealing a smooth, circular stone that rested in his palm. "I found this in Mill Creek one day while we were fishing." He handed the stone to Sadie, who readily accepted it. "I thought it was really something else. See, it's a perfect circle. And it's completely smooth from the water rushing over it for centuries." Isaac sheepishly rubbed the back of his neck, wishing he had something of greater value for Sadie, especially after all she'd done for him and his mother. "It was just so unique, so I plucked it out of the creek and saved it for you. I knew if anyone would appreciate it, it would be you."

Sadie stared down at the flawlessly circular stone in her palm and said nothing for quite some time, causing Isaac's regret to flourish. He really should have gotten her something more substantial. Maybe a pair of binoculars she could use during her time spent birdwatching or perhaps a book about plants would have been better gift ideas. Too late now, he grumbled at himself, wishing with all his might that Sadie would see his good intentions.

Sadie finally looked up, causing a tear to roll down her cheek. "This is the most special gift I've ever received. I'll cherish this always." She closed her palm around the stone, then pressed it against her heart. "*Denki*, Isaac."

Relief swept through Isaac, and he now wondered why he'd doubted himself. Things always seemed to work out when it came to Sadie. "I'm glad you like it." He beamed, feeling heat still radiating from his face. "I knew you'd see the beauty in it."

"*Jah*," she replied in a near whisper that could barely be heard above the sound of raindrops pelting leaves. "Seems like we both did."

Isaac cleared his throat, taken aback by the sudden fluttering sensation in his chest. "We're always on the same page," he pointed out, the corners of his mouth twitching. Whenever Sadie was near, he couldn't seem to stop smiling. Just the thought of her spunky nature and pretty face was enough to trigger a grin that would last the whole day.

"*Jah*, we usually do think alike…except for now," she proclaimed with an impish grin. Using her free hand, she reached up, grabbed one of the tree branches above them and gave it a good shake, sending a torrent of water down on Isaac.

Isaac gasped and tried to step out of the way of the deluge. He hadn't expected a lighthearted prank so shortly after their sentimental moment. Sadie cackled as Isaac shook off the water that had collected on the top of his straw hat. Once Isaac placed the hat back on his head, he reached for another branch to shake some water on Sadie. Seeing what was coming, Sadie darted forward, attempting to run past Isaac and dodge his playful retaliation. As she dashed around him, she lost her footing on the wet ground and let out a shriek. Jumping into action, Isaac lurched forward, catching Sadie before she hit the ground.

Startled by the commotion and by the stirring deep in his heart, Isaac gazed down at Sadie, still cradled in his arms long after she had regained her balance. With their faces so close, Isaac's eyes searched Sadie's as he treasured this moment. Holding her safely in his arms felt completely natural, like she belonged close to his heart. As the rain continued to pour around them, Isaac's lips met Sadie's, and he felt like he was home. With his heart pounding in his ears, Isaac's instincts told him to pull away. But when Sadie rested her cool hands on both sides of his face, Isaac knew that he had been worried for nothing. A second sweet kiss followed the first, which felt like the warmth of summer sunshine.

When their lips parted, Sadie stood on the tips of her toes, gently pressing her forehead against Isaac's, her eyes fluttering shut.

The monsoon-like conditions went unnoticed by the pair, still wrapped in an embrace. Stunned by the unexpected events of the day, Isaac continued to hold Sadie close. A part of him desperately scrambled to understand what this unexpected affectionate moment meant for their relationship. Another part of him never wanted their embrace to end.

As if she'd been struck by a sudden epiphany, Sadie gasped and stepped back. Her eyes snapped open and promptly glistened with tears. "I'm… I'm so sorry," she nervously sputtered. As if her heart had been freshly broken, her lower lip trembled like she was thoroughly riddled with sorrow. She spun around, hiked up the hem of her dress and bolted into the rain, charging through the drenched meadows like a startled mare.

Bewildered by Sadie's abrupt departure, Isaac stood motionless, alone beneath the cluster of trees. In one moment, their souls had lined up perfectly, and in the next, Sadie had run away as if her life depended on it. Had he done something wrong? Isaac started forward but stopped himself before chasing after Sadie. How could he comfort her without knowing what had upset her?

"Sadie!" He called for her several times before accepting that she wasn't coming back. *This is what I get for thinking I might find love again*, Isaac scolded himself, watching as Sadie's silhouette grew smaller and smaller in the misty distance.

Chapter Sixteen

❧

"Care for another slice of cake?" Mim asked Sadie after giving Ruth a second helping.

"Nee, denki," Sadie quietly declined, doing her best to hide her searing heartbreak. She was pleased to see Ruth looking so well. Isaac's mother had come a long way since Sadie had first met her, but that wasn't enough to lift her spirits. She had barely been able to choke down one of the sandwiches her mother had brought to the party, let alone a second slice of cake.

"You sure, sis? Mim's cake is legendary, and we're celebrating our birthdays after all," Mose prodded from across the table. He forked a hunk of chocolate cake into his mouth before wiggling his eyebrows at her.

Sadie nodded and tuned out the lively conversation that was happening around the table. Mose, *Daed* and Susannah chatted about Mose's newest horse while Mim and *Mamm* talked about some of the articles they'd recently read in *The Budget*. Ruth eagerly listened as she ate her cake. Sadie stole a glance at Isaac and flinched when she saw him staring at her. He shot her a concerned, pleading look before she turned away, excusing herself to the washroom, lest she suddenly begin to weep in front of everyone.

As she left the table and hurried down the hallway, Sadie pressed her hand against her mouth to muffle the sobs that ached to be released. She entered the bathroom and shut the door just as the dam that held back her tears crumbled away. She pressed her back against the door, then slid to the floor in anguish. Letting her head fall into her hands, she wept as she recalled the events of the afternoon.

After her unexpected kiss with Isaac, Sadie had found time to run home, change into clean, dry clothes, and have a good cry in the privacy of her bedroom before it was time for her family to pile into their buggy and set off toward Mim's house. Since it was still raining cats and dogs, Mose couldn't take his open courting buggy, which meant the family of five had to crowd into the boxy, gray rig. It was a tight squeeze, especially in the back seat where Mose, Sadie and Susannah had to sit together, packed in like sardines, but Sadie didn't care. She had far too much weighing on her mind and heart to fret over an uncomfortable seating arrangement.

As the horse and buggy had rumbled down the quiet country lane, Sadie had tuned out the chatter of her family and the splashing of the buggy's wheels through the puddles. Instead, her mind had replayed the sweet kiss she'd shared with Isaac on what seemed like a never-ending loop, and each time she pictured the moment, another piece of her heart disintegrated into dust. She knew now, without a doubt, that she was in love with Isaac, much to her chagrin. She had agreed to court the man to avoid her parents' matchmaking and the pity-filled stares of her community, and she'd been foolish enough to have fallen in love. She was downright embarrassed, knowing that she'd given her heart to someone who only saw her as a friend. Surely, Isaac had only been caught up in the quiet, intimate moment under the shelter of the maple trees. More than likely, his kiss was nothing more than an impulsive mistake. Yet here Sadie was, in love with a man who would never be hers, and that hurt more than any physical pain she had ever endured.

"Hurry up, Sadie! Mim says it's time for gifts!"

Susannah's excited voice and her rapid knocking on the door brought Sadie back to the present. "I'll be right there," she responded as she scrambled to her feet. Thankful that her church district allowed for indoor plumbing, Sadie ran some cool water and splashed it against her face in an attempt to hide the evidence that she'd been crying. After patting her face dry with her apron, she took a deep breath before rejoining the festivities.

When Sadie entered the sitting room, she took a seat next to Susannah on the floor since all of the other seats were occupied. Mose had just been given high-quality work gloves from their parents, and he was now tearing the newspaper wrapping off a shiny new pocketknife from Isaac. Then Susannah presented Mose with the gift that she and Sadie had both chipped in on; a battery-powered lantern, which was something he'd mentioned wanting not too long ago.

Next, it was Sadie's turn. "Happy birthday, *dochder*." Anna smiled as she handed her eldest girl a gift. "This is from your *daed* and me."

Though Sadie was in no mood to celebrate her

twenty-second birthday, she gratefully accepted the gift from her parents. She tore away the pink tissue paper to unveil a lovely leather journal. She flipped through the pages and noticed that a different scripture verse was printed on each page. She thanked her parents for the thoughtful gift before Susannah handed her a paper bag. Sadie peered inside and pulled out a battery-operated bird clock. A different bird's song would play each hour, on the hour. Susannah proudly stated that this gift was from her and Mose. Sadie thanked her siblings warmly. Finally, Mim handed Sadie a small basket filled with various floral-scented soaps. Sadie expressed her appreciation for the scented gift.

Finally, it was Ruth's turn for gifts. After Mim presented her sister with a pretty stationery set and Isaac gave his mother an ivy plant that he'd recently purchased at the greenhouse, Sadie stood and hurried into the kitchen, where she'd left the cloth bag containing Ruth's gift. When she returned to Mim's sitting room, she avoided Isaac's tense stare. Though her heart was broken beyond repair, she was determined to put on a pleasant smile. Sadie knew she would have to break off her pretend courtship with Isaac now that she had fallen in love with him, and this might be her last time spending time with his mother. She was determined to make this interaction with the dear woman a cheerful one, for Ruth's sake.

Sadie sent up a quick prayer for emotional strength and knelt on the floor next to Ruth's rocking chair. "I made this for you," she explained, unfolding the colorful blanket. "It's a lap quilt."

Ruth draped the small quilt across her knees and

ran her hands over the hearts and flowers Sadie had stitched into the fabric.

Sadie had to admit that the lap quilt looked quite different than any Amish quilt she'd ever seen. The pattern of hearts and flowers was almost chaotic. Because she found no pleasure in quilting, she didn't have as much experience as other Amish women her age. The stitches she made were noticeably uneven, though she had done the best she could when sewing it.

Ignoring her self-doubt, Sadie quietly pointed out features of the quilt to Ruth, explaining the thought behind each detail. "The flowers are to remind you of the ones we planted earlier this year, and the hearts are to remind you of how loved you are. I noticed you wear a lot of blue dresses, so I used as many shades of blue fabric as I could find."

Ruth's eyes shone with tears as her fingers traced one of the hearts on the blanket. She glanced at Sadie as her lips formed a trembling smile. She let out a little gasp, then stood and pulled Sadie into a warm, motherly embrace.

Sadie felt her own eyes filling with tears for what felt like the hundredth time that day. She not only loved Isaac, but she loved Ruth as well. Though Ruth had never uttered a single word to her, she felt like a second mother to Sadie. They understood each other without words, and Sadie knew in her heart that Ruth loved her. She was certain that this would make distancing herself from Isaac even more impossible than it already felt, but it was something that had to be done.

"Who's up for a game of Scrabble," Mim suggested, ending the bittersweet moment.

"I'll play," exclaimed Susannah as she collected all

of the discarded wrapping paper. Ruth smiled and nodded in agreement, and Anna also stated that she thought a board game sounded like fun.

Amos stood and patted his stomach several times. "Think I'll have another slice of that cake."

"*Jah*, me too," Mose added, following his father into the kitchen.

"You both already had two slices," Anna protested in exasperation.

"We're celebrating, ain't so? I never heard of a celebration where folks limit themselves on sweets," Amos retorted, causing a round of chuckles from most of those in the room.

As they all filed back into the kitchen, Sadie felt someone tap her shoulder. Knowing it was Isaac, she didn't turn to face him. She knew she wouldn't be able to look him in the eye without falling to pieces, so she pretended to not have felt his touch.

"Can we talk, Sadie?" Isaac asked, his voice lowered so that only she could hear it. He reached for her again. This time he took hold of her hand, forcing Sadie to acknowledge him.

In her opinion, there was no need to discuss what had happened earlier that day. She loved him, and now Isaac knew it. Since he didn't love her in return, there was no use in hashing through things. "What's there to talk about?"

Isaac's eyebrows climbed high on his forehead and disappeared under his bangs. "I think you know."

Sadie glanced toward the kitchen table where a game of Scrabble was beginning between the women and where her father and brother were eating their third slices of cake. This was not the time to have a personal discussion, or for her to succumb to yet another puddle of tears. Giving her hand a strong shake to free herself from Isaac's touch, she shot him a pained glare. "Please, not here."

Isaac's mouth opened but before he could say something more, Sadie rushed away and joined the game of Scrabble.

The talk around the table remained just as lively as it had been earlier, though Sadie didn't contribute much to the conversation. Her heart felt so heavy that she felt like she couldn't breathe and had trouble paying attention to the game. Whenever it was her turn to play a word, she either played the most simple word she could, or opted to pass to the next player. She glanced up from her letters and noticed Isaac sitting with her father and Mose. Instead of joining in their conversation, he stole several sad glances at Sadie, like he was an abandoned puppy dog.

As evening approached, the Stolzfus family began to say their goodbyes and thank Mim, Ruth and Isaac for the nice afternoon they had shared. After a quick farewell to Mim and Ruth, Sadie slipped out of the house, hopefully unnoticed. Carrying her birthday gifts, she dashed through the rain and into Mim's barn, where her family's horse happily munched on oats in one of the empty stalls. Soon her father would come out to the barn and hitch the horse to the buggy, and her family would be on their way home. Then she would get ready for bed and do her best to forget this, the most sorrowful day of her life.

Isaac couldn't believe it when Sadie quietly exited the house as her family lingered, having some final conversations with Mim. He felt as if he'd been slapped across the face by the way she'd acted toward him this afternoon. Didn't Sadie have anything to say about the kiss they'd shared under the trees, or her emotional exit afterward? Why had the tender moment upset her so much? How were they to go about their lives when such a delicate problem had wedged its way between them?

Deciding that he couldn't let her leave without clearing the air, Isaac excused himself from the kitchen, shoved his feet into his boots and rushed out to the barn. Running between the raindrops, he did his best not to slide through the mud in the barnyard. Sadie's *daed* had tucked their carriage into the barn to keep it out of the rain, so he was sure Sadie would be nearby. When he entered the barn, he felt his heart stop for a moment when he laid eyes on Sadie as she stroked the face of her family's horse, looking downright miserable. He'd never seen such a dejected look on her lovely face, and quite frankly, it scared him to his core.

"Sadie," Isaac called, nearly tripping over his untied bootlaces. "We need to talk."

Seeing him, she quickly climbed into the boxy buggy and planted herself in the back seat.

Bounding up to her rig, Isaac grabbed one of the buggy's wheels to keep it from carrying Sadie away, even though there was no horse hitched to the rig. The pair stared at each other, neither one of them saying anything for a time. It was dim in the barn, but there was enough gray light spilling in from the wide-open doors to allow him to see something unfamiliar in Sadie's eyes. Unease. Despair.

"That was a real nice lap quilt you gave *Mamm* for her birthday," he started, trying to break the ice between them. "I was surprised since I thought you didn't like to quilt."

"I don't," Sadie replied glumly as she fiddled with the hem of her dress apron, yanking on a thread that had come loose.

"Why'd you sew a little quilt, then?"

"Because I love her. Love changes people."

Once again, Sadie's direct answer floored Isaac. Rather than continuing their small talk, he decided to get to the point. "I'm sorry about…what happened earlier."

Sadie hung her head for a moment. "Don't be sorry." Picking her head up, she gazed at Isaac with the most feeble smile he had ever seen. "I guess for a moment we both thought our courtship was real," she whispered as tears began to well up in her eyes.

Taken aback by Sadie's explanation of their kiss, Isaac let go of the buggy wheel. She'd hit the proverbial nail on the head. Oh, his heart nearly shattered at the sight of her looking so sullen. He longed to climb into the buggy, gather her into his arms and soothe whatever was making her so sorrowful. Wondering if embracing her would do more harm than good, Isaac heaved a sigh, unsure of what to say or do. "*Ach*, Sadie."

Sadie wiped her eyes on the sleeve of her dress, then cleared her throat. "Ready to go?" she asked in a much lighter tone. Isaac turned to see who she was talking to and was disappointed to see the rest of the Stolzfus family running into the barn to get out of the rain.

"*Jah*, we'll just hitch up Samson and be on our way," Mose called back to his twin. He and Amos made quick work of readying the horse to leave while Susannah and Anna joined Sadie in the buggy.

The sudden arrival of Sadie's family forced an end to the conversation that Isaac was having with Sadie. Whatever had gone wrong between them was still unresolved, and Isaac hated to let Sadie leave on a bad note. But with her family there to hear every word they would say, what else could he do? He helped Mose and Amos prepare their horse, then followed the buggy out of the barn as it departed.

For the second time that day, Isaac watched Sadie leave as he stood alone in the rain. While the horse and buggy clip-clopped down the drive, then out to the lane, Isaac felt sick with anxiety. What in the world had upset Sadie so much? Did she regret their kiss? Dragging his hands down the sides of his face, Isaac felt like a piece of him had died, and he wondered if he'd lost his dearest friend.

Isaac hauled himself back into Mim's house, then without saying a word to his mother or aunt, he went upstairs to his dark bedroom. Without even taking off his wet boots, Isaac collapsed against the mattress. He stared up at the ceiling, emotionally drained and too exhausted to fret anymore.

Some time later, Isaac turned when his door creaked open ever so slightly. Mim and her gas lantern peeked into his room with the silence of a church mouse. As if she'd expected him to be asleep, Mim let out a little gasp when she saw her nephew stir. "Sorry, just making sure you're *oll recht*. We didn't see you after Sadie and her family went home."

"I'm fine," Isaac fibbed to not worry his dear aunt. "Just tuckered out." He noticed Mim was wearing her nightgown and robe and her hair was in its usual bedtime braid. Several hours must have passed since he'd come upstairs.

"Hmm," Mim responded, sizing up Isaac as if she didn't quite believe him. She noiselessly stepped into the room and took a seat in the rocking chair near the window. "Sadie's an awful nice girl, *jah*?"

Isaac bit his tongue. Had Mim come to pry? Frankly, he was far too exhausted to discuss Sadie's positive attributes. "*Jah*, she sure is." Sitting up, he slid to the foot of the bed in order to better see his aunt. Might as well get this conversation over with.

Mim paused before speaking again, seemingly to choose her words carefully. "Before Sadie started paying visits around here, your *mamm* barely functioned. Do you remember how she'd lay in bed all day, not even getting up to eat?"

"*Jah*, of course," Isaac replied solemnly, wondering why Mim had chosen to bring up such a grim topic.

"Through her actions, Sadie showed the love of the Lord to your *mamm*. It took some time, but when she allowed Sadie to love her, she started coming out of her shell."

Still uncertain of the purpose for Mim's midnight visit, Isaac voiced a question that he'd asked himself every day for the past two years. "Do you think *Mamm* will ever speak again?"

Mim smiled lovingly at her nephew, her wrinkles appearing deeper in the glow of the lantern. "I don't know, Isaac. We can pray for that." She stood and shuffled across the room, hesitating by the door. "Sometimes a person just needs to let themself love another person. The harder you fight love, the more difficult you'll make your life." Mim shrugged, as if her vague advice could be taken or left, then walked out of the room. *"Gut nacht,"* she said silently, closing the door behind her.

Still seated on the edge of his bed, Isaac's sight re-adjusted to the darkness now that Mim and her lantern had left. With his elbows planted on his knees, he cradled his head in his hands. Mim was absolutely correct. He'd unknowingly complicated the future when he'd invited Sadie into a false relationship. Life had been difficult since he began repressing his feelings for her. The courtship of convenience had turned into a major inconvenience, now that serious emotions were involved.

How would he ever smooth things over with Sadie? Was there any hope for them as a real couple? Dozens of questions swirled in Isaac's mind, but there was one thing he was certain of.

He loved Sadie Stolzfus with all of his heart.

Chapter Seventeen

On the following Tuesday afternoon, after the scholars had left the little one-room schoolhouse, Sadie and Rhoda entered the classroom armed with cleaning supplies. Rhoda would be filling in as the substitute teacher for the next two weeks while the usual teacher, her sister, Sarah Mae, recovered from a sprained ankle.

Rhoda had decided to clean the schoolhouse from top to bottom as a gesture of kindness, and she had politely enlisted Sadie as an assistant. Always eager to lend a hand to anyone who asked for help, and even those who didn't, Sadie had readily accepted the invitation. The chore of tidying the schoolhouse that she had attended years ago would hopefully bring on cheerful, nostalgic memories. Thoughts of a happier time might allow her to escape from the constant gloom that had plagued her over the past few days, all of which had felt dismally endless.

First, Rhoda washed the windows while Sadie polished each one of the wooden desks. Then they moved on to washing the chalkboard and filling the gas lamps. After the shelves were dusted and every inch of the floor had been swept, Rhoda and Sadie gave the time-worn floorboards a good scrubbing. As they washed the floor, Rhoda talked about her sister's injury and the upcoming double date that she and Mose had planned with Leah Beiler and her beau, Daniel. Sadie, however, was feeling far less sociable. She did her best to keep up with Rhoda's chatter, but her mind continued to drift to painful thoughts of Isaac.

Since their unexpected kiss, not an hour had passed without an image of Isaac popping into her thoughts. She felt that she was at her breaking point, and had firmly decided that the only way to carry on with her life was without Isaac. The notion that she cared so deeply for him but would never truly be his was enough to make her nauseous. Unfortunately for Sadie, Isaac wasn't going to let go of their friendship without an explanation as to what had gone wrong between them. Yet Sadie couldn't bring herself to look Isaac in the eye, declare her love for him, then face certain rejection.

That past Sunday had been particularly difficult since Sadie had been forced to be near the man who lingered in her mind and haunted her dreams during the church gathering. Countless times she'd felt Isaac's cheerless gaze land on her, and she found it impossible to concentrate on the preaching. On that particularly stressful Lord's day, Mose had sheepishly approached Sadie before the church meal with a message from Isaac. "He just wants to know if you're all right."

Assuming that her twin brother knew nothing of their fractured relationship, Sadie had put on her bravest smile and replied with a single word. *"Jah."*

Tears rushed into Sadie's eyes as she recalled the events of the past week, and she scoured the schoolhouse floor with even more vigor. Was it wrong to simply disappear from Isaac's life without an explanation? As cruel and painful as it was for both of them, Sadie saw no other option. *Oh, Lord, help my aching heart to heal*, she prayed as tears fell from her cheeks and splashed into the sudsy water on the floor.

"We've got quite a lot done in here, so I think we deserve a break." Rhoda sat back on her heels as she wiped her brow with her wrist. "I brought some chocolate-mint whoopie pies for a snack. Would you care for one?" When Sadie didn't answer, Rhoda glanced at her friend, deep concern quickly spreading across her freckled face. "*Ach*, Sadie! *Was iss letz?*"

"I've… I've got to confess something to you, Rhoda," Sadie stammered, unable to stop her flow of tears. "It's just *baremlich*!"

Rising from her spot on the floor, Rhoda hurried over to Sadie and sat beside her. "What's terrible?" she asked, drying her hands on her black apron.

Sadie was on the verge of hyperventilation and it took several moments before she was able to speak. "What do you know of my friendship with Isaac?"

"*Ach*, I don't know!" As a blush spread like a wildfire across her entire face, Rhoda's brow creased, like she sensed something was amiss. "You two are a couple, ain't so?"

Sadie hung her head, her heartbreak intensifying when she saw that she had deceived her friend with her actions, despite the fact that she hadn't told a single lie. "Isaac and I have been courting, but only for show." Rhoda tilted her head as if she didn't fully understand. Sadie choked on a sob and wiped away the tears that flowed down her flushed cheeks. "Earlier this summer,

Nancy Beiler was on the hunt for a beau, and she set her eyes on Isaac. Do you remember?"

Rhoda chuckled quietly, which took Sadie by surprise. "*Jah*, of course I remember. She caused quite a scene over him on a few occasions."

Sadie took a deep breath and shuddered, unable to control her weeping. "Isaac was still recovering from the loss of the girl he'd planned to marry. When Nancy showed that she was interested in Isaac, he asked me to fake a courtship with him, just until Nancy lost interest and set her sights on someone else."

"But Nancy moved on to chasing Johnny Glick not too long ago. You're saying you kept this up for…what, nearly two months?" Rhoda asked.

Sadie winced as she was filled with regret and embarrassment. "*Jah*, we did."

Rhoda smiled sympathetically, brushing a tear away from Sadie's clammy cheek. "Why?"

"It hurts knowing I'll never get married or have a family of my own. It hurts knowing that I don't belong anywhere, and everyone else knows it too. My parents threatened to play matchmaker and fix me up with someone in our church district." Sadie hiccupped, feeling like a wagon wheel that was stuck in a deep mud puddle. She exhaled with exasperation, feeling like she had no tears left to cry. "I'm so ashamed of myself. I wish I'd never agreed to court Isaac just for show."

"I'm sorry you're hurting so much. Sounds like you were only trying to help a friend who was in a sticky situation, while also being stuck in one of your own," Rhoda whispered, inching closer to her tearful companion. She embraced Sadie, stroking her back and allowing her to cry. "I just wish you knew that you were never truly alone."

Though she was not comforted by Rhoda's kind words, Sadie appreciated her friend's devout support and understanding. "*Denki*, Rhoda."

The two young women continued sitting on the floor while Rhoda patiently allowed Sadie plenty of time to compose herself before she spoke again. "Can I be very frank with you, Sadie?"

"Of course!"

Rhoda's fair, rosy cheeks flamed an almost auburn color, which let Sadie know that she was about to say something that might be difficult to hear. "Isaac is a good man, and I don't think he intended to hurt you. But, in his pain, I don't think he realized that asking you to be his fake *aldi* isn't at all fair to you." She paused, apparently gauging Sadie's reaction. "It also wasn't fair for you to court him just to keep folks from pitying you."

Truth be told, Rhoda wasn't wrong. None of this was fair to either of them, though spending so much time with Isaac for appearance's sake had never felt like a chore to Sadie. In fact, those months had been the most joyful time in her life. A small spark reignited deep in her soul and she felt the need to defend the phony courtship. "It wasn't all bad. We had a lot of fun and got to know each other real well."

Rhoda mulled over Sadie's argument. "But what if… what if there is some fellow out there who is genuinely interested in courting you? He wouldn't be able to do so because of this…arrangement…that you've got with Isaac."

Staring down at the nearly dry, spotless floor, Sadie

shrugged and flung her scrubbing rag into the nearby bucket. "That'll never happen."

"Don't say that." Rhoda attempted to reason with her dejected friend. "You don't know if another man will strike your fancy someday!"

"It won't happen," Sadie protested confidently.

"Sadie…"

"It won't happen because… I… I love Isaac!" Saying aloud the private words that she'd kept hidden in the deepest corner of her heart summoned a fresh round of tears. "I can't imagine ever loving anyone else as much as I love him!"

"That's *wunderbar*," Rhoda exclaimed with a squeal. Her sudden cheer was certainly a stark contrast to Sadie's misery. "You're already practically a couple. You should be honest with him and tell him how you feel. Wouldn't that solve everything?"

"It's not that simple." Sadie moped as she accepted the handkerchief Rhoda handed her. Rhoda didn't know about their kiss, and how Isaac apologized for it. An apology meant he regretted that special moment with her. Sniffling like she had a severe cold, Sadie shook her head. "How am I supposed to tell him how I feel? We were supposed to be faking a relationship, not experiencing a real one!" Noticing a loose thread at the hem of her evergreen dress, she yanked on it hard, causing a small tear. "He'll think I'm pathetic, if not downright ridiculous."

Rhoda frowned, seeming to fully understand the weight of Sadie's emotional burden. "This can't go on forever, though. Won't you continue to suffer unless you confront this situation?"

"I don't know." Sadie rubbed her temples. "I'm at my

wit's end." It only then dawned on her that she had more
to worry about than simply avoiding Isaac until she
figured things out. "What about Mose? If you thought
Isaac and I were courting, he probably does too."

Rhoda fondly placed her hand on Sadie's shoulder. "Nothing to fret over. He's your *bruder*." Rhoda's
mouth contorted like she was suppressing a wide grin.
The thought of her beau probably tickled her pink, but
she respectfully kept her excitement at bay. "If anyone
would understand, it would be your twin. I never saw
siblings who have a closer relationship than you two."

Staring down at the torn hem of her dress, Sadie
heaved a weighty sigh. "We've always been so truthful
with each other. He'll be disappointed in me."

"I don't think you need to worry, but how about I
explain everything to Mose?"

Sadie nodded wistfully, truly grateful for Rhoda's
sincere compassion. "*Denki*, Rhoda. You're the truest
friend anyone could ever ask for."

Rhoda's silver eyes lit up at Sadie's compliment.
"Friends pray for each other, *jah*? Let's pray right now
that both you and Isaac will find peace."

They bowed their heads in silent prayer as they sat on
the squeaky-clean schoolhouse floor. The gesture was
severely needed, though something restless in Sadie
doubted that prayer could help their struggles at this
point.

Chapter Eighteen

The start of the harvest season was just beginning and Isaac noticed a farmer and a team of mules working in the fields at nearly every farm his buggy passed by. The earthy scent of the ground being woken from the calm summer growing season was a welcome comfort to Isaac's weary soul, and he was certain that his mother felt the same way. This short errand to the Mennonite owned bulk foods store was her first trip out of Mim's house since they had arrived in Bird-in-Hand, besides church meetings, and she seemed to be thoroughly enjoying their noontime outing.

Mamm leaned out of the buggy ever so slightly and tilted her face upward, deeply inhaling the fresh air that was filled with little hints of the coming autumn. A smile crossed her lips as she closed her eyes when the sunshine warmed her face.

Sadie would do the same thing, Isaac was certain. Maybe that's why she and his mother felt drawn to each other. It was a bittersweet notion. This outing was a substantial positive step for his *mamm*, which normally would have thrilled Isaac, but how could he be truly content when things felt so bleak between him and Sadie?

It was only the last week of September, but the past ten or so days felt unseasonably chilly, though Isaac knew that it seemed bitter and endless due to the absence of Sadie's spiritual warmth. After he'd sent two letters and a vague message through Mose, then one through Rhoda, Sadie still remained unresponsive. Twice he had traveled to Sadie's house to demand to speak with her, and both times he'd turned his buggy around before it reached the Stolzfuses' driveway, fearing that he would only push her farther away with an unannounced visit. Regardless, things were coming to a boiling point and soon Sadie would have to hear him out, or else he would just have to accept that love just wasn't meant for him. He'd given his heart to two different women, and wouldn't give it away a third time.

As they entered the grocery shop, Isaac held the door open for his mother. The gentle hymns that played in a bluegrass style over the store's speakers offered a rare dash of peace, which Isaac's soul absorbed immediately. He decided that the mellow praise music was a sign from the Lord that he should take comfort. It was a sunny day and his mother had willingly accepted his invitation to leave the house. Though his heart longed for Sadie to the point that his chest ached, he was determined to be content, if only in this moment at the bulk foods store.

When he approached a small selection of local dairy products, Isaac stopped in his tracks. There was Mose Stolzfus, staring grimly at the coolers filled with rows of local milk. Mose suddenly turned, probably hearing the squeaky wheel on Isaac's shopping cart, and his face brightened with a welcoming grin. *Oh, great. So much for not thinking about Sadie right now.*

"Isaac! Ruth! How are you?" Mose's eyes grew as large as the watermelons in the nearby produce section when he saw Isaac's mother, but he graciously didn't mention the surprise he was certainly feeling.

"We're doing *gut*," Isaac fibbed for the sake of his mother. "Figured we'd run some errands for Mim since we're finally having a sunny day after that rainy spell."

"Jah." Mose bobbed his head. "When I get back to the house, I'm fixing to help my *daed* harvest our north tobacco field."

Isaac rubbed his chin. "Sounds like a good idea. Maybe I'll help Mim in her vegetable patch when we get home. It's a shame that she has about sixty acres of empty pasture just going to waste." He shrugged. "I tried convincing her to let me farm it for her, but she thinks it's too much work for me to do alone. She's getting up in years and can't pitch in with that sort of labor."

Mose nodded understandingly. "Well, maybe in the future she'll change her mind. Where the Lord leads, He always provides."

"Jah," Isaac agreed so quietly that he barely heard his own response. *"Mamm,"* he began while turning to his mother, "would you mind if Mose and I talked privately for a spell?" Ruth said nothing but smiled and nodded as she took the shopping cart from Isaac and pushed it away. Once his mother was out of earshot, Isaac turned his attention back to Mose. "What's got you looking so worried?"

Mose scoffed and waved a hand through the air as if he wasn't truly bothered by anything. "Milk prices aren't so good right now." He gestured toward the cooler, pointing at the listed prices. "It's starting to worry me since I'll be partnering with my *daed*'s dairy operation next month." Mose shuffled his feet and peered around the corner as if to make sure that they were still alone. "Rhoda and I are getting hitched come the wedding season, so I wanna make sure I can provide for her. Please keep that under your hat, though."

Isaac did his best to muster a genuine smile for his friend. Indeed, he was truly happy that Mose and Rhoda had found love, though he couldn't swallow the hard lump of jealousy that formed in his throat. "That's *wunderbar*, Mose! Don't worry yourself too much about the future." Isaac recited Mose's earlier proverb with a reassuring grin. "Where the Lord leads, He always provides."

The two men stood silent and politely smiled as an *Englisch* customer passed by with two curious children. After the brood had moved on, Mose nodded toward Ruth, who was studying the wide selection of generic cereals at the other end of the long aisle. "It's real nice to see your *mamm* out and about. Don't think I've ever seen her outside of church, or looking so well, for that matter."

Isaac inhaled so quickly that it caused him to have a short coughing fit. His spell was brought on by thoughts of Sadie stampeding into his mind. He'd been able to focus on the small talk between himself and Mose, but now Sadie was at the front of his mind again, which derailed Isaac's ability to keep his emotions in check. He cleared his throat several times, doing his best to keep his tears at bay. They itched to be shed, but he refused to give in to his anguish, since doing so ran the risk of his mother noticing.

Mose immediately noticed Isaac's dramatic shift in mood. *"Was iss letz?"*

Isaac cleared his throat once more. "It's Sadie. It's her gentle, kind ways that nursed *Mamm*'s spirit back to health."

Mose smiled, though his grin seemed cautious. "That does sound like our Sadie."

Isaac pinched the bridge of his nose and closed his eyes. "It's not just my *mamm*'s progress, though. Sadie made everything better for her, and for me too." He opened his eyes. "She made everything whole, and I broke it."

"The fake courtship, *jah*?"

Unable to make eye contact with Mose, Isaac stared into the freezer, feeling as cold as the contents kept frozen inside it. "She told you about that, did she?"

Mose shook his head. "No, Rhoda filled me in on those details. I guess it was bothering Sadie so much that she spilled the beans to Rhoda. Sadie was so upset that she couldn't bring herself to tell me, so Rhoda shared the news." Mose rolled his eyes. "Silly, though. Sadie knows she can trust me with anything. I'm her twin."

Isaac shifted uncomfortably and he glanced over his shoulder to make sure his mother was still too far away to overhear their sensitive, quiet conversation. "I'm at a loss, Mose. Sadie won't respond to any of the letters I've sent. I also tried to reach out to her through both you and Rhoda." Exasperated, Isaac took a moment to catch his breath. "It's like…like the best thing that ever happened to me has gone missing, and I'll never find it again!"

One corner of Mose's mouth turned upward. "Sounds like your fake courtship was more real than you expected."

Isaac let out a pent-up sigh. "*Jah*, I love Sadie. More than anyone or anything else."

Mose's crooked smile straightened into a full-on grin, though it quickly faded into a much more serious expression. "Can I give you some advice?"

"Sure," Isaac replied, eager to hear words of wisdom from someone who had known Sadie for his entire life.

"Collect your thoughts. Pay Sadie a visit, and be honest with her. Tell her how you feel, before you lose her forever."

Isaac thanked Mose for his advice, though he wondered if it had been given just a little too late.

"Sure thought Ruth and Isaac would be back by now," Mim commented to Sadie as they sat in side-by-side rocking chairs on her front porch. "I thought they were only going to Bird-in-Hand Bulk Foods, but knowing Isaac, he probably stopped to treat Ruth to lunch. She's been doing so much better lately, so it wouldn't surprise me if he's trying to get her out of the house for as long as possible."

Sadie took a sip of the meadow tea Mim had given her, gripping the glass with a trembling hand. As much as she enjoyed socializing with Mim, that wasn't the purpose of her visit. She was there to officially break off her feigned courtship with Isaac, and prolonging this dreaded visit was making her antsy. When she'd arrived several hours ago and Mim had told her that

Isaac wasn't there, Sadie'd had half a mind to turn and head for home. Knowing that she would only have to work up the courage to face the uncomfortable conversation once again, she'd decided to stay and try to enjoy Mim's company until Isaac returned.

"I'm awful glad to hear that Ruth's feeling so much better," Sadie finally replied after finishing her drink. "She looked like she was doing real well at the last church services. Maybe soon she'll start to speak again."

"We can pray for that." Mim let out a contented sigh. "The Lord still works miracles, *jah*?" Sadie didn't comment on Mim's expression but nodded in agreement. A few silent seconds passed while Mim glanced at Sadie's empty glass. "Can I get you more to drink?"

Sadie shook her head, fearing that her nervous stomach wouldn't settle if she had another glass of tea. *"Nee, denki."*

"Just holler if you change your mind." Mim slowly stood with a grunt and made her way toward the screen door. "The Lapp *kinner* usually stop by for a visit after school and I don't have any sweets to give them, so I better start baking. Wouldn't want to disappoint those cute little faces," Mim said to herself more than to Sadie.

"Want me to lend a hand?" Sadie offered half-heartedly, not wanting to appear rude.

"No need," Mim declined. "Besides, you're here to see Isaac, and you'll want to know the minute that he arrives home. I can tell you've got something important to discuss." Sadie glanced up at Mim, her eyes sparkling with surprise, startled by her observation. "It will be *oll recht*," Mim declared as she gave Sadie a reassuring pat on the shoulder. "Talk to the Lord about it, not just my nephew." With that, she headed inside to start her baking.

Sadie glanced around the now empty porch, noticing as a breeze gently nudged one of the porch swings into a swaying motion. How she wished that Mim had remained outside with her until Isaac arrived. Now that she was alone, she had no distraction and was all the more jittery.

Alone. Alone on the porch and alone for the rest of her life. Unless Isaac suddenly made a declaration of love for her, Sadie would spend the rest of her days without a husband or a family of her own. The time had come to finally give up on her dream of sharing her life with someone whose heart sang the same song as hers. If she couldn't spend her life with Isaac, she wouldn't spend her life with any man.

Refusing to succumb to self-pity, Sadie took Mim's advice and decided to spend some time in prayer. As she closed her eyes and bowed her head, she thanked the Lord that He had finally given her the courage to confront the moment she had been avoiding, and for the strength to face each new day knowing that she would never find reciprocated love.

The clip-clopping of a horse's hooves and the rumble of buggy wheels caused Sadie's eyes to snap open. With her heart pounding so strongly that it echoed in her ears, Sadie lifted her head. She instantly recognized the horse as Shadow, with his unmistakable gray coloring. Isaac and Ruth had finally returned home from their outing.

"Lord, please guide my steps and guard what's left of my heart from breaking," Sadie whispered as she stood from the rocking chair. She took several deep breaths in an attempt to settle her nerves. The time had come.

The joyful, satisfying, comfortable days that she spent with Isaac were about to come to an end. She started forward, taking the porch steps two at a time. One step closer to her future as an old maid. One step closer to being alone, she thought as tears formed in her eyes.

A ray of sunshine peeked around a passing cloud, warming Sadie's face as she plodded onto Mim's front lawn. At that moment, the heart-to-heart conversation that she and Rhoda had shared while cleaning the schoolhouse shot to the front of her mind. Sadie repeated Rhoda's sentiment aloud, suddenly seeing it in a new light. "I wish you knew that you are never truly alone."

At the time of their conversation, she'd assumed Rhoda had been referring to herself, and maybe Mose or the other members of her family. No, Rhoda had been referring to the Lord, Sadie realized with a bittersweet smile that stopped her flow of tears. With the company and love of her creator, she would never truly be alone. For the first time in weeks, Sadie felt an unfamiliar yet unmistakable sense of peace about her relationship with Isaac, and about her future, regardless of what might lie ahead.

Though she was only halfway across Mim's expansive front yard, Sadie halted in her tracks, bowed her head and allowed herself to fully submit to her Heavenly Father. "You've loved me since You created me," she whispered as peace surrounded her, releasing her fear and loneliness to Him. "Thy will be done, Lord."

Putting on her bravest face and comforted by the presence of her Heavenly Father, Sadie marched toward the barnyard where Isaac's buggy was coming to a halt. Whatever happened next, she knew that she had indeed found true love, even if it wasn't coming from Isaac.

Chapter Nineteen

As Sadie approached Isaac's buggy, she breathed a sigh of relief. Isaac hadn't seen her while unhitching Shadow from the rig. He'd led the animal toward the entrance of the barn, then was promptly swallowed up by the large structure and disappeared from sight.

When his *mamm* stepped out of the buggy, Sadie almost couldn't believe her eyes. Ruth looked more contented and healthy than Sadie had ever seen her. Perhaps while focused on her own pain, Sadie hadn't noticed that Ruth had put on some weight and no longer seemed so frail and gaunt. If she hadn't been paying attention, Sadie could have easily mistaken the woman for someone else.

"Hi, Ruth! You're looking so well," Sadie gushed as they approached one another. "Don't think I've ever seen so much sunshine in your face!" Sadie gestured toward the clear plastic shopping bag that Ruth held in one hand. "I know you went to the bulk foods store, but it looks like you purchased some fabric at a dry goods store too. Seems like you had a nice, full afternoon."

Ruth smiled broadly and nodded. She took Sadie's

hand and started for the house, probably wanting to show Sadie everything she'd bought during her outing.

"I'm awful sorry, I can't right now. I need to talk to Isaac as soon as possible," Sadie protested, not allowing Ruth to guide her toward Mim's large farmhouse.

Ruth stopped in her tracks and turned to Sadie, studying her young friend with a puzzled expression. She'd undoubtedly picked up on the unfamiliar bleak tone in Sadie's voice.

Feeling her eyes start to water, Sadie cleared her throat to keep her tears at bay. "I really enjoyed all the time we spent together," she confessed just above a whisper, hoping that Isaac's *mamm* would understand just how sincerely she was loved.

Ruth's brow furrowed as she continued to gawk at Sadie. With motherly concern evident across her face, her lips parted and she took in a breath as if she was about to say something.

"Sadie! I didn't know you were here." Sadie spun around to see Isaac, who had emerged from the barn. His mocha eyes twinkled with nervous expectation and he looked her up and down like he couldn't believe she was real. "It's real *gut* to see you."

"We need to talk," Sadie sighed, anguished by Isaac's tender words. She turned back to face Ruth. "I'll see you at the next church gathering." She smiled weakly, nodding reassuringly to emphasize how much she cherished their special connection.

Ruth's grimace couldn't hide her worry. She reached for Sadie's hand and gave it a few supportive squeezes before turning and slowly heading toward the house.

"Wanna take a walk to Mill Creek? I'm sure Mim won't mind if you borrow her fishing pole." Isaac grinned down at Sadie as if her sudden appearance was the highlight of his day.

Did he believe that everything was right as rain between them, just because she'd sought him out to talk?

Sadie shook her head. "*Nee*, not today." She knew it wasn't a good idea. Once she said what she had to say, she would want to leave as quickly as possible. No sense dragging out the awkward, heart-wrenching moment. She glanced at the house and spotted both Ruth and Mim standing on the porch, their necks craned toward the barnyard. "Could we go into the barn to talk?"

"*Jah*, of course," Isaac agreed, his broad smile beginning to droop. "After you." He motioned, allowing Sadie to step into the barn first. The pair went deep into the mostly empty barn and turned toward the cow stalls. Mim's two Holsteins were outside grazing, leaving Isaac and Sadie totally alone for their private conversation.

"Seems like it's been a long time since we've seen each other," Isaac suddenly declared, charging at the elephant in the room. "I've been thinking about you a lot over the past two weeks."

Sadie now knew that he was aware something was wrong, and that he'd decided to avoid unnecessary small talk. She stared at the ground as she walked beside Isaac, unable to meet his gaze. "I've been thinking about you as well."

Isaac abruptly stopped in his tracks and turned his body to face her. "I've also been thinking about the day of the birthday party, and I know that was the day that you started distancing yourself from me." He paused, studying Sadie with imploring eyes. "What happened between us when we went for that walk in the rain?"

Sadie knew the answer to that question. They had shared an unexpected, perfect kiss, and afterward, Sadie had realized that she was in love with a man she could never have, a man who'd specifically mentioned several times that he would never allow himself to love another woman.

"Sadie?"

Unable to rally the strength to answer Isaac's query, Sadie collected herself. She lifted her eyes to meet Isaac's. "We need to end our courtship."

Isaac took a step back as if he was in shock. "What? We agreed to court for six months. It hasn't even been half that long yet."

Sadie mustered a half-hearted shrug. She gazed up at the rafters, noticing a barn swallow leave its nest and swoop out of the barn, wishing she could fly away with it. "*Jah*, well…things have changed. Better to end it now before things get more complicated than they already are."

Isaac let out a loud scoff before he threw his hands in the air. "What's changed? What's so complicated? You and I have always been close, and I see no reason why we can't just move forward with the way things are!"

Sadie blinked against threatening tears. "Please don't make this difficult, Isaac." A wave of nausea brewed throughout her middle, the gut-wrenching goodbye making bile rise in her throat. "I wish you, your *mamm*…all of you…the very best." Unable to face the man who she was certain was her soul mate for a moment longer, Sadie spun and dashed toward the barn's exit.

"Sadie! Wait just a minute, will you?" Isaac dashed after her, keeping hot on her heels. "You know how much I care about you! Please tell me what's got you so upset! Was it our kiss?"

Hearing Isaac's clomping footsteps behind her, and his direct question, Sadie stopped in her tracks, which sent Isaac nearly crashing into her.

"I don't want to pretend anymore!" The truthful explanation had come out in a near shout. Sadie stood as still as a statue for several moments, somewhat embarrassed by her outburst but also nearly relieved that she'd given Isaac some vague insight into her emotions. She couldn't pretend to be his sweetheart when she truly loved him with every bit of her being.

Glancing over her shoulder at Isaac, who stood behind her, mouth agape and clearly stunned speechless, Sadie stepped out of the barn and out of Isaac's world.

After a completely restless night, caring for the animals at dawn and picking at the breakfast that Mim forced him to eat, Isaac dashed to the barn to get Shadow. His hands shook as he hitched the horse to his buggy, and he nearly misplaced his footing and fell hard on the ground when he scrambled to get into the carriage. He was on an urgent mission, and there was no time to waste.

Yesterday's shocking conversation with Sadie had turned his world upside down. He knew that something had been troubling her, but he'd been absolutely dismayed that she was upset enough to part ways. And all of this after they'd shared what he'd thought to be a loving kiss. Sure, he'd taken a huge risk by initiating the tender moment, but Sadie had returned a gentle kiss of her own. Had she realized that she had no romantic feelings toward him after all and panicked since they were technically a couple? Isaac's frazzled mind explored that and several other possibilities as he slapped the reins and rushed his horse out onto the road, ignoring the rattling of the buggy as it sped down the lane.

What was he going to say to Sadie when he arrived at her house? Even if he was able to articulate just how desperately he needed her back in his life, Sadie might just interpret whatever he said as only meaningless words. Besides, after yesterday's visit, she might not even be willing to hear him out. Still, Isaac knew that he had to try.

When Isaac pulled his buggy into the Stolzfus barnyard, he wasted no time in his search for Sadie. "Anyone home?" he called out. He strained to hear if anyone returned his urgent greeting, though it was almost impossible to detect anything over Shadow's hoof stomping and labored breathing.

When Isaac hollered again, he was relieved to see Mose peek out of the barn. "I was expecting to see you sometime this week," he cheerfully announced as he approached Isaac's buggy, a peppy spring in his step.

Isaac's already rapid heartbeat intensified. "Why's that?" he asked anxiously, pulling back on Shadow's reins as the animal urged forward, still energized from the race to the Stolzfus farm.

Mose's brows drew together. "Well, because Sadie's been in better spirits this morning." Mose's welcoming smile suddenly faded. "Figured you two had worked things out."

Isaac shook his head, or at least he thought he did. Both his mind and body seemed paralyzed. Mose was still talking, but Isaac was unable to hear what his friend was saying. In any other circumstance, Isaac would be

glad to know that Sadie was feeling better after a pe-
riod of gloominess. But this…this was different. First,
she'd terminated their feigned relationship, and now
her brother was saying that her melancholy mood had
suddenly lifted like a spring fog. Riddled with guilt,
Isaac shuddered and hung his head. Was Sadie better
off without him?

Once Isaac realized that he was in love with Sadie,
he'd always assumed that her best interests would be at
the front of his mind. But what if that meant she would
be happier, more at peace, without his presence? Her
tone in yesterday's conversation made it sound like she
didn't even want to continue their friendship. Isaac had
raced to the Stolzfuses' farm without a speck of doubt
that he was willing to fight for Sadie, for her love. But
was he willing to walk away, if that's what was best
for her?

"You *oll recht*, Isaac? You're looking mighty pale."

"Where is she?" Isaac's question sounded more like a
demand, disregarding Mose's concern for his wellness.

Mose jerked his head toward the house. "She was
around back of the house, in her garden, last time I
saw her."

"Hold these," Isaac muttered as he handed the reins
to Mose and stumbled out of his buggy.

Like a newborn colt standing for the first time,
Isaac's legs were unsteady as he started toward the im-
pressive two-story stone house. His speed picked up as
he rounded the side of the Stolzfus home, and by the
time he reached the immaculately kept backyard, he
was running as fast as his legs could carry him. There
was Sadie, pretty as ever, kneeling near a large patch of
dirt where she appeared to be planting several yellow

mums. Unable to slow the beating of his heart or the pounding of his feet against the ground, Isaac charged for the garden. He was galloping toward his future, knowing that this conversation would change his life forever. One way or another.

"Sadie!" Isaac shouted as he neared the garden, feeling like his lungs were about to collapse. Sadie flinched and looked up from her work, apparently startled by Isaac's sudden, loud appearance. "I wasn't happy with how our conversation ended yesterday," Isaac panted as he struggled to catch his breath. He waited on pins and needles for Sadie's response, half expecting her to rise and flee from him.

Sadie's slight shoulders shrugged as she removed the disposable pot from one of her mums. "Neither was I, but it was time to let you know what was on my mind."

Surprised by her unruffled response, Isaac watched Sadie in disbelief as she quietly resumed transferring her mums from their disposable containers into the rich soil. He cleared his throat, realizing that in his panic-fueled state, his tone had been far too harsh. He released an exasperated sigh before continuing. "What am I supposed to make of this? You show up after nearly two weeks of ignoring me, only to break off our courtship… our special friendship…with barely an explanation?"

Sadie didn't look up from the ground as she tucked some dirt around one of the freshly planted autumn flowers. "What do you want me to say?" Her voice quivered. She sniffled and wiped her nose on the back of her wrist.

"What do I want you to say? I want to know where we stand," Isaac pleaded, his voice rising though he did his best to control its volume. "After how close we were...after our walk in the rain...?"

Sadie glanced up at him for a fraction of a second, her vibrant green eyes matching the vivid hue of the grass that surrounded her. "I'm done faking a courtship. Thought I was pretty clear about that." She looked up at him again. Her previous stern grimace had been replaced with a tranquil expression. "I'm not mad at you or anything. I just got to thinking that it was wrong to get ourselves tangled up in a courtship for show." A small, pained smile crossed her rosy lips. "We were both suffering, albeit for different reasons. Could've saved us lots of trouble if we'd gone to the Lord instead, *jah*?"

Isaac was dumbfounded. So Sadie had indeed come to terms with her chronic singleness. She didn't need him anymore. The wisdom that flowed out of her never failed to impress him, but Sadie's wisdom wasn't what Isaac had raced to see her for. "But what does that mean for us? We were friends before I asked you to be my *aldi*."

Sadie's eyes fluttered shut. As if carefully collecting her thoughts, she took her time before answering. Though the ribbons of her *kapp* rustled in the gentle breeze, her perfect stillness reflected a new inner tranquility that Isaac envied.

When he could stand the suspense no longer, Isaac begged for an answer. "Sadie?"

"I'm done putting on a show."

Isaac stood motionless in disbelief. "But what does that mean? You've always been so direct with me, so why can't you be direct with me now? What about our friendship? You...you're the best friend I've ever had!"

Sadie said nothing as she clambered to her feet. Wiping her dirty hands on her chore apron, she gazed into the depths of Isaac's soul. "You were my best friend too." She inhaled deeply, as if suppressing a heavy sadness. "Excuse me." She brushed past him, the scent of her lavender soap lingering behind her even after she left the garden.

"So that's it," Isaac grilled her, following in her footsteps as she headed toward the house. "You're done with me?"

Sadie stopped and spun around so abruptly that Isaac almost stepped on the back of her sneakers. "I'm done… putting…on…a…show." She said the words slowly and firmly, like she was filled with conviction. "I told you yesterday… I can't pretend anymore!"

"Is this really what you want?" Isaac reached out for her mud-stained hand, catching it as she bounded up the porch stairs.

Isaac expected Sadie to pull her hand away, but she didn't. "No, but I've prayed for peace and understanding, and my prayers were answered."

Well, there it was. Sadie, although still mourning something, was all right. She appeared far more serious than the Sadie he'd first met that rainy day in the greenhouse parking lot. She certainly wasn't happy, but she'd managed to find a hint of peace amid the chaos of their relationship, the chaos he'd created by suggesting a phony courtship in the first place.

A bittersweet flood of emotions washed over Isaac. There was immense relief in seeing that Sadie was on the mend. On the other hand, he felt himself succumbing to an intense grief that he'd prayed to never battle again. When he released Sadie's hand, Isaac's stomach soured as he came to grips with the realization this touch had been their last. *Sadie, I love you so much that I'll let you go*, he confessed inwardly.

Doing his best to keep his emotions in check, Isaac swallowed against the lump in his throat. How was he supposed to say farewell to the woman who'd mended his spirit and given him a second chance at love? His world had been shattered when Rebecca had died, and now its pieces were smashed beyond recognition because he'd lost Sadie too. Several silent moments passed before Isaac was able to assemble some parting words. "Well, we had a good run."

Sadie's head bobbed and she sniffled several more times as she glanced down at Isaac from her spot up on the porch. "*Jah*, the best."

Isaac reached to rub the back of his neck. "I'll see you around, I guess." He quickly turned to leave, not sure if he would be able to bear hearing Sadie's lovely voice bidding him farewell.

"Isaac?"

He turned on his heels, his vision becoming blurry with unshed tears. Sadie stood beneath the doorframe, halfway into the large farmhouse. Halfway out of his life. "*Jah?*" he questioned, fearing that his voice would fail him.

"I'll always love you."

The otherwise comforting words were anything but a balm to soothe his wounded spirit. The love of friendship wasn't enough. Unsure of how to respond, Isaac decided that a small dose of honesty couldn't hurt. "I'll always love you too."

Deciding that there was nothing left to say, Isaac turned again and plodded to the barnyard. Mose was no longer in sight. He'd probably retreated somewhere deep within the barn to allow his sister and her visitor as much privacy as possible. Isaac valued Mose's kind consideration, especially now that he doubted he'd want to make conversation ever again.

Isaac carelessly flung himself into his rig. Taking the buggy's brake off and limply picking up the reins, he clicked his tongue to get Shadow moving. The horse started with a lazy walk, and Isaac allowed his snail's pace to continue since he was in no hurry to go anywhere. What was the point, especially when Sadie was no longer by his side?

The future was beyond grim. Unfortunately for Isaac, the loss of love had become all too familiar. He'd survived it once, but how would he carry on now that his heart had been shattered for a second time? Sadie had been a blessing from *Gott*, appearing in his life when he'd needed her most. In the privacy of his buggy and with only Shadow to hear, Isaac gave in to the tears that had built up since the day of the birthday party. He wept bitterly as Shadow clopped down the lane, away from Sadie, away from his closest friend, and the soul he desperately loved.

Chapter Twenty

"Another rainy day."

Isaac glanced toward the screen door from his seat on one of the porch rocking chairs. There was Mim, grinning compassionately at him from behind the mesh door. Not in the mood for conversation, Isaac nodded and returned his focus to the water that was splashing down from the eaves above. He'd been sitting there staring at the rain for at least an hour, if not two, but the time spent with only his thoughts for company had been anything but peaceful.

Mim opened the creaking screen door, stepped outside and took a seat next to her nephew. "You've been sitting here since breakfast, and now it's almost time for the noon meal." One of her wispy eyebrows climbed higher than the other. "How's a person supposed to work up an appetite just sitting around all day?"

"Please, Mim." Isaac rubbed small circles into his temples. He was certain that his aunt was only teasing, but his soul ached something terrible and even her jolly, playful banter wasn't enough to make him crack a smile.

"What's your *mamm* up to? She went outside before

the rain started this morning and hasn't come back inside," Mim mentioned, causing Isaac to wonder if she was trying to goad him into a conversation.

"I told her that I saw a new batch of kittens in the barn when I was feeding the animals this morning, and I think she went out to see them."

Mim let out a soft chuckle. "When she was a little *maedel*, Ruth always loved fussing over newborn animals. Seems like she takes one step toward her old self with each day that passes." She leaned forward, loosening the shawl wrapped around her shoulders. "Thought it'd be cooler out here for a late-September day. Things are starting to warm up."

"Uh-huh."

"But not warm enough to chase away the chill in your heart, *jah*?"

Isaac whipped his head in Mim's direction so quickly that his neck loudly cracked. He winced, massaging the spot that was now sore. "I guess not."

Mim smiled affectionately at him as she reached to brush a lock of sandy hair away from his eyes. "None of my business what the young folks are up to, of course, but it's plain to see that your joy seemed to disappear around the same that Sadie stopped visiting."

Isaac shuddered. Mim was absolutely correct. According to the community's tradition, her peeking into his romantic life was wildly unusual. But he felt more lost than a needle in a haystack, and if Mim had some providential words to share, who was he to stop her? He waited impatiently for his aunt to continue, watching her as she gazed into the intensifying rain shower.

"Whenever we face an impossible obstacle, the Lord has already placed the solution right in front of our nose. Sometimes we just need to open our eyes to see it." Mim stood and started toward the door. "Anyway, I'll have lunch on the table shortly. Please run and get your *mamm* in a couple of minutes, but grab some umbrellas before you do. Don't want either of you getting soaked to the bone in this weather!" With that, she retreated indoors.

Isaac harrumphed and crossed his arms over his chest. A damp breeze lapped against his skin as Mim's words rattled around his mind. What solution could there possibly be, unless Sadie loved him in return?

In an attempt to force a distraction, Isaac slapped his knees, sprang up from his chair and wandered across the porch. Leaning on the hand railing, he stared at the soggy ground, noticing for the first time that Mim had planted several yellow mums. Sadie's favorite color, Isaac reminded himself. He hung his head and chuckled at the irony. Reminders of Sadie were everywhere, all of the time.

If Mim knew about this, she'd say it was a "solution from the Lord." Isaac scoffed at the notion, but that rapidly morphed into intense reflection. Were both Mim and the Lord working together to get him to study this from another angle?

Wicking away droplets of water, Isaac skimmed his hand across the railing as he pondered this further. Surely, if Sadie loved him, she would have given him some sort of hint. Had she been giving him clues that he'd missed?

The first memory that came to mind was of their unexpected, tender kiss. That moment had lit a fire in his heart. Had Sadie been warmed by the same spark?

True, she had fled from him moments later, but before that, she'd willingly returned a soft kiss of her own.

She'd said we'd both been caught up in the moment, Isaac sternly reminded himself. She'd said we must've both thought our courtship was real. He continued gawking at the brightly colored flowers as he stood at the edge of the porch, hanging on to the railing to support himself. What did all of this add up to?

Isaac sighed as he ambled back across the porch to his empty chair. Was he just clinging to any glimmer of hope? If only Sadie knew just how much he'd come to love her.

I'll always love you.

Sadie's final words to him echoed through Isaac's mind. At the time, he'd been certain that Sadie was referring to the love one Christian has for all other people. She had a sweet spirit, so that was to be expected. But she kissed him back. She'd said she was done putting on a show. She'd said she would always love him.

Isaac dropped back into his chair with a thud, feeling like he might pass out. Sadie loved him, and he loved her! They could have a life together, a joyful, loving life! Against all odds, love had found two unlikely hearts and woven the threads of their lives together in the most complicated yet perfect way possible. During a summertime downpour, a gorgeous, quirky stranger had emerged from the rain and walked into Isaac's life, and she would become the woman he wished to marry. Now, during another rain shower, he'd come to realize that his unusual, patient, lovely best friend was his soul mate.

Isaac snapped out of his musings when he saw the barn door slide open in the distance. Mim was ringing the supper bell from the backyard. His mother must've heard its clanging and assumed that it was time for lunch. "Wait a second, *Mamm*! I'll bring you an umbrella," Isaac called, cupping his hands around his mouth to amplify his voice. He stood, but before he could turn to fetch the umbrellas, he noticed something unusual out of the corner of his eye.

As Ruth emerged from the barn, she suddenly came to a stop and turned her face up toward the sky. She smiled as raindrops landed on her face, and much to Isaac's surprise, she even stuck her tongue out to catch a few. Then, as if she hadn't a care in the world, she skipped toward an already sizeable puddle growing in a low spot on the lawn. To Isaac's total shock and complete amusement, Ruth splashed around in the puddle, kicking her bare feet through the water. She stretched out her arms and spun around as the rain drenched her clothing. Her smile widened and she let out a laugh that soon turned into a fit of giggles.

Isaac couldn't believe his eyes and ears as he stood on the porch, gawking at his *mamm*'s playful outburst. What a blessing the sound of her laughter was! It had been years since she'd last laughed. Tears rushed to his eyes as a flood of happiness and a torrent of gratefulness washed over him while the rain washed over his mother. Isaac dashed into the rain, needing to celebrate this monumental step forward in his mother's recovery.

Hearing her son's heavy footsteps splashing through puddles, Ruth stopped her spinning, though her smile was still broad enough to stretch across Lancaster County. She held her arms out to receive his embrace with the unmistakable expression of a concerned parent. When Isaac reached her, she looked into his red eyes and wiped away a tear before it could be mixed with the raindrops that pelted his face.

"It's *oll recht, Mamm*. I'm just so happy!" Isaac held his mother's cool hands in his, without feeling the need to hide his emotions from her for the first time since Rebecca's death. "I'm just so thankful to hear you laughing again." He sniffed, unashamed of his joyful tears. "Sadie really had an effect on both of us, *jah*?"

Ruth nodded as she held both of her son's hands in hers. "Go to her."

The moment that his mother's words left her lips, Isaac let out a delighted whoop. He embraced her so tightly that her feet left the ground. He'd nearly forgotten the calming sound of his mother's voice, and hearing it again was truly an answered prayer. For the longest time, he'd feared that he would never hear another word from her, and that anxiety had just been crushed by her three small words. Her first words, advising him to go after Sadie, put an official end to over two years of pain, misery and loneliness for both mother and son.

"Go to her," Ruth repeated, her voice cracking and shaky after not being used for years. "Go to your Sadie."

"I'm heading over to Rhoda's. Her *daed* is planning a small addition onto his workshop and I offered to lend a hand," Mose announced as he entered the kitchen with a noisy yawn and a tall stretch. "Do you wanna come with me?"

Sadie shook her head as she pulled a large plastic mixing bowl from the cupboard. "*Nee, denki.* I think I'm gonna try to bake something this afternoon."

Mose's mouth dropped open and he studied her inquisitively. "That sure doesn't sound like my twin talking."

Sadie shrugged and chuckled softly at her brother's visible shock. "*Jah*, I'm a whole new woman."

"*Ach*, no need for that! We like you just the way you are." Mose smiled, though Sadie could see the concern that was poorly hidden behind his grin. "Are you sure you don't want to come along? I know Rhoda would enjoy your company."

Sadie let out a pent-up breath. With her parents out to lunch with the *Englisch* neighbors and Susannah at the schoolhouse, she was looking forward to spending some time alone. "I love Rhoda, but I don't think I'd be good company for anyone," Sadie explained gently, hoping her brother would catch the hint.

Mose nodded sympathetically. "I gotcha." He headed for the door and explained that he would be staying at Rhoda's for dinner. He bid Sadie farewell and stepped outside only to return a few seconds later. "I can tell that something has your heart hurting awful bad, but I'm real proud of how strong you've been."

Sadie's heart was warmed by her brother's tender, supportive words. "It's strength given to me from above."

Mose agreed, and after another goodbye, he headed back outside.

Despite her best efforts to hide her gloom and carry on with life's daily activities, Sadie's broken heart was apparently still visible to others. Though she prayed daily for peace, the deep melancholy never seemed to lessen. For that reason, she'd been going out of her way to keep her mind and hands busy, reasoning that a busy person had less time to focus on her woes.

After rooting through the cabinets to see what supplies were available, Sadie decided to whip up a batch of chocolate chip cookies. It was the only recipe that she knew how to bake reasonably well, and she didn't want her efforts to be wasted on something that might turn out to be inedible anyway.

While she was mixing the dry ingredients, Sadie thought she'd spied some movement outdoors. Leaning closer to the window above the counter, she watched as the family's golden retriever bolted out of the barn and raced toward the long, tree-lined driveway. That wasn't particularly unusual. Buster had a lot of energy and enjoyed chasing squirrels and rabbits. The dog's adorable, almost goofy expression seemed quite wound-up, as it often did when a member of the family arrived home after being away for several hours. Maybe *Mamm* and *Daed* were back from the restaurant.

By the time she was pouring the chocolate chips into the mixture, she heard the sound of buggy wheels rumbling over the drumming of raindrops against the window. Now that she thought of it, it certainly wasn't her parents returning home since they'd gone to the restaurant by car. Maybe Mose had come back to fetch her at Rhoda's insistence, or maybe someone had come calling for an afternoon visit.

Sadie curiously peered out the window again and worried that her eyes might be playing a terrible trick on her. She immediately noticed the visiting horse's unusual gray coloring. The only gray buggy horse that she knew of was Shadow, who belonged to Isaac. Sadie used a nearby cloth to wipe some steam from the window. She pressed her nose against the glass pane and squinted to be absolutely sure that the scene outside wasn't just a manifestation of what her heart longed for most. Sure enough, it was Isaac sitting in his buggy, laughing as Buster jumped in to greet him.

Sadie placed a hand over her heart, trying to stop its racing. What in the world was Isaac doing here? What more was there to say? She backed away from the window, unsure if she was willing to meet her visitor. Part of her wanted to dash up the stairs to her bedroom, jump onto her bed and hide beneath her quilt until Isaac left. Taking a moment to slow her breathing, she closed her eyes and inhaled deeply. *I am never truly alone*, she reminded herself. Revitalized with the comfort of *Gott*, Sadie hurried outside without stopping to grab her shawl or umbrella.

She skipped down the porch steps and darted across the lawn, unable to dodge the raindrops as she made her way toward the barnyard to help Isaac unhitch Shadow and settle the animal in the barn.

As she approached the buggy, Buster stuck his head out of the rig at the sound of her hurried steps through the puddles. With his tongue lolling and tail wagging, he let out a woof and hopped out of the buggy. Sadie scratched the dog behind his damp ears, taking comfort in the faithful canine's affection.

The buggy creaked a bit as Isaac clambered out of it, his masculine but gentle features nearly stopping Sadie's heart. For a moment, they stared at each other through the rain, neither one of them speaking. Though Sadie hated to admit it, it was tremendously wonderful to see Isaac again.

Pushing away the longing that she knew would never fully leave her, Sadie noticed that Isaac was completely drenched, as if he'd been standing in the rain for far longer than these few moments. "You're downright soaked."

Isaac looked down at his sopping shirt, the movement of his head causing all of the water atop his hat to rush to the brim. "It's raining, just like the day we met, *jah*?" Isaac studied her with a look she hadn't seen from him since the day of the birthday party. "My…uh…my *mamm* started speaking again today."

Sadie immediately felt tears rush to her eyes. Were they brought on by seeing Isaac again, or from the happy news that Ruth had fully recovered from her condition? "*Ach*, that's *wunderbar*." She nodded, feeling her warm tears mix with the cool September raindrops on her flushed cheeks.

Isaac took a step forward but then seemed to hesitate. "It is *wunderbar*!" He stared at the ground, the brim of his hat hiding his face.

"Why did you come here?" Sadie asked him point-blank.

Isaac turned toward Shadow, running his hand along the horse's back, which sent even more water droplets flying through the air. "I can't be without you by my side."

Sadie tilted her head, fearful that she would misinterpret what Isaac was conveying. "We can be friends again."

"No," Isaac retorted almost immediately as he rushed closer to her, now just inches away. "How can I be only friends with the woman who changed my life, who makes me feel truly alive, even after I thought my spirit was dead?" He reached for her hand, then pulled her close enough for her to feel his heartbeat. "I love the woman who chases lightning bugs and who bakes the strangest cookies I've ever seen." His eyes shone brighter than the harvest moon on a crystal clear night. "I love the woman who eats pies like an apple and who brings joy to every life that she touches. I love you, Sadie, and I want you to be my wife."

With her cheek pressed against his chest, Sadie was unable to control her tears of joy. Her heart had found a home, and it was warm and welcoming. Isaac continued to hold her, resting his head on top of hers while she wept.

Finally, Sadie managed to compose herself. She looked up, causing the beating rain to wash away her tears as a lifetime of loneliness was rinsed away as well. "I love you too, Isaac! I can't wait to be your wife."

Smiling down at her, Isaac kissed Sadie's damp forehead and then each of her cheeks. Sliding his hand under her chin, he tilted her face upward. Their lips met, and for the first time in her life, Sadie felt like she was home. When their lips parted, Isaac embraced her again. "Sadie Stolzfus," he whispered in her ear, his cheek pressed against hers, "you taught me to love the rain."

Epilogue

"I must say, I can't remember ever baking fourteen pies in a single morning," Mim stated as she shoved her hands into her quilted oven mitts. She opened the door of her oven, reached inside and pulled out two apple-crumble pies that looked like they could have been featured on the cover of a cookbook.

Sadie studied the previous dozen pies, all of which stood cooling, lined up like ducklings across Mim's counter. "I can't remember ever making something that looks so *appenditlich*!"

Mim chortled as she placed the last two pies on the end of the counter. "They do look delicious! You've been practicing a lot lately, and I'm sure everyone will enjoy these pies at Mose and Rhoda's wedding tomorrow." Mim took off her oven mitts, then hung them on their designated hook on the wall. She moved to the sink and stopped to peer out of the small window above the faucet. "Looks like a car just pulled in and someone's getting out of it with several suitcases." She craned her neck toward Sadie and issued her a mischievous grin. "I reckon it's a taxi bringing someone from the bus station in Lancaster. Wonder who that could be?"

Knowing that Isaac was to return from his trip to Indiana, Sadie let out a squeal and charged out the door. Isaac had traveled to Shipshewana with his mother several weeks ago. Once his mother was settled in back home, Isaac had planned to pack up all of his belongings and return to Bird-in-Hand, though this time he would be returning for good.

"*Willkumm* home!" Sadie shouted as she threw her arms around Isaac's neck. He dropped his suitcases and wrapped Sadie in a warm embrace, which felt so loving that it nearly brought tears to her eyes.

Isaac lifted her off the ground and spun her in several tight circles, causing both of them to laugh.

"*Ach*, it's *gut* to be back in Lancaster County," Isaac declared as he placed Sadie on the ground. "Indiana certainly doesn't feel like home anymore."

"*Jah*, and you're back just in time to see Mose and Rhoda get married tomorrow, though I'm sorry your *mamm* will miss the wedding," Sadie replied, feeling a hint of disappointment. She'd missed Ruth ever since she'd left Bird-in-Hand, though she knew she would see her future mother-in-law again someday.

"Well, I've got some exciting news to share," Isaac replied with one of the biggest smiles that Sadie had ever seen. "*Mamm*, *Daed* and all of my unmarried sisters are moving to Lancaster County as well. *Daed* is coming into town next week and he and I are going house hunting for them. Then we'll find a shop for rent, where he can run his woodworking business from."

"That's *wunderbar*," Sadie exclaimed, clapping her

hands together. "I can't wait to meet the rest of your family."

Isaac's grin fairly sparkled as he and Sadie each picked up one of his suitcases and headed toward a nearby bench that rested beneath a weeping willow tree. "You should've heard *Mamm* excitedly talking *Daed*'s ear off about how successful his business will be with all the Lancaster tourists stopping by. Truth be told, it doesn't matter what *Mamm* talks about. We're all simply overjoyed just to hear her voice again."

"The Lord has a way of working everything out," Sadie mused with a pleasant sigh. She and Isaac took a seat on the bench, and Isaac promptly draped his arm around her shoulders, as if to protect her from the chilly November breeze.

"You've got that right," Isaac agreed as he pulled Sadie to sit closer to him. "Mim's generous offer to pass on the farm and house to us was another blessing that I never expected, and I'm awful glad that you managed to convince her to continue living here even after we're married next month."

Sadie snuggled closer to Isaac and rested her head against his shoulder. "Imagine the day, not so far away, when you'll be working the farm, I'll be tending to the flower beds and our children will be listening to one of Mim's famous stories."

Isaac nodded contentedly and rested his cheek on top of Sadie's head. "If that isn't a happily-ever-after, I don't know what is. How did I get to be so lucky?"

Sadie smiled so widely that her cheeks ached, feeling her heartbeat fall into sync with Isaac's. "I don't think it has anything to do with luck. I believe the Lord led us to each other."

Isaac gently turned Sadie's face up to his. He planted a heart-stopping kiss on her lips before gazing into her eyes with a love that few people ever truly find. "I'll love you forever, Sadie, come rain or shine."

* * * * *

Get 3 FREE REWARDS!

We'll send you 2 FREE Books **plus** a FREE Mystery Gift.

FREE
Value Over
$20

Both the **Harlequin® Special Edition** and **Harlequin® Heartwarming™** series feature compelling novels filled with stories of love and strength where the bonds of friendship, family and community unite.

YES! Please send me 2 FREE novels from the Harlequin Special Edition or Harlequin Heartwarming series and my FREE Gift (gift is worth about $10 retail). After receiving them, if I don't wish to receive any more books, I can return the shipping statement marked "cancel." If I don't cancel, I will receive 6 brand-new Harlequin Special Edition books every month and be billed just $5.49 each in the U.S. or $6.24 each in Canada, a savings of at least 12% off the cover price, or 4 brand-new Harlequin Heartwarming Larger-Print books every month and be billed just $6.24 each in the U.S. or $6.74 each in Canada, a savings of at least 19% off the cover price. It's quite a bargain! Shipping and handling is just 50¢ per book in the U.S. and $1.25 per book in Canada.* I understand that accepting the 2 free books and gift places me under no obligation to buy anything. I can always return a shipment and cancel at any time by calling the number below. The free books and gift are mine to keep no matter what I decide.

Choose one: ☐ **Harlequin Special Edition**
(235/335 BPA GRMK)

☐ **Harlequin Heartwarming Larger-Print**
(161/361 BPA GRMK)

☐ **Or Try Both!**
(235/335 & 161/361 BPA GRPZ)

Name (please print)

Address _____ Apt. #

City _____ State/Province _____ Zip/Postal Code

Email: Please check this box ☐ if you would like to receive newsletters and promotional emails from Harlequin Enterprises ULC and its affiliates. You can unsubscribe anytime.

Mail to the **Harlequin Reader Service:**
IN U.S.A.: P.O. Box 1341, Buffalo, NY 14240-8531
IN CANADA: P.O. Box 603, Fort Erie, Ontario L2A 5X3

Want to try 2 free books from another series? Call 1-800-873-8635 or visit www.ReaderService.com.

HARLEQUIN
PLUS

Try the best multimedia subscription service for romance readers like you!

Read, Watch and Play.

Experience the easiest way to get the romance content you crave.

Start your **FREE TRIAL** at
www.harlequinplus.com/freetrial.